JUVENAL

THE SIXTEEN SATIRES

Third Edition

Translated with an Introduction and Notes by
PETER GREEN

D0012325

PENGUIN BOOKS

PENGUIN BOOKS

Published by the Penguin Group
Penguin Books Ltd, 27 Wrights Lane, London w8 5TZ, England
Penguin Putnam Inc., 375 Hudson Street, New York, New York 10014, USA
Penguin Books Australia Ltd, Ringwood, Victoria, Australia
Penguin Books Canada Ltd, 10 Alcorn Avenue, Toronto, Ontario, Canada M4V 3B2
Penguin Books (NZ) Ltd, 182–190 Wairau Road, Auckland 10, New Zealand

Penguin Books Ltd, Registered Offices: Harmondsworth, Middlesex, England

Original translation first published 1967
Reprinted with revisions 1974
This revised edition first published 1998

1 3 5 7 9 10 8 6 4 2

Set in 9.5/12 pt Monotype Bembo
Typeset by Rowland Phototypesetting Ltd, Bury St Edmunds, Suffolk
Printed in England by Clays Ltd, St Ives plc

PENGUIN CLASSICS

THE SIXTEEN SATIRES

Less is known about the life of JUVENAL (D. Iunius Iuuenalis) than was
once believed – a key source, an inscription naming one Iunius Iuuenalis,
refers to a later descendant, not the satirist – and such evidence as there
is remains sadly inadequate. Much of it comes from Juvenal's own work.
We know that the family was from Aquinum in Latium near modern
Monte Cassino. One ancient Life offers a plausible birth date of AD 55.
Another states that till middle-age Juvenal practised rhetoric, not for
professional reasons but as an amusement, which implies a private income.
Book I of the *Satires* was not published till *c.* 110–12, when the poet
was in his fifties, and is clearly the work of an impoverished and embittered
man who has come down in the world – a hanger-on of wealthy patrons
with a chip on his shoulder – but the precise circumstances of Juvenal's
fall from grace are unclear. The Lives all agree that he was exiled for an
indiscreet lampoon of the jobbing of appointments by a Court favourite.
But they do not agree as to where he was sent or which emperor was
responsible, and Juvenal never refers to the matter. Many doubt whether
he was exiled at all. If he was, it was almost certainly by Domitian, *c.* 93,
to Egypt. In any case he must have lost his patrimony. It is reasonable
to assume that he was recalled after Domitian's assassination in 96. After
Hadrian's accession he seems to have acquired a small farm at Tivoli and
a house in Rome. His last and unfinished (or partially lost) collection
appeared *c.* 128–30. He may have died then: at the latest he is unlikely
to have survived long after Hadrian's death in 138.

PETER GREEN, MA, Ph.D., FRSL, was born in London in 1924, and
educated at Charterhouse and Trinity College, Cambridge, where he
took first-class honours in both parts of the Classical Tripos (1950),
winning the Craven Scholarship and Studentship the same year. After a
short spell as a Director of Studies in Classics at Cambridge he worked
for some years as a free-lance writer, translator and literary journalist,
and as a publisher's editor. In 1963 he emigrated to Greece with his
family. From 1966 until 1971 he taught Greek history and literature in
Athens. Since then he has lived in the USA, with an appointment in
Classics on the faculty of the University of Texas at Austin, where since
1983 he has been the Dougherty Centennial Professor (now Emeritus).

He is currently Visiting Professor of History at the University of Iowa, where his wife holds a permanent position in the Classics department. Among his many publications are *Alexander of Macedon: A Historical Biography* (1974), *Classical Bearings* (1989), *Alexander to Actium: The Historical Evolution of the Hellenistic Age* (1990, revised edition 1993), *The Greco-Persian Wars* (1996) and *Apollonios Rhodios: The Argonautika* (1997). He has also translated *Ovid: The Erotic Poems* (1983) and *Ovid: The Poems of Exile* (1994) for Penguin Classics.

CONTENTS

PREFACE TO
THE THIRD EDITION

It is almost exactly thirty years since I finished the original edition of this book. That is a good life for the average translation. Times change, as the old anonymous tag reminds us, and we certainly change with them. I have a vivid memory of working on Juvenal's later satires in smoky winter tavernas on Lesbos, or between spells of Aegean spear-fishing: my old tattered sandy-brown copy of Knoche's 1950 text still carries a faint tang of sea-salt, faded stains of country wine and what was once the best olive-oil in Europe. By lucky accident my family and I missed the Anglo-American Sixties, and got by far the better of the bargain. I was then a free-lance writer and translator. I was also thin, deeply tanned, muscular, and as healthy as I have ever been. My classical training at Cambridge had put down roots in the here-and-now of Hellenic soil, and was infinitely improved by the change. A natural outsider, I had found my proper fulcrum, and was ready to shift the world. Juvenal – another outsider – and I got together at just the right time. My translation was energetic, impertinent, modernist, and took risks I would never have taken, then, as an academic.

It was also, of course, despite our being out of the Anglo-American loop, a quintessentially Sixties version: I might not be around any more in London or Cambridge, but the books kept flowing in, and without even realizing it I picked up a good many of the ideas and mannerisms of the era. In Athens I was also lured back into part-time academic teaching at university level. Fate was getting ready to hand me a special line in irony. Four years later I left Greece, and my free-lance existence, as it turned out, for ever: new job, new marriage, new life. Before, I had been a flail of the professors: now I suddenly had to adjust to being a full-blown professor myself. It was as radical a metamorphosis as any that Ovid envisaged; and of course over the years it brought about deep-sea changes in my psyche, my social attitudes, my writing style, and a good deal else.

The most obvious changes were visible in my revisions to books. The coffee-table biography of Alexander that I had published in 1970 reappeared several years later trebled in length, and equipped with a heavy scaffolding of notes and references. My Juvenal translation acquired, for its 1974 second edition, a good deal of fairly up-to-date scholarship. By 1990, when I published my history of the Hellenistic age, *Alexander to Actium*, the transformation was complete. This volume ran to over 900 pages, of which a third consisted of detailed scholarly notes, synoptic date-lines, genealogical tables and a vast analytical index that I compiled myself, by hand. Over the years I had become about as academic as you could get. My younger unregenerate self still peeped out often enough to scare the nervous, but there I was (and still am) a hard-working, paid-up member of the professoriate.

When my editor asked if I would consider bringing *Juvenal: The Sixteen Satires* up to date for a revised third edition, I thought the job would be simple: a little rewriting of the Introduction to take new evidence and ideas about the author's life into account; perhaps some fine-tuning of translation and notes at points where textual and allied research had modified either the Latin or scholarly interpretation of it. A pushover, I told myself cheerfully, and set an optimistic deadline for completing my revisions.

That was plain hubris, and I should have known better.

The truth of the matter was, I hadn't looked at the notes since 1974 (and not seriously then), while the translation itself (as opposed to the text, which I continued to teach) was much as I'd sent it to press in 1967. Though I referred to it on occasion, I hadn't really *re-read* it since then. Then Fate gave me another serendipitous nudge: out of curiosity I picked up Niall Rudd's translation (he being a scholar I've always taken seriously) to see how *he'd* gone about some of the problems. The place to start, obviously, was the Translator's Preface. Before I was through the second paragraph I had one of the biggest surprises of my literary career. Rudd was talking about the problems of formal discipline, and in particular, that of line-equivalence: should one exactly match one's author line for line? Well, *of course*, I thought, having done so myself on principle (to the best of my knowledge) in any classical translation where this applied: Juvenal, Ovid's amatory and exilic poetry and, most recently, the *Argonautika* of Apollonios Rhodios. I read on. 'Juvenal's first satire,' Rudd continued, 'has 171 lines (ignoring possible lacunae).' Right. 'Humphries renders it in 164, Green in 200 –'

Excuse me? I blinked, and looked again. There it was. Irritated, I got my copy out and did a count for myself. 201. (I'm still not sure which of us is right.) Incredible: for a while I really found it hard to believe. But it was true. I tried Satire II: 170 lines of Latin, and again my version ran out at 202. Things got better as I went on: my Satire IV was only 168 to 154 for the Latin. But if anyone had asked me, I would have sworn I'd done a line-by-line version. So the first, quite unexpected, task confronting me – a huge one, as things turned out – was to turn my translation into the line-by-line one I'd so long believed it was. In the process I found myself making innumerable other changes, very often to get my version back far nearer to the Latin, both in sound and sense: it kept skipping off in all directions (very Sixties, this), with an unpredictable and insouciant life of its own. The final version that has emerged from this radical reassessment is in ways, and at times, very different from my original text. While trying to preserve the latter's essential characteristics, I have also worked very hard to bring it closer to Juvenal. There is scarcely a line that has not been subjected to close scrutiny at every level.

Equally modernist, and another thing Rudd, quite rightly, complained about (p. xxxiv) was the slangy urban argot with which I'd laced a fair amount of Juvenal's rhetoric. After citing several egregious examples, he went on to 'wonder whether this can be the poet whose distinctive quality was described by Dr Johnson as "a mixture of gaiety and stateliness, of pointed sentences [i.e. sharp epigrams] and declamatory grandeur"'. Well, no, I decided, it probably couldn't; and so I set myself to keep the gaiety, but to bring out more of the 'declamatory grandeur'. But over his complaint about my 'silent glosses' and 'functional substitutes' (see Introduction, pp. lxv–lxvi), I have – one or two minor concessions apart – held my ground. Rudd crams every name in, known or unknown. As he says (p. xxxiii), 'there are numerous places where guessing is no good. In such instances, the reader of the present translation will have to refer to the notes, even if he happens to know some Latin. This is regrettable.' Just how regrettable, only those who have tried it over the long haul will fully appreciate. The number of beats in my Lattimore-style pseudo-hexameter still remain variable, too. Making up for the absence of that fixed-quantity metrical schema (which in Latin, of course, provides a ready-made counter-point) calls for every known trick at the English prosodist's disposal.

As far as the notes are concerned, I have found most help from scholarship done in the Seventies and Eighties. Study of Roman satire, for reasons at which one can only guess, seems at present to be somewhat in the doldrums:

perhaps (cf. Introduction p. xxviii) the systematic elimination of any real moral standpoint from the literary criticism of writers such as Juvenal has robbed them to a great extent of their original attraction. I am particularly grateful for the commentaries of Courtney and Ferguson, which, as it happens, complement one another in the most remarkable way. Ferguson's is, as the phrase goes nowadays, user-friendly. It cannot be said of it, as Housman said of J. E. B. Mayor's commentary, that one turned to it for many things, but not for help in trouble. Courtney's, on the other hand, is primarily directed at fellow-scholars, and deploys the cumulative work of his predecessors, ancient and modern, to provide the essential perspective for attempts, very often successful, to solve a whole series of baffling cruces. Without these two fundamental texts my own work would have been made enormously more difficult. What I owe to other scholars in the field will be readily apparent from my notes.

As before, I have based my translation on Clausen's text of 1959 (minimally revised, and not always for the better, in 1992), and Knoche's of 1950. I have also regularly consulted Housman's second edition of 1931, as well as those of Courtney (1984) and Martyn (1987). At the eleventh hour I managed to obtain a copy of the long-awaited new Teubner edition (1997) by J. A. Willis. However, my reasonable anticipation that this would necessitate much radical rethinking of Juvenal's text proved largely groundless. As his dedication to the memory of Günther Jachmann reveals, Willis is an enthusiastic interpolationist: his text is dotted with shorter or longer italicized passages that he regards as spurious. Despite an epigraph by Alfred Gercke, to the effect that a modern editor's first concern must always be with the way his chosen text was treated in antiquity, Willis is in fact far more interested in modern editorial controversy: significantly, he assures us that those who (during the first third of this century) believed in the genuineness of the 'O Passage' in Satire VI did so, not on rational grounds, but because (Preface p. xlv) 'they feared fulminating Housman's heavy hand' (*fulminantis magnam manum Housmanni tremebant*).

Willis's entire preface, veering uneasily between the pedantic and the jocular, and written in the flattest of pseudo-Ciceronian Latin, reveals a buoyant belief, as obvious as it is erroneous, that Juvenal's reasoning faculties exactly duplicate those of his editor. The result is disastrous. Again and again, Willis pronounces with confidence, and ponderous academic logic (so alien to Juvenal's *pointilliste* mode of thought), on the irrational shortcomings of the MS tradition whenever the latter offends his rigid picture of what the satirist must, or could not possibly, have written. (On the whole problem of interpolations and lacunae see section V of my Introduction.) The one real service this edition performs is to correct a number of misreadings in previous collations; and even here, anyone consulting Willis's *apparatus criticus* must plough their way through endless deletions and emendations, for the most part otiose, proposed by earlier editors. For all its elaborate scaffolding of scholarship, this work did not induce me to change my mind over a single reading.

My bibliographies, like my translation and notes, have been radically revised. Each separate satire now has its own; most (but not all) documentation in the notes to any particular satire will refer to that satire's bibliography – listed in each case as 'Useful General Studies' – rather than to the general one, and (except in the very few cases where a work has both general and specific application) entries are not duplicated from one category to the other (e.g. the items in the bibliography to Satire I will not figure in the general bibliography). These bibliographies make no claim whatsoever to being exhaustive: they simply represent works I have found of particular value (or as holding stimulating views, whether I agree with them or not). In general, I have set myself to bring *Juvenal: The Sixteen Satires* into line with my two Ovidian volumes in this series: that is, while primarily having the intelligent general reader in mind as my audience, I have also done everything I can to make this new edition helpful to students, for whose use the augmented notes and bibliographies are designed. My professional colleagues will find little here that they do not already know; if even once or twice I succeed in shedding a little light on problems that have vexed them and their predecessors, I shall be content. That they and other readers find fewer errors and inconsistencies than they might otherwise have done can be attributed to the vigilance of my persistent (and witty) copy-editor, Monica Schmoller. For any that remain I assume sole responsibility.

As always, and on this occasion more than most, I am conscious of the profound debt I owe, accumulated over so many years, to the penetrating and original discourse on Latin literature – Varro, Sallust, Lucan and the satirists above all – of Professor C. M. C. Green: part of an on-going dialogue between us that has formed one of the most rewarding and illuminating threads in the complex fabric of a busy, happy and endlessly surprising marriage.

Peter Green

Austin, April 1997

INTRODUCTION

I

In the whole of Roman literature there is no more personally elusive character than Juvenal. His work – in marked contrast to the satires of his predecessors Horace and Persius – contains almost no autobiographical material. Of his contemporaries, only the epigrammatist Martial ever refers to him. It has been argued that he was a pupil of Quintilian's, and that the *Institutio Oratoria* alludes to him among 'contemporaries of promise', but this is pure speculation. After his death – it is unlikely that he long survived the accession of Antoninus Pius in AD 138, and may not have lived that long – the *Satires* drop out of sight absolutely for about a century. Since both the vices and the literary fashions which Juvenal castigated became increasingly popular with the Imperial Court towards the close of the Antonine period, this neglect is understandable. Marcus Aurelius would scarcely have relished Juvenal's xenophobic attitude to all things Greek any more than his son, Commodus, would have tolerated a satirist who attacked nobles with a penchant for appearing as gladiators. No critic or grammarian in the second and third centuries AD, though they make frequent references to other Roman poets, ever mentions Juvenal.

Ironically (since Juvenal's view of foreign religions was something less than respectful), his earliest rediscoverers seem to have been the Christian apologists, who raided his arsenal of moral invective for their own sectarian purposes. Tertullian (*c.* AD 160–220) does not mention the satirist by name, but has clearly absorbed some of his more pithy tags. The first direct reference to Juvenal by a Christian writer comes early in the fourth century AD. Lactantius quotes with approval the last lines (365–6) of Satire X ('Fortune has no divinity, could we but see it: it's we, / we ourselves, who make her a goddess, and set her in the heavens'), and foreshadows the traditional view of Juvenal as a distinguished pagan moralist with a genius for crisp epigrams.

The first non-Christian interest in the *Satires* hardly pre-dates the fourth century, and may have been stimulated by the work of two Christian poets, Ausonius and Prudentius, who adapted and imitated them. Perhaps soon after 350 the first ancient commentary was produced; by 390 the historian Ammianus Marcellinus could observe that certain contemporary aristocrats, who had no time for literature in general – Juvenal's attraction has always been at least as much moral and political as artistic – were devouring him with some enthusiasm. At the same period Servius, the great commentator on Virgil, was at work in Rome: he alludes to the *Satires* on more than seventy occasions, thus breaking the complete silence of his predecessors. The waspish gadfly from Aquinum had reached a wide public at last, after centuries of neglect; from then on his fame never wavered.

But the years of darkness left a legacy of ignorance and neglect behind them which still bedevils any attempt to establish exactly what Juvenal wrote, let alone the details of his life. When the *Satires* were resurrected, it was natural that those who studied and admired them should want to know something about their author. But if, as seems probable, they had nothing to go on but one manuscript lacking its final pages, biographical details could only be sought from the *Satires* themselves. There are some thirteen late Lives extant, mostly derived from that preserved in the commentary of Probus; with the exception of the first sentence there, all the details look as though they were derived from a study of Juvenal's own text.

This first sentence tells us that Decimus Iunius Iuuenalis was either the son, or the adopted son, of a wealthy freedman, and 'practised rhetoric till about middle age, more as an amusement than as a serious preparation for teaching rhetoric or pleading in the courts' (cf. T. E. S. Flintoff, *WS* 8, 1974, 156–9). His works bear this out: he makes frequent, knowledgeable, and accurate references to various aspects of the juridical system, indeed sometimes offers us the only evidence outside the Digest for certain features of Roman law (Marongiu 1977, 167 ff.). The Lives generally agree that his birthplace was Aquinum, a hill-town near Monte Cassino, some eighty miles south-east of Rome; that he was exiled for attacking an actor with influence at court; and that this exile was spent in Egypt, though some Lives opt for Scotland. The emperor who banished him is variously given as Trajan or Domitian. There is one incredible tradition (perhaps based on the fact that Satires XV and the incomplete XVI were assumed to be the last he wrote) that his exile to Egypt took place when he was eighty years old, and was combined with a military command (see below, p. xxii). Apart from his parentage and alleged exile – this last, to add to our frustration, and in sharp contradistinction to Ovid, he never mentions himself – there is nothing here that could not have been invented in the fourth century by some scholar who simply read the *Satires* and then looked through his history-books for an appropriate context.

Only one of these Lives attempts to supply the date of his birth, and none tells us when he died. The year AD 55 may be a guess, but it is a plausible one, and fits the rest of our evidence: moreover, if the compiler of the Life had intended to fabricate evidence of this sort, he would in all likelihood have added a supposititious date of death as well. There is a tradition that he survived, worn-out with old age, for some time (but we are not told how long) after the death of Hadrian in AD 138. Some sources believe that he died in exile, others that he returned to Rome, but pined away because his friend Martial had returned to his native Spain in AD 98. This last assertion, irreconcilable with the chronology of the poems, is obviously based on the evidence of Martial's poem to Juvenal from Bilbilis (12.18), and reinforces the suspicion that the biographers were making bricks with such straw as they had. One, unfortunately, asserts that he 'amplified his satires in exile and made many changes in them', a claim which may well have derived from the confused state of the text, and has provided a splendid loop-hole for adventurous modern editors.

The biographies do not tell us whether Juvenal ever married or had children; indeed, apart from his rich freedman father, plus the persistent tradition of his exile, and its cause, there is hardly anything in them – e.g. his military service, or his supposed presence in Britain and Egypt – which could not have been inferred from his own words. The variants on the story of his exile suggest that even this was preserved without any real explanatory facts, and that Egypt or Britain may have been selected as its locale simply because he shows knowledge of them both in the *Satires*.

An examination of Juvenal's writings tends to confirm such a view. The biographical or chronological evidence which the *Satires* yield is singularly small. The First Book, consisting of Satires I–V inclusive, contains allusions to the banishment of Marius Priscus, a corrupt provincial governor, whose trial was held in AD 100 (I 40–50); to the death of Domitian in 96 (IV 153); and perhaps to the publication of Tacitus' *Histories*, between 104 and 109 (II 102–3). Satire II contains further allusions to Agricola's campaign in the Orkneys and his plan for reducing Ireland (159–61), and to Domitian's assumption of the office of Censor (30, 63, 161). Both of these events can be dated to AD 84/5, and yet Juvenal treats them as recent and topical. The impression conveyed by the Book as a whole is that some of the material (especially Satires II and IV) may well have been composed in private draft during the reign of Domitian, and circulated more freely after his murder in 96, when Nerva called off the Terror and brought back the political exiles. If the reference to Tacitus is upheld, the publication of Book I will have taken place about 110/112.

Book II consists entirely of one work, the gigantic and virulent Sixth Satire directed against women. Here we find (407 ff.), as a specifically topical allusion, mention of floods and earthquake in the East, and a comet 'threatening princes in Armenia, maybe, or Parthia'. Just such a comet was visible at Rome in November 115, the year before Trajan's Parthian campaign; and in December of the same year there was a famous earthquake at Antioch, which endangered the life of the Emperor himself. This provides us with a plausible *terminus post quem*. Once again there are earlier datable references which suggest that parts of the draft had been written, or sketched, some time before: the mention of Trajan's German and Dacian victories in 97 and 102/3, the allusion to the Capitoline Games founded in 86, the lovingly accurate description of a complicated feminine hairstyle which had vanished for twenty years when Satire VI appeared (VI 204−5, 387 ff., 486 ff.: for Flavian coiffures see Paoli 1963, 111 and pl. 35).

Book III consists of Satires VII−IX. It is from here on that one begins to detect a subtle change of tone, as many scholars have remarked (e.g. Lindo 1974, 17 ff., Gérard 1989, 265 ff.), from savage vituperation (though this still recurs at times) to a more tempered and reflective irony. It is tempting to connect this with the apparent improvement − not great, but sufficient − in his personal circumstances, already (it would seem) well established by the time he came to write Satire XI.

Satire VII begins with some twenty lines praising 'Caesar' as the one hope for the arts, the only patron writers and literature can depend on in these troubled and philistine times. The introduction has every appearance of an afterthought or revision, tacked on to an already existing draft: the bulk of the satire is devoted to a survey of the poverty and humiliation which not only writers, but lawyers, rhetoricians and schoolteachers have to endure. There is, moreover, a distinct flavour of ironic ambiguity about the compliment Juvenal pays his Imperial patron. On every count it seems likely that the Emperor in question was Hadrian, and that the publication

of Book III took place between his accession in 113 and his departure for
a tour of the provinces in 121 (see below, p. 164). Satire VII is the first
occasion on which Juvenal refers to an Emperor in anything but disparaging
terms; Satire VIII, even more surprisingly, is dedicated to a young nobleman
just going out to govern a province, and is a lecture on the theme of 'Virtue
the one true nobility'. Satire IX, the sad tale of a discarded male gigolo,
looks like early work (so Highet 1954, 212).

Book IV (Satires X–XII) contains no evidence which would enable us
to guess its date of publication with any accuracy. In Satire XII there is a
description of the inner harbour basin which Trajan constructed for the
port of Ostia (75–81). We know that this basin was built in 104; the
knowledge, however, does no more than give us an obvious *terminus post
quem* for the date of the satire's composition. But in Satire XI Juvenal
speaks of himself as an old man with wrinkled skin – too old, indeed, to
stand the noise and dust and heat of the Games – who prefers to sit quietly
at home and sun himself. Also, his material circumstances have clearly
changed. The nightmare obsession with poverty and degradation that
permeates his earlier work has disappeared, and much of his lethal invective
with it: now, he reveals, he is the owner of a modest competence – a farm
near Tivoli, at least three slaves. It is not much, and he is conscious that
snobbish guests might despise his bone-handled cutlery and frugal menu
(129 ff., 203 ff.); but he is no longer the snarling, indigent, chip-on-the-
shoulder flay-all of the First Book. By Satire X, as Courtney (13) nicely
puts it, 'the motive for writing is no longer anger, but irony based on
cynical laughter; the goal of life is *tranquillitas*.' Satire XII, indeed, a poem
which celebrates the safe return of a friend after near-shipwreck, suggests
that Juvenal may have begun to take on a few of the characteristics he
previously despised. When he slips into the grand manner one is no longer
always quite sure that he is parodying it; and his periphrastic mythological
allusions become less mocking, more turgidly Alexandrian.

With Book V we are on only slightly firmer ground. This contains
Satires XIII–XVI, and was, it seems clear, the last work Juvenal published.
Satire XIII is generally dated to AD 127 by the fact that the addressee,
described as sixty years old, was born in the consulship of 'Fonteius'. This
person is most often, and plausibly, identified with the consul of AD 67 –
who, however, is known only by his cognomen of 'Capito', acquiring
'Fonteius' through identification (again, plausible, but not certain) with
the legate of Germany in 68 (Courtney 1–2). There are, moreover, two

other possible consular contenders: Fonteius Capito in 59, and C. Fonteius Agrippa in 58. Thus though other considerations tend to confirm the 127 date for Satire XIII, it *may* be as early as 118 or 119.

The events described in Satire XV are dated by Juvenal to the consulship of Aemilius Juncus – that is, again, to 127 – and are described as having taken place 'lately', though the word *nuper* was capable of much stretching. Highet further argues, very ingeniously, that the reference in Satire XIV (96–106) to young Romans becoming Jewish converts and undergoing circumcision provides us with a *terminus ante quem* for Book V's publication. In 131/2, largely as the result of Hadrian banning the practice of circumcision, a violent Jewish rebellion broke out. 'Therefore,' Highet argues, 'Juvenal could not have brought out a book complaining about the custom as being too easy and too common, if it had been made illegal and difficult before the book was published.' There is, then, a fair presumption that Book V appeared between 128 and 130. If this is so, we have a consistent and plausible chronological sequence of publication, as follows: Book I, *c.* 110–12; Book II, *c.* 116; Book III, *c.* 118–20; Book IV, ?*c.* 123–5; Book V, *c.* 128–30.

Now this picture assumes an unnaturally short creative span, and thus confirms the late biographical tradition that Juvenal only began his career as a satirist when already middle-aged: he himself, in the programmatic First Satire (25), speaks of his youth as something over and done with. If the birth-date of AD 55 represents something fairly near the truth, as I believe it does, then Book I will not have appeared till Juvenal was in his mid-fifties, and Book V when he was well over seventy. If he was still alive after Hadrian's death, he must have been about eighty-three or eighty-four when Antoninus Pius assumed the purple. Such a life-span fits in very well. with his special preoccupations. Born a year after Nero's accession, he would have been an impressionable fourteen during the terrible 'year of the four emperors' (AD 69), when, after Nero's assassination in July 68, Galba, Otho and Vitellius were successively toppled and murdered, leaving Vespasian the undisputed occupant of the Imperial throne. Twenty-six at the time of Domitian's accession in 81, he would have just turned forty when a Palace conspiracy finally removed the tyrant in 96. Such a pattern is not susceptible of complete proof, but does at least make consistent sense.

At some time during this period Juvenal made the acquaintance of the epigrammatist Martial, a man some fifteen years older than himself, whose first eleven books of *Epigrams* appeared between AD 85/6 and 98, at which point he left Rome for Spain. There is at least a possibility that Juvenal himself was a Spaniard. Syme has pointed out that there were a large number of Iunii in Spain, and that many of them settled – like our Juvenal – at Tivoli; the cognomen 'Iuvenalis' suggests either foreign or lower-class antecedents, and in fact two owners of it were freedmen from towns near Aquinum. (There was also one consul during the period, in AD 81, who had this cognomen: I have sometimes wondered whether 'Iulius Iuvenalis' should not in fact be 'Iunius Iuvenalis'.) Martial twice refers to Juvenal in Book VII of his *Epigrams*, published in the autumn of 92 (7.24, 91): long before the satirist had gone public with his invective, the two were, evidently, close friends.

Martial sends Juvenal a holiday present of 'Saturnalian nuts' from his smallholding. He inveighs against some unknown mischief-maker's attempts to cause trouble between them. Later, in 102, under Trajan, from his Spanish rural retreat he provides his old friend with a rather gloating little sketch of Bilbilis and its rural pleasures (*Epigr.* 12.18), prefaced by a contrasting picture of what Juvenal himself may be assumed to be doing: pushing through crowds in the noisy Subura, or trudging uphill, sweating under the folds of a full-dress toga, to kick his heels in the ante-rooms of the great. The earlier poems had described Juvenal as *facundus*, or 'eloquent', a term regularly applied to barristers and speech-makers, and one which confirms the tradition that he practised *declamatio* as a young man. The later epigram, composed during the gestation of Book I of the *Satires*, agrees in detail with the picture Juvenal draws there of the squalid and humiliating life endured by the 'client', or retainer, of some wealthy patron.

Now the passage I have quoted from the Life specifically emphasizes that Juvenal's practice of rhetoric till 'about middle age' was not dictated by the necessity of earning a living; it was an *amusement*, the pastime of a *rentier* living on a gentleman's income. The tone of Martial's two earlier epigrams is quite consistent with such a supposition: Juvenal is a man to whom he sends little presents, whose friendship he is determined not to lose. But the note from Spain contains an unmistakable note of spiteful triumph: one gets the impression that Fortune (Juvenal's favourite bugbear), at some point between 92 and 102, has reversed their positions. This, of course, brings us back to the enigmatic problem of the satirist's exile. Time, I fear, has done little to resolve the enigma. In 1967 I believed, with Highet, that Juvenal was exiled to Egypt by Domitian, between 93 and 96, for an indiscreet reference to an actor, a former favourite of the emperor's. By 1989 (Green, *JR* 248–51) I had almost convinced myself that the exile never took place at all. Now I have come back, with modifications and for different reasons, to a position more or less identical with my original one. The trouble is, what little evidence we have is both dubious and, too often, inconsistent.

Highet's thesis has come under heavy attack since 1954. It is argued, with some plausibility, that the savagery exhibited by Domitian during his latter years, in response to real or imagined slights, makes it inconceivable that Juvenal would have suffered mere exile rather than a death-sentence for his *lèse-majesté*: Helvidius Priscus and Hermogenes of Tarsus had lost their heads for far less serious offences (Suet. *Dom.* 10, Tac. *Agric.* 45, Plin. *Ep.* 8.14.7, cf. Coffey, *Roman Satire* 121 and n. 18). Similarly, Juvenal would hardly have been so rash, in such a climate, as to wantonly provoke the Imperial wrath after so many years of discreet silence; and had Juvenal in fact incurred Domitian's wrath in 93, that cautious trimmer Martial would never have made public admission of their friendship. I agree. Yet in fact these objections add up to very little. Domitian's savagery was tempered by an equally erratic, and decidedly macabre, sense of humour: as we shall see, it may well have been exercised at Juvenal's expense on this occasion. The poet almost certainly did not *publish* the offending lines, but, at worst, *recited* them to friends ('in exilium missus quia *dixit* uersum illum', says the scholiast on I 1), and was reported by an informer. Since the relevant book of Martial's *Epigrams* was published in the autumn of 92, there was no reason for him to avoid mentioning Juvenal, whose disgrace (according to Highet's thesis) did not take place till the following year. We may note, however, that this is the last time Martial refers to his bosom friend for ten years; and when he does break silence, his tone is by no means so friendly. Could the nameless *provocateur* who came between them in 92 have been warning Martial to drop a potentially dangerous acquaintance?

The ancient Lives, which contradict each other so maddeningly on almost every detail of Juvenal's alleged exile, are nevertheless united in the assertion that he did, somewhere, at some time, for some reason, suffer banishment. If we challenge this assertion, as is now the fashion (see, e.g., Courtney 5–9), we still need to explain how it gained credence in the first place. It is true that Juvenal himself (in striking contrast to the loud complaints of Cicero and Seneca during their brief relegations, and *a fortiori* to Ovid in Tomis: see Green, *JR* 248 with n. 33) never says one word about being exiled: but this could just as easily argue for discretion as against the fact of exile.

What does the earliest Life allege? First, that in middle age Juvenal uttered a short pasquinade of a few verses satirizing Paris the *pantomimus* and his jobbing of commissions. There is no clear indication whether this Paris was the one who performed under Nero, or his successor at the court of Domitian: to confuse matters further, both were executed by their respective Imperial masters, the first in 67, the second in 83 (Dio Cass. 63.18, 67.3; Suet. *Nero* 54, *Dom.* 3.10). The lines actually cited (VII 90–92) are the following:

> What nobles cannot bestow, an actor will. Why bother
> to appear in great patricians' spacious reception-halls?
> Prefects and tribunes alike are appointed by ballet-dancers.

Praefectos Pelopea facit, Philomela tribunos: Thyestes' daughter Pelopea and Procne's sister Philomela – both, interestingly, victims of rape – were popular lead roles for dancers: as we shall see, Domitian remembered this line. Yet the quotation is general, it attacks no one by name. It is lines 87–9 that would have imperilled Juvenal, and would surely have been quoted by any scholar trying to manufacture a good case:

> he'll starve, unless he can sell his virgin libretto to Paris –
> Paris, Director of Ballet, the jobber of high commands,
> who hands out poets their six-month carpet-knighthoods.

No commentator mentions them in this context, and there is no proof that they even existed when Juvenal's original lampoon was in circulation. At that time, *tum*, says the Life, 'there was an actor [unnamed, be it noted] who was a court favourite, and many of his fans were being promoted daily'.

But at *what* time? It is generally assumed that if such an attack was made, it had to be aimed, before 83, at Domitian's still-living favourite, and kept very private, in the manner of *samizdat* literature today, enjoying at the very most a limited underground circulation. As far as the secrecy goes, the Life offers confirmation: 'For a long time he did not venture to entrust anything even to quite a small audience.' The question is, for how long?

We are not told. But Martial was quite happy to claim Juvenal as a close friend in 92, which he would hardly have done were the friend a former exile (and why should Domitian have reprieved him anyway?). Thus 93-6 still remains by far the most likely period for exile. One Life states that Juvenal was sent to Egypt as a kind of joke, 'to match his trivial and humorous offence' ('ut leui atque ioculari delicto par esset'). I suspect that this is the truth, and that our confused tradition is in fact based on Domitian's grim witticism at the poet's expense. Another Life records the *mot* he allegedly uttered when consigning Juvenal to the Great Oasis: 'Well, Philomela's promoted *you*, too' (cf. Suet. *Dom.* 11; Dio Cass. 67.1-3). But exile there meant *deportatio*, the harshest form of banishment, involving loss of civil rights, confiscation of property, and severe limitation on movement.

If we accept this theory, Juvenal will have been exiled to Upper Egypt in 93, and returned to Rome in 96/7, after the accession of Nerva and the recall of the political exiles. We know, on his own testimony, that he had visited Egypt, and loathed the Egyptians, with a xenophobic ferocity that eclipses even his distaste for the Greeks. His knowledge of the country is extensive and peculiar: it includes, again, a collection of vivid details – the negresses of Meroë whose breasts are bigger than their babies, the earthenware skiffs used on the Delta canals, the chap-fallen, wrinkled, elderly female baboon. But even three years of exile here could leave its mark on a man. Gregory Nazianzen saw Hero, the philosopher, when he was released after a four-year sentence in the Oasis, and said that he looked like Lazarus come back from the tomb. And this exile was only the culmination of fifteen nightmare years under Domitian. The psychological effect on such men was brilliantly described at the time by Tacitus, in his *Agricola* (ch. 3), in terms that recall Dostoyevsky's *House of the Dead*:

Now at long last our spirit revives . . . Public security, ceasing to be merely something hoped and prayed for, is as solid and certain as a prayer fulfilled. Yet our human nature is so weak that the cure lags behind the disease. Our bodies, which grow so slowly, perish in a flash; and so too the mind and its interests can be more easily crushed than brought to life again. Idleness develops a strange fascination of its own, and we end by loving the sloth that at first we loathed. Think of it. Fifteen whole years – no mean fraction of our human life – taken from us. Many have died a natural death, all the most irrepressible have fallen victims to the cruelty of the Emperor. Even we few that survive seem to have outlived, not only our fallen comrades, but our very selves, in those years stolen from our man-hood that have brought us from youth to age, from age to the far end of life's journey – and no word said.

Penniless, his position and career in ruins, seared by exile and the Terror, Juvenal came back, turned forty, to a Rome of jumped-up guttersnipes and decadent aristocrats: too proud to work, conditioned by his upbringing beyond any hope of adaptation, resigned to the humiliation of a client's life. Who in such circumstances – as he himself asked – could help writing satire? And who could refrain from making the various instruments of his downfall the main targets for his invective?

There is one more piece of evidence, tantalizingly fragmentary, which both confirms the tradition that Juvenal's family was – as he himself makes clear (see Satire III 318–21) – from Aquinum, and suggests that the poet, in his youth, may have been relatively well off. Two inscriptions (*CIL* 10.5382, 5426), recorded in the eighteenth century but now lost, were found near the modern Aquino, both dealing with a certain [Iu]nius Iuuenalis. The text is in places uncertain (Courtney 3–4 offers a careful analysis), but the general sense is clear. The first stone commemorated his gift of an altar or shrine to Ceres, the second was a vote of thanks from the citizens of Aquinum to 'their benefactor', and a resolution to set up a tablet and statue of him to put his generosity on record. This Juvenal was a man of parts: commanding officer of a cohort of Dalmatian (Yugoslav) auxiliaries, joint-mayor of Aquinum during the census year (which implied extra responsibilities), and 'Priest of the deified Vespasian'.

It has always been clear that this man must have been a close relative, since he came from the poet's home-town, and was similarly associated with the cult of Helvine Ceres. (Ceres, incidentally, as Highet acutely points out, is almost the only Roman deity whom Juvenal consistently treats with anything like respect.) Attempts to identify him as Juvenal himself have of necessity been more speculative: the breaks in the stone preclude this, and have led to more or less tendentious attempts at restoration. But the final blow to this identification has to be the fact (Courtney 5 with further reff.) that military cohorts of Dalmatians seem not to have been raised prior to the Marcomannic Wars (AD 166–72, 177–80) of Marcus Aurelius. Consequently we no longer need to worry about saddling the author of the *Satires* with the career of a solid local civic dignitary, or reconciling Juvenal's classic civilian-oriented anti-militarism with military

service in command of Dalmatian auxiliaries. The inscription must refer
to a relative, but one of much later date: all we can deduce from it for our
Juvenal is a family tradition of fairly prominent provincial respectability. If
he was, in fact, the son of a wealthy Spanish freedman, the family had put
down Latin roots with remarkable speed and effectiveness; and much of his
fundamental attitude to life suggests rather the familiar lineaments of a *déclassé*
gentleman (see below, pp. xxxi ff.). Another enigma to add to the rest.

What we know or can surmise, then, is considerably less than seemed
possible thirty years ago. The birth-date of AD 55 still seems the most likely.
Of the three quasi-independent facts supplied by the Lives – a rich freedmen
father, a period of political exile, oratory as a hobby until middle age –
only the last carries complete conviction. Though I maintain the possibility
of the second, it is in the uncomfortable knowledge that it might well yet
prove fictional. The first, on the face of things plausible, is considerably
weakened by analysis of the *Satires* themselves for what Winkler (1983,
14–17), in an even-handed attempt to mediate between author and persona,
defines as 'a point of view consistent in itself, uncontradictory and coherent',
and identifies as 'the voice of the author rather than the persona'. Notable
in this category, of course, are Juvenal's rancid xenophobia, his jaundiced
view of patronage, and the shift of emphasis from anger to amused cynicism
and subversive irony in the later satires. Such characteristics tell us a good
deal more than, say, his frequency of references to Britain (border warfare,
chariot-fighting techniques, Richborough oysters, whales off the Atlantic
coast).

Up to a point we can speculate. For some years he will have divided his
time between the capital and his home-town, practising declamation,
cultivating influential friends, and – very privately – trying his hand at
satirical sketches to relieve his feelings. He made the acquaintance of another
literary Spaniard, Martial, and was much influenced by his outlook and
subject-matter. If he married, there is no evidence for it. His published
work suggests that he was fond of children, but disliked smart society
women and coterie homosexuals. It is interesting that all three of Martial's
epigrams addressed to him contain mild sexual improprieties which we can
presume were to the recipient's taste. The delights of country living that
Martial enumerates for his city-bound friend include an adolescent *uenator*,
'a huntsman, the sort that you'd want to have off in some secret glade'
(*Epigr.* 12.18.22–3). This instantly reminds us of Juvenal's own recommendation – set parenthetically in a misogynistic torrent of abuse against

women and marriage – that it's much better to sleep with boys, who don't quarrel with you in bed, nag you for presents, or complain because your sexual athleticism lacks a truly Priapic dimension (Satire VI 34–7). Martial, it seems clear, knew his friend's tastes.

But, it will instantly be objected, what about Juvenal's notorious *attacks* on homosexuality? Close scrutiny of these at once reveals that, insofar as the satirist is castigating sexual perversion *per se* (rather than hypocrisy, avarice, meanness, or breach of class protocol), what excites his anger and contempt – a highly conventional reaction – is the adult invert, the transvestite queen, the middle-aged or elderly *fellator*, above all the habitually sodomized, those whom Aristophanes labelled the *euryproktoi*, with their smooth, enlarged and depilated rear passages (Green, *JR* 251 with n. 54). For Naevolus, the 'two-legged donkey' (*bipedem asellum*), the bisexual male prostitute of Satire IX, Juvenal has nothing but sympathy, as a short-changed fellow-client; it is the donkey's stingy employer, the bitch-queen Virro, who really excites his fury. Here, as in so many other respects, Juvenal shows himself a stickler for respectable ancient convention. Like any Greek gentleman of the archaic or classical period, he restricted the legitimate object of homosexual affection to the adolescent boy, *eromenos* or *pusio*, prescribed by that tradition which cast the adult male mainly as penetrator. Beyond the first beard lay forbidden territory.

It is possible that late in Domitian's reign, not earlier than 93, a squib of Juvenal's on the sale of commissions became known to the authorities, and he was exiled to the Great Oasis (or Syene) in Upper Egypt, with loss of property and civil rights. Recalled by Nerva after Domitian's assassination, he fell into the squalid and humiliating life of a *déclassé* hanger-on – an existence which supplied incomparable material for the first three books of the *Satires*. Soon after his return, in 98, Martial abandoned the urban rat-race and went back to Spain (borrowing his fare off the Younger Pliny), from where he sent Juvenal a short poetic epistle of the *suave mari magno* variety, contrasting his own rustic relaxation with Juvenal's barren and obsequious daily round.

During this period Juvenal was working at, and polishing, what he finally issued (*c.* 110–12) as Book I of the *Satires*. Book II followed about five years later, and Book III shortly after the accession of Hadrian. From now on the tone of Juvenal's work underwent a marked change, and this may well have been due to the improvement in his material circumstances. He seems to have had a small farm at Tivoli, and a house in Rome where he

could entertain friends to a modest but pleasant meal. It is very likely that
he benefited in some way by Hadrian's patronage of the arts; perhaps the
emperor gave him a pension and a small estate, as Augustus had done for
Horace. If so, it is not hard to see why Juvenal thereafter dropped his
stringent attacks on bad literature; Hadrian's taste was far from impeccable,
and his touchiness over aesthetic matters notorious. (Yet Juvenal, like
Ovid, simply could not resist the occasional mischievous jab, as the insertion
of the lines into Satire VII that supposedly got him exiled, an appeal to
Hadrian for artistic support, nicely demonstrates.)

Two more books of *Satires* appeared, in 123/5 and 128/30. By now
Juvenal was a septuagenarian, who must have recalled, with some irony,
his own vivid descriptions of old age in Satire X. He probably survived
Hadrian by a year or two, to die, leaving few friends and little reputation,
about AD 140 – in the middle of what Gibbon described as 'the period in
the history of the world during which the condition of the human race
was most happy and prosperous'.

II

'On the death of Domitian,' the Younger Pliny wrote, with characteristic
candour, 'I reflected that here was a signal and glorious opportunity to
punish guilt, to avenge misfortune, *and to bring oneself into notice.*' The reader
of Juvenal's *Satires* cannot help but feel that their author (who may have
been on bad terms with Pliny) envisaged an identical programme. Satire I,
his manifesto, and probably the latest composition in the First Book,
announces (85–6) *indignatio* as his driving motif, and the world at large as
his subject-matter:

> All human endeavours, men's prayers, fears, angers, pleasures,
> joys and pursuits, make up the mixed mash of my book.

But in fact this programme is never carried out. Juvenal writes from a very
limited viewpoint, and the traverse of his attack is correspondingly narrow.
Throughout his life, so far as we can tell, he never once questioned the
social structure or the moral principles of the regime which had treated
him so shabbily. (Any crypto-Republicanism one can detect in his work
is no more than a reflection of the fashionable Stoic shibboleths current

throughout his lifetime.) All that he asked of the Imperial administration was that its rulers should behave according to the dictates of virtue and morality; as for the upper classes, he seems to have hoped for no more from them than that they should set a good public example and avoid activities liable to tarnish their image with the plebs.

Thus his approach to any social problem is, basically, one of static conservatism. He may have thought that the client-patron relationship was fundamentally degrading, but he never envisaged its abolition. He attacked wanton cruelty to slaves, but did not query the concept of slavery itself (another characteristically Stoic attitude). His most violent invective, whether borrowed from the common rhetorical stockpot or the fruit of his own obsessions, is reserved for those who, in one way or another, threaten to disrupt the existing pattern of society, to inject some mobility and dynamism into the class-structure. It follows, *a fortiori*, that he will display especial animus against those who have robbed him, and his kind, of their chance to achieve what they regard as their birthright *within that framework*. This is one of the main keys to an understanding of the *Satires*.

Another depends on the much-vexed question of Juvenal's satirical persona, whether single or multiple. When I first studied Juvenal, no one had yet come forward to inform us, with peremptory assurance, that authorial intention was irrelevant, that the work was, literally, in the eye of the beholder, that critical reader-response and *Rezeptionsgeschichte* were what mattered, that judging the literary value of a poem or play in any abiding sense was a self-deluding mirage, that a menu or seed-catalogue could be deconstructed in just the same way as the *Iliad*, that the apparent 'character' of author or narrator must always be viewed as a mere literary mask, a persona, an artificial manipulation of traditional formalized *topoi*, i.e. rhetorical commonplaces. Juvenal, as readers of W. S. Anderson will be well aware, has been no more immune than the next man to this kind of treatment.

I would be the first to concede that the movement has corrected several patent and egregious fallacies associated with the 'biographical nexus', and in so doing has rendered a valuable service to literature. Clearly the poetic 'I' is no more *necessarily* identical with the lyric poet than are their dramatic characters with the playwright or novelist who created them (and never mind Flaubert's famous declaration: 'Emma Bovary, c'est moi!'). There is also the constant hazard of circular argument. As Winkler (1983, 4) says of Highet, 'he extracts pieces of information concerning the life of Juvenal from the author's works, constructs his "biography", and then returns to the works for "evidence" to support his hypotheses'. Satirical convention also posits the self-evaluated 'one honest man' as narrator, and sanctions every kind of evasion and exaggeration to shock an audience with revelations of vice: the construct is artificial, creating a vehicle for propaganda which aims at the same time to be a work of art. As J. P. Sullivan said, 'at its lowest level, it was a matter of projecting a literary personality'. Hence the satirical narrator, whether anonymous or in character. No one would argue with this, and Highet (1974), despite some strong incidental arguments, made a bad mistake in taking up an extreme position that virtually denied the existence of the persona.

Unfortunately, the extremism has been far from one-sided. If Highet tried to discount the persona, too many contemporary critics have done their level best to eliminate the author: both seem to me equally wrong-headed. I have dealt elsewhere (Green, *JR* 245-6) with the general social implications of this latter trend, and do not need to repeat my arguments here. What concerns me is the effect on Juvenal, which has been to turn the *Satires* into a series of contrived, semi-dramatic performances, structurally exotic and wholly removed from real life, performed by a literary quick-change artist with a bundle of formal masks behind which to hide, and a bagful of moral bromides and stock rhetorical tropes or literary allusions to suit every occasion. The expression on the mask may change from savage indignation (Satires I–VI) to transitional uncertainty (VII–IX) and, finally, Democritean amusement with a touch of recurrent asperity (X–XVI); yet the poet himself remains as elusive as the Cheshire Cat's grin. Worse, in course of time the process of deconstruction attacks the persona too, undercutting Kernan's principle (*The Cankered Muse*, 16) that 'the satirist always presents himself as a blunt, honest man with no nonsense about him'. For Susanna Braund Juvenal's narrator has become 'a spineless and petty bigot' (*JS I* 110–21, cf. 234–5), thus subverting any moral standpoint that the *Satires* may originally have had.

Now though a creative writer – the dramatist or novelist in particular – may indeed project a variety of fictionalized mouthpieces for his or her own purposes, a recognizable personality still tends to pervade them all: in a very real sense the writer *is* all his characters (Flaubert again). Thus though it is no accident that persona-theorists unduly stress the dramatic element in works (such as Juvenal's *Satires* or Ovid's *Amores*) which, on the face of it, offer a unified voice more or less congruent with that of the author, this does not make nearly as much difference as they suppose. In cases especially where the writer's life is well documented – Byron, say, or Eliot, who make a nice contrast in this respect – it is clear that public and private face are symbiotically related. To be sure, Byron is not identical with Juan, any more than Eliot *is* Prufrock; but we only need try to imagine a Prufrock by Byron or a Juan by Eliot to sense the creative limits that authorial personality imposes. Eliot as hedonist, Byron as puritan: these are paradoxical humours that no one, in the face of a clear biographical record, would reasonably attempt to assert.

The danger comes when, as in the case of Juvenal, the personal evidence is scanty and, in places, implausible or plain contradictory. Despite occasional nuggets of hard fact, the numerous extant Lives give the impression of having been cobbled together, for the most part, either from one another or after an imperceptive gleaning through Juvenal's own work, by a group of dim scholiasts desperate for a few crumbs out of which to construct a potted biography. Even so, the kind of rule-of-thumb blanket rejection of such evidence which now appears to be *de rigueur* (it has been applied, famously, by Mary Lefkowitz to the lives of the Greek poets) represents an abrogation of reasoned judgement in the specific instance. As Winkler admits (1983, 15), 'As much as art can shape life, life is always the creative force behind an artist, literary or other.'

Satire I is rightly regarded as a programme-piece. In it Juvenal deploys most of the main themes to which he afterwards returns – vapid, cliché-ridden literature and rhetoric; various kinds of social and sexual obnoxiousness; above all, the corrupting power of wealth. But the attack is both calculated and highly selective: in each case there is a special, and revealing, motive behind it. Juvenal's main point about mythological platitudes, acute enough in itself, is that they served as a handy refuge for writers anxious to avoid dangerous contemporary issues: that their unreality is due to deliberate escapism. Readers must draw their own conclusions. Juvenal neither attacks the rhetorical system of education, nor the civilization which produced it, on principle. Instead he works through a cumulative list of significant illustrations. But his main thesis, developed with passionate intensity through the first three books, is (to put it in economic terms) the appalling influence which mobility of income can have on a static class-structure.

The actual figures whom Juvenal presents on the stage, both here and in subsequent satires, fall into three broad stylized categories. First, and most interesting as a pointer to Juvenal's own preoccupations, there is the decadent aristocrat – of either sex – who has in some way or other betrayed the upper-class code, whose conduct fails to reach those well-defined social and moral standards imposed on the governing classes as a complement to their privileges. This scapegoat figure is accused of many things, from extortion to miscegenation, from outrageous homosexuality to public appearances in the gladiatorial arena: what is common to each case is the *abrogation of responsible behaviour* which it implies. A governing class that lowers its standards and neglects its traditional duties constitutes a positive danger to the social structure over which it is set.

This is what lies behind Juvenal's occasional blurring of social and moral criticism, as when the consul who demeans his office by driving his own gig in public is bracketed with forgers and adulterers, while Nero's crimes rise from mere murder to the climactic horror of his appearances on the stage. The rhetorical anticlimax is a device which Juvenal (like De Quincey in 'On Murder as One of the Fine Arts') employs to some effect: but it is hard not to feel the real and passionate animus behind examples of this sort. Juvenal flays upper-class shortcomings all the harder because he sees his world in peril: his terror of social change made him treat infringements of accepted manners or conventions on a par with gross major crimes.

In a sense his instinct was sound. Collapsing social standards are as sure a sign of eventual upheaval as the ominous drying up of springs and wells which heralds a volcanic eruption. In the famous Sixth Satire against women, what Juvenal really objects to is not so much licentiousness *tout court* as the breaching of class and convention. All his examples are chosen from ladies of high society; and what most arouses his wrath against them is that they contract liaisons with lower-class persons such as musicians, actors, or gladiators. (One gets the feeling that he would have no particular objection to a little in-group wife-swopping provided it was done discreetly.) These great ladies are several times compared, disadvantageously, to their social inferiors, who bear children instead of having abortions, and would never indulge in such unfeminine pursuits as sword-play or athletics.

Balancing this picture, and in sharply dramatic contrast to it, is that of the wealthy, base-born *parvenu*, a figure whom Juvenal clearly found both sinister and detestable – with good reason, since as a phenomenon he directly threatened Juvenal's own social position, and that of every *rentier* in Rome. The rise of the freedman class forms one of the most significant elements in the history of the early Empire. These coarse, clever, thrusting ex-slaves, most often of foreign extraction, suffered from none of the crippling conventions and moral beliefs that every upper-class Roman inherited as part of his emotional luggage. What enabled them to amass such gigantic fortunes, and to force their way into positions of immense political power, was by no means only their native ability. They were cashing in on their masters' ignorance of, and contempt for, a world ruled by commerce and industry.

Since the middle-class Equestrian Order, to which Juvenal aspired, was mainly a matter of the right property qualification, freedmen and their descendants began to monopolize all the best posts that it offered. It is no accident that Satire I draws so blistering a portrait of the Commander of the Praetorian Guard and the Prefect of Egypt. These were the supreme prizes of any Equestrian's career: in Juvenal's poem they are both held by Egyptians – a jumped-up fishmonger called Crispinus, and a Jew, Tiberius Julius Alexander, whose statue, Juvenal suggests, should be used as a public latrine. He is always referring, enviously, to the capital sum of 400,000 sesterces which was required for admission to the Order. He and his shabby-genteel friends are kept out of the seats reserved for Equestrians, while the sons of panders, auctioneers and gladiators are entitled to them. It is significant that while Martial merely laughs at these social climbers, Juvenal attacks them in deadly earnest (Malnati 1988, 133 ff.): to him they represented a real threat.

He attacks those who are irresponsible enough to fritter away their capital and become *déclassé* – a charge he also brings against the aristocrats, but for a different reason: since wealth now is the sole criterion of acceptance and power, they are imperilling their position of authority by destroying the *de facto* foundation on which it rests. Yet though Juvenal regarded enough capital to qualify for Equestrian status as the *summum bonum*, he never indicates in any way that he would consider working to obtain it. He vaguely hopes for it as a gift from God, or 'some godlike human', presumably a periphrasis for Imperial patronage. Here we hit on a central and vital factor in his attitude to life. Juvenal was a bred-in-the-bone *rentier*, with all the characteristics of his class: contempt for trade, indifference to practical skills, intense political conservatism, with a corresponding fear of change and revolution; abysmal ignorance of, and indifference to, the economic realities governing his existence; a tendency to see all problems, therefore, in over-simplified moral terms, with the application of right conduct to existing authority as a kind of panacea for all ills.

His particular dilemma, like that of many another *laudator temporis acti*
yearning for some mythical Golden Age, is that he is living by a set of
moral and social assumptions that were obsolete before he was born. The
only occupations he will recognize are those of the army, the law and
estate-farming. He is as rigidly and imperceptively snobbish about trade as
any nineteenth-century rural squire, and with even less justification. Highet
(1954, 136) offers a sharp run-down on his position:

Since his ideal is the farm which supports its owner in modest comfort (or the
estates which make a man a knight), he does not realize that Italy now lives by
imports. And he will not understand that the Greco-Roman world was built up by
the efforts of the shrewd, energetic, competent men who made harbours, highways,
aqueducts, drainage-systems, and baths; who cleared the forests and set up the
trade-routes; who exchanged the products of the far parts of the globe and ventured
on innumerable dangerous voyages.

All he can see in the immense commercial activity of his day is a frantic
scrambling after quick profits, stupid luxuries, or wheat to keep the rabble
quiet.

He is ready to admire Trajan's splendid new harbour at Ostia, but the
socially inferior men who built and planned it elicit nothing from him but
a quick, dismissive gibe about making money out of privy-contracts –
'These are such men as Fortune, by way of a joke, / will sometimes raise
from the gutter and make Top People' (Satire III 39–40). His ideal is not
so far from that of Naevolus, the ageing homosexual gigolo (IX 140–46):
a small country home bestowed by some wealthy patron; 'A nice little
nest-egg at interest / in gilt-edged stock'; a life of cultivated idleness, the
Victorian 'genteel sufficiency'. 'What can I do in Rome?' cries Juvenal's
friend Umbricius, in a famous and much-quoted section (41 ff.) of Satire
III; and the reader is so carried away by the rhetorical brilliance of the
passage that it never occurs to him to answer, briefly: 'A useful job of work'
(cf. Marache 1989, 17). Nor, indeed, does it occur to Juvenal.

It is sometimes said that Juvenal is a very modern figure, and this is true;
but in ways he is far more like a nineteenth-century phenomenon such as
Dickens. Indeed, it could be argued, without stretching the paradox too
far, that George Orwell's essay on Dickens is the most illuminating introduction to Juvenal in existence. The social parallels are so numerous and
striking that they cannot be ignored. Again and again it might be the

Roman poet rather than the English novelist that Orwell is analysing. Juvenal, like Dickens, 'displays no consciousness that the *structure* of society can be changed' (cf. Reekmans 1971, 117 ff.). Like Dickens again, he lived in 'a city of consumers, of people who are deeply civilized but not primarily useful'. He too records 'pretentious meals and inconvenient houses, when the slavey drudging fourteen hours a day in the basement kitchen was something too normal to be noticed'. He too 'knows very little about the way things really happen . . . As soon as he has to deal with trade, finance, industry or politics he takes refuge in vagueness, or satire'. He too sees revolution as a monster, and is acutely aware of the irrational bloodlust and opportunism of the mob, the *turba Remi*. He too has a special compassion for children: like Dickens, he attacks bad education without proposing a better alternative.

Juvenal's xenophobia may be closer to Thackeray: but what he shares with Dickens more than any of Dickens's own contemporaries – and for much the same reasons – is that special horror of slums and poverty, that ignorance of, and distaste for, the urban proletariat which stand high among 'the special prejudices of the shabby genteel'. Like Dickens, he frowns – as we have seen – on social miscegenation: he objects to Eppia running off with her ugly gladiator for exactly the same reason that Dickens objects to Uriah Heep's passion for Agnes Wicklow. He too is a caricaturist; and as we know, it is fatal when a caricaturist sees too much. He too (like every urban Roman of his age) was 'out of contact with agriculture and politically impotent'. He too 'only succeeds with [the landowning-military-bureaucratic] class when he depicts them as mental defectives'. He too (and this is both his strength and his weakness as a satirist) in the last resort 'sees the world as a middle-class world, and everything outside these limits is either laughable or slightly wicked'.

The *rentier* and the caricaturist combine to produce a comic yet night-marish *reductio ad absurdum* of the dole-queue at some great man's house which in fact is the core and centre of Satire I. It is a vivid and brilliant piece of work, memorable – Dickensian echoes again – for its 'turns of phrase and concrete details': wildly exaggerated, yet embodying social truths along with the personal fears and obsessions. The *sportula* ('dole' is an inadequate translation) has degenerated from a friendly *quid pro quo* into an impersonal soup-kitchen hand-out: one of Juvenal's most valid points against excessive money-grubbing is the way it corrupts personal relation-ships. In this Kafka-like crowd of greedy and obsequious hangers-on, impoverished aristocrats on the way down (including a consul and a praetor) jostle for precedence with a Syrian chain-store magnate on the way up, who remarks, unanswerably from his own point of view (106–9): 'So what's in a purple border, / what's it really worth, if a Corvinus is reduced / to herding sheep up-country, while I have more in the bank / than any Imperial favourite?' Juvenal's comment is one of dejected and cynical resignation: 'Then keep the Tribunes waiting, / let money reign supreme', he remarks (109–10), adding that though the Romans – who were much addicted to deifying abstractions – had not as yet raised an altar to Cash, still 'Of all gods it's Wealth that compels our deepest / reverence' (112–13).

But this, of course, was just as true of Juvenal and his class of cultured *rentiers* as of anyone else: once again he provides us with that nice touch of moral ambiguity which makes him so enjoyable to read. However much he might inveigh against the corrupting influence of money, he would never have admitted for one moment that it could possibly corrupt *him*. He not only yearned with fervent and frustrated longing for the financial portion that would admit him to the company of the elect, but regarded it as his moral prerogative – a not uncommon phenomenon among individuals or groups who lack the ability to obtain what they want by native talent. The idea that financial acumen should dictate the size of one's bank-balance seemed to him not only outrageous but quite irrelevant (cf. Gérard 1985, 273 ff.). He seethed with impotent fury – as did many of his class – to find himself shouldered aside and outsmarted by the kind of shrewd, vulgar millionaire that Petronius depicts so memorably in the *Satyricon*; worse still was the sinister political influence wielded over successive emperors by Greek freedmen, to whom men of parts were forced to kowtow in the most humiliating manner. His introductory Satire, with its forgers, gigolos, informers and crooked advocates, is a threnody on the theme of collapsing social values, on the impotence of the old middle classes when confronted by a ruthless, unprincipled and commercially talented opposition.

It is significant that Juvenal's programme-satire hinges round the caricature of a patron-client relationship because, fundamentally, it was the only relationship – certainly the only business relationship – that he was capable of understanding. At one level, the *quid pro quo* concept was built into Roman manners as a basic principle: it permeated the formalized structure of *amicitia* (which means both more and less than the English word 'friendship'), and was extended to men's relationships with the Gods. Here, as so often, Juvenal betrays his inability to see beyond the *status quo*. This was not really his fault, and Orwell, again, makes us see why: 'Given the fact of servitude,' he remarks, 'the feudal relationship is the only tolerable one.'

If any single statement can illuminate and resolve the whole social content of Juvenal's work, this is it. He saw the feudal relationship everywhere: between master and slave, between patron and client, between the jobber of army commissions and the hopeful military careerist. Roman society formed a vast pyramid, with the Emperor – the most powerful patron of all – at the top, and the rabble roaring for bread and circuses at the bottom; in between came an interlinked series of lesser pyramids, where one man might play both roles, patronizing his inferiors and toadying to those above him. This is one of the points which Juvenal brings out and exaggerates in his caricature, and refers to again later (V 137–8) when describing Trebius' ultimate ambition – 'to be / a magnate, a patron of magnates'.

It is curious that all Roman writers of this period, Juvenal included, should so despise the *captatores*, the professional legacy-hunters, because, in a sense, legacy-hunting was the only occupation of the leisured classes: sinecure appointments, the *sportula*, a modest competence on retirement – it all came to the same thing in the end. Petronius recognized this: he remarked that in Croton there were only two sorts of people, the rich and their sycophants. Perhaps the *captatores* were despised – in a way like the merchant-freedmen – for being efficient professionals, in whom the cold and relentless pursuit of wealth had destroyed all human feeling. This is certainly what Juvenal felt. He regards it as necessary to emphasize, when celebrating the survival of his friend after a storm, that his motives are altruistic – not those of the legacy-hunter (XII 93–130). He believed in the feudal relationship; it was the only one he knew, and he was aware that it had originally expressed, in formal terms perhaps, a personal, human relationship that contained a good deal more than mere reciprocal expressions of obligation. But what he now saw was the systematic reduction of this feudal concept into pure financial huckstering, at all levels, where both parties – without any thought of personal contact, let alone affection – were angling to secure the biggest possible profit.

When Juvenal writes, as he so often does, about the corrupting effect of wealth, this notion is never very far from his mind. Money corrodes sexual relationships by encouraging, not only infidelity, but knowing complaisancy in the cuckolded husband; money destroys social stability by turning ex-slaves into titular middle-class gentlemen; money excuses vulgarity, buys favourable discrimination, corrupts true friendship, procures false sycophancy, leads to perjury, murder, fraud; money has become the criterion for winning professional respect; we mourn its loss with more heartfelt tears than we would the death of a friend or a lover. Once client and patron had had a genuine mutual relationship, based on trust, obligation and service: now all we see are retainers whose friendship was bought with the meal-ticket (Seager 1977, 40 ff., Marache 1989, 616 ff.). What is more, the whole idea of altruistic obligation is actively despised, with dire effects on society as a whole:

> When you tell a young man that only fools give presents
> to friends, or relieve the debts of a poverty-stricken relation,
> you're simply encouraging him to rob and cheat, to acquire
> riches by any crime . . . (XIV 235–8)

Juvenal devotes three entire satires to demonstrating the way in which, at various levels, this relationship has become a corrupt parody of its original self. (Coherent though it is, his account of the client-patron relationship almost certainly overlays social fact with literary hyperbole – see Cloud 1989, 205 ff. – but nevertheless contains a solid core of observed behaviour.) In Satire IV we see it from the apex of the pyramid, where Domitian and his Imperial Privy Council are on show: cold sadist and cowardly sycophants, discussing, not the situation on the frontiers, but what to do with a giant turbot. In Satire V it is the same story, but the props have been changed: the sadist is now a wealthy patron giving a dinner-party for his hangers-on, and deliberately torturing them with the contrast between what he is served and their own insultingly cheap entertainment. In Satire IX this principle is applied to the field of sexual relationships (it is also apparent at intervals during Satire VI) and taken to the ultimate point in human degradation, with a homosexual patron who grudges every penny he pays his gigolo, and puts sex on an exclusively cash basis (39–40):

> 'I paid you that *then*, more later, and more that other time –'
> he figures, butt twitching.

The homosexual's name is Virro; so is that of the host at the dinner-party. Whether Juvenal was pointing at a real person or not, he clearly intended his readers to link the two characters – and with good reason. But the pessimism goes further, since – as Juvenal so clearly sees – it takes two to make, or corrupt, a relationship; and those grovelling courtiers, those greedy free-loaders, that professional male prostitute, have all encouraged the intolerable situation in which they find themselves by abandoning their self-respect, their basic *humanitas*. Vicious host and decadent parasite, both are equally to blame.

The moral dilemma that Juvenal presents, here and elsewhere, lies at the heart of his position as a satirist, and has a very personal application to his life. Like his friend Umbricius, like all decent, educated *rentiers* of the middle class, who stick by their moral principles and expect certain traditional privileges and monopolies in return, Juvenal finds that the historical process is threatening to sweep him into oblivion. 'There's no room in this city for the decent professions,' Umbricius laments, before retiring to rural Cumae; and a study of Books I–III of the *Satires* shows us exactly what he means. Lawyers with principles are being ousted by cheap, flashy shysters, as crooked as the clients they defend. Posts in the army or the civil service are handed out by Greek freedmen, and obtained by former Egyptian fishmongers. Writers are at the mercy of ignorant, contemptuous patrons. Teachers are despised, bullied and paid a miserable pittance.

Poverty, indeed, is now so general a condition for poets that it is no longer (as it once was for Horace, *Epist.* 2.2.51–2) the main spur to satirical writing: plain resentful anger (*indignatio*) has taken its place (Fabrini~Lami 1981, 163 ff.). The traditional ruling classes are frittering away their money and their authority, and a new class of greasy and unprincipled upstarts is threatening to replace them. Worst of all, the 'humane professions' have been invaded by a flood of sedulous, slippery, quick-witted Greeks,

> all of them lighting out for the City's classiest districts
> and burrowing into great houses, with plans to take them over.
> Quick wit, unlimited nerve, a gift of the gab that outsmarts
> a professional public speaker – that's them. So what do you take
> that fellow to be? He's brought every profession with him –
> schoolmaster, rhetorician, surveyor, artist, masseur,
> diviner, tightrope-walker, magician or quack, your hungry
> Greekling is all by turns. Tell him to fly – he's airborne! (III 71–8)

Juvenal's xenophobia is not so much of the old-fashioned nationalist variety as that which we find in a trade unionist who sees his job threatened by immigrant labour. In this new urban rat-race he and his kind had either to compromise their principles, and beat the Greeks and new freedmen (*could he have been the son of one?*) at their own game, or go under. He could no longer rely on the benefits of Imperial preference.

The classic example of survival by compromise is, of course, Juvenal's elder contemporary Martial, the fashionable social pornographer, Rome's equivalent of a scandal-sheet gossip-columnist. His gross adulation of Domitian was only matched by the neat volte-face he performed after that Emperor's assassination, when he flattered Nerva, in equally lavish terms, for being above flattery. Juvenal felt unable to take this way out: perhaps, in any case, his specialized talent would have made heavy weather of Martial's feather-light political insincerities. At all events, he preferred to endure the grinding and humiliating indigence of a client's life, attending upon great men, stomaching snubs and insults, in return for a bare subsistence dole and the occasional dinner-invitation. Perhaps, with luck, a patron might sometimes lend him a peeling hall in the outer suburbs for a public recitation of his work-in-progress. The tragedy was that no conceivable alternative existed for him. He knew, all too well, the degradation involved: but a *déclassé* gentleman had to make his choice between subservience and the gutter:

> are there no sidewalks or bridges, no share in a beggar's mat
> for you to make your pitch from? Is dinner worth such insults?
> Are you *that* famished? Wouldn't your self-respect do better
> out there, shivering cold, and chewing on mouldy dog's bread? (V 8–11)

Echoes of Dickens are always cropping up in Juvenal. Just as his attitude to contractors much resembles that of Dickens to the ironmaster in *Bleak House*, or the dust-contractor in *Our Mutual Friend*, so here I am reminded of Scrooge's famous question: 'Are there no prisons? Are there no workhouses?'

Pity the poor *rentier*: robbed of his perquisites by clever foreigners, despised and humiliated by the upstart *nouveaux riches* who have replaced his traditional patrons both in the professions and at court, caught between the twin horrors of beggary and moral self-abasement. We see this wretched creature snubbed by scornful gigolos, shoved off the ladder of preferment by crooks and con-men, scrambling for scrappy hand-outs from contemptuous patrons, in competition with ex-slaves, public officials and malingerers; too honest to lie, too class-bound to do a job of work, sneering at astrology, saddled with a conscience that refuses to aid and abet adulterers, murderers or provincial governors on the make; bitching away about slippery Greek *arrivistes*, Stoic informers and the *captatores* who do poor clients out of hoped-for legacies; exposed to unpleasant ridicule on account of his dirty patched toga, his split and cobbled shoes; living in hope of a favourable glance from some scornful patron, indifferent if not actively sadistic; scared in his garret at the prospect of being roasted alive in one of Rome's all-too-frequent fires, or having a jerry-built apartment house collapse about his ears; deafened by Rome's ceaseless clamour, mud-spattered and crowded in the streets, the target for slops and worse from upper windows, and physical assault at the hands of brutal young thugs; fobbed off at dinner with cheap and nasty food while his so-called host gorges himself on rich delicacies; snarling away at the mercenary rapacity of women, as cynical as Dr Johnson over the hazards and meannesses of literary patronage, the niggardly rewards won by poets; sniping enviously, in the name of virtue-the-true-nobility, at blue-blooded pedigrees. *Tranquillitas*, we may feel, does not arrive one moment too soon.

What we hear from Juvenal, in the earlier satires at least, is the *cri de coeur* of a doomed class. Later, the tone sheds its hysteria and asperity: once Juvenal has achieved the *rentier*'s 'modest competence', much of the impulse for his satirical invective fades away. Though this does not make it any the less forceful or valid, his moral indignation had highly personal motives behind it; and these – as is inevitable – both modify and illuminate his moral, religious and philosophical outlook.

III

Like so many writers who feel that the world they inhabit is out of joint, Juvenal is continually harking back to the distant past: the Golden Age before Saturn's fall, the semi-mythical period that followed Rome's foundation by Romulus, the early Republic of Livy's zealously Imperial propaganda. He never loses an opportunity to contrast the thrift, abstemiousness, simplicity, patriotism and moral rectitude of the good old days with the selfish hedonism and social flux he sees all around him. (The topic is well discussed by Winkler, ch. ii, 'The Good Old Days in Juvenal's Satires', 23–58, though I do not share his conviction that the poet's attitude to the Golden Age was one of *total* cynical mockery: a clever writer will often subvert what half his mind yearns for.) This well-worn rhetorical device had been done to death by almost every Roman poet since the close of the Republic; but Juvenal's handling of it deserves attention on at least two counts.

To begin with, from his point of view there was a great deal of truth in it. The trouble with literary commonplaces, especially when they are sedulously imitated from one generation to the next, is that we tend to write them off as mere stage-properties. But the two or three centuries before Juvenal's lifetime *had* radically transformed Roman civilization and *mores*; a vast and sudden influx of wealth *had* corrupted former standards of behaviour and promoted reckless ambition; the Republic, however venal and inefficient, *had* been replaced by a despotism, however benevolent and enlightened; the average Roman citizen *had* lost effective political power; foreign upstarts *had* obtained a stranglehold on some of the most influential positions in the Empire; such members of the old aristocracy as had survived the Civil Wars and subsequent Imperial purges *were*, very often, taking refuge in hell-raking or philosophical quietism. Juvenal, as they say, had a case.

What he has been most often criticized for is the way he proposed to present it. Towards the close of the first Satire he remarks that the blunt outspokenness of a satirist such as Lucilius would be impossible today: put the finger on a successful murderer, let alone an Imperial favourite, and you are liable to end as a human torch in the arena. Therefore the oblique approach must be cultivated (I 168–71):

> So ponder these things in your mind
> before the trumpet sounds. Any later's too late
> for a soldier. I'll try my hand on the famous dead, whose ashes
> repose beside the Latin and the Flaminian Ways.

This disclaimer has produced a whole host of interpretations. Juvenal is being flippantly evasive, and refusing to commit himself; he is covering his line of retreat against possible libel actions, and in fact has every intention of attacking contemporary figures; his indignation is the synthetic flourish of the mere rhetorician, and his disclaimer a clumsy imitation of similar stock apologias by Horace and Persius. Such historical instances as he presents – and there are fewer of them than one might suppose – are mostly taken from the reigns of Claudius, Nero and Domitian. What is more, it is argued, his Satires were published – whatever the date of their original composition – under emperors whose humane and liberal attitude would, surely, have made such elaborate precautions unnecessary. The arbitrary despotism of the Terror, with its police spies and informers, had been swept away, had it not? Why, critics ask, does the fellow keep hedging in this pusillanimous fashion?

Till quite recently the most favoured answer was Kenney's (1963): that Juvenal does not so much make specific attacks against the dead (except in Satire IV, which is an isolated, and probably early, exception) so much as use them as exempla, pegs on which to hang a moral generalization. This was a common practice among satirists and rhetoricians, and had the specific authority of Quintilian to back it. But Juvenal's use of it also throws light on his attitude to the Imperial civilization under which he is forced to live. Again, he does not criticize the structure of his society as such; all he sees is a steady decline in moral integrity from the Golden Age to his own day. If his solution – let men pursue virtue and all will be well – seems to us intolerably naïve, at least he saw the crucial flaw at the heart of his society, and expressed it in memorable terms. Highet's summing-up of such an attitude (57–8) is excellent:

One evil emperor to him was like another. Every corrupt nobleman resembled his ancestors, having merely grown worse. Over a century earlier, Horace had pointed to this process, and said, in one of the gloomiest of his poems, that the morals of his countrymen were growing worse from father to son, uninterruptedly. Now, looking gloomily back, Juvenal saw the long slope reaching to his feet. He realized (although perhaps his audience did not) that it would be trivial to satirize only the men and women of his own time. They were end-products of a process which began with the lash of Julius Caesar and the wet sword of Augustus, which ran on through the lunatic Caligula, through Nero and the civil wars, to the fiendish emperor of yesterday and perhaps another monster tomorrow. This realization was one of his chief contributions to satire.

It was indeed: despotism has no guarantee of benevolence (though the Stoics tried to make their moral precepts a kind of inoculation against excess) and Juvenal at his gloomiest hardly foresaw some of the Imperial horrors in store for posterity. (It is an ironical gloss on his theory of parental influence that such a philosophical paragon as Marcus Aurelius should have produced, in his elder son and successor Commodus, precisely the kind of brutalized gladiatorial thug whom Juvenal most detested.) But the satirist's pessimism is prescient: he knows, only too well, that one good emperor does not bring the millennium. The central problem remains unchanged, and must be treated *sub specie aeternitatis*. This realization is one of his major claims to be treated as a classic.

There is, however, another side to the problem of taking examples from the dead, and a quite different reason for doing so, which gives a somewhat less high-minded motive to the writers of the day, and suggests that Juvenal may have come closer to Martial in his dealings with officialdom than has generally been supposed. In a brilliant and highly original essay, 'Juvenal and the Establishment', E. S. Ramage (1989) sets out at length, with a wealth of documentation, the use by the Flavian and Antonine emperors, not only of well-placed eulogy, but – more important for our purposes – the systematic *denigration of chosen predecessors*, to make themselves shine all the more brightly by comparison. Was Juvenal, like Martial, serving the new regime? It looks uncommonly like it, and the uncomfortable realization that Trajan and Hadrian, liberal propaganda notwithstanding, had their own secret police and short-order executions lends an uncomfortable edge to the possibility. *Laudatio* of the new star was best served by *damnatio memoriae* of the old. Satire IV is of course Ramage's prize exhibit (692–704), with its craven councillors and savage tyrant, not to mention 'the lack of freedom under [Domitian], his promotion of the *delatores* and his desire for *adulatio*, his activities as censor, his self-proclaimed divinity, and his military activities'. These last had been eulogized to a huge degree, and Trajan, whose own successes, like Domitian's, lay along the Rhine and Danube, might well have encouraged a literary propaganda campaign to minimize his predecessor's victories and add extra lustre to his own. Attacks on the more lurid or *outré* Julio-Claudian dynasts would not come amiss either.

It is hard to re-read the early satires after studying Ramage's essay without these considerations coming to mind at almost every turn. Ideologically Juvenal fitted in very well with the new regime: 'This agreement with the ideological and propagandistic purposes of the emperors under whom he was writing shows how he as an outspoken satirist could exist under what was perhaps the most totalitarian regime to date. He adapted his writing to the times in which he wrote' (706). Proclaim the virtues of the new freedom, but eschew vulgar eulogy: praise indirectly, by a blackening of earlier monarchs and their associates. The survival of genius could be justified by expediency. When he drew his portrait of Crispus (Satire IV

81–93), did Juvenal remember Horace's deadly little phrase 'Fabula de te narratur'?

Against this background it is well worth examining his attitude to religion, in particular the concept of Fortune or Destiny. Stoic orthodoxy identified Fortune with God, and Nature, and Reason: this uneasy compromise reflected a prevalent mood of fatalism, which felt that the world must be ruled either by blind and random chance, or else by immutable destiny. At the lowest level this trend was exemplified by the common passion for astrology and fortune-telling: for thinking people, especially those living within the shadow of the Imperial throne, it posed some very disturbing questions on the existence of free will. Tacitus felt the dilemma acutely. Is it true, he wonders, that 'the friendships and enmities of rulers depend on destiny and the luck of a man's birth?'. May not our personalities play some part in determining our lives? Under Augustus it had been easy enough to believe in a benevolent Destiny directing the affairs of Rome and her citizens; by the time Lucan came to write his *Pharsalia*, Fortune looked far less appealing. Juvenal accurately reflects this ambivalent attitude. At times he portrays Destiny as a capricious, immutable deity, playing hopscotch with our careers; but he also, with great emphasis and some shrewdness, declares, at the end of Satire X (365–6): 'Fortune has no divinity, could we but see it: it's we, / we ourselves, who make her a goddess, and set her in the heavens.' Ethically, Juvenal feels, as did most Stoics, that man must pursue virtue by his own efforts: though uncommitted to any specific philosophy, he had mopped up, in a piecemeal fashion, most of the popular intellectual attitudes of the day. These included a briskly flippant cynicism towards the myths and ritual of traditional Roman religion, and a creed of moral self-help which, by implication, left little scope for divine interference.

What he never seems to have realized is that this detached urban sophistication of his struck at the very roots of the high-minded Republican *pietas* which he professed to find so admirable. Even when lauding his rude forefathers to the skies, he cannot help sneering wittily at their shaggy, acorn-belching primitivism: all his descriptions of the Golden Age have an unmistakable note of civilized latterday mockery running through them. There is, in fact, a radical split detectable between Juvenal's moral ideals, and the fashionable intellectual scepticism which he shared with most educated Romans of his day and age. This dichotomy sets up tensions and cross-currents throughout the *Satires*: it is nowhere so obvious as in Juvenal's dealings with Roman deities or mythology.

In the old days, he tells us, the numinous power of the Gods was nearer to Rome, and no one ever dared to scoff at divine power. It does not seem to occur to him that he never loses an opportunity of scoffing at it himself. He pokes fun at Jupiter's sexual escapades, and Numa's assignations with Egeria: he mocks Mars for being unable to keep robbers out of his own temple, and offers us a hilarious glimpse of life on Olympus before King Saturn 'exchanged his diadem / for a country sickle, when Juno was only a schoolgirl' (XIII 39–40); he pooh-poohs anyone who is naïve enough to believe in Hades, and repeatedly debunks traditional mythology, which he sees, in his superior middle-class fashion, as a collection of mildly ridiculous and unedifying *contes drôlatiques*.

In short, Juvenal falls into an error very common among intellectual moralists, that of proclaiming a social ideal with his rational mind, and then destroying any hope of its fulfilment by the emotional attitudes he brings to it. He, and those like him, who upheld *sapientia* – a word which embodies both the reasoning faculty, formal logic, and moral philosophy – against Fate, superstition and all the messy irrational magma which bedevils men's minds everywhere, made one cardinal error. They totally ignored the cohesive social binding power of irrational and emotional factors on the human mind; they genuinely believed that men could be made wise and good by taking thought, and needed no other stimulus. There are, in any age, some people of whom this is true: but they always remain a small, if articulate, minority. By mocking religious traditionalism, the Stoics were undermining the very foundations of those antique virtues they sought to promote. Cash may have been a despicable deity; but it was hardly more despicable than the collection of blind, arbitrary, indifferent or bloody-minded figures of fun which Juvenal presents in the *Satires*. Philosophical self-help has always been a dubious substitute for religion; as the rallying-cry for a national regeneration of morals it is laughable. One suddenly realizes what a tiny proportion of Rome's population Juvenal was addressing, how narrow his terms of reference were.

In this connection, I think the significance of his penchant for satirical parody has received less attention than it deserves. Juvenal uses this device, not only to point the contrast between heroic past and degenerate present by decking out the latter in borrowed antique plumes, but also as an escape-valve for his own highly ambivalent feelings about the past. He is full of sly literary allusions: Statius, Calpurnius Siculus, above all Martial, constantly peep through his phraseology, and the effect (as so often with

Eliot today) is to undercut, parody or subvert what might otherwise be taken at its face value (Townend 1973, 148 ff.). This process, by availing itself, not only of earlier authors, but also of philosophical commonplaces, mythological *exempla* and popular moral or rhetorical tags, is so all-pervasive that after a while it becomes hard to take Juvenal seriously at all (Fredericks 1979, 178 ff.).

The parody kicks both ways. At one point in Satire IX Juvenal makes a male prostitute the recipient of an address which echoes Virgil's exhortation to a similarly orientated, but somewhat more genteel, literary shepherd. 'The unlovely reality of Naevolus,' as Lelièvre demurely remarks, 'placed alongside a romanticized conception of the passion in which he deals, may be felt to represent an astringent comment on the conventions of pastoral poetry.' If there was a tragic grandeur in the mythical past, it is long gone. Again and again Juvenal sees 'contemporary society as aping the heroic characters from epic and drama, and the result is a bizarre joke' (Smith 1989, 822).

Perhaps it is more than that. Juvenal parodies a number of authors – Horace (Duret 1983, 201 ff.), Ovid, Statius, Homer and Lucretius among them – but I do not think it accidental that his favourite target is grandiloquent epic (Hellegouarc'h 1992, 269 ff.), nor that the author he makes more fun of than all the rest put together is Virgil, the mouthpiece of Augustus, the singer of Rome's Imperial destiny. Virgil announced, in the *Georgics*, that mythological topics were obsolete, and that 'Caesar' (i.e. Augustus) would be his theme; Juvenal makes a similar declaration, but – significantly – as *his* alternative topic opts for vice and crime. Where Virgil glorifies, Juvenal belittles: with symbolic appropriateness, he uses more diminutives than almost any other Roman poet. He delights in transferring a heroic phrase to a mundane context. The cannibalistic Egyptian riot of Satire XV is a kind of anti-epic battle, and I have often wondered whether the spear-flinging ape on goatback at the end of Satire V was not meant to recall the equestrian manoeuvres of the *lusus Troiae* in Book V of the *Aeneid*. Juvenal may think that Rome has been rotted by long peace, but the glories of battle and conquest hold singularly little appeal for him either.

I have said that he had no concept of altering the structure of his society, and this is true; on the other hand he was very prone to indulge in the backward-looking wish-fulfilment dream – something very different. *If only* is the keynote of his fantasy: *if only* Rome had never acquired an empire, *if only* we were still the small, simple, agricultural community that we were in the days of the Kings, *if only* there had not been that dreadful influx of wealth and clever foreigners to corrupt our morals, tempt us with luxury, give us the appetite for power! (cf. Hellegouarc'h 1971, 233 ff.). When Juvenal looks back to the Golden Age, he is lamenting the loss of innocence. His real hero is not so much Cicero – though the career of that provincial-made-good must have whetted his own ambitions in more ways than one – as Cato the Censor. Cato was a walking embodiment of the old semi-mythical virtues: husbandry, piety, service to the State. His xenophobia was at least as marked as Juvenal's, and as a moral Jeremiah he left the satirist standing. He even, more appropriately than perhaps he knew, went to the length of giving the Roman sewerage system a radical overhaul. (So, in a sense, did Juvenal.) His official post as Censor was one to which every satirist unofficially aspired.

But what made Cato particularly interesting to the intellectuals of a politically impotent age was the fact that he offered an almost unique example of morality, without any strings attached, actually controlling and changing the course of political events. Seneca had argued that only differences of character and behaviour distinguished the king from the tyrant: it followed as a necessary corollary that the one safeguard against despotism was the inculcation of moral virtue in the ruler. Under the early emperors there was an obvious political explanation for this alarmingly *simpliste* attitude. What one cannot abolish, one must take steps to improve.

Besides, no one had forgotten the bloody chaos and anarchy that had accompanied the death-throes of the Republic. The Romans might have sacrificed their freedom, but they had won peace, prosperity and stable government in exchange. It was not difficult for the Emperor's supporters to argue that any show of independence, any talk of 'liberty', directly threatened the *pax Romana*. We have seen such arguments in our own day. The only alternative was the complete political quietism of thinkers such as the ex-slave Epictetus, who openly stated that philosophy's concern was with personal problems and emotions, whereas Caesar could be left to guarantee men's social security. (This did not stop Domitian banishing him in AD 89: there were three purges of 'philosophers' during this period, by Vespasian in 71, and by Domitian in 89 and 93.) This was the intellectual legacy that Juvenal inherited. It would, I think, be true to say of him, as M. L. Clarke says of Tacitus, that 'his heart was on the side of the republican past, his head on the side of the Imperial present'.

If we try to pin down any coherent philosophy in Juvenal's work, we soon find ourselves forced to admit defeat. Juvenal himself (XIII 120–24) expressly denies allegiance to any of the three major groups of his day, the Stoics, Epicureans and Cynics – which does not mean that he refrained from raiding their commonplaces, in an eclectic fashion, whenever it happened to suit his book. His attitude to marriage resembles that of the Cynic, his cultivation of friendship has an Epicurean flavour, his aphorisms on such topics as virtue and fortitude and destiny are forceful expressions of Stoic doctrine, often more striking than anything composed by more professional thinkers. But he had little formal knowledge of philosophy as such, and scant aptitude for sustained rational argument: like A. E. Housman, one surmises, he found abstract thought irksome. His attitude to the whole business, fundamentally, was that of the caricaturist who formed so large an element in his creative personality: he saw life as a series of vivid, static, distorted snapshots.

This has caused much argument as to whether his general picture of Rome under the Flavians is truth or rhetorical fiction. Grimal, for example (1986, 2 ff.), argues, persuasively, that while employing all the old traditional rhetorical clichés taught in the schools, by sheer poetic originality he uses this material to create a vivid world where reality is constantly exaggerated and caricatured into semi-fictional burlesque. As Gérard asks, only half rhetorically, at the outset of his long investigation into the problem (Gérard 1976, iii): 'Quoi de plus incertain et de plus changeant que la réalité?' It has, indeed, often been alleged (see, e.g., Courtney 32 ff.) that Juvenal's picture differs so radically from that to be found in the correspondence of his exact contemporary, the Younger Pliny, as to cast serious doubt on the accuracy of the satirist's observation. Melodramatic fiction, in fact, served up by a Jeremiah-like persona who tears into corruption with all the relish of a vulture working its way through ripe carrion.

Now no one would doubt – to take a modern example – that George Orwell and Harold Nicolson both recorded their honest impressions of England in the Thirties and Forties, or that they enjoyed a very similar upper-class education: yet they happened to inhabit radically different worlds. So did Rudyard Kipling and Baron Corvo; and the odds are that Juvenal and Pliny did too. The well-heeled and well-connected administrator-cum-*littérateur* who corresponded with, and undertook diplomatic missions for, the Emperor Trajan, saw a very different side of things from the peevish threadbare urban scribbler, the anti-militaristic civilian, the nasty misogynist and nagging moral grumbler in pursuit of hand-outs and patronage who emerges from the *Satires* themselves.

My own feeling is that the scene this person draws for us is limited, selective and often prejudiced; that it leaves out a great deal – the happy, virtuous, hard-working majority are not alas, the stuff which inspires great satire – and exaggerates much of what it includes; but that ultimately it is based on fact, and presents a truly observed, if highly partial, portrait both of Rome itself and of aberrant upper-class *mores* during Juvenal's lifetime. A satirist may resort to caricature; but he seldom tilts at exclusively paper windmills. The 'intellectual image', as W. S. Anderson rightly reminds us, does not exist in Juvenal: it would be very strange if it did, since the cast of mind which it implies is wholly alien to Juvenal's method of exposition. Philosophers, for Juvenal, were primarily eccentric individuals, who spent their time laughing, weeping, living in tubs, or avoiding beans. When he came to deal with contemporary upper-class Stoics, it was in the same personal terms. He shows us a group of hypocritical crypto-homosexuals with crew-cuts, aping Cato's sternness and shagginess, but in fact corrupt shams, whose knowledge of the philosophers is limited to the plaster busts they have on display in their houses. Juvenal does not work out a coherent ethical critique of institutions or individuals: he simply hangs a series of moral portraits on the wall and forces us to look at them.

IV

Le style, as Buffon said, *c'est l'homme même*; and when we examine the style, imagery and structure of Juvenal's *Satires*, we find an almost uncanny congruence between what we can deduce of the author's personality and the form of self-expression he chose. Satire had, originally, been a literary medley, a loose sequence of isolated scenes. Intellectual exponents of the art such as Horace and Persius had tightened up its structure a good deal: but for a writer of Juvenal's temperament, who worked through images rather than by logic, the old form was far more congenial. He picked a theme, and then proceeded to drive it home into his reader's mind by a vivid and often haphazard accumulation of examples. Juvenal's sense of overall structure – as so often with an artist who dislikes abstract concepts – is sketchy, to say the least of it. Very often his work reads like a series of paragraphs that bear only a token relationship to each other, written at different times and stitched together without much concern for tidiness or coherence.

If Juvenal ever read Quintilian's remarks about the need for economy and order in one's presentation of a subject, they cannot have made much impression on him. He announces a topic for later treatment, and then forgets all about it. He is full of abrupt jumps (some of them probably due to lacunae in our text) and splendidly irrelevant digressions. He prowls all round his subject, with the purposeful and disjunctive illogicality of a monkey exploring its cage. The cumulative effect is impressive: at times Juvenal seems to anticipate the techniques of cinematic montage, and if he had been alive today it is a fair bet he would be making his living as a scriptwriter at Cinecittà. This is especially apparent in Satire III, with its fast-moving, well-edited shots – arranged, we may note, in chronological sequence – of street-scenes in the City. We can almost hear the cutting-room shears at work as we move from the fatal accident (pedestrian crushed under waggonload of marble) to the victim's home, and from there to Hades' bank, for a glimpse of the brand-new ghost awaiting Charon the ferryman; or from the bedroom of an insomniac bully to the dark street where he picks his quarrel with an innocent passer-by.

But since Juvenal was well acquainted with the rules of rhetoric – and since (perhaps more important) classical scholars are themselves tidy-minded intellectuals with a great gift for logical analysis – it has too often been assumed that the *Satires* must follow a *rational* structure and pattern if only we had the wit to see it. 'An abrogation of form,' says Helmbold (1951), 'is unthinkable for a professional writer of Juvenal's attainment.' This seems a very dubious assertion, besides begging the question of what can be defined as 'form'. Behind it one glimpses that old ghost which still haunts classical studies, however often right-minded scholars may exorcize it: the feeling that ancient authors achieved a perfection which somehow places them above common literary error, that they cannot be criticized, only explained and justified.

Tu nihil in magno doctus reprehendis Homero? Horace asked – 'Tell me, do you, a scholar, find nothing to cavil at in mighty Homer?' Such an attitude, besides betraying a fundamental misconception of the way Juvenal worked, has had unhappy consequences for his text. When the German scholar Ribbeck argued that the second half of the *Satires* was so different in tone from the first that it must be the work of a late forger, he meant what he said. Any passage which fails to measure up to an editor's preconceived standards of Juvenalian perfection, from the standpoint of aesthetics, rhet-oric, structure, content or even – on occasion – of decency, is liable to be excised from the canon as an interpolation, on the grounds that 'Juvenal could not possibly have written it'. So of recent years the *Satires* have been laid on a Procrustean bed of structural analysis: this has produced some useful insights, and a great deal of disagreement.

In Satire II, for instance, Juvenal has two loosely related themes, homosexuality and hypocrisy, which he develops by something not very short of random association. Our philosophers are hypocrites because they mask their homosexuality behind a pretence of virtue. They are aristocrats, and therefore doubly reprehensible. Domitian is the arch-hypocrite: despite his, and his relatives', sexual excesses he assumes the role of Censor. In any case, homosexuality is progressive and contagious, a symptom of our corruption: if a man joins the philosophical coterie he will end up at drag-parties and homosexual 'marriages'. Our conquests abroad contrast shamefully with the canker at the core: Rome corrupts all who live there. Now there is no overall logical pattern about this development, but it remains remarkably effective nevertheless: the apparent inconsistencies which some writers have found (e.g. between the supposedly unrelated topics of hypocrisy and perversion) melt away on inspection.

Satire III is so splendidly orchestrated that the lack of logical sequence seems not to have bothered critics as much as one might expect. It falls loosely into two halves, on the vicissitudes of a poor but honest *rentier*, and the discomforts and actual dangers of city life; but even so, Juvenal moves from one train of thought to another exactly as the fancy pleases him. As always, he obtains his effects by the piling up of visual effects, paradoxical juxtaposition rather than step-by-step development, a series of striking contrasts between the decent, innocent Roman (a kind of Candide-like observer) and the crooks, Greeks, draymen or other *canaille* who push ahead of him, bang him in the ribs, splash him with mud, beat him up at night, steal his job, drop slops on his head, and leave him to beg in the gutter when his apartment burns out.

If Juvenal can confine himself to a single theme, and then expand it by means of one extended dramatic illustration, his form is neat and logical enough: what Anderson and others call a 'frame' presentation, with the exemplum topped and tailed by introduction and coda. Two good instances of this are Satires V and XV, where in each case the dramatic illustration – a clients' dinner-party, a grisly fight in the desert – forms a simple core or maquette round which the entire poem is articulated. It is no coincidence that the most satisfying satires, structurally speaking, tend to be the shortest.

Juvenal's only idea of structural enlargement is repetition, adding one 'frame' to another until he runs out of material. His dilemma bears some resemblance to that of Russian composers when endeavouring to make use of traditional themes: as Constant Lambert said, 'the whole trouble with a folk song is that once you have played it through there is nothing much you can do except play it over again and play it rather louder'. Anyone who doubts this should look at Tchaikovsky's Fourth Symphony and see what he does with the 'Little Fir Tree' motif.

But – and this is equally significant – there is no correlation between regularity of form and literary excellence in the *Satires*. The most dramatically vivid of them, that little *tour de force* Satire IV, is a broken-backed affair which has defied even the most ingenious attempts to unify its parts. Once again we see the principle of random selection at work, a train of thought which proceeds from one enticing image to another like a man leaping from tussock to tussock across a bog. Juvenal begins with an anecdote about his favourite *bête noire*, Crispinus, the commander of the Praetorian Guard. Crispinus has bought a giant mullet for 6,000 sesterces, an outrageous price. But the mention of one giant fish reminds Juvenal of another; he drops Crispinus and sails into a spoof-epic sketch of Domitian and his Cabinet solemnly debating what could be done with a giant turbot presented to the Emperor by an Ancona fisherman. Some scholars have found 'connecting ideas between the two parts in the ways in which Crispinus and Domitian use their big fishes and in the similarities of the two men's characters', which is little more than a ratification of the free-association principle.

This is nowhere more apparent than in what is arguably Juvenal's greatest, as well as his longest, achievement: the enormous diatribe against women and marriage which forms Satire VI, and was published by itself as Book II of his complete works. There have been innumerable attempts to extract a coherent pattern from this unwieldy monster, but all have broken down on points of detail. Highet describes the overall theme as the futility of marriage, and claims that the poem has a 'good bold simple structure, ending in a powerful climax'. But even he admits that 'the chief difficulty in it is to find some reason for the arrangement of the various types of married women's folly, in 352–591, and here the manuscripts appear to have been badly disturbed'. (When in doubt, blame the text.) Anderson, on the other hand, declares that 'the structure of Satire 6 is conclusively against an interpretation of the central theme as that of marriage. The subject of the satire is Woman, Roman Woman, and her tragedy. She has lost her womanhood . . .; in its place she has adopted viciousness.' Both are right, both wrong: the two themes co-exist in the satire, and Juvenal moves between them as the fancy takes him.

He opens with a semi-ironic portrait of the Golden Age, when Chastity had not yet retired from earth: adultery, he reflects, is man's longest-established vice. Why marry, he asks, when so many handier forms of suicide are available? You'll be lucky to find a virgin, and even a virgin will soon change her ways when she starts moving in the society of young upper-class Roman matrons. From voyeuristic orgasms at the theatre she'll soon graduate to liaisons with actors, musicians or gladiators. Two caution-ary illustrations follow: the senator's wife who runs off with a swordsman, Messalina's activities in the brothel.

So far the sequence has been orderly enough. But Juvenal's powers of concentration never seem to extend much beyond a hundred lines, and here, as usual, free association begins to creep in. After a couplet on sex crimes so irrelevant that some critics think they should be transferred to the end of the poem, Juvenal observes that the peccadilloes of rich wives are condoned because of the dowry they bring: the cash-motif has appeared again. There follows a cutting little sketch which illustrates Juvenal's favour-ite theme, the corruption of personal relationships, and – as in Satires IV, V and IX – attacks both parties with equal vigour. This episode has never, I think, had quite the attention it deserves. Sertorius and Bibula are a cynical *reductio ad absurdum* of the marriage of pure self-interest. Bibula may be a mercenary gold-digger who takes Sertorius for all he's got; but Sertorius, equally, is a cold sensuous hedonist whose only interest in Bibula is a physical one, and who dumps her, ruthlessly, the moment her charms begin to fade. The marital relationship has been pared down to calculating exploitation: no human emotion remains in it. Here we have the same psychological theme that reappears in the commination on legacy-hunters at the end of Satire XII:

> So long live legacy-hunters, as long as Nestor himself!
> May their possessions rival all Nero's loot, may they pile up
> gold mountain-high, love no man, and be loved by none.

Selfish greed, selfish indulgence are, between them, destroying all human intercourse and affection. The individual now stalks through life as though it were some sort of no-man's-land, in armoured isolation, out solely for what he can get, giving no quarter and expecting none. Even marriage has become the same battleground in miniature. Hell, as Sartre said, is other people; but it is also oneself.

Nevertheless, Juvenal goes on, there is no way out for a prospective husband: if the corrupt woman is a bitch, the virtuous woman is a bore. Who would want to marry such a high-minded noble prig as Cornelia, 'Mother of the Gracchi', and burden himself with that insupportable legacy of noble rectitude? (Here, for once, the urban sophisticate shows through the moralist's mask: I suspect that this represented Juvenal's basic attitude to the whole Republican myth.) Virtuous pride is far from easy to live with, and brings its own retribution – look what happened to that sow-like breeder Niobe. With which reflection, Juvenal suddenly switches to an attack on Greek fashions. From this point the montage technique comes increasingly into play, and the pace quickens with a kind of hysterical frenzy. Women torment you and run your life, forcing you to discard old friends and make bequests to your wife's lovers. There are quick shots of a wife bullying her liberal husband into torturing a slave, a mother-in-law pandering to her daughter's adultery. A preamble on female litigiousness and quarrelsomeness leads into some vivid glimpses of upper-class ladies practising swordplay. Women nag in bed, we are told, and talk their way out of anything.

At this juncture Juvenal stops and asks what produced the decline in morals: wealth, he concludes, and too many years of peace (this is rather like the pre-1914 journalism of Belloc and Chesterton and W. E. Henley). Then he is off again on alcoholism, orgies and supposedly gay go-betweens who turn out to be strongly heterosexual in bed. The final sections of the poem present a series of stylized portrait-sketches: the woman who is mad on the Games, the well-informed busy-body who talks back to generals, the hearty drinker with her dog-whip and her obliging masseur, the tyrant in the boudoir, beating the slave-girl who dresses her hair, the astrology-fans and devotees of exotic cults. With some final sulphurous remarks about abortions, aphrodisiacs and parricide for profit, the satire grinds to a snarling but essentially unresolved halt. The reader has been not so much reasoned into agreement as battered into submission.

This technique may indicate a defect in Juvenal's constructive powers: but it seems to me a fundamental part of his satirical equipment. If it is a weakness, the weakness has been turned to the best advantage, and with considerable ingenuity. Here Juvenal stands poles apart from a naturally architectonic poet such as Virgil or Horace. The writer he far more resembles, not only in his pessimism and sense of moral purpose, but also in style and technique, is Lucretius. Both have the same urgent, nagging, neurotic method of exposition; both use the hexameter as a weapon to bludgeon their audience. Both, we may note, share that odd preoccupation with the Golden Age of rural primitivism from which they themselves, by temperament and habitat, were so far removed.

Source-hunting in literature is, on the whole, an unprofitable game: but Juvenal was a noticeably bookish writer, and his debts were more interesting than most, since he turned them to such good use. He must have known Martial's *Epigrams*, for instance, almost by heart, since there is scarcely one of the earlier satires but contains some echo of them; yet Juvenal's borrowings are far from indiscriminate, and reveal a keen sense of judgement. He saw, clearly, that Martial's supreme quality was his gift for direct observation, his pointillist use of the occasional piece to build up a composite, Mayhew-like portrait of Roman life and manners. Juvenal took the technique (and some of the descriptions) but adapted it to his own purposes, changing not only the context but also the phraseology. Furthermore, as Lelièvre (1958) has pointed out with some acuteness, Juvenal's deliberate echoes of earlier writers very often serve the same purpose as do those employed by T. S. Eliot in *The Waste Land*: they are touchstones to intensify the sense of moral decadence.

Orwell, in the essay I mentioned earlier, remarked that Dickens's genius emerged most clearly from 'turns of phrase and concrete details'. Broadly speaking, the same is true of Juvenal, though temperamentally he was far removed from Dickens, and altogether lacked the novelist's generous scope and warmth. Juvenal is, *au fond*, a miniaturist, and his greatest gift – whether in a dramatized scene, a piece of invective, or a moral statement – is for vivid and memorable concision: apt instrument to convey the vision of 'a society that is hollow at its core and has lost its sense of the future', for which the past off which it is living comes across as 'a wretched congeries of dead traditions, absurd legends, rhetorical exempla, topoi, and lies' (Wiesen 1989, 709). His language, however casual and demotic it may appear, has been distilled, refined, crystallized. Dubrocard (1970) points out that, of the 4,790 words in the *Satires*, no fewer than 2,130 are *hapax legomena*, i.e. occur here once only, and nowhere else. It is not surprising that his whole lifetime's output barely exceeded 4,000 lines of verse. Seldom can one man's body of work have had less spare fat on it. We see this most clearly and obviously in the famous aphorisms which, even in Latin, have become part and parcel of the Western European inheritance: *panem et circenses, quis custodiet ipsos custodes?, rara avis, mens sana in corpore sano*, and many others, such as *maxima debetur puero reverentia*, which are less well known since the decline of Latin as a pillar of secondary education.

This gift of Juvenal's extends to his invective, in particular to his cold, quasi-clinical handling of sexual misdemeanours. He never once uses the Latin equivalent of a four-letter word (in which he provides a striking contrast to Martial); but as Highet says, when it comes to turning your stomach with a couple of well-chosen phrases, there is almost no one to touch him. While lambasting Domitian in Satire II (32–3) he throws off the following couplet:

> . . . cum tot abortiuis fecundam Iulia uuluam
> solveret et patruo similes effunderet offas.

> (his too-fertile niece gabbled pills, brought on a messy abortion,
> and every embryo lump was the living spit of Uncle.)

I have printed the Latin here because no translation on earth could do full justice to Juvenal's revoltingly skilful use of language and rhythm. The first hexameter, with its predominantly spondaic feet, its repeated 'v's, 'o's and 'u's, moves forward in a series of slow, sluggish heaves that irresistibly suggest uterine contraction; the second begins and ends with an explosive burst (*solveret, offas*) which represents the actual expulsion of the embryo. Finally, there is the vulgar term *offa*, which not only sounds disgusting, but carries unpleasant associations, since it is most commonly used in connection with pigs or sows.

This is no isolated instance. Perhaps Juvenal's greatest poetical achievement is his ability to marry sound, sense and rhythm into one organic whole. His ear for the nuances of vowel-sounds and consonantal patterns is acute, and few Roman poets can equal his absolute control over the pace, tone and texture of a hexameter. The garrulous bluestocking in Satire VI (434 ff.) elicits the comment: 'Such a powerful rattle of talk, / you'd think all the pots and bells were being clashed together'. In the Latin you can actually *hear* them: 'uerborum tanta cadit uis, / tot pariter pelues ac tintinnabula dicas / pulsari'. With apparently careless ease he catches the crackle of a fire, the cooing of doves on the roof-tiles, an old man greedily gulping his food, the belch and eructation of a gluttonous Palace trimmer, the drunken dancing of Egyptian villagers, a tittering Greek, the heave and lurch of seasickness, the harsh, abrupt, staccato rattle of a bully's questions suddenly fired at his victim, the scrannel, hen-like piping of a counter-tenor. Examples could be adduced from every satire.

One of the first things I realized about Juvenal, over half a century ago, was this superb mastery of verbal poetics, of the subtle rhythms and rhetoric of the hexameter, which in his hands became an instrument to match, and often beat, Milton's blank verse at its best. Jenkyns' curious belief (1982, 151 ff.) that in my generation we were all, having been brought up on Palgrave's *Golden Treasury*, deaf to the poetics, not only of satire, but of virtually everything outside lyric, I treasure as one of those monumental absurdities that only a cloistered Oxonian could perpetrate. No one needs his kindly guidance to be moved by a famous passage like that describing the fall of Sejanus (X 58–64), with its powerful movement, its disturbing sound-effects, its dense, hard verbal brilliance:

> descendunt statuae restemque sequuntur,
> ipsas deinde rotas bigarum impacta securis
> caedit, et immeritis franguntur crura caballis;
> iam strident ignes, iam follibus atque caminis
> ardet adoratum populo caput et crepat ingens
> Seianus: deinde ex facie toto orbe secunda
> fiunt urceoli pelues sartago matellae.

> The ropes are heaved, down come the statues,
> axes demolish their chariot-wheels, the unoffending
> legs of their horses are broken. And now the fire
> roars up in the furnace, now flames hiss under the bellows:
> the head of the people's darling glows red-hot, great Sejanus
> crackles and melts. Those features, once second in all the world,
> are turned into jugs and basins, frying-pans, chamber-pots.

Verbal dexterity is reinforced by a sparing, but dramatic, use of simile and metaphor: the informer who could slit men's throats with a soft whisper; the lofty but gimcrack tower reared by ambition; the father who is destroyed by the son he has himself trained in vice, like a lion-tamer who vanishes into the maw of his own lion; the senator's wife who drinks and vomits

like a big snake that has tumbled into a vat. Sometimes the implications
are very subtle. It took Anderson (1982) to make us see that 'the metaphors
in VII 82 ff. transform the inanimate epic of Statius into a very attractive
female, whose allure resides entirely in her sex' – the point being, of course,
that Statius is prostituting his art by pandering to popular taste (and, we
might add, compromising his integrity by selling ballet-scenarios to Paris
in order to make a living). We have already seen something of Juvenal's
penchant for the diminutive and the anticlimax as devices for satirizing
contemporary littleness: here, too, the effect is prepared for with great
verbal skill, so that the deflationary punch-line, or even word, catches
readers with their defences down and forces them to *think*:

> what squalor, what isolation would not be minor evils
> compared to an endless nightmare of fires and collapsing
> houses, the myriad perils encountered in this brutal
> city – and poets reciting their epics all through *August*! (III 6–9)

A few shocks of this sort, and we begin to ask ourselves whether, socially
speaking, the amateur gladiator of distinguished family, the muleteer-consul
or the stage-struck Emperor are not symptoms of more deep-seated flaws
in the body politic than might at first be supposed.

But for the modern reader, whose interest in Juvenal is to a very large
extent antiquarian rather than moralistic, the prime quality of the *Satires* is
their ability to project the splendour, squalor and complexity of the Roman
scene more vividly than the work of any other author, Horace and Cicero
included. This, of course, is particularly true of Satire III, on which J. W.
Mackail wrote a paragraph in his *Latin Literature* which I can no more resist
quoting than could Duff:

The drip of the water from the aqueduct that passed over the gate from which the
dusty, squalid Appian Way stretched through its long suburb; the garret under the
tiles, where, just as now, the pigeons sleeked themselves in the sun and the rain
drummed on the roof; the narrow, crowded streets, half choked with the builders'
carts, ankle-deep in mud, and the pavement ringing under the heavy military boots
of guardsmen; the tavern waiters trotting along with a pyramid of hot dishes on
their heads; the flower-pots falling from high window-ledges; night, with the
shuttered shops, the silence broken by some sudden street brawl, the darkness shaken
by a flare of torches as some great man, wrapped in his scarlet cloak, passes along

from a dinner-party with his long train of clients and slaves: these scenes live for us in Juvenal, and are perhaps the picture of ancient Rome that is most abidingly impressed on our memory.

Yet this is only a fraction of the motley scene which Juvenal paints, with quick, bold, economic strokes: the 'smoke and wealth and clamour' of Rome which Horace described are here, and its smells too, and above all its colourful, polyglot inhabitants, caught in one vivid phrase after another, glimpsed for a moment and then gone – the African poling his felucca up the Tiber, with a cargo of cheap rancid oil; the plump, smooth successful lawyer riding above the heads of the crowd in his litter; the homosexual fluttering his eyelids as he applies his make-up, or wearing a chiffon gown, near-transparent, to plead a case in court; the ageing gladiator, straight out of Hogarth or Rowlandson, with 'a helmet-scar, a great wen on his nose, an unpleasant / discharge from one constantly weeping eye'; a lady of quality, her large thighs wrapped in coarse puttees, panting and blowing at sword-drill; the downtrodden teacher and his resentful pupils, conning lamp-blackened texts of Virgil before daybreak; the sadistic mistress who sits reading the daily gazette or examining dress-material while one of her slaves is being flogged in the same room; the would-be poet giving a recital in a cheap, peeling hired hall, with his claque of freedmen distributed at strategic points through the audience (only Juvenal would have added the realistic touch of placing them at the ends of the rows); the fat, horsy consul Lateranus, swearing stable oaths, untrussing his own hay or boozing with matelots and escaped convicts in some dockside tavern; the contemptible trimmers hurrying down to boot Sejanus' corpse in the ribs ('and make sure our slaves watch us') while sneering at the rabble for its opportunism; the miser hoarding fish-scraps in September; the squad of slaves with fire-buckets guarding a millionaire's *objets d'art*; the court martial presided over by a group of hobnailed old colour-sergeants; the temple-robber scraping gold-leaf from the statues of unprotesting deities; the sizzle of sacrificial offerings, the roar of the crowd at the races, beggars blowing kisses, the carver flourishing his knives, fortune-tellers, whores, confidence-men, politicians – it is an endless and kaleidoscopic panorama. But it was not so much human endeavours that obsessed him – he had always been rather hazy about what people actually *did* – so much as humanity itself, that marvellous ant-hill which he hated and loved with equal fervour, and from which he never succeeded in tearing himself away.

V

It is a curious and infuriating paradox that we possess, probably, more manuscripts of Juvenal than of any other classical author, including Homer, but that only one of these – P, the Codex Pithoeanus-Montepessulanus, preserved in the Medical School of Montpellier – derives from a relatively sound and intelligent tradition. We know that an edition was prepared between 350 and 400 by a pupil of the great grammarian Servius: it is on this that P (itself of the ninth century AD) depends, and the worst omissions and corruptions which P repeats are likely to have been already embodied in the text on which that editor worked. But at about the same time as Servius' pupil was preparing his edition, another and far less intelligent scholar also set about the text of Juvenal. Repeatedly he 'introduced changes which he thought would make Juvenal more intelligible and orderly, and usually made him much stupider. It is a common fault of strong-willed editors to assume that their author had no more imagination and less sense of style than they themselves' (Highet 187). As one of C. P. Snow's characters has reminded us, in the world of scholarship we needs must choose the dullest when we see it; and with an infallible instinct posterity pounced on the inferior edition, which was disseminated in something like 500 manuscripts. Only P (apart from the so-called 'fragmenta Aroviensia' and some ninth-century anthology snippets preserved at St Gall) represents the relatively uncontaminated 'Servian' text; and P mysteriously vanished for several centuries after the Renaissance, only reappearing about 1840, when it served as the foundation for Otto Jahn's edition of 1851.

But P (as Housman pointed out, with acid wit, in the preface to his own edition), though the best manuscript, is by no means free from corruption, and in many places inferior manuscripts supply a correct reading where P does not. The situation was rendered more complicated (in my opinion, for the most part unnecessarily) by Jachmann (1943), who posited wholesale interpolation, including up to one-third of the transmitted text. Too many scholars follow this line, if not to such a radical extent. As I hope to have made clear in my notes, I believe the real textual problem to be the precise opposite of interpolation: i.e., lacunae. The history of the 'O Passage' in Satire VI (see below) should warn us of the possible pitfalls still awaiting editors.

In 1950 the German scholar Ulrich Knoche produced a text based on the widest collation of manuscripts yet undertaken, and his *apparatus criticus* is an essential tool for any future student of Juvenal. It was largely utilized by W. V. Clausen in his Oxford Classical Text edition of 1959 (revd 1992); Clausen had the further advantage of personally collating P, which Knoche did not do, and as a result was able to correct a number of traditional mis-statements about its readings. My version of Juvenal is based, broadly speaking, on Clausen's text, though I have diverged from it on a number of occasions. Wherever I have done so the fact is attested in a note. Housman's revised edition (1931) *editorum in usum* has been at my side throughout; I have also learned much from J. R. C. Martyn's refreshingly adventurous recension (Amsterdam 1987). Willis's new Teubner edition is discussed in my preface. Otherwise there has been relatively little editorial work – or indeed work of any sort, compared with the previous two decades – done on Juvenal.

I have also, predictably, differed from Clausen on a number of occasions about what should be secluded in square brackets [ ] as spurious or interpolated matter. The 'interpolation theory', as a convenient panacea for explaining textual difficulties, has been coming back into fashion again lately; Knoche expunged over a hundred lines from the text, and Clausen, with more caution, about forty. Courtney (1975) upholds the majority of Housman's and Clausen's deletions. Willis (1997) is even more prone, as a Jachmann *epigonos*, to find spurious matter everywhere. Fortunately, since there are no fewer than 297 lines that fail to meet his criteria, he italicizes rather than deletes them. Here – as should be apparent from my notes – I stand more with Vahlen, Housman, Duff, Griffith, Highet and Ferguson, and against Clausen, Courtney, Braund and Willis. Though interpolations do exist in Juvenal, they are far fewer than critics such as Jachmann would have us believe; and all attempts to prove an interpolation on purely aesthetic or even logical grounds must be regarded with deep suspicion. It is no argument to say that because a line is weak, otiose or inappropriate, *therefore* Juvenal could not have written it: the ghost of classical perfectionism walks in odd places. 'Moralists', as Housman observed, 'are often flat, and poets of the silver age redundant; and although for Juvenal's sake we may hope that these lines are spurious, we are not entitled to believe them so.'

Normally, in Penguin Classics, it is not necessary to go into textual matters at such length. But Juvenal is something of a special case when it comes to translation. To begin with, his text, even after the labours of many editors, still contains many dubious or unresolved readings. Now in

the nineteenth century it was the fashion to emend a corrupt passage by
hook or by crook; but today scholarly caution is the watchword. Editors
may be ready to throw out passages as spurious on what seem fairly flimsy
grounds; but if they are confronted by a textual crux which, for one reason
or another, cannot be submitted to this treatment, they are prone to
advertise their critical restraint by obelizing the passage – that is, by isolating
it within daggers † † like some infectious case of illness, and leaving it as
it stands. Whatever one's feelings about this editorial practice in principle,
one can scarcely regard it as a help to the translator. The one thing no one
can do with an obelized passage, almost by definition, is to translate it.
Unlike a cautious editor, the translator is bound to produce some sort of
coherent sense: he is not allowed to hedge his bets. This awkward fact
must serve as a partial excuse for the number of occasions on which I have
either accepted emendations proposed by others, or – when all other
recourses failed – have tentatively supplied my own.

Another awkward textual hurdle for any translator is this problem of
lacunae. If critics have been overwilling to find interpolated matter in
Juvenal, they have also tended to underestimate the number of occasions
on which passages from the interior of the Satires may have been lost in
transmission, or deliberately excised, at a very early period. Here we must
move with caution, since disjointed abruptness or illogical switches of
topic in a poet with Juvenal's temperament may be evidence of creative
idiosyncrasy rather than of a defective text. But there are many passages
where it is reasonable to assume a lacuna of one or more lines: for examples
see Satires I 131–2, 156–7, III 112–13, IV 4–5, VI 118–19, 510–11,
VII 205–6, XII 3–4, XVI 2–3. It is interesting, and may not be wholly
coincidental, that with two exceptions all these lacunae are to be found in
Books I–III, and that of the exceptions one is an obvious scribal error,
while the other occurs in a satire on a politically explosive subject. Throughout these first three books, as we have seen, Juvenal was working at white
heat: it is just possible that the lacunae were the result of deliberate editorial
censorship – perhaps as much on moral as on political grounds.

Considerable support for such a thesis appeared in 1899, when a young
student named E. O. Winstedt, examining an eleventh-century manuscript
of Juvenal in the Bodleian Library, discovered, to his astonishment, that it
contained 36 lines – 34 of them one continuous passage – which existed
in no other text, and the absence of which had never been so much as
suspected. The lines in question occur in Satire VI: they were inserted

between lines 365–6 and 373–4. To complicate matters still further, they were obscure, corrupt, and of such sophisticated obscenity that Housman could write, truthfully, in his preface that 'until I translated and emended this fragment . . . no one had any notion what it meant'. His account (xxix–xxx and xxxix–xl) of how this fragment was preserved in one Beneventan manuscript, and the process by which the text was battered into some sort of shape after the passage had been lost or excised, is still the *locus classicus* on the subject.

As soon as the lines were published, there was a strong movement among certain scholars to prove them a spurious insertion or forgery. Until the last war this opinion more or less held the field. Since then intensive work on the 'O Passage', as it is generally known, has reversed the position, and the case for these lines being Juvenal's work may be regarded as sound (Luck, Courtney and Ferguson all regard them as genuine; Willis has renewed, unconvincingly, the arguments for their being spurious). They certainly are stamped with Juvenal's authentic tone and technique: if he did not write them, it is hard to conceive who else could have done so. But the whole episode, as I have suggested, sheds a lurid light on the concealed pitfalls which Juvenal's text may contain at any point. Critics are too fond of talking about the stupid, irrelevant, flat or otherwise otiose interpolation: *the one they can see.* Why should all interpolators (an improbable breed at the best of times) be congenital idiots? What editors should be worrying about far more is the insertion they *can't* see: the clever, appropriate, stylistically impeccable (and undetectable) pastiche – or, worse, and far more likely, the dropped passage that, with or without the help of later scribes, leaves the text making some sort of sequential sense.

'I should not be surprised', Highet wrote in 1954, 'if a new manuscript of Juvenal turned up tomorrow with half a dozen new passages (several of them shocking) and with a totally irregular provenance and descent.' That was optimistic, and perhaps a tad over-dramatic (did he see himself being televised on prime-time news about the shocking revelations?). Forty years have passed, and there has, alas, been no sign of such an interesting epiphany: disappointment has probably been outweighed in the academic community by relief. It isn't an impossibility, but it remains a great deal less likely than Highet seems to have thought.

Textual problems apart, the translator of Juvenal is hampered by two main difficulties in achieving a version which will both convey the force and flavour of its original, and have immediate relevance for a modern, non-Latinate audience. One of these difficulties I have already discussed above. No translator can hope to capture the condensed force of Juvenal's enjambed hexameters, his skilful rhythmic variations, his dazzling displays of alliteration and assonance and onomatopoeia: here I can claim no more than that I have recognized the problem, and done what I could to surmount it in a wholly different medium. It is hard to estimate the gulf which lies between an inflected, mosaic language such as Latin, and an uninflected language like English, with its plethora of controlling particles. Furthermore, the vowel-lengths in Latin are fixed quantities, whereas those in English are variable according to stress and context: we may say, broadly speaking, that whereas Latin verse is ruled by metre, English verse adapts itself elastically to rhythm.

It follows that the first casualty in any version of Juvenal (or Virgil, or Lucretius) will be the strict hexameter. All attempts to acclimatize this growth on English soil (even such a brilliant *tour de force* as C. S. Calverley's experimental fragment of Book I of the *Iliad*) have ultimately failed, for one simple and insurmountable reason. A stress-hexameter, lacking the counter-tensions set up by the metrical framework of its Latin or Greek original, produces such a cumulative effect of dead, clumping monotony that two or three pages will normally be enough to send the reader to sleep – or in search of something less stultifying. On the other hand, translating Juvenal into blank verse, let alone elegiac couplets, sets up alien associations which one should be at pains to avoid. (I have treated this topic at some length in *Essays in Antiquity*, 1960, 185–215, and in *Classical Bearings*, 1989, 223–39, 256–70: interested readers can pursue the argument there.) Prose is out of the question: despite Juvenal's chatty, discursive technique he is, first and foremost, a poet, a master of language and rhythm, who exploits the hexameter with a virtuosity perhaps only rivalled by Virgil.

The best compromise solution, it seems to me, is the variable six-stress line first employed (so far as I know) by Cecil Day Lewis in his admirable version of the *Georgics*, and afterwards developed by Richmond Lattimore in translations of Hesiod and Homer. It was applied to Juvenal, with excellent results, by Highet in the illustrative quotations scattered throughout his *magnum opus*. By allowing great latitude over the position of the caesura (the natural rhythmic break in a line), and the stresses governing the six 'feet', and indeed the number of stresses, that dead monotony can be broken up to a surprising extent, while at least something of the hexameter's overall form can be retained. English falls naturally into iambic rhythms rather than into the dactylo-spondaic pattern of the hexameter (which may be why English translators have always succeeded comparatively well with Greek tragedy); it follows that many of the six-stress lines which Day Lewis, Lattimore and I employ to represent hexameters are really iambic Alexandrines in disguise. This seems to me the lesser of two evils. Any solution to the hexameter problem is bound to be a compromise; and at least the present one can reproduce one vital device – enjambement – which Juvenal uses constantly and with striking effect.

But there still remains another hazard, historical rather than literary. If English translators have succeeded with Greek tragedy, they have almost always come a dreadful cropper over Greek comedy: not so much on technical or aesthetic grounds, as because of the unfamiliar names, the obscure topical or historical allusions that they are for ever having to break off in mid-passage and explain to the layman. Nothing is calculated to annoy a reader more – or indeed to produce a stiffer, more pedantic flavour – than a text where every other line requires, and gets, some detailed marginal gloss before it can be understood. In this respect Juvenal must be counted a translator's nightmare. He is full of recondite references that he takes for granted his reader will understand; he is writing for educated Romans who knew their own myths and history, and were at least as familiar with prominent public figures – both at leader-page and gossip-column level – as an assiduous newspaper-reader or TV-scanner would be nowadays.

I cannot pretend to have eliminated this difficulty altogether, but I have reduced it as far as possible by the use of two simple devices. One of these I call the 'silent gloss'. If a difficulty can be made clear by the addition of a brief phrase, I insert that phrase in the text of my version, without comment. For example, at VI 440–42 (an example we have already studied in another context) the bluestocking's jabber, Juvenal says, would make you 'think all the pots and bells were being clashed together'; there follows a baffling reference to one woman acting 'as lunar midwife'. Here I have tacitly inserted the phrase 'when the moon's in eclipse': just enough (I hope) to remind the average educated reader of a widespread primitive superstition – making a loud noise to scare demons during the moon's rebirth – without their needing to hunt down the allusion in a note.

The other device is what might be termed 'functional substitution'. Juvenal is very fond of citing well-known names from history, not for any specific purpose, but as *representative types* of some virtue, vice, occupation or personal characteristic. This is a regular practice among Roman writers, and was taught as part of the rhetorician's stock-in-trade. But for its effectiveness it depends on one's audience being familiar with the various touchstones employed. To modern readers most of the names would mean nothing at all, and the device, far from calling up clusters of mental associations as it was meant to do, would become a baffling private code to which they lacked the key – thus totally defeating its own ends.

For instance, at I 35–6 we read of an informer 'quem Massa timet, quem munere palpat / Carus et a trepido Thymele summissa Latino'. Who, the bewildered reader well may ask, are Massa and Carus? What is the relation of Thymele to Latinus, and just what is Latinus making her do? With the help of the ancient commentaries, and an acquaintance with the historical context, a specialist can, more or less, tease out the answer to this puzzle: but what Juvenal was aiming for when he packed these lines with – to him and his contemporaries – highly-charged proper names was the delighted shock of instant recognition, and such an emotion is not liable to be induced by an explanatory notes. Now in fact Massa and Carus were type-figures of the small-time informer, the minnows who circled round the big fish Juvenal is sketching here; and Latinus was an actor who saved his own skin by pushing his wife into this sinister creature's arms. Such is the sense which Juvenal is conveymg, and he means it as a perennial generalization: I therefore translate accordingly. We lose the associative image, but at least we gain unhampered clarity: 'Lesser informers, terrified, stroke him with bribes: / nervous actors send their wives round to do the stroking for them.' Another, slightly different, instance occurs in Satire II (24–8):

> quis tulerit Gracchos de seditione querentes?
> quis caelum terris non misceat et mare caelo
> si fur displiceat Verri, homicida Miloni,
> Clodius accuset moechos, Catilina Cethegum,
> in tabulam Sullae si dicant discipuli tres?

Here we have a whole battery of historical allusions without any purpose except to provide type-figures and point a contrast. The Gracchi are brought in, simply and solely, as radical revolutionaries, Verres as the classic rapacious governor, Milo as a political assassin, Clodius as an adulterer, Catiline and Cethegus as traitors, and Sulla as a dictator. There is no other reason whatsoever for their presence in this passage, and, once again, I have preferred to substitute the function for the name (those who prefer every name, however recondite, kept and glossed, should try Niall Rudd's translation: cf. above, p. ix).

VI

With a satirist in particular we need to know the individual motives, *uotum*, *timor*, *ira*, *uoluptas*, the overall moral and psychological stance determining his angle of attack, his special prejudices and obsessions. Where, as they say, is Juvenal coming from? The random, ad hoc quality noticeable in so much modern scholarship on his work is largely due to a failure to face this fundamental problem. Deconstruction of authorial intention, plus heavy over-use of the persona-principle (perfectly legitimate in itself), and the moral relativism which these habits almost inevitably induce, have between them too often reduced the satires to little more than a meaningless literary game.

This move to cut the author loose from his work, while (I repeat) a salutary corrective to biographical literalism – Bundy's work on the formal and encomiastic nature of the Pindaric ode is a splendid example of the theory's virtues as well as its excesses – can also be seen as a profoundly ahistorical symptom, part of the persistent current assault on so-called 'bourgeois objectivism', the deliberate undermining of the concept of actual and retrievable truth, a phenomenon so often acutely embarrassing to prophets, theorists or ideological system-makers. If literature is no part of the historical process, but a mere intellectual game of which the rules can be refashioned by any player, wherein does its value lie, except as a suspect vehicle for academic careerism? And how can it be related to the beliefs and cultural evolution of the society that generated it, let alone to the individual whose vision drew it into being?

There are in fact many theses and articles about the *Satires* that make much more sense when viewed against the central – and highly modern – paradox of his character (cf. Green, *JR* 254 and n. 69 for examples). Juvenal was a typical product of his age in that he regarded his society, above all its class-system, as a fixed, immutable datum. This was one of the first facts I ever grasped about him. He may have thought that the client-patron relationship had been debased from its original grounding in genuine, if formal, *amicitia*, but the idea of *abolishing* it would never have occurred to him. As I remarked earlier (p. xxxiv), his most savage attacks are reserved, precisely, for those who looked as though they might disrupt the existing pattern of society. (He was typical in this attitude: no accident that the words in both Greek and Latin for 'make a revolution' – νεωτερίζειν, *res nouare* – simply mean 'innovate', 'do something new'.) Hence the invective against *arrivistes*, clever foreigners and social climbers, all of whom of course threaten not only the fixed order of things, but Juvenal's own position as a *déclassé*, but still gentlemanly, *rentier*. If he *was* a freedman's son – let alone a *Spanish* freedman's son, and the more I think about it, the less likely this seems to me – then, paradoxically, it remains true that freedmen's sons, as a class, were among his most dangerous competitors.

The real paradox, of course, lies in the irreconcilable contrast between his simultaneously romanticized and mocking-cynical view of the past (from which, whatever its faults, the present always, in the *Satires*, represents a moral decline), and that detached urban sophistication to which he was heir, and which constantly drove him to debunk the traditional myths and shaggy primitivism that formed part and parcel of the *mos maiorum*, the peasant Republicanism of the old days that he was always – tongue not entirely in cheek – proclaiming as his ideal. This is a dilemma with which we are uncomfortably familiar today: our emotions, too, demand comforting traditional beliefs, against which our intellect and reason (not to mention our sense of humour) so often obstinately rebel.

The antique code of conduct on which Juvenal bases his moral judgements is summed up in Book III of Cicero's *De Officiis* (cf. Courtney 23 ff.): those farming virtues of small-town thrift and hard work that had scant relevance to what Horace termed 'fumum et opes strepitumque Romae' (*Odes* 3.29.12), the smoke and wealth and clamour of the City. A perilous gap had opened up between sentimental moral dream and political reality. Hence the yearning back to a Golden Age, the endless charges of corruption and decline, the jeremiads against Rome's socially destructive loss of simplicity and poverty, the commercialization of *officium* (public and personal responsibility), the emergence of moneyed upstarts, the abrogation of principle by scions of the old aristocracy. Juvenal (Courtney 25) can neither understand nor tolerate 'the fact that change in Rome's role necessarily changed the nature of the community and the city; Roman writers, convinced that "moribus antiquis res stat Romana uirisque" [Rome's welfare was rooted in her ancient traditions and manpower] often seem to wish to put the clock back without surrendering the time gained'.

Juvenal's complex and dramatic sense of irony failed to perceive the inherent contradiction in which he was involved. But we can understand it today, all too well; and on that understanding – social and moral even more than literary – any real appreciation of the *Satires* must, ultimately, be based. I am sure (as I wrote in 1967) that my understanding of Juvenal has been deepened by the sheer discipline involved in translating (and now to a considerable extent retranslating) him, however imperfect the final result of that discipline may be. Visiting him again in our common old age – these days I too prefer peaceful sunbathing to the races – has largely reinforced my original estimate of all his idiosyncrasies. I do not think my opinion (as opposed to my literary assessment) of him has really changed – except in one respect – since the summing-up which I first wrote over forty years ago, and published, with modifications, in 1960 (*Essays in Antiquity*, 184). I thought, then, that 'the writer must command our respect; but the man can never command our affections'. The respect he still commands; but I was wrong about the affections. Over the years he has imperceptibly become an old friend. As I write these last words I am conscious of my heart warming towards him.

That paragraph, then, with one excision, will serve again as an appropriate coda to this Introduction:

'Yes; Juvenal is a writer for this age. He has (in spite of his personal preoccupations) the universal eye for unchanging human corruption; he would be perfectly at home in a New York dive or a rigged political conference, ready to pillory the tycoons or degenerates who were elbowing him out of an easy job in some international organization. Bureaucrats have taken over from aristocrats, but his cry still goes up; and if we finally weary of its savage brilliance, it is simply because the thought underlying it is so utterly negative, and, in the last resort, so ignoble in its purpose . . . Nevertheless, Juvenal remains an historical no less than a literary landmark. He crystallizes for us all the faults and weaknesses we have watched gaining strength at Rome through the centuries; when his minatory voice dies away there is nothing left but to sit in silence, and listen to Gibbon's great rhetorical epitaph on a nation that sold its soul to win the fruits of the known world.'

Peter Green

Harlton – Redgrave – Methymna – Pholegandros –
Athens 1958–66
Revised Iowa City and Austin 1996–7

THE SIXTEEN SATIRES

SATIRE I

Must I *always* be stuck in the audience, never get my own back
for all the times I've been bored by that ranting *Theseïd*
of Cordus? Shall X go free after killing me with his farces
or Y with his elegies? No come-back for whole days wasted
on a bloated *Telephus*, or *Orestes* crammed in the margins,   5
spilling over on to the verso, and *still* not finished?
I know all the mythical landscapes like my own back-room –
the grove of Mars, Vulcan's cave near Aeolus' rocky island;
what the winds are up to, which phantoms Aeacus
is tormenting, from where old what's-his-name's carrying off   10
the golden fleecelet, the size | of those ash-trees the Centaurs
      hurled –
rich Fronto's plane-trees and quivering marble statues
echo such rubbish non-stop: recitation cracks the columns.
You can expect the same from established | poets as from tyros.[1]
I too have winced under the cane, concocted 'Advice   15
to Sulla': *The despot should now retire into private life,*
take a good long sleep.[2] When you find such hordes of scribblers
all over, it's misplaced kindness *not* to write. The paper
will still be wasted. Yet why drive my team down the track
which the great Auruncan[3] blazed? If you have the leisure   20
to listen and reason calmly, I will enlighten you.

    When a flabby eunuch marries, when well-born girls go crazy
for pig-sticking up-country, bare-breasted, spear in fist;
when the barber who rasped away at my youthful beard has risen
to challenge good society with his millions; when Crispinus –   25
that Delta-bred house-slave, silt washed down by the Nile –
now hitches his shoulders under Tyrian purple, airs

a thin gold ring in summer on his sweaty finger
('My dear, I couldn't *bear* to wear my *heavier* jewels') –
30 it's harder *not* to be writing | satires; for who could endure
this monstrous city, however | callous at heart, and swallow
his wrath? Here's a new litter, crammed with that shyster lawyer
Matho.⁴ Who's next? An informer. He turned in his noble patron,
and soon he'll have gnawed away what little remains on the bone
35 of nobility. Lesser informers, terrified, stroke him with bribes:
nervous actors send their wives round to do the stroking for them.
We find ourselves elbowed aside by men who earn legacies
in bed at night, who these days scale the heavens
via that best of all routes – a well-fixed old trot's bladder.
40 Her lovers divide the estate: Proculeius gets one-twelfth,
but Gillo the rest, a fair match for the size of their – services.
All that sweat deserves *some* reward: they're both as pallid
as though they'd trodden barefoot on a snake, or were waiting
their turn to declaim, at Lyons, in Caligula's competitions.
45 Need I tell you how anger burns in my heart when I see
the bystanders jostled back by a mob of thugs, whose master
has debauched and defrauded his ward? The verdict against him
was a farce. What's infamy matter if you keep your fortune?
Exiled, the governor drinks | the day away, revels in heaven's
50 wrath: it's his province that suffers, though it won its case.⁵
     Are not such themes well worthy of Horace's pen? Should I
not attack them too? Why rehash Hercules' labours, or what
Diomedes did, all that bellowing in the Labyrinth, or the legend
of the flying craftsman, and how his son went splash in the sea?⁶
In an age when each pimp-husband takes gifts from his wife's
55   lover
(if she can't inherit by law): and is adept at watching the ceiling,
or tactfully snoring, still wide awake, in his wine,
will such things suffice? When a rake who's lost his family fortune
on racing-stables still reckons to get his cohort? Watch him
60 race down the Flaminian Way like Achilles' charioteer,
reins bunched in one hand, showing off to his mistress
who stands beside him, wrapped in his riding-cloak!
Don't you want to cram whole notebooks with scribbled
        invective

when you stand at the corner and see some forger carried past
exposed to view on all sides, in an all-but-open litter,   65
on the necks of six porters, lounging back with the air
of Maecenas himself? A will, a mere scrap of paper,
a counterfeit seal – these brought him wealth and honour.
Do you see that distinguished lady? She has the perfect dose
for her husband – old wine with a dash of parching toad's blood.   70
Locusta's a child to her;[7] she trains her untutored neighbours
to bury their blackened husbands, ignore the gossip.
If you want to be someone today, dare acts that could earn you
prison or island exile. Probity's praised – and freezes:
gardens, palaces, furniture, those antique silver cups   75
with their prancing *repoussé* goats – crime paid for the lot of
        them.
Who can sleep easy today? Avaricious daughters-in-law
and brides are seduced for cash, schoolboys are adulterers.
Though talent be wanting, yet indignation will drive me
to verse such as I – or any scribbler – can manage.   80
All human endeavours, men's prayers, fears, angers, pleasures,   85
joys and pursuits, make up the mixed mash of my book.[8]   86

    Since the days of the Flood, when Deucalion first ascended   81
that mountain-top in his vessel, and looked for a sign,
and slowly the hard stones warmed into living softness,
and Pyrrha confronted those early | males with their naked mates,   84
when has there been so abundant a crop of vices? When   87
has the purse of greed yawned wider? When was gambling
more frantic? Today men face the table's hazards
with not their purse but their strong-box open beside them.   90
Here you'll see notable battles, with the croupier for squire,
stakes for arms. Isn't it crazy to lose ten thousand
on a turn of the dice, yet grudge a shirt to your shivering slave?
In the old days who'd have built all those country houses, or
        dined
off seven courses, *alone*? Now citizens must scramble   95
for a little basket of scraps on their patron's doorstep.[9]
He peers into each face first, scared stiff that some imposter
may give a false name and cheat him: you must be identified
before you get your ration. The crier has his orders:

even the Upper-Ten must answer his summons, they're
100   scrounging
along with the rest. 'The praetor first, then the tribune –'
but a freedman blocks their way. '*I* got here first,' he argues,
'Why shouldn't I keep my place? Oh, I know I'm foreign:
look here, at my pierced ears, no use denying it – born
105   out East, on the Euphrates. But my five shops bring in
four hundred thousand, see?[10] So what's in a purple border,
what's it really worth, if a Corvinus is reduced
to herding sheep up-country, while I have more in the bank
than any Imperial favourite?' Then keep the Tribunes waiting,
110   let money reign supreme; we can't have a Johnny-come-lately,
the chalk just off his feet, flout this sacrosanct office![11]
Why not? Of all gods it's Wealth that compels our deepest
reverence – though as yet, | pernicious Cash, you lack
your own temple, though we've raised | no altars to Sovereign
        Gold
115   (as already to Honour and Peace, to Victory, Virtue
and Concord – where storks' wings rattle as you salute their nest).
        When the Consul himself tots up, at the end of his year,[12]
what the dole is worth, just what it adds to his income,
how are we poor folk to manage? Clothes and shoes must be
        bought
120   from this pittance, *and* food, *and* fuel. But a throng of litters
gets in line for the hand-out; a husband even, sometimes,
will go the rounds with a sickly or pregnant wife in tow,
or better (a well-known dodge) pretend she's there when she isn't,
and claim for both, displaying a curtained, empty sedan.
'My Galla's in there,' he says. 'Let us through! You doubt me?
125   Galla!
Put out your head! Don't disturb her – she must be sleeping –'
        The day's marked by its prescribed and fascinating routine.
Dole first: then attendance down in | the Forum, where Apollo-
as-jurisconsult surveys the Law Courts, and triumphal
130   statues abound, including a jumped-up Egyptian Pasha's,[13]
whose effigy's only fit for pissing on – or worse.
131A   [Experienced clients follow their patron home again],[14]
hoping in desperation (what expectancy lasts longer?)

for that invitation to dinner which never comes: worn out,
they drift away, poor souls, to buy cabbages and kindling.
But their lord meanwhile will loll alone at his guestless   135
dinner, scoffing the choicest produce of sea and woodland.
These fellows will gobble up whole legacies at one sitting,
off the finest, the largest, the rarest | antique dining-tables:
soon there won't be a parasite left. But who could stomach
such meanness in gourmands? What gross greed it takes to dine   140
off a whole roast boar – a creature meant for banquets!
But you'll soon pay a heavy price, when you undress and waddle
into the bath, still full of undigested game-meat –
hence sudden deaths, and old age interrupted.
The story goes round as the latest dinner-table joke,   145
and your funeral procession draws mocking cheers from your
            'friends'.
To these habits of ours there's nothing more, or worse, to be
            added
by posterity: our grandsons will share our deeds, our longings.
Today every vice has reached its ruinous zenith. So hoist
your sails, cram on all canvas! But where, you may wonder,   150
is a talent to match the theme? and where our outspoken
ancestral bluntness, that wrote at burning passion's behest?
'Whose name do I dare not utter?' Lucilius cried: 'Who cares
whether the noble Consul forgive my libel or not?'
But name an Imperial favourite, and you'll blaze, a human torch,   155
bound upright, half-choked, half-grilled, your calcined carcase
leaving a broad black trail as it's dragged across the sand.[15]
      What price the man who's poisoned three uncles with
            belladonna?
Is *he* to ride feather-bedded, and look down his nose at us?
Yes; and when he approaches, put a finger on your lips –   160
just to say *That's the man* will brand you an informer.
It's safe enough to retell how Aeneas fought fierce Turnus;
no one's a penny the worse for Achilles' death, or the frantic
search for Hylas, that time he plunged in after his pitcher.[16]
But when fiery Lucilius rages with Satire's naked sword   165
his hearers go red; their conscience freezes with their crimes,
their innards sweat in awareness of unacknowledged guilt:

hence wrath and tears. So ponder these things in your mind
before the trumpet sounds. Any later's too late
170   for a soldier. I'll try my hand on the famous dead, whose ashes
repose beside the Latin and the Flaminian Ways.[17]

SATIRE II

Northward beyond the Lapps to the frozen Polar ice-cap
is where I long to escape when I hear high moral discourse
from raging queens who affect ancestral peasant virtues.
An ignorant crowd, too, despite all those plaster busts
of Stoic philosophers on display in their houses: 5
intellectual perfection in their case means hanging up
some original portrait – Aristotle, or one of the Seven Sages.
Appearances are deceptive: every back street abounds
with solemn-faced humbuggers. *You're* castigating vice,
you, the most notable dyke among all our Socratic fairies?   10
Your shaggy limbs and the bristling hair on your forearms
proclaim a fierce spirit; but the surgeon who lances your swollen
piles breaks up at the sight of that well-smoothed passage.[1]
Such creatures talk in a clipped, laconic fashion, crop
their hair as short as their eyebrows. Give me the open, honest   15
eunuch priest: gait, gestures proclaim his twisted nature.
He's a freak of fate – indeed, his wretched self-exposure,
the very strength of his passion, demands our forgiveness
and pity. Far worse is the one who attacks such practices
with hairy masculine fervour, but after much talk of virtue   20
cocks his dish like a lady. 'What? *I'm* to respect *you*,
when you're in the trade?' cries the hustler – 'So what's to choose
between us? Let whites mock blacks, or hale men cripples!'
Who'd stand for a radical carping at revolution?
Wouldn't you think the world had turned itself upside-down   25
if embezzlers condemned extortion, or gangsters murder,
if rakes fingered adultery, traitors denounced treason,
and dictators inveighed against all purges and proscriptions?

Or take that more recent case, the adulterer with a tragic
30   incestuous twist, so busy reviving those stern decrees,
a threat to everyone – even | to Mars and Venus! Meanwhile
his too-fertile niece gobbled pills, brought on an abortion,
and every embryo lump was the living spit of Uncle.[2]
Then isn't it right and proper for even the worst sinners
35   to despise these false moralists, bite back when castigated?

    Laronia[3] couldn't stomach one such cross-patch's endless
litany ('Where, oh where, are our marriage-laws now sleeping?').
'How lucky we are today,' says she with a grin, 'in having
you to look after our morals! Rome had better behave –
40   a real killjoy, a new Cato, has dropped from the skies! But tell me,
just *where* did you buy that heavenly perfume I can smell
on your bristly neck? Don't blush to name the boutique!
If we *must* rake up old laws, surely our list should be headed
by the Sodomy Act? You should first examine the conduct
45   of men, not women. Men do worse,[4] but their numbers
protect them. They all close ranks, shields overlapping,
and queers stick together like glue. Besides, you will never find
our sex indulging in such detestable perversions –
we're not in the habit of giving | tongue to each other's parts!
50   But Hispo pleasures youths *both* ways, turns doubly pallid.[5]
Do we women ever take briefs, set ourselves up as experts
in civil law, or deafen the courts with our pleading?
Few women wrestle in Rome, few are meat-eaters –
but *you* spin your yarn with a will, and come back home
55   with baskets crammed; you twist the swelling spindle
as Penelope would, or the spider-girl Arachne,
or that unkempt drab in the play, astride her block.[6]
Everyone knows why "The Delta" willed his entire estate
to a freedman, though while he lived | it was his girl who enjoyed
60   rich gifts. It pays well to sleep third in the marriage-bed.
Get wed, keep mum: discretion spells diamond ear-bobs.
How can *you*, with such a record, denigrate women?
You censure the dove, yet absolve the perverted raven.'[7]

    Plain home-truths, these: the pseudo-philosophers fled
65   in confusion. Not one lie for them to refute. But just where
will men draw the limit, after | they see a high-born lawyer

dress in transparent chiffon, to public amazement,
to prosecute loose-living women? If they're whores, bring in
a guilty verdict: yet even a proven whore wouldn't dare
to rig herself out like *that*. 'But it's mid-July,' he complains,   70
'I'm boiling –' Then plead stark naked: it's crazy, but less
      shaming.
Is *this* an appropriate costume in which to move or expound
laws to triumphant troops, their battle-scars still fresh,
or to mountain peasants who've left | their ploughs to hear you
      speak?
What wouldn't *you* say if you saw a judge dressed up   75
like that? And just imagine a *witness* in chiffon!
You, the keen, untiring defender of Roman freedom
and law are a walking transparency! Infection spread this plague,
and will spread it further still, just as a single
scabby pig in the field brings death to the whole herd,   80
or the touch of one blighted grape will blight the bunch.[8]
In time you'll sink to worse things than your chiffon garment:
no one reaches his nadir straight off. You'll be taken up, over
      time,
by a very queer brotherhood. In the secrecy of their homes
they put on ribboned mitres and three or four necklaces,   85
then disembowel a pig and offer up bowls of wine
to placate the great Mother Goddess. Their ritual's all widdershins:
here it is *women* who may not cross the threshold:[9]
none but males can approach this altar. 'Away, profane
women!' they cry, 'no flute-girls here, no booming conches!'   90
(Such secret torch-lit orgies were known in Athens once,
when the randy Thracian priests outwore the Goddess herself.)
You'll see one initiate busy with eyebrow-pencil, kohl
and mascara, eyelids aflutter; a second sips his wine
from a big glass phallus, his long luxuriant curls   95
caught up in a golden hairnet. He'll be wearing fancy checks
with a sky-blue motif, or smooth green gabardine,
and he and his slave will both swear by women's oaths.[10]
Here's another clutching a mirror – just like that fag of an
      Emperor
Otho, who peeked at himself to see how his armour looked   100

before riding into battle. A heroic trophy *that* was,
fit matter for new annals and recent histories,
a civil war where mirrors formed part of the fighting kit!
To knock off an imperial rival[11] *and* keep your complexion fresh
105   demands consummate generalship; to camp in palatial
luxury on the battlefield, *and* give yourself a face-pack
argues true courage. No Eastern warrior-queen
(say the archer Samiramis), not ill-starred Cleopatra
aboard her flagship at Actium[12] matched such behaviour.
110   Here's no restraint of speech, no decent table-manners;
these are the Goddess's minions, here shrill affected
voices are quite in order, here the white-haired priestly dervish
who conducts the rites is a rare | and memorable instance
of the open throat, a teacher | worthy of hire. Yet one
115   Phrygian act they baulk at – slashing off that useless member.
        What about the noble Gracchus, who 'married' some common
                performer
on horn or straight trumpet – and brought him half a million
as a bridal dowry? The contract was signed; the blessing
pronounced, the blushing bride hung round 'her' husband's neck
120   at a lavish wedding-breakfast. Shades of our ancestors!
Is it a Censor we need, or an augur of evil omens?
Would *you* be more horrified, or think it a more ghastly
portent, if women calved, or cows gave birth to lambs?
This former priest of Mars, who once sweated under his nodding
125   sacred shield,[13] was now decked out in bridal frills
complete with train and veil! O Father of our City,
what brought your pastoral people to such perversion?
Great Lord of War, whence came this prurient itch upon them?
Here's a wealthy, well-born man married off to a man,
and you don't shake your helmet, or pound the ground with your
130   spear,
or complain to your father! Away with you then, clear off
from the Roman Field you neglect, that bears your name![14] 'I
        must go
down-town tomorrow first thing: a special engagement.'
'What's happening?' 'Need you ask? I'm going to a wedding –
        old X

and his boy-friend: just a few friends.' Very soon such things will
    be done,   135
and in public: they'll even angle for mention in the Gazette.
But still they have one large painful problem: they can't
hang on to their 'husbands' by producing babies.
Nature knows best, will not indulge their passions
with any physical issue. They die sterile: all in vain   140
they sample fat Greek Lyde's fertility potions,
or hold out eager hands to be struck by the wolf-boys' goatskins.[15]
But the worst remains to be told: our male bride took a trident,
put on the net-thrower's tunic, and dodged about the arena
in a gladiatorial act.[16] Yet this was the man whose blood-line   145
ran the truest of blue, whose Republican ancestry
outshone them all – the privileged ringside spectators,
even the noble patron in whose honour the show was staged.

    That ghosts exist, or subterranean kingdoms
and rivers, or black frogs croaking in Styx's waters,   150
or one punt ferrying thousands, not even children –
except those young enough to get a free bath – still credit.[17]
But just *imagine* it's true – how would our great dead captains
greet such a new arrival? And what about the flower
of our youth who died in battle, our slaughtered legionaries,   155
those myriad shades of war? If only they commanded
sulphur and torches in Hades, and a few damp laurel-twigs,
they'd insist on being purified. Yes: even among the dead
we're paraded to public scorn. Though our armies have advanced
to Ireland, though the Orkneys are ours, and northern Britain   160
making do with the shortest nights, these conquered tribes abhor
the vices that flourish throughout their conquerors' capital.[18] Yet
we hear of one Armenian who outstripped our most effeminate
young home-grown Roman pansies: *he* surrendered his person
to the lusts of a *tribune*. A good deal more than the mind   165
is broadened by travel: he came to Rome as a hostage,
but Rome turns boys into men. If they stay here long enough
to catch her sickness, they'll never go short of lovers.
Trousers, sheath-knives, whips, even bridles, are cast aside,
and they carry back upper-class Roman | habits to Ardaschan.[19]   170

SATIRE III

Despite the wrench of parting, I applaud my old friend's
decision to make his home in lonely Cumae,
and give the Sibyl at least *one* fellow-citizen!
A charming coastal retreat, this, and the gateway to Baiae –
5   though myself, I'd prefer a barren island to down-town Rome:[1]
what squalor, what isolation would not be minor evils
compared to an endless nightmare of fires and collapsing
houses, the myriad perils encountered in this brutal
city, and poets reciting their epics all through *August*!
10   While his chattels were being loaded on to one small waggon,
my friend stood by the damp arches of the old Capuan Gate,
where King Numa had nightly meetings with his mistress.
(But these days Egeria's grove and shrine and sacred spring
are rented out to Jews, their gear a Sabbath haybox:[2]
15   each tree's under orders to pay rent to the City,
the Muses have been evicted, the wood's turned mendicant.)
       From here we strolled down to Egeria's valley, its grotto
modernized past recognition. (What a gain in sanctity
and atmosphere, if green-grassed banks surrounded
20   the pool, if no flash marble affronted our native limestone!)
Here Umbricius[3] stood. 'There's no room in this city,' he said,
'for the decent professions:[4] their emoluments are nil.
My resources have shrunk since yesterday, and tomorrow
will eat away more of what's left. So I am going
25   where Daedalus put off his weary wings,[5] while as yet
I'm in vigorous middle age, while active years are left me,
while my white hairs are still few, and I need no stick
to guide my tottering feet. So farewell Rome, I leave you

to sanitary engineers and municipal architects, fellows
who by swearing black is white find it easy to land   30
contracts for a new temple, swamp-drainage, harbour-works,
river-clearance, undertaking, the lot – then pocket the profit
and fraudulently file their petition in bankruptcy.
These creatures used to be horn-players, stumping the provinces
in road-shows, their puffed-out cheeks a familiar sight; but now   35
they stage gladiatorial games, and at the mob's thumbs-down
will butcher a loser for popularity's sake, and then
move on to lease public privies. But why draw the line at that?
These are such men as Fortune, by way of a joke,
will sometimes raise from the gutter and make Top People.   40
    'What can I do in Rome? I'm a hopeless liar. Supposing
a book is bad, I can't puff it, and beg for a copy. Astral
motions I never learnt. Guaranteeing a father's death –
that I cannot and will not do. I have never meddled
with frogs' guts;[6] others know more about bearing adulterers'   45
letters – and presents – to wives. I won't be an accomplice
in larceny – *ergo*, no governor will take me on his staff:
it's like being a paralysed cripple, right hand useless.
Who today gets taken up if he's not in the know,
mind seething with private matters, never to be revealed?   50
Harmless secrets bear no obligations, nor will the person
who imparts them to you do *you* any favours thereafter;
but if Verres[7] promotes a man, that man has the screws on Verres
and could trash him at will. Not all the gold washed seaward
with the silt of shady Tagus is worth the price you must pay   55
to be racked by insomnia, feared by your high-placed friends –
and for what? Too-transient prizes, unwillingly resigned.
    'Now let me turn to that race[8] which goes down so sweetly
with our millionaires, but remains my special pet aversion,
and not mince my words. I cannot, citizens, stomach   60
a Greek Rome. Yet what fraction of these dregs is truly Greek?
For years now eastern Orontes has discharged into the Tiber
its lingo and manners, its flutes, its outlandish harps
with their transverse strings, its native tambourines,
and the whores pimped out round the racecourse.[9] (That's where
        you go   65

if you fancy a *foreign* pick-up, in one of those saucy toques;
while every rustic today wears dinner-pumps – *trechedipna* –
and *niceteria* – medals – round his *ceromatic*, or mud-caked,
neck.) They flock in from high Sicyon, or Macedonia's uplands,
70   from Andros or Samos, from Tralles and Alabanda,
all of them lighting out for the City's classiest districts
and burrowing into great houses, with plans to take them over.
Quick wit, unlimited nerve, a gift of the gab that outsmarts
a professional public speaker – that's them. So what do you take
75   that fellow to be? He's brought every profession with him –
schoolmaster, rhetorician, surveyor, artist, masseur,
diviner, tightrope-walker, magician or quack, your hungry
Greekling is all by turns. Tell him to fly – he's airborne!
The inventor of wings for men was no Moor or Slav, remember,
80   or Thracian, but born in the very heart of Athens.[10]

    'Time to get out, when such men put on the purple,
when louts blown into Rome along with the figs and damsons
precede me at dinner-parties, or for the witnessing
of manumissions and wills[11] – *me*, who drew my first breath
85   among these Roman hills, and was nourished on Sabine olives!
What's more, there's none can match their talent for flattery:
dummies they laud as eloquent, the ugly they call handsome,
a scrag-necked weakling they liken to Hercules, hoisting
the giant Antaeus aloft, way off the earth. They go
90   into ecstasies over some shrill and scrannel tenor
who cock-a-doodles worse than a rooster treading his hen.
We can make the same compliments, but *they're* the ones
people believe. Who can beat them in any performance
of female parts, as courtesan, matron or slave-girl?[12]
95   No mantle, either; you'd swear that what you saw and heard
was a woman, not an impersonator: no bulge
beneath the belly, all smooth, with even a suggestion
of the Great Divide. Yet, back home, even the most famous
of these tragedy queens and dames will pass unnoticed.
100   They're a nation of actors. Laugh, and they'll out-guffaw you,
split their sides. When faced | with a friend's tears, they weep
            too,
though totally unmoved. If you ask for a fire in winter,

the Greek dons his cloak; if you say | "I'm hot", he'll begin
    sweating.
So we're not on an equal footing: he has the great advantage
of being able, night or day, to borrow his expression   105
from another man's face, to raise his hands and applaud
when a friend burps loudly, or pisses right on the mark,
with a splendid drumming sound from the upturned golden
    basin.[13]
Besides, nothing's sacred to him and his randy urges,[14]
neither the housewife, nor her virgin daughter, nor her   110
daughter's still beardless fiancé, nor her hitherto virtuous son –
and if none of these is to hand, he'll lay his friend's grandmother.
[They want to worm out secrets, get a hold over people.][15]

    'And while we're discussing Greeks, let us consider,
not the gymnasium crowd, but some bigwig philosophers,   115
like that elderly Stoic informer who destroyed his friend and pupil:
he was brought up in Tarsus, by the banks of the river
where Bellerophon fell to earth from the Gorgon's flying nag.[16]
No room for honest Romans when Rome's ruled by a junta
of Greek-born secret agents, men who – like all their race –   120
never share friends or patrons, but keep them to themselves.
One small dose of venom (half Greek, half personal) dropped
in that receptive ear, and I'm out, shown the back-door,
my years of obsequious service all gone for nothing. Where
can a hanger-on be ditched with less fuss than here in Rome?   125
    'Besides (not to flatter ourselves) what use are *our* humble
    efforts,
dressing up while it's dark still, hurrying along,
when the praetor's kicking his lictor into racing ahead
to greet two maiden ladies (who've been up and about for hours),
and scared stiff lest his colleague manage to get there first?   130
Here a citizen's son is shouldered off the sidewalk
by some rich man's slave, who'll hand out a legionary tribune's
pay to his aristocratic amateur call-girl
for jerking off quickly in her. But when some common-or-garden
garish scrubber attracts *you*, you dither and hesitate: 135
Can I afford to accost her? It's the same with court witnesses:
morals don't count. If Numa or Scipio took the stand –

and *he* escorted the Mother Goddess to Rome! – or Metellus
who rescued Minerva's image from her blazing shrine, the
      immediate
140   question would still be: "*How much is he worth?*",[17] with only
an afterthought on his character. "How many slaves does he keep?
What's his acreage? How big, how good, is his dinner-service?"
Each man's word is as good as his bond – or rather, the number
of bonds in his strong-box. A pauper | can swear on every altar
145   between Samothrace and Rome – he'll *still* pass for a perjuror
(though the Gods themselves forgive him), a defier of heaven's
      wrath.
The poor man's always a target for everyone's mocking
laughter, with his torn and dirt-encrusted top-coat,
his grubby toga, one shoe agape where the leather's
150   split open – those clumsy patches, that coarse and tell-tale
stitching no more than a day or two old. The hardest
thing that there is to bear about wretched poverty
is the fact that it makes men ridiculous. "You! Get out
of those front-row seats," we're told. "You ought to be
      ashamed –
155   your incomes are *far* too meagre! The law's the law. Make way
for some pander's son and heir, spawned in an unknown brothel;
yield your place to the offspring of that natty auctioneer
with the trainer's son and the ring-fighter's brat applauding beside
      him!"
All the fault of that idiot Otho and his Reserved Seat Act.[18]
160   What prospective son-in-law ever passed muster here
if he couldn't match the girl's dowry? What poor man ever
      inherits,
or is hired by the Office of Works? All low-income citizens
should have marched out of town, in a body, years ago.
Nobody finds it easy to get to the top if restricted
165   resources cripple his talent. But in Rome the problem's worse –
inflation swells the rent of your miserable flat, inflation
hits the keep of your hungry slaves, your own humble dinner.
You're ashamed to eat off earthenware – yet if transported
to a rural peasant regime, you'd be content enough
170   to wear a hooded cloak of coarse blue broadcloth.

Throughout most of Italy – let's admit it – no one is seen
wearing a toga until he's dead. Even on public
holidays, when last year's shows are cheerfully staged
in the grass-grown theatre, when peasant children, sitting
on their mothers' laps, shrink back in terror at the sight   175
of those gaping, whitened masks, you'll still find the entire
audience – top row or bottom – dressed exactly alike.
Even the highest magistrates feel themselves entitled
to no better badge of status than a plain white tunic.
But in Rome we must toe the line of fashion, spending   180
beyond our means, and often on borrowed credit.
It's a universal failing: here we all live in pretentious
poverty. To cut a long story short, there's a price-tag
on everything in Rome. What does it cost to greet Cossus,
or extract one tight-lipped nod from Veiento the
          honours-broker?[19]   185
X's beard is being trimmed, Y's dedicating his boy-friend's
kiss-curls: the house is full | of venal barbers.[20] So swallow
your bile, and face the fact that all we hangers-on
have to bribe our way, swell some sleek menial's savings.

   'Who fears, or ever feared, the collapse of his house in cool   190
Praeneste, or rural Gabii, or Tivoli perched on its hillside,
or Volsinii, nestling amid its woodland ridges?[21] But here
we inhabit a city largely shored up with gimcrack
stays and props: that's how | our landlords postpone slippage,
and – after masking great cracks in the ancient fabric – assure   195
the tenants they can sleep sound, when the house is tottering.
Myself, I prefer life without fires, without nocturnal panics.[22]
By the time the smoke's reached the third floor – and you're still
          asleep –
the heroic downstairs neighbour is roaring for water, shifting
his stuff to safety. If the alarm's at ground-level,   200
the last to fry is the wretch among the nesting pigeons
with nothing but tiles between himself and the weather.
What did Cordus own? One divan, | too short to bed a dwarf in;
six mugs on a marble-topped sideboard; beneath it, a pitcher
and an up-ended bust of Chiron; one ancient settle   205
crammed with Greek books – though by now uncultured mice

had gnawed their way well through his texts of the great poets.
Cordus had just about nothing – who'd deny it? – yet that
      nothing
the wretched man lost *in toto*. Today the final

210   straw on his load of woe (broke, begging for crusts) is, no one
will give him a roof and shelter, no one will buy him food.
But if some great man's mansion is gutted, women go crazy,
top people put on mourning, the courts go into recess:
then we deplore urban hazards, complain about fires!

215   *Then* contributions pour in while the shell is still ash-hot –
construction materials, marble, fresh-gleaming sculptured nudes.
One friend provides antique bronzes by Euphranor and Polyclitus,
another, old icons looted from some Asiatic temple;
a third, bookshelves and books, with a study-bust of Minerva;

220   yet another, a sackful of silver. And so this dandified
bachelor more than makes good his losses, till a rumour –
well-founded – gets around that he set the fire himself.[23]

    'If you can tear yourself loose from the Games, a first-class
house can be purchased, freehold, in any small country town

225   at the price of a year's rent, here, for some shabby, ill-lit attic.
A garden plot's thrown in, a well with a shallow basin –
no rope-and-bucket work when your seedlings need watering!
Fall in love with that two-tined hoe, work and plant your
      allotment
till a hundred vegetarians could feast off its produce.

230   It's quite a feat anywhere, even out in the backwoods,
to have made yourself master of – well, a single lizard.

    'Insomnia causes most deaths here (the complaint itself
being brought on by indigestion, rich food lying heavy
on a stomach sour with heartburn): show me the apartment

235   that lets you sleep! In this city sleep costs millions,
and that's the root of the trouble. The waggons thundering past
through those narrow twisting streets, the oaths of draymen
      caught
in a traffic-jam, would rouse a dozing seal – or an Emperor.[24]
If the tycoon has an appointment, he rides there in a big litter,

240   the crowd parting before him. There's plenty of room inside:
he can read, or take notes, or snooze as he jogs along –

those drawn blinds are most soporific. Even so
he outstrips us: however fast we pedestrians may hurry
crowds surge ahead, those behind us buffet my rib-cage,
poles poke into me; one lout swings a crossbeam   245
down on my skull, another scores with a barrel.
My legs are mud-encrusted, from all sides big feet kick me,
a hobnailed soldier's boot lands squarely on my toes.
Do you see all that steam and bustle? A hundred hangers-on,
each followed by his scullion, are getting their free dinners.   250
A strongman could scarcely tote those outsize dixies,
all the gear one poor little servant must balance on his head,
trotting briskly along to keep the charcoal glowing.

   'Newly-patched tunics are torn again. Here's the tall trunk
of a fir-tree swaying past on its waggon, behind it a dray   255
stacked high with pine-logs, a nodding | threat to the populace.
Just suppose that the axle supporting that cartload of marble
were to snap, and the whole lot avalanche down on them –
what would be left of their bodies? Who could identify fragments
of ownerless flesh and bone? The poor man's flattened carcase   260
would vanish along with his soul. The folk at home, meanwhile,
are cheerfully scouring dishes, blowing the fire to a glow,
clattering greasy scrapers, filling oil-flasks, laying out towels.
But already, while his houseboys bustle about their chores,
himself, the latest arrival, is sitting there on the bank,   265
scared of that filthy old ferryman. No crossing the muddy
channel for *him*, poor devil, with no fare-coin in his mouth.

   'There are various other nocturnal perils to be considered:
it's a long way up to the rooftops, and a falling tile
can brain you.[25] Think of all those cracked or leaky vessels   270
tossed out of windows – the way they smash, their weight,
the damage they do to the sidewalk! You'll be thought most
      improvident,
a catastrophe-happy fool, if you don't make your will before
venturing out to dinner. Each open upper casement
along your route at night may prove a death-trap: 275
so pray and hope (poor you!) that the local housewives
drop nothing worse on your head than a pailful of slops.

   'Then there's the drunken bully, who's found no victim,

and lies there in agony, tossing and turning all night,
280   like Achilles after his friend Patroclus' death.[26]
[He can't doze off otherwise; for certain individuals]
only a fight brings sleep. Yet however flown with wine
our young hothead may be, he carefully keeps his distance
from the man in a scarlet cloak, the man surrounded
285   by torches and big brass lamps and a numerous bodyguard.
But for me, a lonely pedestrian, trudging home by moonlight
or with hand cupped round the wick of one poor guttering
        candle,
he has only contempt. Hear how this wretched quarrel starts
(a *quarrel*? when you're the fighter, and I'm just punchbag?):
290   he blocks my way, tells me to stop. I have to obey him –
what else can you do when attacked | by a raging tough who's
        stronger
than you are? "Where have *you* sprung from?" he shouts. "Ugh,
        what a stench
of beans and sour wine! You've been round with some
        cobbler-crony,
scoffing a boiled sheep's head and a dish of chopped spring leeks!
295   Nothing to say? Speak up, or I'll kick your teeth in!
Tell me, where's your pitch? What synagogue do you doss in?"
Whether you try to answer or back away in silence
makes no odds, you're beaten up anyway – then your irate
        "victim"
takes *you* to court! Such, then, is the poor man's "freedom":
300   after being slugged to a pulp, he may beg for his last few
remaining teeth to be left him, as a special favour.

    'Nor is this the sum of your terrors: when every building
is shuttered, when shops stand silent, when doors are chained,
there are still cat-burglars in plenty waiting to rob you, or else
305   you'll be knifed – a quick job – by some street-apache. Whenever
the swamps and forests[27] are cleared out by armed patrols,
such folk make headlong for Rome, as though into a warren.
Our furnaces glow, our anvils are weighted down with chains –
310   that's where most of our iron goes nowadays: one wonders
whether ploughshares, hoes and mattocks may not soon be
        obsolete.

How fortunate they were (you well may think), those early
forebears of ours, how happy | the good old days of kings
and tribunes, when Rome made do with one prison only![28]

    'There are many other arguments I could adduce: but the sun   315
slants down, my cattle are lowing, I must be on my way –
the muleteer has been signalling me with his whip
for some while now. So goodbye, don't forget me – and
      whenever
you get back home to Aquinum for a break from the City,
invite me over from Cumae, to share your fields and coverts:[29]   320
I'll make the trip – in boots – to those chilly uplands,
and hear your *Satires* – if *they* think me worthy of that honour.'[30]

SATIRE IV

Here's Crispinus again,[1] and I shall have frequent occasion
to bring him on stage – a monster without one single redeeming
virtue, a sick voluptuary strong only in his lusts,
which draw the line at nothing except unmarried girls . . .[2]
. . . So what are they worth in the end – those mile-long
5   colonnades[3]
and shady parks through which he drives with his carriage
and pair, his countless mansions, his property near the Forum?
No bad man is happy, least of all the seducer – and he
sacrilegious as well – with whom a virgin priestess, lately,
10 lay, to be buried alive, the blood still hot in her veins.[4]
But now to a lighter topic – though if any other man
had acted that way, he'd have had | the authorities on his tail:
for what would be reprehensible in Citizen A or B
was fine for Crispinus. But what's to be done, when the man
        himself
15 eclipses all charges in foulness? He purchased a red mullet
for sixty gold pieces – or ten to each pound weight
(as they'd say who always try to make things more impressive).
A shrewd investment, perhaps, if he'd used it to persuade
some childless dotard to name him | a principal legatee;
20 or, better still, offered it to his expensive mistress,
who rides in her cave-like sedan, blinds drawn over big windows.
But no: for himself he bought it. We see things done nowadays
undreamed-of by that poor cheapskate Apicius.[5] Did *you*
pay *that* much for fish-scales, Crispinus, you who once
wore your native papyrus as loin-cloth? The fisherman would
25   have cost

less than the fish. At that price you could have purchased
most of Provence, or a vast Apulian plantation.
What kind of banquet was it that the Imperial Person himself
guzzled, I wonder, when all that gold – a merest
fraction of the whole cost, a modest side-dish – was   30
belched up by this clapped-out Palace buffoon in purple,
this Senior Knight, no less, who once went bawling his wares,
cheap job-lots of catfish – Alexandrian, like their hawker.
Calliope, Muse of Epic, begin! You can hold forth seated
and singing's out, truth's in. Say on, Pierian girls!   35
(And I hope that calling you 'girls' will work to my advantage.)
      In the days when the last Flavian was flaying a half-dead
            world,
and Rome was in thrall to a hairless Nero, there barrelled
into a net by Ancona, where the shrine of Venus stands
on her Adriatic headland, an eye-popping giant of a turbot,   40
as huge as those tunny that spend | all winter under the frozen
Sea of Azov, and finally, when the spring sun melts
the ice, are borne down-current to the mouth of the Black Sea,
torpid with sloth, and fat from long hibernation.[6]
This splendid catch the owner | of boat and trawl has earmarked   45
for Rome's Pontifical Majesty – since who'd dare auction
or buy such a fish, when the very seashore swarms
with narks and informers? Every Inspector of Seaweed
from miles around would pounce on this defenceless boatman,
all quoting law, to wit, that the fish was a fugitive,   50
a former regular feeder in the Imperial stews, and having
fled thence, must now be restored to its former master.
If the masters of jurisprudence are to be trusted,
everything rare and lovely that swims in the ocean,
wheresoever, belongs to the Crown. So make it a present   55
rather than perish![7]
                    Now pestilential autumn
was yielding to frosts; now patients were hoping for milder fevers,
and harsh winter's icy blasts kept the turbot refrigerated.
On sped the fisherman, as though blown by a south wind,
till below him lay the lakes where Alba, though in ruins,   60
still guards the flame of Troy and the lesser Vestal shrine.[8]

A wondering crowd thronged round him, briefly blocking his
        way,
till the smooth-hinged doors swung inward, the crowd fell back,
and the senators – still shut out – saw the fish admitted
65   to the Epic Presence. 'Accept,' the fisherman said, 'this gift
too large for a private kitchen. Keep holiday today,
purge your stomach forthwith of its last square meal
and prepare to eat a turbot saved to adorn your reign –
it insisted on being caught.' Gross flattery, and yet
70   the Imperial Crest surged up: there is nothing godlike power
will refuse to believe of itself in the way of commendation.
But alas, no big enough dish could be found for the fish. A
        summons
went out to the Privy Council, each of whom quailed beneath
the Emperor's hatred, whose drawn white faces reflected
75   that great and perilous 'friendship'.[9] First in response to the call
of the chamberlain – 'Hurry! He's seated!' – and clutching his
        cloak
came Pegasus,[10] new bailiff to the bewildered City
(what else, then, were Prefects but bailiffs?). Still, Pegasus made
as righteous a jurist as any – though he held that those troubled
        times[11]
80   constituted a warrant for Justice pulling her punches
on every occasion. Next came the aged, genial Crispus,[12]
whose manners – like his morals – were mild and pliable. No
        one
could better have served to advise a monarch with absolute sway
over seas and lands and nations – if only he had been free,
85   under that scourge, that plague, to speak out against cruelty,
tender honest advice. But what could be more capricious
than a tyrant's ear, on whose whim there hung the fate of a friend
who'd been chatting about the rain, or the heat, or the spring
        showers?
So Crispus never swam upstream against that raging torrent,
90   wasn't the kind of citizen to speak his mind freely, proffer
an honest private opinion, or stake his life on the truth;
and so he survived many winters, to reach his eightieth year,
safeguarded, even in *that* Court, by such defensive techniques.

Another elderly statesman, Acilius, hurried in next,
with his son, who ill-deserved the harsh, too-imminent fate   95
in store for him, cut down by Authority's sword.[13] Long life
and breeding together today are so rare, I'd rather be
a son of the soil, a shrimpling brother to giants.
Poor wretch, the trouble he took – stripped off, at close quarters,
sticking Numidian bears in that private country arena![14]   100
No good. Such patrician gambits are common knowledge
today; who's still taken in by the well-tried ancient tricks
old Brutus knew? Too easy to gull a bearded monarch.[15]

Next, no more cheerful-looking, despite his plebeian blood,
came Rubrius, once condemned for a crime best not referred
          to[16] –   105
yet still possessing the gall of a faggot scribbling satire.
Next, Montanus'[17] gross paunch | appeared, with dragging belly,
and – reeking of morning unguents, more aromatic
than two funerals put together – Crispinus; then Pompeius,[18]
who outmatched him in ruthlessness, whose whisper slit men's
          throats;   110
Fuscus,[19] who dreamed of battle while lolling in marbled villas,
his guts a predestined feast for Romania's vultures;
Veiento the trimmer,[20] and deadly Catullus, burning
for love of a girl he had never seen, a monster –
even by current standards – in a category of his own,   115
blind fawner and ominous Secretary for Bridges:
well suited to beg at carriage-wheels outside Ariccia,
blowing kisses to every coach as it lumbered down the hill.[21]
His double-take at the turbot was unsurpassed, he went on
and on about it, staring left – though the creature   120
was on his right. (He'd also give boxing commentaries[22]
or track the hoist that whisks boy-acrobats to the awnings.)
But Veiento, unyielding, like some frenzied acolyte
of Bellona, erupts in prophetic | utterance. 'A mighty
omen!' he cries, 'a sign of great and glorious triumph!   125
You will capture some king – perhaps Arvíragus of the Britons
will fall from his chariot:[23] the creature's foreign too –
just look at the spines down its back!' All that Veiento
failed to point out was the turbot's age and birthplace.

      'Then what's your advice? Cut him up?' 'No, no!' Montanus
130   exclaimed,
'Spare him that last indignity! Procure a deep casserole
big enough for its fragile walls to contain his massive bulk!
Some mighty Prometheus[24] is needed, at once, to make such a
     dish!
Quick, fetch clay and a wheel – but henceforward, Caesar,
135   let potters always be numbered among your retinue.'
      Motion carried – and worthy of such a proposer. He'd known
the old Imperial Court and its luxuries, Nero's midnight
banquets that kindled new appetites, when veins were on fire
with vintage wine. No man in my time was a greater
140   gourmet: he knew, and could tell you, at the very first bite,
just where an oyster came from – whether it was raised in
Circeii, the Lucrine pond, or the sea-beds of Richborough:
the lowly sea-urchin he placed with a single glance.[25]
      All rose. The meeting was over, the Councillors dismissed.
145   Yet their mighty master had sent an emergency summons
which brought them post-haste, and panic-struck, to his castle,
as though with news of the Rhinelanders, or the ferocious
Prussians;[26] anxious dispatches might have been pouring in,
on precipitate wing, from all parts of the empire.
150   Yet would that he'd rather devoted all his savage instincts
to such trifles! He robbed Rome of her most illustrious
and noblest sons, unopposed. No hand was raised
to avenge them. He could welter in Lamian blood. But once
the commons began to fear him, then he was done for.[27]

SATIRE V

If you're still unashamed of your life-style, Trebius,[1] still
    convinced
that the highest good's scraping crusts from another man's board;
if you can put up with what would not have been tolerated
by Augustus's wits and jesters, down below the salt – why then
I'd be shy of accepting your evidence, even on oath!   5
Nothing I know asks less than the gut: yet supposing
even the little that's needed to fill its void is absent –
are there no sidewalks or bridges,[2] no share in a beggar's mat
for you to make your pitch from? Is dinner worth such insults?
Are you *that* famished? Wouldn't your self-respect do better   10
out there, shivering cold, and chewing on mouldy dog's bread?

    Get one thing clear from the start: a dinner-invitation
settles the score in full for your earlier services.
What this great 'friendship' yields is – food. Your lord scores
    meals,
however infrequent, scores them to square his accounts. So if –   15
after two months during which his client is quite forgotten –
with the bottom place to be filled at the lowest table,
he says 'Be my guest', you're in heaven. What more could
    Trebius
hope for? He has his reward – though it means a short night's
    sleep,
and rushing out, shoelaces trailing, all in a pother for fear   20
lest the whole crowd's been round already, paid their respects
before the stars have vanished, at that early hour
when the frosty Waggon is lazily circling the heavens still.

    Yet – what a dinner! The wine's so rough that sheep-clippings

25   wouldn't absorb it; you'll see guests turn Corybants.
      At first it's only insults – but soon a regular battle
      breaks out between you and the freedmen, cheap crockery flies
      in all directions, you're hurling cups yourself
      and mopping the blood off with a crimsoned napkin.
30   Virro's[3] own wine was bottled when the consuls wore long hair:
      those grapes were trodden during the Social Wars – and yet
      not a spoonful will he send to a friend with heartburn!
      Tomorrow he'll choose some other vintage, the best,
      from the Alban or Setine hills,[4] a jar so ancient, so blackened
35   with hearth-soot, that source and date are both illegible:
      such wine our Stoic martyrs would toss down, garlanded,
      on the birthday of Brutus or Cassius.[5] The goblets that Virro
      drinks from are regular tankards, amber-encrusted,
      studded with beryl. But *you* get no golden vessels –
40   or if you do, a waiter is stationed close beside you
      to count the jewels, check your sharp fingernails.
      Please excuse him: that jasper's a fine piece, much admired.
      Virro, like many others, has transferred his gems from fingers
      to cups. (Our ancient heroes – such as the youth preferred
45   over green-eyed Iarbas – fronted their scabbards with them.)
      But the cup *you* drink from, the sort with four big nozzles –
      named after Nero's long-nosed | cobbler from Beneventum[6] –
      will be shoddy and cracked, crying out for cement to mend it.
          If my lord's stomach is heated by wine and victuals, then
50   boiled ice-water's brought him, chiller than mountain snow-drifts.
      Did I complain just now that different wine was served you?
      You don't drink the same *water*! *Your* cups are proffered
      by some Saharan groom, or in the bony hand
      of a blackavised Moor, whom you'd much prefer *not* to meet
55   while driving uphill, at night, past the tombs on the Latin Way.
      But himself has the flower of Asia before him, a youth
      purchased for more than warrior | Tullus, Ancus – indeed,
      all the early Roman kings – could scrape up between them,
      cash and chattels together.[7] So, when you're thirsty, you must
60   catch your black Ganymede's eye. A boy who cost thousands
      won't mix drinks for the indigent – though such youth, such
              beauty

excuse his disdain. Will he ever get round to you?
If you ask him for hot or cold water, do you think he'll fetch it?
No way: he resents attending to some ancient hanger-on –
resents your requests, resents even | standing while you're seated.   65
[Great houses are always crammed with these supercilious
      flunkeys.]
Here's another: look how he grumbles as he offers you the bread,
though it's almost too hard to break, solid lumps of old mouldy
dough that crack your grinders sooner than let you bite them.
But snowy-white, fresh-baked from the very finest flour,   70
is the loaf reserved for my lord. And remember to keep your
      hands
to yourself, show reverence for the bread-pan. If you're daring
enough to reach for a slice, someone's there to make you drop it:
'The impertinence! Kindly keep to your proper basket
if you don't mind, remember the colour of your bread!'   75
'Was it for this,' you wail, 'that daily I abandoned
my wife to go scrambling up the steep and chilly
Esquiline streets,[8] through violent | springtime Jupiter's
      hailstorms,
or some sudden cloudburst that drips from my sodden cloak?'
    Observe the size of that crayfish: it marks out a platter   80
reserved for my lord. Please note the asparagus garnish
heaped high around it, the peacocking tail that looks down
on the guests as it's brought in, borne aloft by some tall waiter!
But *you* get half an egg that's stuffed with a single prawn,
and served in a little saucer, like some funeral offering.[9]   85
Himself drizzles his fish with the finest oil, but *your*
colourless boiled cabbage (poor you!) will have an aroma
of the lamp; the stuff you're offered as a dressing
came to town in some sharp-prowed felucca. One good sniff,
and you know why Africans empty the public baths.   90
Rub it on you, and poisonous snakes will give you a wide berth.
    My lord will have his mullet, imported from Corsica
or the rocks below Taormina: home waters are all fished out
to fill such ravening maws, our local breeding-grounds
are trawled without cease, the market never lets up –   95
we kill off the fry now, close seasons go by the board.

The provinces keep our kitchens supplied with gourmet items
that legacy-hunters purchase, and their spinster quarry sells back.
Virro is served with a lamprey: no finer specimen ever
100 came from Sicilian waters. When the south wind's in abeyance,
drying damp wings in his cell, then hardy fishermen
will dare the wrath of Charybdis. But what's in store for you?
An eel, perhaps (though it rather resembles a water-snake),
or a grey-mottled river-pike, born and bred in the Tiber,
105 bloated with torrents of sewage, a long-term *habitué*
of those cesspools underlying the slums of the Subura.[10]

A word with himself now – if he will deign to listen.
'Nowadays no one expects such generous presents
as the old Republican gentry once used to lavish
110 on their humbler friends. In those times such largesse
brought more honour than title or office. All we're asking
is – dine with us as an equal. Do this, and no one'll care
if, like too many, you hoard | your wealth, act poor to your
          friends.'[11]

Himself is served with a force-fed goose's liver,
115 a capon the size of the goose, and a boar, all steaming-hot,
such as Meleager slew. Afterwards, if it's springtime,
and thunder's answered men's prayers for this luxury extra,
truffles appear.[12] 'Ah, Africa!' cries the gourmet,
'keep your grain, unyoke your oxen – just send us truffles!'
120 Meanwhile, to ensure no cause for resentment is lacking,
watch the carver prancing about, with *brandissements* of his flying
knife, and carrying out each last one of his master's
instructions: no small matter to make a nice distinction
between the proper gestures for the carving of hares and hens!

125 If you ever dare to hold forth as though you had a title,
you'll be dragged by the heels, and bounced from the front-door
like Hercules' victim Cacus.[13] When, pray, will Virro
make a toast to *you*, or offer to drink from the cup
your lips have touched? And which of you is so reckless,
130 so utterly lost as to call 'Drink up!' to your patron?
There's a lot that mere threadbare retainers can never express.
but if some god, or mere godlike | human, kinder than Fate,
capitalized you for knighthood[14] – *then* see how you'd rise

from nowhere to the position of Virro's dear, dear friend!
'Give Trebius this! A helping | of that for Trebius! Will you   135
try some tenderloin, brother?' O Cash, it's you he honours,
you who are truly his brother. But if your ambition's to be
a magnate, a patron of magnates – don't have a small Aeneas
playing around the house with his young, enchanting sister:
barrenness in your wife makes for cheerful, attentive friends.   140
But as things are now, even should your wife present you
with triplets, still Virro will offer congratulations
on your squalling brood, send each a green baby-coat,
and later play uncle to them with peanuts and pennies
whenever the little freeloaders turn up at dinner-time.   145
     For the lower-income guests, some dubious toadstools:
for my lord, a rare mushroom, the kind that Claudius guzzled
(until his wife fed him one that wrote finis to his eating).
For himself, and his fellow-tycoons, friend Virro will order
the choicest fruits to be served, their scent a feast in itself,   150
fruit such as grew in Phaeacia's eternal autumn,[15]
or might, you feel, have been rifled from the Hesperides.
For yourself, a rotten apple, the sort munched on the
         Embankment[16]
by monkeys with shield and helmet, cringing beneath the whip
as they learn to throw spears from the back of some shaggy
         she-goat.   155
     Perhaps you think Virro's close-fisted? No way. He does it
to make you suffer. What farce, what pantomime could elicit
bigger laughs than your pleading gullet? His whole idea –
in case you didn't get it – is simply to reduce you
to furious tears, an endless grinding of molars.   160
You see yourself as a free man, your lord's invited guest;
but *he* assumes you've been hooked by the smell from his
         kitchen –
and he's not far wrong. For what self-respecting person,
however down-and-out, whether born to the purple
or a simple peasant, would put up with Virro *twice*?   165
It's the hope of a good dinner that lures you – 'Surely he'll give us
a picked-over hare, or some scraps from the boar's butt-end?
Surely a chicken's carcase will come our way?'[17] So you sit there,

the lot of you, speechless, expectant, clutching untasted rolls.
170   He has taste who treats you thus. If you really can swallow
all that, why then, you deserve it. Some day you'll find yourself
sticking out your shaven head to be banged, like a public buffoon,
inured to the whip, most worthy | of such feasts, of such a
'partner'.[18]

SATIRE VI

During Saturn's reign I believe that Chastity still lingered
on earth, and was seen for a while, when draughty caves
were the only homes men had, hearthfire and household
gods, family and cattle all shut in darkness together,
when hillbilly wives would spread their woodland beds   5
with dry leaves and straw, and the pelts of those wild beasts
caught prowling the area – a far cry from Cynthia,
or the girl who wept, red eyed, for that sparrow's death.[1]
Their breasts gave suck to big strong babies – indeed,
very often they out-bristled their acorn-belching husbands.   10
Once, when the world was young, and the sky bright-new still,
men's lives were different: born from rock and oak,
or moulded from living clay,[2] they had no parents.
Some few traces, perhaps, of Chastity's ancient presence
survived under Jove – but only while Jove remained   15
a beardless stripling, long | before Greeks had learned to swear
by the other man's head, when no one was scared of thieves
in the vegetable-patch or orchard, when gardens were still
        unwalled.
Thereafter, slowly, Justice | withdrew to heaven, together
with Chastity – both sisters beating a common retreat.[3]   20
    It's an old well-established tradition, Postumus, to bounce
your neighbour's bed, outrage matrimonial sanctity.
All other crimes came later, with the Age of Iron –
but the Silver Era witnessed our first adulterers.
And here you are *today*, man, getting yourself engaged,   25
fixing marriage-covenant, dowry; soon some high-class barber
will be fixing your hair, perhaps | you've already got the ring

on her finger! But *marrying*, Postumus? You used to be quite
     sane –
what Fury's got into you, what snake has stung you up?
30   Why stand such bitch-tyranny when there's rope available,
when those dizzying top-floor windows are all wide open,
when there's a bridge near by from which you can make your
     jump?[4]
Supposing none of these exits catches your fancy,
don't you think it better to sleep with a pretty boy?
35   Boys don't quarrel all night, or nag you for little presents
while they're on the job, or complain that you don't come
up to their expectations, or demand more gasping passion.[5]
     But Ursidius, you say, upholds | the Family Encouragement
          Act,[6]
wants a sweet little heir, will forgo fat pigeons
40   and bearded mullet, the bait of the legacy-hunting market.
I'll credit anything, friend, if a woman's led to the altar
by Ursidius, if that once most notorious co-respondent,
who hid in more bedroom cupboards than a comedy juvenile
     lead,
is sticking his silly neck out for the matrimonial halter?
45   And as for his quest for a wife with antique morals – man,
his blood-pressure's up, he needs cupping by a doctor!
Such fastidiousness! If you're in luck, if you find a chaste partner,
well may you go down prostrate, kiss the Tarpeian shrine's
threshold, and slaughter a gilt-horned heifer for Juno!
50   Few girls are fit to serve the Corn-Goddess, or have fathers
who wouldn't shrink from their kisses.[7] Hang up garlands
on your doorposts, wreathe thick ivy over the lintel!
Is one man enough for Hiberina? You'd sooner torture
that bitch into being content | with one eye! Some young lady
55   brought up on Daddy's country estate has a spotless
character? Let her live in a village, even, as once
she did in the country – *then* I'll believe in that paternal
estate! But who's going to swear that nothing ever came off
in caves, or up mountains – are Jove and Mars *that* senile?
60   Look around the arcades, can you pick out a woman worthy
of your devotion? Go through every single theatre –

will they yield one candidate you could love without a qualm?
While that queen of a dancer Bathyllus[8] is miming Leda,
one woman lets go of her bladder, another whinnies: 64
your country girl looks, and learns: country girl, country matters.   66
Others in winter, when the theatres are closed, the scenery
packed away, when only the lawcourts go droning on,
will yearningly fondle souvenirs of their favourite actor,
their tragedy king – his mask, his thyrsus, his jock-strap.   70
That queen who brings down the house as Actaeon's mother
in the late-night show – poor Aelia's crazy about him. Such
women will pay, and pay well, to defibulate counter-tenors,
ruin singers' voices. Hispulla's in love with a tragic lead –
surprised? You think she'd prefer a professor of rhetoric?[9]   75
Marry a wife, and she'll make some smart guitarist
or flute-player a father, not you. Or, when you erect
long stands in the narrow streets, and hang your front-door
with outsize laurel wreaths, it'll all be to welcome an infant
whose face, in the tortoiseshell cradle, under its canopy,   80
recalls some armoured thug, some idol of the arena.
    When that senator's wife, Eppia, eloped with her fancy
        swordsman
to Pharos and Nile and the Alexandrian stews,
Egypt itself cried out at Rome's monstrous morals.
Husband, family, sister, the bitch forsook them all,   85
country and tearful children, as well as – this *will* surprise you –
the public games, and her favourite matinée idol.
Luxury-reared, cradled by Daddy in swansdown,
brought up to frills and flounces, Eppia nevertheless
made as light of the sea as she did of her reputation –   90
not that our pampered ladies set any great store by *that*.
Boldly she faced the Tuscan waves, the booming
Ionian swell, heart steadfast, despite the constant
chop and change of the sea. When a woman faces danger
in a good cause, then chill terror ices her heart,   95
her knees turn to water, she can scarcely stand upright;
but wicked audacity breeds its own fortitude.
To go aboard ship at a husband's bidding is torture:
then bilge-water sickens, then the sky wheels dizzily round.

100　　But a wife going off with her lover suffers no qualms. The one
　　　pukes on her husband, the other eats with the sailors,
　　　takes a turn round the deck, enjoys hauling on rough sheets.
　　　What was the youthful charm that so fired Eppia? What
　　　was it hooked her? What did she see in him that was worth
105　　being mocked as a fighter's moll? For her poppet, her Sergius
　　　was no chicken, forty at least, with one dud arm that held
　　　　　promise
　　　of early retirement. Deformities marred his features –
　　　a helmet-scar, a great wen on his nose, an unpleasant
　　　discharge from one constantly weeping eye. What of it?
110　　*He was a gladiator.* That makes anyone an Adonis;
　　　that was what she chose over children, country, sister,
　　　and husband: steel's what they crave. Yet this same Sergius,
　　　once pensioned, would soon have begun to seem – a Veiento.[10]
　　　　Do such private scandals, do Eppia's deeds, appal you?
115　　Then consider the Gods' rivals, hear what Claudius
　　　had to put up with. The minute she heard him snoring
　　　his wife – that whore-empress – who dared to prefer the mattress
　　　of a stews to her couch in the Palace, called for her hooded
　　　night-cloak and hastened forth, with a single attendant.
120　　Then, her black hair hidden under an ash-blonde wig,
　　　she'd make straight for her brothel, with its stale, warm coverlets,
　　　and her empty reserved cell.[11] Here, naked, with gilded
　　　nipples, she plied her trade, under the name of 'The Wolf-Girl',
　　　parading the belly that once housed a prince of the blood.[12]
125　　She would greet each client sweetly, demand cash payment,
　　　and absorb all their battering – without ever getting up.
　　　Too soon the brothel-keeper dismissed his girls:
　　　she stayed right till the end, always the last to go,
　　　then trailed away sadly, still | with burning, rigid vulva,
130　　exhausted by men, yet a long way from satisfied,
　　　cheeks grimed with lamp-smoke, filthy, carrying home
　　　to her Imperial couch the stink of the whorehouse.
　　　What point in mentioning spells, or aphrodisiac potions,
　　　or that lethal brew given to stepsons? Sexual compulsion
135　　drives women to worse crimes: they err through excess of lust.[13]
　　　　'Censennia's husband swears she's the perfect wife: why so?'

Because she brought him a million. In exchange he calls her
        chaste.
Venus' shafts do not waste him, nor Love's fires burn him up:
it was avarice lit that torch, her dowry fired those arrows –
her freedom was bought. She flirts openly, writes love-notes: 140
rich women who marry cash-seekers have widows' privileges.
    'Then why does Sertorius burn with passion for Bibula?'
When you get to the truth, it's her face, not her, that he loves.
Just let a few wrinkles appear, or her skin go dry and slack,
her teeth begin to blacken, or her eyes lose their lustre, then: 145
'Pack your bags!' his steward will tell her, 'and get yourself out of
        here!
You're a nasty bore, always blowing your nose. Get out,
and double quick: there's a snot-free replacement coming.'
But for now she's hot, she's the princess, wheedling ranches,
        vineyards,
prize sheep – herdsmen and all – from her husband. Yet that's
        nothing: 150
she demands all his slave-boys, his field-gangs: if a neighbour
owns any item they don't, it has to be bought at once.
In misty December, when | the mural of Trader Jason
is hidden, armed sailors and all, by white canvas market stalls,[14]
she goes on a shopping spree: huge crystal vases, outsize   155
myrrh-jars, and a famous diamond ring – once flaunted
by Berenice, which adds to its price: a gift from her brother,
that barbarous prince Agrippa, a token of their incest,
in the land where monarchs observe the Sabbath barefoot,
and tradition leaves pigs to attain a ripe old age.[15]   160
    'Not one woman, out of so many, who meets your standards?'
Assume one with beauty and charm, wealthy, fecund, her hall
crammed with ancestral portraits, grant her virginity
more intact than in all those dishevelled Sabine maiden
peacemakers,[16] make her a rare bird, a black swan or the like –   165
who could stomach such wifely perfection? I'd far far sooner
marry a penniless tart[17] than you, Cornelia, Mother
of Statesmen, so haughty a prig | for all your virtues, your dowry
weighted down with triumphs. As far as I'm concerned
you can take your battle-honours – Hannibal, Syphax,   170

the whole Carthaginian myth – and get lost with them, madam.[18]
    'Apollo, be merciful; Artemis, lay by your shafts,'
Amphion prayed. 'The children are not to blame –
strike down their mother!' But Apollo still drew his bow.
So Niobe lost, at one stroke, both quiverful and husband –
all through the boast that she was nobler in her offspring
than Leto – and more prolific than the white Alban sow.[19]
    What beauty, what decorum are worth having thrown in your
        face
day in day out? What pleasure remains in such lofty
180 and rarefied perfection, when pride of spirit has turned it
from honey to bitter aloes? What man is so besotted
that for half the day, or more, the wife upon whom he bestows
such praise, in reality doesn't give him cold shivers?
    Often it's trivial faults that most offend a husband.
185 What could be more sickening than the way no Italian girl
will believe in her own beauty till she's tarted up *à la grecque*,
Sulmo done over as Athens? Now everything's Greek-style
[though what should make them blush is their slipshod Latin].
This is the language they use to express fear, anger, joy
190 or worries, each innermost secret thought – they even
make love the Greek way. Young schoolgirls might be excused
for behaving like this; but when you're in your mid-eighties
are you *still* talking Greek? Such language is quite indecent
coming from an old woman. When you mouth lascivious phrases
195 like *Zoé kai Psyché* – 'My life, my soul!' – you're using
bedroom language in public.[20] Such naughty, caressing
        endearments
have fingers, they'd start a twitch in any man's groin.
But don't get excited: even if your voice were softer
than any gay actor's, your age is still scored on your face.
200   So if it's the case that a signed and sealed marriage-partner
won't win your love, there doesn't seem any reason
to marry at all: why waste | good money on a reception,
or those cakes handed out at the end to your well-gorged guests?
Why lose a salver of mint-new golden guineas –
205 victory issues, too – on the first-night bridal offering?[21]
But if your mind is set, with uxorious obsession,

on one woman and one only, then bow your neck to the yoke
in voluntary servitude. No woman spares a lover;
she may be on fire herself, but it's her lover's torments
and the spoils of war that give her real pleasure. The better bargain   210
you are as a husband, the less you get out of your wife.
Want to give someone a present? Sell property? She maintains
her veto on all such transactions; she even controls your likes
and dislikes: lifelong companions, regular visitors
since boyhood – these may find the door slammed in their faces.   215
Ringmasters, pimps, all the riff-raff of the arena
have a free hand with their wills. But *you* must include
two or three of her lovers amongst your legatees.

MR rong the household

    'Crucify that slave!' 'But why does the slave deserve it?
What witnesses are there? Who's charged him? Give him a
            hearing –   220
no delay can be too lengthy when a man's life is at stake.'
'So a slave's a *man*, is he, you crackpot? He's done nothing? So
            what?
I want, I *command* it: let my will suffice as reason.'
So she dictates to her husband. But soon she leaves this kingdom,
switches houses, wears out her bridal veil; in the end   225
back she comes to the bed she abandoned, leaving
a freshly garlanded house, the bridal hangings
not yet removed, the boughs still green on the threshold.
Score up another husband: that makes eight
in under five years: it ought to go on her tombstone.   230
    No marital peace for you while your mother-in-law still lives.
She gives advice on how to strip you bare – and enjoy it,
on the subtlest, least obvious way to answer billets-doux
from would-be seducers. It's she who hoodwinks or fixes
your servants, she who takes to her bed when she's well,   235
who lies tossing under the sheets till the doctor makes his visit.

Wein Arm their mothers

Meanwhile, all hot impatience, hidden behind the scenes,
her daughter's lover sits silent, tugs at his foreskin.[22]
Do you really think any mother will pass on better morals
than those she learnt herself? Besides, it's profitable   240
for an old whore to bring up her daughter to the trade.
    There's scarcely one court-hearing in which the litigation

wasn't set off by a woman, as defendant or plaintiff,
ready to deal with a brief single-handed, full of advice
245   to counsel on opening his case, or presenting special points.[23]
   Women in purple track-suits, women who wrestle in mud –
these are a common sight. So are our lady-fencers –
we've all seen *them*, stabbing the stump with a foil,
shield well advanced – just the right training needed
250   to blow a matronly horn at the Floral Festival,[24]
unless their aim is higher, to make the real arena.
But then, what modesty is there in some helmeted hoyden,
a renegade from her sex, who adores male violence – yet
wouldn't want to *be* a man, since the pleasure is so much less?
255   What a sight, if one's wife's equipment were sold at auction,
plumes, baldric, armlets, and one half of a left-leg
shin-guard! Or if the other fashion of fighting attracts her,
how happy you'll be when the dear girl sells off her greaves![25]
(And yet these same women have such delicate skins
260   that even sheer silk chafes them; they sweat in the finest chiffon.)
Hark how she snorts at each practice thrust, bowed down
by the weight of her helmet; see the big coarse puttees
wrapped round her ample hams – then wait for the laugh,
when she lays her weapons aside and squats on the potty!
265   Tell me, you noble ladies, descendants of Lepidus, blind
Metellus, 'Gut' Fabius[26] – what gladiator's woman
ever dressed up like this, or gasped at the fencing-stump?
   The bed that contains a wife is always hot with quarrels
and mutual bickering: sleep's the last thing you get there.
270   In bed she attacks her husband, worse than a tigress
robbed of its young, and to stifle her own bad conscience
bitches about his boy-friends, or weeps over some fictitious
mistress. She always keeps a big reservoir of tears
at the ready, and waiting for her to command in which
275   manner they need to flow: so you, poor worm, are in heaven,
thinking this means she loves you, and kiss her tears away –
but if you raided her desk-drawers, the letters, the assignations
you'd find that your green-eyed adulteress has amassed!
Then what if she's caught in bed with a slave or a knight? *Quick,*
      quick,

Quintilian, find me a pat excuse! But *I'm stuck*,[27] says the Maestro,   280
Solve this one yourself. And she does. 'We agreed long ago
you were free to do as you pleased, and in the same way I
could indulge myself too. I don't care if you bawl the house
    down –
I'm human too.' For sheer nerve, there's nothing beats a woman
caught in the act: guilt fuels her fury and defiance.   285
    Whence, you ask, come such monsters? From what source?
Their lowly fortune held Latin women to chastity
in the old days: their poor huts were kept free of vices
by hard work, little sleep, hands horny from carding
fleeces, by Hannibal's presence close to the city-gates,   290
and their menfolk standing to arms on the Colline ramparts.
Now the ills of long peace afflict us: luxury, a more deadly
incubus than warfare, avenges the world we subdued.
No visitation of crime or lust has been spared us since
Roman poverty perished. From then our Seven Hills   295
have been flooded out by Sybaris, Rhodes, Miletus,
and unruly Tarentum, wine-flown and garlanded.[28]
Filthy lucre it was that first brought loose foreign morals
amongst us, effeminate wealth that with vile self-indulgence
destroyed us over the years. What conscience has Venus tipsy?   300
Our inebriated beauties can't tell head from tail
at those lavish oyster suppers served around midnight
when the best wine's laced with perfume, and tossed down neat
from a foaming conch-shell, while the dizzy ceiling
spins round, and the tables dance, and each light shows double.   305
Why, you may ask yourself, does the notorious Maura
sniff at the air in that knowing, derisive fashion
as she and her dear friend Tullia pass by the ancient altar   307
of Chastity? What, pray, is Tullia whispering to her? Here,
at night, they reel from their litters, here they relieve themselves,
pumping out their piss, in long bursts, on the Goddess's statue.   310
Then – the Moon watching their motions – they ride each other
    in turn,
and finally go home. So you, on your way next morning
to some great house, will splash through your wife's piddle.
    We know the Good Goddess's secrets,[29] when loins are stirred

315 by the flute, when Priapus's maenads, wine-flown, horn-crazy,
     sweep along in procession, howling, tossing their hair –
     ah, what a vast mounting passion fills their spirits
     to get themselves mounted! Such lustful yelps, such a copious
     downflow of vintage liquor splashing their thighs!
320 Off goes Saufeia's wreath, she challenges the call-girls
     to a contest of bumps and grinds, emerges victorious,
     herself admires the shimmy of Medullina's buttocks:[30]
     so the ladies win all the prizes – skill rivalling pedigree.
     No make-belief here, no faking, each act is performed
325 in earnest, the genuine article, fully guaranteed
     to warm the age-chilled balls of a Nestor or a Priam.
     Delay breeds itching impatience, boosts the pure female urge,
     and from every side of the grotto a clamorous cry goes up:
     'It's time! Let in the men!' If a lover's sound asleep,
330 his young brother is told to get dressed and hustle along.
     If they draw blank there, they try slaves. If enough slaves cannot
               be found
     the water-carrier's hired. If they can't track him down, either,
     and men are in short supply, they're ready and willing
     to go down on all fours and cock their dish for a donkey.
335 Would that our ancient rituals (at the very least in their public
     observances) were untouched by such nastiness! But every
     Moor and Hindu knows well which 'lady'-harpist it was
     brought a tool as long as both those anti-Catonian
     pamphlets of Caesar into the sanctuary where
340 all images of the other sex must be veiled, where even
     a buckmouse, ball-conscious, beats an embarrassed retreat.[31]
     What man would once have despised divine power? And who
     would have dared to sneer at King Numa's earthenware bowls,
     black pots, and brittle platters of Vatican clay? But now
345 what altar does not attract its Clodius in drag?[32]
O 1   In every house where there lives – and plays – a Professor
     of Obscene Arts, his hand-twitch a broad signal,
     you'll find a disgusting crowd, camp if not actually queer.
     People let them defile their meals, sit down at the sacred
O 5 family board; let glasses | be washed that should be destroyed
     when La Courgette's drunk from them, or The Bearded Cowrie.[33]

[handwritten marginal note:] what about the mysteries that sexual things & ancient things must & must then function?

The *lanista*[34] runs a cleaner, more decent house than yours:
he quarters the fag targeteers and the armoured heavies
well away from each other; net-throwers aren't required
to mess with convicted felons, nor in the same cell   O 10
does he who strips off to fight discard his shoulder-guards
and defensive trident. Even the lowest scum of the arena
observe this rule; even in prison they're separate.
But the creatures your wife allows to share your cup!
A dyed-blonde washed-up whore working the graveyards   O 15
would gag at drinking from it, whatever the vintage.
Yet on *their* advice great ladies | will marry – or, presto! divorce;
it's with them they relieve the boredom of daily existence,
revive their flagging spirits, learn to shimmy their hips,
as well as other tricks known only to the teacher –   O 20
and him you can't always trust. He may line his eyes with kohl,
wear a yellow robe and a hairnet – but he's an adulterer!
That affected voice, the way he scratches his bottom,
one arm akimbo, should never lull your suspicions.
Once into bed, he'll prove a champion performer,   O 25
dropping the role of Thaïs for that of the skilled Triphallus.
'Who are you fooling? Keep | this act for others! I'll wager
you're one hundred per cent a man. It's a bet. Will you admit it?
Or must the torturer rack your maids?'[35] Oh, I know
the advice my old friends would give, on every occasion –   O 30
'Lock her up and bar the doors.' But who is to stand guard
over the guards themelves? They get paid in common coin
to forget their mistress's sex-life: both hide the same offence.
Any shrewd wife, planning ahead, will first turn the heat on them.   O 34
All women now, high or low, share the same lusts: the peasant   349
trudging barefoot over black cobbles is no better   350
than the lady who rides on the necks of tall Syrian porters.

    To go to the Games, Ogulnia hires dresses,
attendants, a carriage, cushions, a baby-sitter, companions,
and a little blonde slave-girl to carry her messages. Yet
what's left of the family plate, down to the last salver,   355
she'll hand out as a present to some smooth athlete.
Many such women lack substance – yet poverty gives them
no sense of restraint, they don't observe the limits

their resources impose. Men, on the other hand,
360 sometimes at least show providence, plan for the future
in a practical way, learn by the ant's example
to fear cold and hunger. But an extravagant woman
never knows when she's overdrawn. None of them reckon
the cost of their pleasures, as though, when the strong-box was
          empty,
365 more money would grow there, the pile replenish itself.
      There are girls who adore unmanly eunuchs – their kisses
always delectably smooth, with no trace of a beard,
and no worry about abortions! But the highest pleasure
comes from one who was fully-grown, a lusty black-quilled
370 male, before the surgeons went to work on his groin.
Wait, therefore, until the testicles drop and ripen,
let them fill out till they hang | like two-pound weights; then
          what
the surgeon chops will hurt no one's trade but the barber's.
373A (Slave-dealers' boys are different: pathetically weak,
373B ashamed of their empty bag, their lost little chickpeas.)
What a specimen, everyone knows him, making his public entry
375 to the baths, endowed in a way to challenge Priapus! And yet
he's a eunuch. His mistress arranged it. So, let them sleep
          together –
but Postumus, don't ever trust your Dionysiac boy-friend,
just out of adolescence, to the – mercy of such a eunuch!³⁶
      If your wife has musical tastes, no professional singer's
fibula can resist her. She's forever handling
their instruments, her bejewelled fingers sparkle
over the lute, she practises | scales with a vibrant plectrum
once used by some elegant player – it's her mascot,
her solace, she rains kisses on it, the darling object.
385 A certain patrician lady, blue-blooded on both sides,
made enquiry of Janus and Vesta, offering wine and cakes,
to learn if her lutanist Pollio could aspire to the oakwreath prize
at the Capitoline Festival.³⁷ What more could she have done
if her husband was sick, or the doctors shaking their heads
390 over her little son? She stood at the altar – no shame at
veiling her face for a lute! – made the proper responses

in traditional form, and blanched as the lamb was opened.
Tell me now, I beg you, most ancient of deities,
Father Janus,[38] do such prayers get answered? Lots of leisure,
the way I see it, in heaven: you Gods have nothing to do.   395
X solicits your aid for her comedy lead; Y pushes
her tragic ham: the diviner will soon get varicose veins.

   Yet a musical wife's not so bad as some presumptuous
flat-chested busybody who rushes around the city
gate-crashing all-male meetings, talking back straight-faced   400
to a uniformed general – *and* in her husband's presence.
She knows all the news of the world, what's cooking in Thrace
or China, the secrets of stepson and stepmother
behind closed doors, who's in love, which gallant is all the rage.
She'll tell you who got the widow pregnant, and in which month;   405
she knows each woman's endearments, her favourite positions.
Any comet threatening princes in Armenia, maybe, or Parthia,
she's the first to spot; she picks up | the latest gossip and rumours
at the city-gates.[39] Some she invents, alleging that Niphates[40]
has overflowed and is inundating entire countries –   410
towns are cut off, land sinking, disaster, floods! Such stuff
she'll unload at street-corners, on anyone she encounters.

   Yet even this is not so unbearable as her habit,
when woken up,[41] of grabbing some poor-class neighbour
and belting him with a whip. If her deep slumbers   415
are broken by barking, 'Fetch me the cudgels,' she roars,
'And be quick about it!' She orders the owner a thrashing,
then one for the dog. No joke to meet that hideous face.
In the evening she visits the steam-bath, has her oil-jars and
            quarters
transferred there then, loves sweating amid the hubbub.   420
When her arms drop, exhausted by the weighty dumb-bells,
the masseur takes over, fingers | caressing her little crest
from the top of her thigh, and making her yelp as she comes.
Her unfortunate guests, meanwhile, are nearly dead with hunger.
At last she appears, all flushed, with a three-gallon thirst,   425
enough to empty the brimming jar at her feet
without assistance. She knocks back two straight pints
on an empty stomach, to sharpen her appetite: then

throws it all up again, souses the floor with vomit
430 that streams across the terrazzo. Her gilded jordan
stinks of sour wine. Like some big snake that's tumbled
into a wine-vat, she drinks | and spews by turns. Quite sickened,
eyes shut, her husband somehow holds down his bile.[42]

Worse still is the well-read menace, who's hardly started
dinner
435 before she's praising Virgil, forgiving the doomed Dido,
comparing rival poets, Virgil and Homer suspended
in opposite scales, weighed up one against the other.
Critics surrender, academics are routed, everyone there
falls silent, not a word from lawyer or auctioneer –
440 or even another woman. Such a powerful rattle of talk,
you'd think all the pots and bells were being clashed together
when the moon's in eclipse. No need now for brass or trumpets:
one woman can act, single-handed, as lunar midwife.[43]
But wisdom imposes limits, even on virtue, and if
445 she's so determined to prove herself eloquent, learned,
she should hoist up her skirts and gird them above the knee,
offer a pig to Silvanus, scrub off in the penny baths.[44]
So avoid any woman's company at a dinner-party
who affects a rhetorical style, who hurls well-rounded
450 syllogisms like slingshots, who has all history pat:
far better one who *doesn't* | grasp all she reads. I detest
the sort who are always thumbing – and citing – some standard
grammar,
whose every utterance follows the laws of syntax,
who with antiquarian zeal quote poets I've never heard of:
such matters are men's concern.[45] Let her castigate the language
of her bumpkin friend: a husband should be left his solecisms.

There's nothing a woman denies herself, her conscience is nil,
once she's adorned her neck with that emerald choker, once
she's weighted down her ear-lobes with vast pearl pendants.
460 (What's more insufferable than a wealthy female?)
But earlier she's a sight both hilarious and appalling,
her face bread-poulticed, or greasy with vanishing-cream
that clings to her husband's lips when the poor man kisses her –
though it's all wiped off for her lover. When does she take trouble

about how she looks at home? It's with her lover in mind   465
that she purchases all those imported Indian scents and lotions.
First one layer, then the next: at last her actual features
begin to emerge, and are freshened with asses' milk:
if her husband's posted North, into Hyperborean exile,
then a bevy of young she-asses will travel with them.[46]   470
But after she's been plastered with all these medicaments
and various treatments − not least the wads of damp dough −
it makes you wonder what's back there, a face or an ulcer.

It's revealing to study the details of such a woman's
daily routine. If her husband, the previous night,   475
has slept with his back to her, then the wool-maid's had it,
cosmeticians are stripped and beaten, the litter-bearer's accused
of not coming on time, gets punished because of her husband's
night off. Rods, straps, cat-o'-nine-tails − all draw blood:
some women pay their floggers an annual salary.   480
During beatings she'll fix her face, or listen to friends' gossip,
consider the width of the hem on some gold-embroidered robe −
Crack! Crack! − or skim the long entries of the daily gazette,
Crack! Crack! − till the flogger's exhausted, she snaps 'Get out!',
and for one day at least the judicial hearing is over.   485
Her household's governed as savagely as a Sicilian court.[47]
If she's made some assignation that she wants to look her best for,
and is in a hurry, and late, for a date in the public gardens,
or (more probably) at the shrine of that procuress Isis[48] − then
the slave-girl fixing her coiffure will have her own hair torn out,   490
poor creature, the tunic ripped from her shoulders and breasts.
'Why is this curl out of place?' the lady screams, and her rawhide
lash inflicts chastisement for the offending ringlet.
But what was poor Psecas's crime? Why blame a slave-girl
for the shape of your own nose? Another attendant   495
combs out the hair on her left side, twists it round the curlers;
the council is reinforced by an elderly lady's-maid
of Mama's, now retired from hair-pins to wool. She delivers
her verdict first; those beneath her in age and experience
declare themselves next, as though | some issue of reputation   500
or life itself were at stake, so fierce their quest for beauty,
so many the tiers and storeys, the weight of hair built up

on her head!⁴⁹ Such heroic stature – the front view, at least: from
          behind
she's much shorter (a different person, you'd think); the effect
505   is absurd if she's really tiny, so lacking in height that she's dwarfed
by a girl–pygmy, the sort | for whom stiletto heels
do nothing, who's forced to stand on tiptoe for a kiss.
Meantime she gives not a damn for all those household
expenses: she lives more like her husband's neighbour –
510   except when it comes to loathing his friends and servants,
or running up bills . . .⁵⁰

                                    . . . Now here come the devotees
of frenzied Bellona, and Cybele, Mother of Gods,⁵¹
with a huge eunuch, a face | for lesser obscenities
to revere. Long ago, with a sherd, he lopped his soft genitals:
515   now neither the howling rabble nor all the kettledrums
can outshriek him. A Phrygian mitre tops his plebeian cheeks.
With solemn rant he warns her of September and its siroccos –
unless she lustrates herself with a hundred eggs
and makes him a present of her old russet dresses,
520   so that any disaster, however sudden or frightful,
may pass into the clothes – a one-shot, one-year expiation.
In winter she'll break the ice, descend into the river,
and thrice, before noon, let the eddies of Tiber close
over her timorous head;⁵² then crawl out, naked, shivering,
525   and shuffle on bleeding knees, by way of penance,
across the Field of Mars. Indeed, if white Io⁵³ so orders,
she'll make a pilgrimage to Egypt's last frontier,
fetch water from tropic Meroë for the aspersion
of Isis's temple, that stands | beside our ancient sheep-pens.
530   She believes herself instructed by the voice of the Lady herself –
just the kind of rare mind and spirit a god *would* talk to at night!⁵⁴
That's why high praise and special | honours accrue to the one
who with his shaven-headed, linen-clad followers
runs through the streets as Anubis, grins at the people's grief.⁵⁵
He it is that makes intercession | for wives who've failed to
          abstain
535   from sex on all the prescribed and ritual feast-days,
exacting huge penalties when the marriage-bed is polluted,

or whenever the silver serpent of Isis appears to nod.
His tears and professional mutterings will guarantee
absolution – that is, after | Osiris has been well bribed   540
with a fat goose and a slice of the sacrificial cake.[56]
The moment he's gone, a palsied Jewess, parking
her haybox outside, comes begging in a breathy whisper.
She interprets Jerusalem's laws, she's the tree's high priestess,[57]
a faithful mediator of heaven on earth. She likewise   545
fills her palm, but more sparingly: Jews will sell you
whatever dreams you like for a few small coppers.
A young lover for the lady, or a good fat inheritance
from some childless millionaire, are predicted (after inspection
of a pigeon's steaming lungs) by Eastern fortune-tellers,   550
who'll unravel a chicken's or puppy's innards, sometimes
even a child's: the seer can always shop his client.
Chaldaeans tend to inspire more confidence: whatever
these astrologers predict comes straight, it's believed,
from Ammon's oracular fountain. (Now that Delphi is silent   555
the human race is condemned to a blacked-out future.)[58]
The most successful are those who've been exiled more than
        once . . .
[like you-know-who with his friendship and horoscopes for hire,
who settled the hash of that great citizen dreaded by Otho . . .][59]
. . . Nothing boosts your diviner's credit so much as a lengthy spell   560
in the glasshouse, with fetters jangling from either wrist:
no one *really* believes in his powers unless he's dodged execution
by a hair's breadth, and been deported to some Cycladic island –
tiny Seriphos, say – and got free after lengthy privations.
Your Tanaquil[60] wants to know why her jaundice-ridden mother   565
takes so long dying (she's enquired about *you* already). When
will she see off her sister, her uncles? Will her present lover
survive her? (What greater boon could she ask of the Gods?)
Yet she cannot tell what Saturn's gloomy conjunction
may threaten, or under which star Venus is most propitious;   570
which months bring loss, which seasons belong to profit.
Remember to dodge any meeting with this sort of woman,
in whose hands you see clutched, not the usual amber scent-ball,
but a well-thumbed almanac! She's not after expert advice:

she's an expert herself, the sort | who won't accompany her
575   husband
overseas – or back home again – if her horoscope forbids it.
When she wants to go out of town, a mile even, she decides
the time from her tables. If she rubs one eye, and it itches,
she can't put ointment on it till she's checked out the almanac.
580   If she's lying ill in bed, she will only take nourishment
at such times as Petosiris, the Egyptian, may prescribe.[61]
Women of lower rank and fortune learn their futures
up and down the race-track, from phrenologist or palmist,
with much smacking of lips against evil influences.
585   Rich ladies send out to hire their own tame Phrygian
prophet, they skim off the cream | of the star-gazers, or pick
one of those wise old parties who neutralize thunderbolts:
plebeian fates are foretold at the Circus or Embankment.
Here, by the public stands and dolphin-columns, old whores,
590   bare-shouldered, with thin gold neck-chains, come for advice –
should they ditch the inn-keeper? marry the rag-and-bone man?[62]

       Yet these at least endure the dangers of childbirth, all
those nursing chores which poverty imposes upon them:
but how often do gilded beds witness a lying-in
595   when we've all the abortionist's arts, so many sure-fire drugs
for inducing sterility or killing an embryo child?
So cheer up, my poor friend, pick out your lethal mixture,
and give her the dose yourself. If she chose to stay pregnant,
to swell her belly with frolicsome infants, you might become
600   some blackamoor's father, then find yourself changing your will
for an heir whose off-colour face you'd rather not see by daylight.

       I say nothing of spurious children, changelings picked up
beside some filthy cistern,[63] and passed off as nobly-born –
false hopes, deluded prayers! – our future priesthood,
605   our bluest patrician blood. Fortune at night-time
is shameless, smiles on these naked babes, enfolds them
one and all in her bosom: then, for a private joke,
deals them out to great families, loves and lavishes
her care upon them, makes them her special favourites.

610   Here comes a peddler of magic spells and Thessalian[64]
philtres, with which a wife can befuddle her husband's wits

till he lets her slipper his backside. If you go stupid, that's why:
that's the source of your mental blackouts, your total forgetfulness
about recent events. Yet all this can be borne, provided[65]
you don't begin to go crazy, like that uncle of Nero's   615
who drank a knock-out mixture brewed up for him by his wife
Caesonia.[66] What woman won't copy a prince's consort?
Certainties went up in flames then, mere anarchy ruled the
        world –
it was just as though Juno herself had driven her husband
insane. (By comparison Agrippina's mushroom   620
was to turn out less lethal: that only stopped the breathing
of one old dotard, saw off his tremulous headpiece
and beslobbered, drooling chops to some nether heaven.)[67] But
this potion meant fire and sword, *this* the torturer's rack,
this mangled Senate and burghers in one bloody heap: 625
such was the cost of one philtre, a single poisoner.

     Wives loathe a concubine's offspring. Let no man cavil,
no man forbid it: today it's *right* to murder your stepson!
You wards, I warn you, who have an ample portion,
should watch out for your lives, accept no dish at dinner: 630
those pies are steaming-black with Mummy's poison! Take care
that another person first nibbles any food you're offered
by her who bore you, make sure that your nervous tutor
tastes every cup beforehand. Do you think this is melodrama?
Am I making the whole thing up, quite careless of precedents,   635
mouthing a lot of claptrap in the grand Sophoclean manner
that's out of place under Italian (much less Virgilian) skies?
How I wish it *was* nonsense! But Pontia[68] cries: 'I did it!
I confess the deed, I gave aconite to my children – the crime
was detected, is public knowledge – but *I* was the murderer.'   640
'What? *Two*, you savage viper? *Two at one meal?*' 'Indeed:
and if there'd been seven I'd have polished *them* off, too.'
Whatever the tragic poets tell us of fierce Medea
and Procne[69] may well be true: I won't dispute it. These
women were monsters of daring in their own day – but not   645
from the lust for wealth. We find such deeds less freakish
when wrath provides the incentive for a woman's crimes,
when white-hot raging passion seizes and whirls her

headlong, like some boulder that breaks from the mountain-top

650   as the ground caves in and the rockface becomes a landslide.
What *I* can't stand is the woman who plans and carries out
her crimes in cold blood. Our wives observe Alcestis[70]
dying instead of her husband: if *they* had a similar chance,
they'd gladly sacrifice their husband's life for their lapdog's.

655   Any morning you'll meet Danaïds and Eriphyles galore;
on every street you can find a resident Clytemnestra.[71]
The only difference is this: whereas Clytemnestra wielded
a clumsy great double-axe in both hands, nowadays
the job's done with an ounce of toad's lung. But cold steel may
        return

660   if our modern Agamemnons follow Mithridates' example,
and sample the pharmacopeia till they're proof against every
        drug.[72]

SATIRE VII

All hopes for the arts, all inducement to write, rest on Caesar.[1]
He alone has shown respect for the wretched Muses
in these hard times, when famous | established poets would lease
an out-of-town bath-concession or a city bakery
to make their living, when others considered it no disgrace   5
to work as auctioneers, when hungry creative artists
deserted the Vale of the Muses for the sale-rooms.
For if you're not offered a farthing in that poets' shady retreat,
you'll have to embrace the title – and income – of the man with
    the hammer,
sell what the auction sells, join battle, flog job-lots   10
to the bystanders – winejars, stools, cupboards and bookcases,
old copies of third-rate plays, a *Thebes*, a *Tereus*.
Better to live thus than swearing before a judge 'I saw it',
when you saw nothing. Leave that | to the knights from Asia
    Minor –   14
galled ankles, revealed by low slippers, betray *their* origins.[2]   16
But no one henceforth will be forced to perform unworthy
labours, who's skilled at shaping eloquent utterance
into tuneful measures, none who have nibbled at laurel.
So at it, young men: your Imperial Leader's indulgence[3]   20
is urging you on, surveying | your ranks for worthy talent.
    But if you had thoughts of obtaining patronage
for your art elsewhere, and in that hope go on scribbling
across your buff parchment, best order a bundle of firewood,
and offer your works to Vulcan;[4] or else just lock them away   25
and let the bookworms riddle them full of holes.
Break your pen, poor wretch, destroy those insomniac

battle-pieces, high art hammered out in a cramped garret
with dreams of a laureate's wreath on a starveling bust!
30   That's the most you could hope for: our skinflint millionaires
only flatter artistic talent, only load it with compliments,
like children admiring a peacock. So the prime of life slips by,
the years when you might have been a sailor, soldier, farmer,
until the spirit grows weary, till your glib yet penniless
35   old age turns in hatred against itself and its art.
       Let me list the tricks to avoid | shelling out on your behalf
played by the patron for whom you deserted Apollo
and the Muses.⁵ He's a poet | himself, second only to Homer –
he thinks – in a thousand years. If the sweet itch for renown
40   stirs you to give a recital, he'll fix you up with some peeling
dump of a hall in the suburbs, its doors all chained,
their hinges squealing like a herd of pigs in a panic.⁶
He'll lend you a claque of freedmen and other hangers-on
to sit at the end of each row, distribute the applause;
45   but none of these nabobs will pay | for hiring seats and benches,
or the upper tiers and the framework of beams that supports them,
the front-row chairs due back right after the performance.
Yet still we keep at it, ploughing a dusty furrow,
turning the seashore up with our sterile coulter. You can't
50   escape [you're caught in the noose of bad ambitious
habit]; there are so many | possessed by an incurable
endemic writer's itch that becomes a sick obsession.
But the outstanding poet, one who mines no common seam,
smelts down no reworked slag, strikes no debased
55   poetic currency, minted | with populist platitudes –
I can't think of one just now, still I'm sure they exist –
such a paragon's life will be free from worries, unclouded
by bitterness; he's a woodland-lover, one fit to drink
at the Muses' fountain. How can grim poverty grasp
60   Inspiration's enchanted wand, how find that singing grotto
if you're forced to scrape and pinch to satisfy the body's
demands for cash? Horace cried | 'Rejoice!'⁷ on a full stomach.
What room for true genius, save in the heart that's devoted
uniquely to poetry, untroubled by other concerns,
65   one that's sustained by Apollo, by Dionysus? It calls

for a lofty spirit, not one that's scared of buying a blanket,
to have visions of horses and chariots, of immortal godhead,
to limn the Fury that once confounded Rutulian Turnus.[8]
For if Virgil had not had one slave-boy[9] and a fairly comfortable
lodging, all those snakes would have dropped from the Fury's hair,   70
her grave trumpet would have been voiceless. Can we expect
a modern playwright to rival the ancient tragic stage
when 'Atreus' is now compelled to hock his coat, and the dishes?
Poor Numitor's nothing to spare for a friend in need – although
his mistress never goes short, and he scraped up enough   75
(remember?) to purchase that tame lion – not to mention
the meat it scoffed. Of course, it comes a good deal cheaper
to feed a lion than a poet: poets have bigger bellies.[10]

  Fame may satisfy Lucan, resting in peace in his marbled
park;[11] but for epic poets less well-endowed, poor starvelings,   80
what's glory, however great, if that and nothing else?
Crowds flock to hear that mellifluous voice, his darling
Theban epic, whenever | Statius delights the City
by promising a performance. The audience sits there spellbound
by such fabulous charm, even the common people   85
are mad to hear him. And yet, | though he brings the house
       down,
he'll starve, unless he can sell his virgin libretto to Paris[12] –
Paris, Director of Ballet, the jobber of high commands,
who hands out poets their six-month carpet-knighthoods.[13]
What nobles cannot bestow, an actor will. Why bother   90
to appear in great patricians' spacious reception-halls?
Prefects and tribunes alike are appointed by ballet-dancers.
yet you need not begrudge the living a poet derives
from the stage. Today the age of the private patron's over:
where will you find the successors to Maecenas and his like?   95
Then genius got its reward; then many found it worthwhile
to go pale with work – and no wine – right through December.[14]

  What about writers of history? Do all *their* labours
bring a better return, or just | use more time and midnight oil?
No limits here: they pile up their thousand pages –   100
plus an enormous account for stationery supplied.
Their vast themes, and the genre, make this inevitable.

But what will the harvest yield, what fruit all your grubbing?
Does any historian pull down even a newsreader's wage?[15]
    'Oh, they're an idle lot, though, too fond of their shady
105   day-beds.'
How about advocates, then? Tell me the sum *they* extract
from their work in court, those bulging bundles of briefs!
They *talk* big enough – especially when there's a creditor
listening, or, worse, they're nudged in the ribs by some dun
110 who's brought his weighty ledger to fuss about a bad debt.
Then they pump out huge lies, huff and puff like a bellows,
spray spittle all over themselves[16] – yet if you check their incomes
(real, not declared), you'll find that a hundred lawyers
make only as much as one successful jockey.
115 Court's in session: you rise, a whey-faced Ajax,
to defend some case of contested citizenship
before a jury of yokels. Burst your lungs, talk till you drop,
collect a green palm-wreath[17] on your garret staircase –
but what's the pay-off? One dry ham hock-end, a jar
120 of pickled fish, mouldy onions – an African's monthly ration –
or five quart bottles of rotgut, fetched from up-river.
Four cases, let's say, bring you one gold piece between them –
but by prior agreement the solicitors take their cut.
'A blue-blooded lawyer gets | the maximum fee, though we
did a better job.' Ah, but look | at that bronze group in the
125   forecourt,
that four-horse chariot, and himself perched on a warlike
charger, threatening with droopy spear, one eye lost,
remote but upright, a dummy dreaming of battles.[18]
That's the way lawyers go bankrupt, this is what will happen
130 to Tongilius, who goes to the baths with his outsize – oil-flask,
of rhinoceros-horn, and his mob of muddy retainers,
and has Thracian slaves to carry his litter through the Forum,
when he shops for slaves or silver, glassware or country-houses:
that extorted gown[19] gets him credit, with its purple weave.
135 [Such display has its uses, though, since purple or amethystine]
robes bring in clients. It pays | these gentry to advertise,
to live well above their means, sell themselves at a premium –
and spendthrift Rome sets no limits | to their extravagance.

Trust in our eloquence, can we? Why, Cicero himself
wouldn't get tuppence these days without a big ring to flash.   140
When a litigant's picking a lawyer, his first thought is, *Have you got
eight slaves, ten freeborn retainers, a litter in attendance,
an escort of citizens?* That was why one advocate rented
a sardonyx ring – and why he made more than his colleagues.
Forensic skill seldom goes with shabby linen. How often   145
can a down-at-heels lawyer produce | some weeping mother in
     court?
Who'll hire *his* eloquence? You'd better take off for Gaul
or, better, Africa – that nurse of hopeful lawyers –
if you really suppose your tongue can earn you a living.[20]

Or do you teach declamation? You need to have iron nerves   150
when a whole large class demolishes 'Cruel Tyrants'!
Each student stands up in turn, and delivers by rote what he's just
learned at his desk: the same sing-song, identical verses,
bubble-and-squeak rehashed, sheer death for the poor master.
What type of case is involved, what's the best approach   155
and the clinching argument, what counter-shots will be fired –
these are things everyone's desperate to learn, but won't pay for.
'What, *pay* you? But what have you taught me?' 'Oh, I suppose
it's the teacher's fault if some rustic backwoods pupil's
heart doesn't beat more quickly week after week, while dinning   160
his awful Hannibal speech into my wretched noddle,
whatever the theme for discussion – should Hannibal march on
     Rome
from Cannae? And after that thunderous cloudburst, should he
play safe, withdraw his drenched and dripping cohorts?'[21]
Name your figure, I'll pay it – what wouldn't I give for any   165
boy's father to hear him as often as I must!' That's
the stock complaint of our teachers when they shelve stuff like
     'The Rapist'
or 'A Case of Poison', or 'The Wicked Ungrateful Husband',
or the one about pounded drugs that can cure chronic blindness –
and sue in the real-life courts for recovery of their fees.   170
So, if he takes my advice, that teacher will forthwith
discharge himself from the Bar, seek some other walk of life,
who's come down to the arena from Rhetoric's playground

for mere peppercorn fees – yet still | the highest he can command
175   in this profession. Go figure out the amount
famous musicians or singers pull down for giving lessons
to top people's sons, and you'll tear up your *Manual of Rhetoric*.[22]
For baths, a magnate will lay out thousands; still more, for a
        covered
cloister to drive around in when it rains – you couldn't expect
        him
180   to wait till the weather clears, or let his pair get muddy –
better here, where his mules' polished hooves will keep their
        lustre.
Elsewhere a banqueting-hall, with lofty Numidian columns,
must be sited to get the best of the winter sunshine;
and, however big an investment his mansion may have been,
185   he must still have a first-class chef and a major-domo.
With such expenses, a tenner's enough, and more than enough
for Quintilian. There's just nothing that comes any lower
than a son on the list when Daddy | is paying out cash. 'Then
        how
did Quintilian come by all those vast estates?' Ignore
190   the fortunate exceptions.[23] Luck makes you handsome and brave,
luck brings brains and breeding, a splendid pedigree, plus
the senatorial crescent to sew on your black shoestraps.
Luck makes a first-class speaker or javelin-thrower, luck
means that you still sing well | with a cold. It all depends
195   under which constellations you utter your first thin squalls
when you're fresh and red from your mother's womb. If Fortune
so pleases, you may rise from teacher to consul;
let her frown, and presto! the consul's a teacher once more.[24]
What about Bassus or Cicero?[25] What brought *them* to the top
200   but the stars in their courses, Fate's | miraculous occult powers?
Fate gives kingdoms to slaves, lets captives triumph – although
such lucky ones are rarer than the proverbial white raven.
Professorial chairs too often prove barren comfort,
bring banishment or death. Cases abound: the wretch
205   who hanged himself, or that other | indigent to whom
Athens dared give nothing but the cup of cold hemlock.[26]
Gods, grant the earth lie easy | and light on our fathers' shades,

with crocus bloom: may their ashes | enjoy eternal springtime,
who held that the teacher stood in place of a parent,
and must be revered as such! Achilles, well-grown, still feared   210
the rod, was still taking singing-lessons in his native mountains,
would never have dared to snicker at the music-master's tail.
But nowadays pupils will sometimes flog their instructor –
it happened to Rufus, known as 'The Cicero of the Backwoods'.[27]

What teacher, however learned, however successful,   215
gets a fitting return for his labours? Yet even this little,
however trifling – and any | professor makes more – is further
whittled away by the pupil's | attendant – *si peu sensible* –
and the cashier taking their cut. Best to give in, then:
make a concession, agree on a lower fee, not unlike   220
the hawker peddling winter rugs, white blankets –
so long as you get *some* recompense for sitting from midnight
in a hell-hole no blacksmith would tolerate, no wool-carder
would put up with for one moment for training apprentices;
so long as you get *some* return for enduring the stink   225
of all those guttering lanterns – one to each pupil,
so that every Virgil and Horace is grimed with lamp-black!
Yet seldom will even this small pittance be obtained
without a court-order. What's more, parents ask quite impossible
standards: the master's grammar must be above cavil,   230
history, literature, he must have all the pundits
pat at his fingertips. They'll expect him to answer questions
on his way to the public baths, tell them straight off the cuff
the name of Anchises' nurse, just who, and from what country,
was Anchémolus' stepmother, how long Acestes lived,   235
how many jars of Sicilian | wine he gave the Trojans?[28]
Demand that the teacher shall mould these tender minds, like an
        artist
who thumbs out a face in wax. Insist on his being
a father to all his pupils, responsible for forestalling
their indecent tricks with each other (though it's no sinecure   240
to keep check on all those darting eyes – and fingers).
'See to it,' you're told, 'and when the school year's ended,
you'll get as much as a jockey | makes from a single race.'[29]

What good are family trees? What point is there in being valued
for the length of your pedigree, Ponticus,[1] or in displaying
ancestral masks and statues – an Aemilius in his chariot,
half of a Curius, a Corvinus lacking one shoulder,

5   or a Galba minus his nose and both ears into the bargain?
Why trace back the ramifications of your kinship
on that ample chart, through innumerable branches,
to smoke-grimed Pontiffs or Masters of Horse, if your own
life is a public disgrace?[2] Why have so many portraits

10   of generals around, if you spend the whole night gambling
under their noses, and only | get to bed at dawn – when *they*
would be up, striking camp, and moving their standards off?
Why should a Fabius, though of Hercules' house, enjoy
ancient rights at the Great Altar, being styled 'Of the Rhône',[3]

15   if he's a greedy numskull and softer than any lambkin,
if his backside is pumiced smooth, a caricature of his hairy
ancestors, if he shames his family honour by traffic
in illegal drugs, and his statue has to be broken up?
You may line your whole hall with waxen busts, but virtue,

20   and virtue alone, remains the one true nobility.
Let a Paulus, a Cossus, a Drusus[4] shape your integrity;
honour *their* images above all your ancestral portraits;
when you are Consul let *them* | go before the lictors. First
you must show me your moral virtues. In word and deed

25   can you be reckoned pure, and firm for justice? If so,
I recognize you as a noble. All hail to you, sir, regardless!
Whatever your ancient line, so rare and distinguished
a scion comes as a benison to his applauding country,

which well may cry 'We have found him! Rejoice!', like the
    people
of Egypt for reborn Osiris.[5] Who'd claim high nobility   30
for one who falls short of his breeding, whose only distinction
is a famous name? But dwarfs get labelled 'Atlas',
a blackamoor's 'Snowball', some ugly misshapen girl
gets known as 'Miss Europe', while bald and scabby mongrels,
listlessly licking the rim of an empty lamp, we nickname   35
'Pard' or 'Tiger' or 'Leo', or anything else (if there is)
that roars more fiercely. So watch it: a patrician title,
when assumed by you, may produce much the same effect.
    At whom is this warning aimed? I'm talking to you, Rubellius
Blandus.[6] You're all puffed up by descent from the House of
    Drusus –   40
as though it were by some act of your own that you are a noble,
that she who conceived you could boast bright Julian blood,
wasn't some weaver for hire by the windy Embankment![7]
'You others are dirt,' you tell us, 'the rabble, the very dregs:
not one of you can prove his own father's citizenship,   45
whereas I claim descent from the kings.' Long life then, m'lord,
and much joy of your pedigree! Yet first-class advocates
may be found in the common herd, men used to handling briefs
for illiterate noblemen; try | the plebeians for a jurist
who's expert at slashing through all legal knots and riddles! 50
That's where our front-line troops are recruited from, brave
    young men
holding the fort in Germany, or the Middle East[8] – but you,
with your blue blood and nothing else, resemble some limbless
Herm: your one advantage is that the statue's noddle
is marble, whereas you, you dummy, are alive.   55
    Tell me, O scion of Trojans,[9] what's the first characteristic
of a thoroughbred? Speed and strength. The horse we most
    admire
is the one that romps home a winner, cheered on by the seething[10]
roar of the crowd. Good breeding doesn't depend on
a fancy pasturage; the thoroughbred earns his title   60
by getting ahead of the field, by making them eat his dust.
But lack of victories means that the auction-ring will claim him,

whatever names from the stud-book adorn his pedigree.
No ancestor-worship here, no respect for the dead. Sold cheap,
65   and constantly changing hands, these slow and plodding
descendants of noble bloodstock will end up turning a mill-wheel,
neck-galled from the collar, fit | for no other work. To make us
respect *you*, not your possessions, show us something
to inscribe on your personal record, to set beside those honours
we paid, and pay still, to the forebears who endowed you with all
70   you own.
        That's enough on the youth who (rumour claims) let his
            kinship
with Nero go to his head, who was puffed up with silly pride:
one seldom finds any decent respect for others
in that class. Ponticus, I don't want to see *you* valued
75   by your ancestors' record, achieving nothing that's worthy
of honour yourself. It's shabby to lean on borrowed renown:
the pillars may totter, the house collapse in ruin –
the trailing vine-shoot yearns for its widowed elm.
So be a good soldier, an honest | guardian, a judge
80   of integrity; if you are called as a witness in some ambivalent
and dubious case, though Phalaris should command you
to lie – and should wheel in his bull while dictating your
            perjuries[11] –
the worst sin still is to rate survival above honour,
by choosing life to lose one's very grounds for living.
85   Who merits death is dead, though he dines off grade A oysters
by the gross, or fills up his bathtub with the costliest perfumes.
        So when you at last obtain that provincial governorship,
you've waited for so long, set some limit on your anger,
curb your avarice, feel compassion for the local inhabitants,
90   whose very bones, you'll find, have been sucked dry of marrow:
observe what the law prescribes, what the Senate decrees, what
            rewards
await the good ruler, the thunderbolt of justice
with which our parliament struck down those governors who
out-pirated the Cilicians.[12] Yet what came of their condemnation?
95   Some native must sell off the threadbare clothes from his back
since Official B has grabbed all Official A had left him –

yet he still keeps quiet: after this | he'd be mad to lose his
    boat-fare.[13]
When our allies were newly conquered, and still flourishing,
they may have complained, but their losses didn't hurt them.
Their houses were stacked roof-high with piles of bullion,   100
with scarlet cloaks from Sparta and Coan purple;
bronzes and paintings, busts | and ivories by the Old Masters,
so vivid they seemed alive, were in every household; rare
the table without fine examples of the silversmith's art. Then came
the conquistadors – Antonius, the whole Dolabella clan,   105
temple-plunderer Verres[14] – and carried off their ill-gotten
loot by the shipload, more trophies in peace than wartime.
But today a few yoke of oxen, a small herd of brood-mares
with their stallion – that's all that a captured farmstead yields,
apart from its household shrine, with perhaps one decent   110
statue, a single god, left in it. Such are the choicest
pickings today, the most valued.[15] Perhaps you despise
the unwarlike Rhodians, the scented sons of Corinth –
and rightly so: what harm can ever befall you
from youths who put on perfume and shave their legs to the
    crotch?   115
But steer clear of rugged Spain, give a very wide berth
to Gaul and the coast of Illyria; avoid those harvesters
who provision a Rome with no leisure save for racing and the
    stage.
(And what return would you get from so dire an outrage, seeing
that Marius, not long since, stripped Africa to the bone? [16])   120
But rule number one is this: take care not to victimize
men both desperate and courageous. Though you rob them of all
their gold and silver, they still possess swords and shields,
helmets and javelins: the plundered keep their weapons.[17]

    What I have just propounded is not rhetoric but truth;   125
my performance, believe me, is taken straight from the Sibyl's
    book.[18]
If your staff are upright and honest – no long-haired pansies
who can fix your verdicts for cash – if your wife's above suspicion,
and doesn't come round on circuit from city to city
like a harpy with crooked talons, a regular gold digger, then   130

you can trace your lineage back to the Woodpecker King – or if
        loftier
names are what you're after, why not load your pedigree
with all those embattled Titans, and Prometheus for good
        measure?[19]
[Borrow your own ancestry from any myth you like.]
135   But if ambition and lust dictate your headlong progress,
if you splinter the rods in blood across provincial backs, if
blunt axes and weary headsmen are your prime delight,
then you will find your noble background itself beginning
to turn against you, to hold | a bright torch to your shamelessness.
140   The higher a criminal's standing, the more public the obloquy
directed against him for all his moral failings.
What's it to me, if you're | a habitual forger, and sign
your fraudulent deeds in a temple your grandfather built,
or by Daddy's triumphal statue? Or if you slip out at night,
145   wrapped in a hooded cloak, to commit adultery?
        Driving flat out past his ancestors' bones and ashes,
there speeds fat Lateranus in his gig, himself, *himself*,
locking the drag on the wheel, the Consul as muleteer![20]
It's night, but the moon can see him, the stars peer down
150   as witnesses – and as soon as his term of office
is ended, why then Lateranus will flourish his whip
in broad daylight, quite shamelessly, flick a cheerful salute
to respectable elderly friends as he passes; he'll untruss
the hay-bales himself, and fodder his weary horses.
155   But though he'll sacrifice 'a dun steer and eke a shearling',
as ancient ritual prescribes, he swears at Jove's high altar
by Epona, whose picture's daubed | on the doors of his reeking
        stables.[21]
And when he decides to show up at one of the all-night taverns,
mine host – some Syrian Jew with greasy pomaded hair –
160   runs out, [a Syrian Jew from the Idumaean Gate,]
calls him 'M'lord' and 'Your Honour', while Cyane the barmaid
hitches her skirt, and uncorks her bottle for action.[22]
        I can hear his supporters' comeback: 'Well, didn't we all
behave like that as young men?' Perhaps; but you kicked the habit

before you reached manhood. Wild oats should be sown and done
    with: 165
some follies should not outlast your first official shave.
Youth rates a certain indulgence; but Lateranus was still going
the rounds of the bath-house bars, with their lettered awnings,
when old enough for Eastern campaigns, for garrison
duty in Syria, maybe, or on the Rhine or Danube,   170
old enough to protect the Emperor's person. Send down
to the docks for your general, Caesar – to the best-known tavern:
you'll find him lolling there beside some hired killer,
with a bunch of thieves and matelots and fugitive criminals,
among hangmen and coffin-makers and a castrated   175
priest who's passed out on the job, still clutching his drums.
It's Liberty Hall here: bed and board are in common,
privilege is abolished, all men are free and equal.[23]
If you came across one of your slaves in such a den, Ponticus,
you'd pack him off to a chain-gang on your country estate: 180
but blue blood looks after its own, condones behaviour
in the upper crust that would shame a humble cobbler.

    One can never, I fear, adduce such vile and shameful
examples that nothing worse remains unmentioned.
His money all spent, Damasippus hired out his voice   185
to the stage, and played the shrieking *Ghost* of Catullus;
spry Lentulus made a hit as *The Crucified Bandit* – a pity
he wasn't nailed up in earnest.[24] A good part of the blame
must rest with the public: they sit there, shamelessly gawping,
while barefoot patricians swop gags and buffooneries,   190
stooging around, all slapstick, getting the big laughs
with their knockabout routine. Does it matter what *price*
they charge for their degradation? They do it – *and* with no Nero
to force them: their honour's for sale, both to stage and arena.[25]
But if *you* were faced with the choice, though – death, or a life on
    the boards –   195
which would you opt for? Has any man so feared death
that he'd rather play jealous husbands, be feed-man to a clown?
Still, with an Emperor-harpist, a comic-lead nobleman
comes as no surprise. What's left | after this but the arena?
Here, too, public scandal awaits you: a Gracchus fighting,   200

and not in full armour, either, with target and falchion –
such gear he can't abide [but condemns and detests it:
no visor to cover *his* face]. What he wields is – a trident!
Once he's gathered his net, and thrown it, with a flick of the
        wrist,
205   and missed his cast, his face exposed to the spectators,
quite recognizable, he bolts | for dear life from the arena.
No mistaking that cloth-of-gold tunic, left open at the throat,
not to mention the tall mitre with its dangling ribbons.²⁶
So the armed swordsman who | was pitted against Gracchus
210   had perforce to endure worse ignominy than wounds.

        If a free popular suffrage were granted, who would be
so crazy as not to prefer a Seneca to a Nero –
Nero, whose proper punishment would need far more than one
monkey, one sack, one serpent to square off *his* account!²⁷
215   Orestes' crime was identical, but circumstances made it
a very dissimilar case – *he* killed with divine sanction,
to avenge a father slain | in his cups. Orestes never
had Electra's blood on his head, he never murdered
his Spartan wife, or mixed up a dose of belladonna
220   for any close relative. *He* never sang on the stage
or composed a Trojan epic – and what, when Verginius,
Vindex, or Galba took over, cried out for vengeance more
of all that Nero wrought in his harsh and bloody regime?²⁸
Such were the acts of this prince of the blood, and such
225   his accomplishments – how he adored inflicting that ghastly voice
on audiences abroad, and winning Greek parsley-wreaths!
So deck his ancestral statues with concert-tour souvenirs,
make offerings of the costumes he wore as Antigone
or Thyestes, the mask in which he played Melanippe,
230   and hang up his harp on his own | colossal marble likeness!²⁹

        Where could you hope to find men of loftier ancestry
than Catiline or Cethegus?³⁰ Yet they planned a night attack
on the City, were ready to fire Rome's houses and temples,
as though they were the descendants of trousered Gauls,
235   daring what would condemn them to fry in the shirt of pitch.³¹
But the Consul was on the alert, and beat back their forces.

This new man from Arpinum – low-born, just come to Rome
as a raw provincial burgher – posted armed guards everywhere,
stopped the panic, alerted the Seven Hills. A civilian,
he won as much fame and honour within the City walls   240
as Octavius' sword, all bloody with endless slaughter,
brought *him* on the plains of Thessaly, at Philippi,
and the battle off Actium.³² But when Rome styled Cicero
his 'fatherland's father', its parent, Rome had freedom still.³³

    Another son of Arpinum once toiled in the Volscian hills,   245
guiding a plough for hire. Later he joined the army –
centurion-bait, his brains | half cudgelled out if he paused
to lean on his spade, take a breather from camp-entrenching.
Yet this same man faced the threat of Cimbrian invasion,
stood up single-handed and saved the trembling City.   250
So when the ravens swooped down to feast on those slaughtered
barbarian corpses, the largest | they'd ever seen, his noble
colleague shared in his triumph, but the cheers were for Marius.³⁴

    Plebeian by name, plebeian in spirit, the Decii still
were accepted by the Earth-Goddess and underworld deities   255
as a worthy self-sacrifice offered for the assembled host
of legions and allied troops, the flower of all Latium.
[So the Decii stood higher than those whose lives they
      preserved.]³⁵

    The last of our good old kings to assume Quirinus' mantle,
the diadem, rods and axes, had a slave as his mother. But   260
the Consul's own sons, who should rather have performed
some great deed in the furtherance of imperilled
freedom, something for men to marvel at – like Cocles,
or Mucius, or that virgin swimming the Tiber – instead
plotted to open Rome's gates to her exiled tyrants.   265
A slave revealed to the Senate all their criminal secrets
(why don't ladies mourn *him*?), and they were justly punished
with the scourge and the axes, first now applied by law.³⁶

    I'd rather you had Thersites for father, so long as *you*
resembled Achilles, and matched up to Vulcan's arms,   270
than to have you sired by Achilles, but become a Thersites.
Yet however far back you can trace your ancestral

pedigree, it began in a kind of ill-famed ghetto;
your first forefather, whatever | his actual name, was either
275   a shepherd – or something I'd much prefer not to mention.[37]

SATIRE IX

JUVENAL: I'd like to know why, whenever we meet, you look so
gloomy, Naevolus, grimmer than Marsyas after his flaying?
Why should you have an expression like Ravola's[1] when caught
right in the act, damp-bearded, going down on Rhodope?
(If a slave takes a lick at a pastry, we give *him* a licking.)   5
Heavens, your face! It looks even more miserable
than a share-pusher's when he offers a triple rate of interest
and can't find one sucker. What's produced all these sudden
lines and wrinkles? You used to take life as it came –
the provincial squire in person, a dinner-table wit   10
whose jokes had an edge of urban sophistication.[2]
What a change today – that sick-hound look, that unkempt
bush of dry hair! Your complexion's lost all the glow
it once got from hot packs of depilatory bird-lime,
coarse bristles sprout unchecked on your hairy thighs.   15
You've lost weight, too, you're thin as some chronic invalid
long burned by a quartan ague, endemic fevers.
A wasting body reveals all moods in the mind it houses,
anguish and pleasure alike: both stamp themselves into
one's features then. You seem to have quite transformed   20
your way of life, to be set on | a totally different track.
Quite recently, I recall, you were working the temples – Isis,
Peace (for Ganymede's shrine), Cybele (her secret grotto
up on the Palatine), Ceres (easy women haunt shrines!).[3]
You laid them by dozens then, and (something you don't
          mention)   25
more often than not you would have their husbands, too.
NAEVOLUS: This kind of life has paid off for many, but it's never

brought *me* fair return for my labours. Sometimes I'll collect
a greasy street-cloak, coarse and crudely coloured,
30   cut from a bolt of loose-woven Gallic fabric,
or some silver-plated gewgaw, lacking a hallmark.
Mankind is ruled by the Fates, they even govern those private
parts that our clothes conceal. If your stars go against you
the fantastic size of your cock will get you precisely nowhere,
though Virro⁴ may have drooled at the sight of your naked
35   charms,
though long coaxing love-letters come all begging your favours,
though – quote – *What naturally draws a man is – a pansy*.⁵
Yet what could be more monstrous than a close-fisted pervert?
'I paid you that *then*, more later, and more that other time –'
40   he figures, butt twitching. 'Well,' I say, 'fetch the accountant
with his reckoner and tables, tot up the total figure:
a miserable five thousand. Now list *my* services.
You think it's easy, or fun, this job of cramming
my cock up into your guts till it's stopped by last night's supper?
45   The slave who ploughs his master's field has less trouble
than the one who ploughs *him*.' 'But you used to fancy yourself
as a pretty young boy,' he says, 'a latter-day Ganymede –'
'Will you ever indulge your followers, your clients,
if you're so mean you won't pay for your own vices?'
50   But you still have to send him gifts – a green parasol, or amber
scent-balls – each birthday, or early in showery spring
when he lolls around on his sofa, examining the private
tributes that he's been given to celebrate Ladies' Day.⁶
     'Hey, sparrow,⁷ who'll inherit all those hills and estates,
55   all those pastures (to fly across which exhausts the buzzards)?
Your Campanian vineyards, the ridge that looks down on Cumae,
desolate Gaurus – these yield you a rich return of grapes:
whose sealed vats offer more long-lasting vintages?
Would it cost you so much to present yours truly with some acres
60   to retire his exhausted loins? Would you honestly rather
pass on that country cottage (the child with its peasant mama,
a puppy scampering round) to some cymbal-bashing boy-friend?'⁸
'You're rude to ask,' says he. But my rent cries *Ask him!* and so
does my single slave (as single as Polyphemus' big eye

which crafty Ulysses exploited to make his get-away.)[9]   65
But one's not enough, a second | will have to be bought, and both
fed and lodged. What's to do in the winter gales? What on earth
can I tell these two when December's winds freeze their shoulders
and naked feet? 'Hold on for summer and the cicadas'?[10]

   'You can hedge if you like, discount all the rest, but don't you   70
think it worth something, Virro, that if I hadn't displayed
true dedication to duty, your wife would be virgin still?
You know well how, and how often, you begged for my assistance,
and what you promised. The girl was actually bolting
when I got her to bed; she'd torn up her marriage-vows   75
and was leaving for good.[11] It took me | all night to change her
        mind,
with you boo-hooing outside – as witness the bed, and yourself
who heard its creaks, and your lady's sudden climax.
In many households adultery's saved a marriage
that was shaky and coming unravelled and all but dissolved.   80
How can you shuffle like this? Where's your sense of priorities?
Does it mean nothing to you, you treacherous ingrate, *nothing*
that you've managed a son and daughter, all by my doing?
You're rearing them as your own, you loved advertising these
        proofs
of your manhood in the Gazette.[12] Hang a wreath from your
        lintel: 85
you're a father, I've given you something to kill the gossip.
You hold parental rights now, I've cleared your status as heir:
you receive the estate tax-free, plus a nice little extra.
But just think of the benefits if I engender another
child, and bring the total score up to three!'[13] JUVENAL: Indeed,   90
just cause for complaint here, Naevolus. What is his answer?
NAEVOLUS: He ignores me, he's after some other two-legged
        donkey.
but remember, please, don't pass a word of this on –
keep my complaints to yourself, they're for your ears only:
these pumice-smooth creatures make | the deadliest enemies.   95
He told me his secrets, and now he feels burning hatred,
as though I'd betrayed what I knew. Oh, he wouldn't hesitate
for one moment to have me knifed | or beaten, to set a torch

against my front-door. And don't underestimate one thing:
100   poison, for the wealthy, is never expensive. So –
copy Mars' Council[14] in Athens, keep all this to yourself.
JUVENAL: Ah Corydon, Corydon dear,[15] what secrets do you
            suppose
a rich man can keep? If his slaves don't tattle, his horses
and dog will, his doorposts, his statues – shut all the windows,
105   pull the curtains tight, bar every door, extinguish
the lamps, get rid of the guests, let no one sleep within earshot,
and *still* whatever he did at the second cock-crow
that barman down on the corner will know by dawn, together
with every rumour started by the great man's kitchen staff
110   from head cook to bottle-washer. Of course they'll slander him;
gossip's their only weapon, their way of getting back
for whippings. And there's always some wino to accost you
at the crossroads, bent on inebriating your wretched ears.
These are the lot you should bind to silence about
115   what you were saying just now. Tattling a secret gives them
a bigger kick than pinching, and swilling, as much good wine
as Saufeia[16] did, while conducting a public sacrifice.
118   First among many reasons for decent living, surely,
120   is the need to be proof against the malice of your slaves:
a bad slave's worst part is his tongue. And yet the master,
in thrall to those he supports with his own cash and bread
is worse served still, is never truly free.[17]
NAEVOLUS: Useful advice, my friend, but a little too general.
125   What's my best move *now*, after all these wasted seasons
and disappointed hopes? The bloom of life will wither
all too soon, our miserable portion on this earth
is running out: while we drink, while we call for garlands,
            perfumes,
and call-girls, old age creeps up on us, unregarded.
130   JUVENAL: Never fear: so long as these Seven Hills stand fast
you'll always have friends in the trade, they'll still come flocking
from near and far, by ship or by coach, these gentry
who scratch their heads with one finger.[18] And here's one more
sound piece of advice: chew colewort, it's a fine aphrodisiac.

NAEVOLUS: Save that stuff for the lucky ones. *My* Fates are
          overjoyed   135
if cock can keep belly fed. Poor little household gods,
whom I supplicate with a pinch of incense or barley-meal,
or a tiny garland – when | will I ever lay by enough
to insure my old age against the indigent beggar's
bed-roll and crutch? A nice little nest-egg at interest,   140
in gilt-edged stock;[19] a small silver dinner-service
(too large, even so, for the old Republic);[20] a couple
of brawny porters, Bulgarians, to convey me in comfort
by sedan, through the crowds, to my seat in the noisy Circus –
what else? A stooped engraver, and a portraitist with the knack   145
of dashing off five-minute likenesses.[21] These are sufficient.
When will my means grow to modest? – not an ambitious
          programme,
but unlikely, even so, to materialize. Whenever
Fortune's invoked for my benefit, she plugs up her ears
with wax from Ulysses' ship, is deaf to all blandishments.[22]   150

SATIRE X

In all the lands that stretch far eastward from Cádiz
to Ganges and the dawn, few indeed there are can distinguish
true good from its opposite, or manage to dissipate
the thick mist of error. Since when were our fears or desires
5   ever dictated by reason? What project goes so smoothly
that you never regret the idea, let alone its realization?
Whole households have been destroyed, at their owners'
        insistence,
by the obliging Gods. Civilian and soldier share this
self-destructive urge. A torrential and over-fluent
10   gift of the gab has killed many; many have perished
through trusting physical beef, their marvellous biceps.[1]
But for most it's the cash they amass with such excessive care
that chokes them, those fortunes that dwarf any normal
        inheritance,
by as much as your British whale exceeds some puny dolphin.
15   So during the Reign of Terror, at Nero's command,
Longinus was banished, Seneca – grown too wealthy –
lost his magnificent gardens, a regiment besieged
Lateranus' mansion.[2] Soldiers seldom raid garrets.
Though you've only a few good silver vessels with you,
when you take to the road by night, you're scared of swords and
20   cudgels,
and quake at the stirring shadow of every moonlit reed:
it's the empty-handed traveller who whistles with footpads
        around.

    The most popular, urgent prayer, well-known in every temple,
is for wealth. *Increase my holdings, please make my strong-box*

wealth destroys

the largest in town![3] But you'll never find yourself drinking   25
belladonna from pottery cups. The time you should worry is
          when
you're clutching a jewelled goblet, when your bubbly flames with
          gold.
They had a point – don't you agree? – those two old philosophers:
one of them helpless with laughter whenever he set foot
outside his house, the other a weeping fountain.   30
The cutting, dismissive sneer comes easily to us all –
but where did Heraclitus find such a reserve of tears?
Democritus' sides were shaken with perpetual laughter,[4]
though the cities *he* knew had no togas, striped or bordered
with purple, no sedans, no tribunal, no rods and axes.[5]   35
Suppose he had seen the praetor borne in his lofty carriage
through the midst of the dusty Circus, in ceremonial dress –
the tunic with palm-leaves, the heavy Tyrian toga
draped in great folds round his shoulders; a crown so enormous
that no neck can bear its weight, and instead it's carried   40
by a sweating public slave, who, to stop the Consul
getting above himself, rides in the carriage beside him.[6]
Then there's the staff of ivory, crowned with an eagle,
a posse of trumpeters, the imposing column of white-robed
citizens dutifully marching beside his bridle-rein,   45
friends bought with the meal-ticket stashed away in their wallets.[7]
Democritus in *his* day, too, found matter for laughter
in all human encounters. His sagacity demonstrates
that the greatest men, our best future models, may still
be born in a sluggish climate, a country of muttonheads.   50
The cares of the crowd he derided no less than their pleasures,
their griefs, too, on occasion: if Fortune was threatening,
'*Up you,*' he'd say, and give her the vulgar finger.
     So our current petitions are pointless – destructive, even?
Then what requests *can* we wax to the knees of the Gods?[8]   55
     Some men are overthrown by the envy their great power
arouses; it's that long and illustrious list of honours
that sinks them. The ropes are heaved, down come the statues,
axes demolish their chariot-wheels, the unoffending
legs of their horses are broken. And now the fire   60

roars up in the furnace, now flames hiss under the bellows:
the head of the people's darling glows red-hot, great Sejanus
crackles and melts. Those features, once second in all the world,
are turned into jugs and basins, frying-pans, chamber-pots.[9]

65   Hàng wreaths over your doors, leàd a big white-chalked bull
up to the Capitol! They're dragging Sejanus along
by a hook, in public. Everyone cheers. 'What an ugly,
stuck-up face he had,' they say. 'Believe me, I never cared
for this fellow.' 'But what was his crime? Who brought

70   the charges, who testified? How did they prove his guilt?'
'Nothing like that: a long and wordy letter arrived
from Capri.'[10] 'Right: say no more.' And what of the commons?
They follow fortune as always, detest the victims.
If a little Etruscan luck had rubbed off on Sejanus,

75   if someone out of the blue had struck down the Emperor's careless
old age, this same rabble would now be proclaiming Sejanus
Augustus. But these days, we've no vote to sell, so their motto
is 'Couldn't care less'. Time was | when their plebiscite elected
Generals, Heads of State, commanders of legions: but now
they've pulled in their horns. Only two things really concern

80   them:
bread and the Games. 'I hear | that many are to be purged –'
'That's right, the oven's a big one, and no mistake.'[11] 'My friend
Bruttidius looked rather pale when I met him in town just now –
our slighted Ajax, I fear, is out for blood, having been

85   so ill-protected.'[12] 'Come on, then, quickly, down to the river –
boot Caesar's foe in the ribs while his corpse is still on show.'
'But make sure our slaves watch us – eyewitnesses can't deny it,
can't drag their quaking masters into court at a rope's end.'
That's how they talked of Sejanus, such was their private gossip.

90   Would you really choose to be courted as Sejanus was? To possess
all he did? To hand out top magistracies, appoint
the Chief of the General Staff, be known as the 'protector'
of a Princeps hunkered down on the narrow crag of Cápri
with his herd of astrologers? You'd love the salutes, the cohorts,

95   a private barracks, crack cavalry[13] – and indeed, why shouldn't
you covet them? Even those who lack the murderer's instinct
would like to be licensed to kill. Yet what fame or prosperity

are worth having if they bring you as much trouble as pleasure?
Would you rather assume the mantle of the wretched creature
being dragged along there, or control some sleepy rural hamlet,   100
inspecting weights, giving orders for the destruction
of short-measure pint-pots, an out-at-elbows aedile?
So you have to admit, the knowledge of what was desirable
eluded Sejanus. His itch for excessive honours,
his pursuit of excessive wealth, built up a towering   105
edifice, storey by storey, so that its final downfall
was that degree greater, the crash more catastrophic.
Take men like Pompey or Crassus – and that other tyrant[14]
who cowed Rome's citizens, brought them under the lash:
what proved their downfall? Lust for ultimate power   110
pursued without scruple – and the malice of Heaven
that granted ambition's prayers. Battle and slaughter
see most kings down to Hades; few tyrants die in their beds.
    The eloquence of Demosthenes or Cicero, their fame,
are what every schoolboy first prays for, right through his
        holidays,[15]   115
though as yet he has only a penny for an offering to Minerva,
and one house-slave to follow behind with his little satchel.
Yet both of these perished because of their eloquence, both
were destroyed by their own overflowing and copious talent.
That talent alone cost Cicero his severed head and hand: 120
no third-rate advocate's blood has ever stained the rostra.
O fortunate Roman State, born in my great Consulate –
had he always spoken thus, he could have laughed Antony's
swords to scorn. I prefer such ridiculous verses
to you, supreme and immortal Second Philippic,   125
so universally praised. A violent end took off
Demosthenes too, who held all Athens spellbound
with his torrential oratory in the crowded theatre.
He was born with the Gods against him and under an evil star,
that boy whom his father – bleary | with soot from red-hot ore   130
sent away from the coals and the pincers, the grime of the smithy,
the sword-forging anvil, to learn the rhetorician's trade.[16]
    Consider the spoils of war, those trophies hung on tree-trunks –
a breastplate, a shattered helmet, one cheekpiece dangling,

135   a yoke shorn of its pole, a defeated trireme's
       figurehead, miserable prisoners on a triumphal arch –
       such things are reckoned the zenith | of human achievement;
              these
       are the prizes for which each commander, Greek, Roman,
              barbarian,
       has always striven; for them he'll endure hard toil
140   and danger. The thirst for glory by far outstrips the pursuit
       of virtue. Who on earth would embrace poor Virtue naked
       if you took away her rewards? Yet countries have come to ruin
       through the vainglory of a few who longed for renown, a title
       that would cling to the stones set over their ashes – although
145   a barren fig-tree's strength would suffice to crack these open,
       seeing that sepulchres, too, have their allotted fate.
              Weigh Hannibal: how many pounds will you find, now, in
                     that peerless
       commander? This is he whom all Africa could not hold,
       from the ocean surf of Morocco east to the steamy Nile,
150   to Ethiopian tribesmen – and new elephants' habitats.[17]
       Now Spain swells his empire, now he leaps the Pyrenees;
       Nature throws in his path high Alps and snowstorms:
       he splits the rocks asunder, moves mountains – with vinegar.
       Now Italy is his, yet still he presses onward:
       'We have done nothing,' he cries, 'till our Punic troops have
155   stormed
       the gates of Rome, till our standard | is set in – the Subura!'
       A fine sight it must have been, fit subject for caricature,
       the one-eyed commander perched on his gigantic beast!
       What an end – alas for glory! – was his: the victor vanquished,
160   the headlong flight into exile, the awesome celebrity
       now a client waiting outside the door of a petty Eastern
       despot, until His Bithynian | Majesty deign to rise!
       No sword, no spear, no stone was to extinguish the spirit
       that once had wrecked a world: what avenged those losses,
165   those rivers of spilt blood, was a ring, a poisoned
       ring! On, on, you madman, over your savage Alps,
       to thrill schoolboys and supply a theme for recitations![18]
              One globe seemed all too small for the youthful Alexander:

unhappily he chafed at this world's narrow confines,
as though caged on some bare rocky Aegean islet. Yet   170
when he entered the city of brick-walled Babylon,
a coffin was to suffice him.[19] Death alone reveals
our puny human dimensions. It's believed that once
sails crowded through Athos (the lies mendacious Greece
spun round her history!), the sea was paved with vessels   175
and chariots drove across it: deep streams, we're told,
and rivers were drunk dry by the Persians for breakfast,
etcetera: get the rest from some sweaty-drunk poet's recital.[20]
But mark the state in which he came back from Salamis –
this barbarian who'd made a habit of flogging the winds   180
with a rigour they'd never suffered in Aeolus' prison-house,
who'd bound Poseidon himself with fetters (and doubtless
thought it an act of mercy that he'd refrained from branding
the deity as well: what God would serve *this* master?) –
so, how *did* he return? With a single vessel, the sea   185
blood-red, the prow slow-thrusting through shoals of corpses.
Such the price he paid for his long-cherished dream of glory.[21]
   '*Grant us a long life, Jupiter, O grant us many years!*'
In health or sickness, this is your only prayer.
Yet how grisly, how unrelenting, are longevity's countless   190
evils! Look first at your face: an ugly and shapeless
caricature of itself. Your skin's now a scaly hide,
you're all chapfallen, the wrinkles you've developed
resemble nothing so much as those carved down the cheeks
of some grandmotherly baboon in darkest Africa.   195
Young men are all individuals: A will have better looks
or brains than B, while B will beat A on muscle;
but old men all look alike, with tremulous limbs and voices,
bald pates, wet runny noses, like a baby's,
and toothless gums with which they must mumble their bread: 200
so repulsive to their wives, their children – indeed, themselves –
that they arouse distaste even in legacy-hunters.[22]
Their taste-buds are shot, neither food nor wine now gives them
pleasure, while long oblivion's blanked out sex – or if
they try, it's hopeless: though they labour all night long   205
at that limp and shrivelled object, limp it remains.

So what can their tired and hoary groins still hope for?
Nothing very exciting. The libido's decidedly suspect
when desire outruns performance. Other senses deteriorate:
210   take hearing. How can the deaf appreciate fine music?
Quality makes no difference: a first-class soloist,
massed choirs in their golden robes – *they* get nothing from them.
What does it matter to *them* where they sit in the concert-hall
when they can barely hear a brass band – horns and trumpets –
215   blowing its guts out? The slave who announces the time,
or a visitor, must shout to let them know his message.

    The blood runs thin with age, too: now nothing but fever
can warm that frigid hulk, while diseases of every type
assault it by battalions. (If you asked me their names
220   I'd find it less trouble to list all Oppia's lovers,
the number of patients Doc Themison kills each autumn,
the partners that X, the wards that Y has defrauded,
the number of men tall Maura goes down on daily,
the number of schoolboys that are laid by Hamillus;
225   I could sooner run through all the country-houses now owned
by the barber who rasped at my chin when I was a stripling.)[23]
Here a bad hip or stiff shoulder, there lumbago;
the stone-blind envy the one-eyed. Here's a fellow
whose pallid lips must accept | food from another's fingers:
230   once accustomed to lick his chops at the prospect of dinner,
if he opens wide today he's like a baby swallow
when its mother flies back with a beakful she hasn't touched
      herself.
But worse than all bodily ills is his mental collapse, when he fails
to remember the names of servants, or recognize the friend
235   who was yesterday's host at dinner, let alone the children
he begot and brought up. A cold-blooded codicil
disinherits his flesh and blood, and the whole estate is bequeathed
to some professional sexpot, whose expert panting mouth –
after years in that narrow archway – earns her a rich reward.
240   If he keeps his wits intact, though, he still must endure
the burial of his sons, the death of his dearly-beloved
wife and brother, urns filled with his sisters' ashes.
Such are longevity's penalties – perpetual grief,

black mourning, a world of sorrow, ever-recurrent
family bereavements to haunt one's declining years.   245
Nestor, the King of Pylos, if we can trust great Homer,
lived longer than any creature save the proverbial crow –
happy, no doubt, to have postponed his death for so many
ages of men, to have counted past one hundred,
to have sampled new wine so many times. But wait   250
one moment – consider his bitter | complaints about Fate's
  decrees,
and his too-long thread of life, while he watched his valiant son
Antilochus burn on the pyre, how he asked his fellow-mourners,
any of them, why he'd survived so long, what crime
he'd committed to deserve such extreme longevity.[24]   255
Peleus made the same plea as he mourned the dead Achilles;
so did Odysseus' father at that seafarer's passing.
If Priam had passed away at a different time, before
the building of those ships for Paris's reckless venture,
he'd have joined his ancestors' shades while Troy still stood,   260
with magnificent obsequies – his coffin carried out
on the shoulders of Hector and Hector's brothers, while
Ilium's womanhood wept, and Cassandra led off the ritual
lament with Polyxena, garments rent in mourning.
So what did length of days bring him? He saw his world   265
in ruins, saw Asia's destruction by fire and the sword;
then put off his crown, took arms, and – a dotard, but a soldier –
fell before Jove's high altar, like some ancient ox
turned off from the thankless plough, that offers its wretched
stringy neck to be severed by its master's knife.   270
This at least was a manly exit: but Hecuba lived on
like a vicious bitch, grinning and barking, stark crazy.[25]
I take our own Marius now – passing over Mithridates
and Croesus (warned by the wise and eloquent Solon
to watch out for the final stretch of a lengthy life)[26] –   275
his exile and prison, his outlaw's life in the marshes,
the conqueror begging his bread through the streets of Carthage:
all through living too long. What more fortunate paragon
had Nature, or Rome, ever bred on this earth, had he drawn
his glorious last breath at the climax of his triumphal   280

procession, after parading those hordes of captured Teutons,
just on the point of stepping down from his chariot?[27]
Providential Campania gave Pompey a fever, which should
have been welcomed; however, the public prayers of so many
285   cities prevailed: Rome's destiny, and his own,
kept him alive for defeat and decapitation – a fate
such as not even Catiline or his fellow-conspirators
suffered: at least they died whole, without mutilation.[28]
     When a doting mother passes the shrine of Venus,
290   she'll whisper one prayer for her sons, and another – rather louder,
more detailed – for her daughters to have good looks. 'What's
       wrong?'
she'll ask you, 'Didn't Latona rejoice in Diana's beauty?'
Perhaps; but Lucretia's fate should warn us not to pray
for a face like hers; Virginia would happily yield her features
295   to Rutila, take on poor Rutila's hump.[29] A physically
handsome son keeps his wretched parents in constant
anxiety: coexistence of good looks and decency
is rare indeed. However old-fashioned his background,
however strict the morality on which he was brought up –
300   and even if Nature, with generous, kindly hand has
turned him out a pure-minded, modestly blushing
youth (and what greater gift, being more powerful
than any solicitous guardian, could she bestow?) –
manliness still is denied him. A seducer will not scruple
305   to lay out lavish bribes, corrupt the boy's very parents:
cash always wins in the end. But no misshapen
stripling was ever unsexed by a tyrant in his castle,
no Nero would ever rape a clubfooted adolescent –
much less one with a hump, pot-belly, or scrofula.
310   Be proud of your handsome son, that's fine – but don't forget
the extra hazards that face him. He'll become a notorious
layer of other men's wives, always scared that some husband's
hot on his tail for revenge. He'll have no luckier star
than Mars did, he can't avoid the toils for ever – at times
315   jealous rage will exact more than jealous rage is allowed
by any law: will horsewhip a rival to ribbons,
stick a knife in his heart, or a mullet up his backside.[30]

So your dream-boy's going to set himself up as the lover
of a married woman? But when she's | been giving him presents a
      while,
soon enough he'll turn to someone he *doesn't* love, take her   320
for her eye-teeth. And remember, there's *nothing* that these
      women,
high-born or not, won't do for their hot wet groins:
when their morals are gone, they've just one obsession – sex.
'But what's wrong with good looks in the chaste?' How much
      use, I ask you,
was stern self-restraint to Hippolytus, or to Bellerophon?   325
Phaedra flushed angry-red, as though disdaining rejection;
Sthenoboea flared up with a passion that matched the Cretan's;
both lashed themselves into a fury.[31] Pure feminine ruthlessness
thrives best on guilt and hatred. What advice, do you suppose,
should one give the young man whom Caesar's wife is determined   330
to marry? This blue-blooded sprig of the highest nobility –
wonderfully handsome, too – is raped and doomed by one glance
from Messalina's eyes. She sits there, waiting for him,
veiled as a bride, while their marriage-bed is prepared
in the public gardens. A million will come as dowry   335
according to ancient ritual; there'll be witnesses, an augur.
You thought these were secret doings, known only to a few?
But *she* wants a proper wedding. So what's your decision?
If you refuse her commands, you'll die before lighting-up time;
if you commit the crime, you'll get a brief respite, until   340
your liaison is so notorious that it reaches the Emperor's ears:
he'll be the last to learn of this family scandal. Till then
better do what you're told, if a few more days' life matters
that much. But whichever way you think quicker and easier,
you'll still have to offer your lily-white neck for the chop.[32]   345
    Is there nothing worth praying for, then? If you want my
      advice,
let the powers-that-be themselves | determine what's most
      appropriate
for mankind, what best suits our various circumstances.
They'll give us not what we want, but what we need; a man
is dearer to them than he is to himself. Led helpless   350

by emotional impulse and powerful blind desires
we ask for marriage and childbirth. But the Gods alone can tell
what they'll be like, our future wives and offspring!
Still, if you *must* pray for *something*,[33] if at every shrine you offer
355   the entrails and holy chitterlings of a white piglet,
then ask for a healthy mind in a healthy body,
demand a valiant heart for which death holds no terrors,
that reckons length of life as the least among the gifts
of Nature, that's strong to endure every kind of sorrow,
360   that's anger-free, lusts for nothing, and prefers
the sorrows and gruelling labours of Hercules to all
Sardanapalus' downy cushions and women and junketings.[34]
What I've shown you, you can bestow on yourself: there's one
path, and one only, to a tranquil life – through virtue.
365   Fortune has no divinity, could we but see it: it's we,
we ourselves, who make her a goddess, and set her in the
          heavens.

SATIRE XI

If Atticus dines in state, he's thought a fine gentleman;
if Rutilus does, he's crazy. What gets a bigger horse-laugh
from the crowd than a gourmand gone broke? Every dinner-party,
all the baths and arcades and theatre foyers are humming
with the Rutilus scandal.[1] He's young still, physically fit   5
to bear arms, and hot-blooded. Gossip claims that with no official
compulsion, but no ban either, he'll sign his freedom away
to some tyrant of a *lanista*, take the gladiator's oath.[2]
You'll find plenty more like him, men who live for their palate
and nothing else, whose creditors – bilked once too often –   10
now lie in wait for them at the entrance to the market.
The most straitened of these are the ones who dine best of all,
as they totter to ruin with light glinting through the cracks.[3]
Meanwhile they ransack the elements for tasty items
with never a thought for expense – indeed, if you look closer,   15
the higher the price, you'll find, the better pleased they are.
So raising more money to squander presents no problem –
they'll hock the family plate, or pledge poor Mummy's portrait,[4]
and spend their last fiver to add relish to their gourmet
earthenware: thus they're reduced to the gladiators' mess-stew.   20
That's why it makes a difference who's host: what in Rutilus
would be spendthrift waste, gets his neighbour a generous
          reputation:
the verdict depends on their means. I despise, and rightly,
that man who knows by precisely how much Atlas
out-tops all the mountains of Libya, yet lacks the wit   25
to measure the difference between a purse and an iron-bound
strong-box. From Heaven descends the maxim *Know Thyself*[5] –

to be taken to heart and remembered, whether you're choosing
a wife, or aiming to win a seat in that august body
30   the Senate. Thersites never laid claim to Achilles' armour:
Ulysses did – and brought public | ridicule on himself.
If you decide to plead a critical case, where vital
issues could go either way, take stock of yourself: what are you,
a talented, forceful speaker or Matho the windbag?[6]
35   A man should know, and study, his own measure
in great things and small alike: even when buying fish
don't go hankering after salmon on an income only suited
to catfish.[7] What end awaits you, if your appetite's expanding
as your funds contract, if you sink all your father's cash
40   and property into a belly capacious enough to swallow
all his herds and estates, family silver, and capital holdings?
The last thing such *rentiers* part with, after everything else,
is their ring: when the finger's bare, why, beggary follows.
It's not an untimely grave that wastrels need to fear:
45   Death holds less terror for them than lingering old age.

     The pattern is pretty constant. They raise a City loan
which the creditors see squandered. When the capital sum
is almost exhausted, and the lender is looking pale,
they skip out down the coast for a cure of oysters.[8]
50   To welsh on your debts these days is thought no worse an action
than fleeing the stuffy Subura for a place on the Esquiline.
There's only one regret that moves these expatriates,
one thing they miss – a whole year of the Circus.
They've forgotten what blushing means. Catcalls pursue
55   Shame out of Rome; few hands are raised to stop her.[9]

     Today you'll discover whether | my life and goods and
        conduct,
Persicus, match up to all my fine exhortations –
whether, while praising beans, I'm a secret glutton,
or say 'porridge' aloud, but privately ask for cheesecake.
60   Now you've promised to be my guest, you'll find me
a very Evander: you | can be Hercules, or, if you're modest,
Aeneas – not quite so classy, but still of divine descent;
and both – one by fire, one by water – were translated to
        heaven.[10]

Here's the menu – all homegrown, nothing from the market:
first, from my farmstead at Tivoli, a plump tender kid,   65
the pick of the flock – too young to have cropped pasture,
or to have dared to nibble low-sprouting willow-shoots –
whose veins hold more milk than blood; mountain asparagus,
picked by my bailiff's wife as a break from her spinning;
big eggs, still warm from the straw in which they were packed,   70
and the pullets that laid them, as well as grapes, preserved
for six months, but still as fresh as when they were gathered;
baskets of Syrian pears and Italian bergamots, fragrant
apples, the equal of any you'd find in an east-coast orchard –
don't worry, winter's ripened them, the cold's dried out   75
their green autumnal juices, made them quite safe for dessert.
     Time was when this would have seemed a luxurious banquet
to our senators. Curius[11] used to raise his own spring greens
on a little allotment, and cook them over his modest hearth.
But today the scruffiest chain-gang ditcher disdains such fare,   80
remembers the smell of tripe in some stifling cook-shop.
Once, as a feast-day treat, it used to be the custom –
or if it happened to be a relative's birthday –
to unrack a side of salt pork or a flitch of bacon,
with maybe a little fresh meat if they'd run to a sacrifice.   85
Some kinsman who'd served the state three times as Consul,
who'd commanded armies or held the Dictatorship,
would stop work sooner than usual to attend such an occasion,
toting the mattock with which he'd mastered the hillside.
When men trembled before the Fabii, or stern Cato,   90
or Fabricius or the Scauri, when even a Censor in office
feared the stern moral code of his inflexible colleague,[12]
then nobody thought it a matter for serious concern
what species of turtle was swimming the seas, to provide
fine adornments for the bedheads of our Trojan-born elite;   95
couches were small in those days, their sides without inlaid work,
their plain bronze headrests displaying a garlanded ass's head
with country children playfully romping round it.
[Houses, furniture, diet were all of a piece throughout.]
Then a soldier was rough, no Greek art connoisseur: 100
when a city was sacked, and as his share of the booty

he got cups signed by great artists, he'd break them up to make
horse-trappings, or to emboss his helmet in relief
with the image of Romulus' She-Wolf (tame, as Imperial
105   Destiny bade), the Quirinal | twins beneath their rock,
and Mars, swooping naked, armed with spear and shield –
appropriate art to display to a dying foeman![13]
These troops ate their porridge from plain earthenware bowls:
any silver they had shone brightly on their armour.
110   (All of which you might envy, if envy took you that way.)
The power of godhead, too, was closer: witness that voice
crying through the silent[14] City, about the midnight hour,
that the Gauls were coming on us from Ocean's shores. Thus the
            Gods
performed the office of prophet; thus Jupiter warned us,
115   such was his constant care for the welfare of Latium,
when his image was baked clay still, still undefiled by gold.
        In those days there were home-grown tables, carpentered
from our own local timber. If a gale uprooted
some ancient walnut-tree, its trunk would serve this purpose.
120   But your modern millionaire cannot enjoy his dinner –
finds the turbot and venison tasteless, the perfume and roses
stinking like garbage – unless his broad table-top[15]
rests on an ivory leopard, rampant, snarling, a stand
carved in the round from tusks such as Assuan exports,
125   and the slippery Moors, and the blacker-than-Moorish Hindu:
tusks that those great beasts shed in some Arabian wadi,
so burdensome they've grown, too big to support.[16] This makes
for *bon appétit* and a strong | digestion. Table-legs
of silver, for them, are as bad as an iron ring.[17] That's why
130   I steer clear of guests who make snobbish comparisons
and despise my non-affluence. There isn't a single ounce
of ivory here, not even my dice or draughtsmen
are fashioned from this material. My knife-handles, too,
are of bone. Notwithstanding, this never turns the victuals
135   rancid, or renders a chicken harder to cut up.
Nor will you find a carver to whom the whole kitchen staff
has to defer, a pupil of the maestro, Trypherus,

in whose classroom a splendid banquet – sow's paunch, pheasant,
    boar,
antelope, hare, gazelle, not to mention the tall flamingo –
is mock-carved with blunt knives upon elmwood dummies,
    making   140
a clatter that loudly resounds throughout the neighbourhood.[18]
My boy has never learnt how to knock off a guinea-fowl's wing
or a slice of venison: he's still an unhandy novice,
always has been: the best he can manage is the odd pork cutlet.
My cups, too, are the cheapest, picked up at bargain prices,   145
handed round by an unpolished youth who's dressed for warmth,
not some Phrygian or Lycian, a prize item bought
from a dealer: whenever you ask | for a double, ask in Latin.[19]
My servants all dress alike, with cropped straight hair
that's only combed today because of the party.   150
One is a tough shepherd's son; another a ploughman's,
homesick for the mother he's been away from so long,
missing their little cottage, the pet kids that he played with.
His expression is frank, his manners decent and modest,
such as ought to be found in one born to the bright purple.   155
He doesn't parade his cute little balls at the bath-house,
his voice is still unbroken[20] – no need to shave his armpits,
or nervously hold an oil-flask in front of his swollen cock.
The wine he'll serve you was bottled among his native
mountains, under whose peaks he wandered as a child.   160
[Servant and wine both share a common fatherland.]

    Perhaps you may be expecting a troupe of Spanish dancers,
gypsy girls with their wanton songs and routines, the climactic
applause as those shimmying bottoms grind to floor-level.
[Brides with their husbands beside them will watch things that   165
any person would be ashamed to speak of in their presence.]
Such shows arouse flagging passions, they're the tycoon's hot
    substitute
for Spanish fly. Yet in fact it's the ladies who derive
more pleasure from them, who reach such a pitch of excitement
at what they see and hear that they void their bladders.   170
No such follies in *my* modest home: I leave them to be heard,
and enjoyed – the clack of the castanets, language so filthy

that a stripped whore under some stinking archway would blush
to employ it, all the arts and obscenities of lust –
175   by the nabob who spits his wine on a floor of Spartan marble.[21]
The rich are forgiven such conduct. Gambling's a disgrace,
adultery too, for middle-class people: the same tricks,
when played by the smart set, are labelled as chic and madly smart.
         At my feast today we'll have very different entertainment:
180   we'll hear the Tale of Troy from Homer, and from his rival
for the lofty epic palm, great Virgil. Does it matter
what sort of speaker recites such immortal poetry?
         Now cast care aside, shelve all your business worries:
you've got the whole day free, so relax and treat yourself
185   to a welcome rest. Don't let's have any mention of money –
and if your wife's in the habit of staying out all night,
if she comes home next morning with clothes suspiciously creased
and spotted with damp, if she's red in the face and ears,
if her hair-do's all anyhow, don't boil with throttled resentment,
190   just forget all your troubles the moment you cross my threshold –
your house, your servants, the losses and breakages
they cause you: forget, above all, the ingratitude of friends.
         Now the spring races are on: the praetor's dropped his napkin
and sits there in state (but those smart nags just about cost him
195   the shirt off his back, one way and another); and if
I may say so without offence to that countless mob, all Rome
is in the Circus today. The roar that assails my eardrums
means, I am pretty sure, that the Greens have won – otherwise
you'd see such gloomy faces, such sheer astonishment
200   as greeted the Cannae disaster, after our Consuls
had bitten the dust. The races are fine for young men:
they can cheer their fancy and bet at long odds and sit
with some smart little girl-friend. But *I'd* rather let my wrinkled
old skin soak up this mild spring sunshine than sweat
205   all day in a toga.[22] Here nobody cares if you visit
the baths an hour before noon – though do so five days running
and you'll very soon find such a life can get just as boring
as any other: restraint | gives an edge to all our pleasures.

SATIRE XII

My birthday, Corvinus?[1] No; a still happier occasion,
on which this gay turf altar awaits the beasts I'd vowed
to the Gods: a snow-white lamb for Juno, Queen of Heaven,
the same for Minerva, her shield armed with the Moorish Gorgon.
But the victim reserved for Tarpeian Jove strains at his taut   5
stretched tether, tosses his head, a mettlesome frisky
young calf, well-grown for temple and altar, for sprinkling
with unmixed wine: high time he was weaned, he feels,
as he fiercely butts at the tree-trunks with his growing horns.[2]
If my means were ample, and matched up to my wishes,   10
I'd have laid on a bull that was bulkier than – Hispulla,[3]
slowed down by his very size: no locally-pastured beast,
but a pedigree Umbrian, bred in lush water-meadows,
with a neck that only the heftiest priest could sever[4] –
to mark the return of my friend, still trembling from the horrors   15
he's undergone, and astonished to find himself safe and sound.
Small wonder: for he avoided not deep-sea perils alone
but being struck by lightning. Thick black clouds blotted out
the heavens: burning and sudden, fire flashed down on the yards,
making each man believe that he had been hit – and soon,   20
thunderstruck, conclude that the grimmest shipwreck was nothing
to this horror of blazing sails. It all resembled
a storm in a poem, exactly the same events,
and just as bad. But I've got yet another crisis to tell you,
and for you to pity again, though the rest is all of a piece,   25
awful, but a disaster experienced by many –
witness those countless votive plaques in the temples:
our artists, everyone knows, owe bed and board to Isis.[5]

This was just the fate that befell my friend Catullus.[6]
30   The hold was half-seas under already, and now
with great waves pounding the vessel from either side,
rocking the mast, the grizzled | old captain's expertise
could hit upon no solution. So Catullus resolved to compound[7]
with the winds, and jettison cargo – thus imitating the beaver,
35   that makes itself eunuch when cornered, in its urge to escape
surrenders its balls: so precious | the drug, it knows, in its groin.[8]
'Heave my goods overboard,' Catullus screamed, 'all of them!'
Willing to throw out even his rarest possessions –
a purple robe, fine enough for any soft Maecenas,
40   and other fabrics made from wool that's been dyed by natural
rich herbage – but also with thanks to some secret property
of the water, and to the climate along the Guadalquivir.[9]
Out went his silverware, too, wrought salvers made to order
for Domitian's chamberlain, three-gallon wine-bowls designed
45   to quench the thirst of a Centaur – or Fuscus' wife;[10]
plus baskets, thousands of dishes, chased goblets out of which
Philip the Crafty had drunk, the man who purchased cities.[11]
But where in the world would you find anyone else who'd dare
to save his skin, not his silver, to set life above property?
50   [Some are so blind with greed that they live for their fortunes
rather than making their fortunes enhance their lives.][12]
    Even when most of the cargo and stores was overboard
the ship made no headway. So, urged | by extreme necessity,
as a last resort, the captain chopped down the mast to solve
55   his dilemma: dire straits indeed, the very worst,
when your vessel has to be rescued by such diminution!
So go, trust your life to the winds, rely on timber planking
with only four fingers' breadth – or seven at most –
of pitchpine as protection between yourself and death.
60   Remember, next time, to take bags of bread, water-bottles,
and axes to chop off a spar with in case of shipwreck.
But luck was with our traveller: after a time the sea
fell calm, and his destiny triumphed over wind
and wave alike. The Fates, in cheerful mood, now spun him,
65   with beneficent hand, a yarn of the whitest wool,

and the wind returned, but as | the mildest breeze, and the
    stricken
vessel ran on before it, propelled by the makeshift aid
of bellying garments, and her single surviving
spritsail. Then, as the southerly storm-clouds dwindled,
fresh hope of survival returned | with the sunshine: soon they
    glimpsed   70
that lofty peak, so beloved | of Ascanius that he preferred it
as home to his stepmother's city Lavinium, called it
The White Mount, after the sow whose thirty dugs and piglings –
a sight never seen before – made light their Trojan hearts.[13]

  At last the vessel entered the harbour of Ostia, passing   75
the Tyrrhenian lighthouse, gliding between those massive
piers that reach out to embrace the deep, and leave
Italy far behind – a man-made breakwater
that no natural harbour could equal. The captain nursed his lame
vessel through to the inner basin, its waters so tranquil   80
that a rowboat could ride there. The crew, with shaven heads,[14]
safe home, took garrulous pleasure in telling their adventures.

  So off with you, lads: show reverence both in thought and
    speech
as you garland the shrines, strew meal on the sacrificial knives,
and dress the fresh new altars of bright green turf.   85
I'll follow you soon. When the main rite's been duly performed,
I'll come back home, where my own small images
are fresh-waxed and adorned with delicate garlands.
I'll make my private oblations to Jupiter, burn incense
for family and household gods, scatter nosegays of every hue.   90
The house is pin-bright, the gateway's decked with branches:
our early-morning lamps join in our thanksgiving.

  But don't mistake my motives, I beg you, Corvinus: the friend
for whose safe return I've raised all these altars possesses
three little heirs. Who'd bestow so much as a croupy   95
old chicken, its eyes just glazing over, on such
a barren acquaintance? Just think of the cost! Fat quails
never go to the men with children.[15] But if some wealthy
spinster or bachelor catches | the mildest fever, the whole
of the temple cloister's soon hung with formal votive prayers: 100

some even promise a sacrifice of a hundred oxen –
but only because there aren't elephants for sale here!
(Neither in Latium, nor anywhere under Italian skies
do these beasts breed, but imported from darkest Africa
105   are pastured in the Rutulian forests once ruled by Turnus:
and these are the Emperor's herd, they're prepared to serve
no private master: their ancestors answered to Tyrian
Hannibal, or King Pyrrhus, or our Roman generals;
bore cohorts on their backs, and – forming no small part
110   of an army – marched into battle, a line of turrets.)[16]
A hardened legacy-hunter wouldn't hesitate, if he could,
to line up one of these tuskers before the altar, slay it
for some maiden lady's household gods: sole victim
worthy of such divinities – or of those who covet their wealth.
115   Just say the word, and this fellow | will vow to sacrifice
the tallest and most good-looking of his numerous slaves,
he'll deck the brows of his houseboys and chambermaids
with the ritual chaplet; and if he happens to have a nubile
daughter like Iphigeneia, he'll sacrifice *her* – though he couldn't
120   hope she'd be switched for a doe, like her tragic predecessor.[17]
    I agree with my fellow-citizen: a legacy far outweighs
even a thousand ships. If a dying man recovers,
he'll cancel his earlier testament, he's caught in the trap
of such remarkable service; may well, in one brief clause,
125   make our legacy-hunter sole heir. *Then* watch the victor
strut cock-a-hoop over his rivals! Now do you understand
how well it paid off to butcher that Mycenaean maiden?
So long live legacy-hunters, as long as Nestor himself!
May their possessions rival all Nero's loot, may they pile up
130   gold mountain-high, love no man, and be loved by none.[18]

SATIRE XIII

All deeds that set evil examples result in unpleasantness
for the doer himself. The first retribution: no guilty
person can win acquittal at the bar of conscience, despite
having suborned some judge to award him a rigged verdict.
What do you think men feel, Calvinus,[1] about this recent   5
outrage against you, this breach-of-trust case? Yet you're not
so poorly off that one modest financial setback
would sink you. Besides, your plight, as everyone knows,
is by no means rare: many others have suffered a similar
mishap – by now it's a cliché, just average bad luck.   10
Let's drop these excessive complaints. A man's anger should never
get overheated, disproportionate to his loss.
But you, my friend, can scarce bear the least, most exiguous
scintilla of trivial trouble: your temper's red-hot, you've a burning
pain in your guts – all because | a friend won't refund the sum   15
you entrusted to him! Should this *really* cause amazement
to someone turned sixty, born | in Fonteius's consulship?[2]
Or has all your handling of property taught you nothing at all?

   Philosophy's fine, its scriptures provide you with precepts
for rising above misfortune: but those who have learnt the hard
   way,   20
in the school of life, to shoulder every vicissitude
without fret or resentment – don't we admire them, too?
What feast-day's so holy it never produces the usual quota
of theft, embezzlement, fraud, all those criminal schemes
for quick gain, glittering fortunes won by the dagger or drug-box?   25

   Good men come rare: count up, you'll scarcely find as many
as there are gates in Thebes, or mouths to the rich Nile.[3]

We live in the world's ninth age, a period still worse
than the age of iron: such evil defies Nature
30   to find a name that fits it, a metal sufficiently base.⁴
And yet we always demand good faith from Gods and mortals
as noisily as a lawyer's speech in court is applauded
by his hired claque. You childish | old booby, can't you see
the passion other folks' money arouses? Can't you see
35   just how naïve and comic a figure you cut these days,
demanding that men should not perjure themselves, should believe
that there's truth in religion, in temples, in bloody altars?
That was how primitive man lived long ago, before
King Saturn was ousted, before he exchanged his diadem
40   for a country sickle, when Juno was only a schoolgirl,
and Jupiter − then without title − still dwelt in Ida's caverns.
No banquets above the clouds yet for Heaven's inhabitants,
no beautiful Hebe or Ganymede there to serve as
cup-bearers;⁵ no Vulcan, still black from the smithy,
45   scrubbing the soot off his arms with spirits of − nectar.⁶
Each God would breakfast in private; there wasn't the rabble
of Gods we've collected today, the stars were content with a few
deifications, and so the firmament rested lighter
on poor Atlas's back. Not yet | had the gloomy realm of the
         nether
50   depths been assigned to grim Pluto and his Sicilian bride;
no Furies, no wheel, no boulder, no black and murderous
vulture: while they'd no king yet, the shades had a high old time.⁷
    In those days the least malfeasance drew shocked attention:
they thought it a heinous offence, to be punished by death,
55   if a young man failed to stand up in his elders' presence, and if
the schoolboy did not defer to the bearded youth. Never mind
whose strawberry-beds were bigger, which store-room held more
         acorns:
that four years' lead ensured one immutable respect,
and manhood's first fuzz shared equal | status with grizzled age.
60   But nowadays if a friend *doesn't* disavow your deposit,
if he returns your holdall with its rusting specie intact,
such honesty's a portent − consult the sacred records,
offer up the sacrifice of a garlanded lamb!

If I discover a decent God-fearing man, I compare him
to a boy with a double member, or fishes found under the plough   65
by some gawping farm-hand, or even a pregnant mule.
It worries me, just as though the sky had rained down stones,
or a swarm of bees had settled in a hanging cluster
on some temple roof-top, or maybe | a river in spate had come
roaring down to its outfall with torrents of blood or milk.[8]   70

   You complain that you've lost, by a trustee's fraudulence,
ten thousand in cash. Yet others may have been bilked like you,
may have lost a secret deposit of two hundred thousand, or more,[9]
such a pile that the biggest strong-box can scarcely contain it.
Easy work to ignore the testimony of the Gods in Heaven –   75
provided no mortal finds out. Just hark at those loud
denials, observe the assurance of that lying face!
He'll swear by the Sun's rays, by Jupiter's thunderbolts,
by the lance of Mars, by the arrows of Delphic Apollo,
by the quiver and shafts of Diana, the virgin huntress,   80
by the trident of Neptune, Our Father of the Aegean;
he'll throw in Hercules' bows and the spear of Minerva,
the armouries of Olympus down to their very last item;
and if he's a father, he'll cry: 'May I eat my own son's noddle –
poor child! – well boiled, and soused in a vinaigrette dressing!'[10]   85

   Some attribute every event to Fortune's hazards,
and contend that the universe has no prime mover,
but that Nature controls the seasons, and day and night;
so they'll fearlessly lay their hands upon any altar.[11]
Others are scared that punishment overtakes an offender,   90
and believe in the Gods, yet still perjure themselves. 'Let Isis,'
they argue, 'dispose of my body as she pleases,
let her strike my eyes and blind me with her vengeful rattle[12] –
I'd forgo my sight to keep | all the cash I've denied receiving.
Consumption, gangrenous ulcers, the loss of half a leg –   95
they'd all be worth it. A penniless champion sprinter,
if he wasn't plain crazy, a case for some smart Greek quack,
would opt for wealth and the gout: where, pray, does
          swift-footedness
get you in terms of cash? Can you eat an olive-wreath?
The wrath of the Gods may be great, but it's certainly slow[13] –   100

and if they make it their business to punish all wrongdoers,
when will they get to me? Besides, I *may* find a God open
to prayer and persuasion, one who forgives such matters. Many
commit identical crimes, yet suffer diverse fates:
105   one earns the cross for his pains, another a diadem.'[14]
      Thus they strengthen their will when terrified and guilty
over their vile misdeeds: when summonsed to swear at a shrine,
they'll charge on ahead, quite ready | to nag and drag *you* along.
For when a bad case is backed by brazen audacity,
110   many will take it on trust. (It's all pure play-acting,
a role like the runaway clown's in that witty farce by Catullus.)
But you, poor soul, exclaim (loud enough to out-shout Stentor
or rival the Mars of Homer):[15] 'How *can* you hear such things,
Jupiter, and not open those lips of yours? Never mind
if they're marble or bronze – say *something*! Otherwise what's the
115   point
of our emptying packets of incense on your sacrificial embers,
or making you all those offerings – chopped calves'-liver,
pigs' chitterlings? Frankly, we might as well honour the statue
of some worthy civic deadhead for all the good it does us.'
120   Now accept such consolation as an individual can offer
who isn't lined up with the Cynics, hasn't swallowed Stoic
            doctrine
(there's only a shirt between them), who holds no brief
for Epicurus, so pleased with the plants in his little garden.[16]
A baffling illness should get top specialist attention,
but *your* complaint could be handled by a first-year medical
125   student.
If you can demonstrate that no more detestable crime
was ever committed, I'm silent. I won't stop you beating
your breast with your fists, or your cheeks with the flat of your
            hand,
since after you've suffered such loss, the doors must be shut,
130   and the household wail louder, make noisier lamentation
over your cash than they would at a family funeral – no one
on such an occasion needs to work up fictitious grief,
or content himself with rending his garments and forcing
a tear or two out – lost cash breeds honest weeping.

   But if you see the courts choked with similar complaints,   135
and if, when your opponent's perused the bond ten times over,
he declares the signature forged, the document waste-paper
(despite the fact that the handwriting's his, *and* the impress
of the sardonyx signet-ring he keeps in that ivory case) –
despite all this, you fusspot, do you *really* suppose your plight   140
merits exceptional treatment just because you're a white hen's
     offspring,
whereas we mere common pullets were hatched from less
     favoured eggs?[17]
Yours is a modest loss – to be borne with moderate choler
when you look at the big-time offences. Just think
of the hired thug, for instance, or the fire that's deliberately   145
started in your front hallway with a well-placed sulphur match!
Or of those who rob ancient shrines of their largest chalices
(the gifts of nations, so holy their very rust should be
     worshipped),
or of crowns that long-dead kings left there in dedication.
If such prizes are lacking, there are small-time desecrators   150
who'll scrape off the gold leaf from Hercules' thigh, from the very
features of Neptune, strip Castor of all his gilding.
[Why not? It's common practice to melt down the Thunderer.[18]]
Think of those who concoct and peddle poisonous drugs,
or the man who's lugged down to the sea in a sack of oxhide,   155
with an innocent ape as his unfortunate companion.[19]
Yet such form the merest fraction of the non-stop crimes
that our City Prefect must hear every day from dawn to sundown.
If you want to find out the truth about mankind's morals, it's all
contained in one courtroom. Spend a few days there, and   160
see if you dare, on return, to complain of *your* misfortunes!
Who's surprised to find goitre in an Alpine canton, or women
from the Sudan with udders bigger than their fat babies?
Who does a double-take at a blond and blue-eyed German,
even when he's twisted his greasy locks into horns?   165
[Let's face it, all of them share the common human condition.]
    When the clamorous clouds of Thracian cranes swoop down
they're charged by the Pygmy warrior in his miniature armour;
but soon – no match for his enemy – he's snatched into the sky

170   by the fierce crane's crooked talons. If you saw such a spectacle
       here on Italian soil you'd just split your sides; but there,
       though such battles are frequently witnessed, nobody ever
       laughs, since the fighting forces all stand about one foot high.[20]
           '*What?*' you exclaim, 'is this crook, this fraudulent swindler,
175   to get off scot-free?' Let's suppose he's been loaded with fetters
       and hustled away, at our instance (what more could your wrath
                   demand?)
       to summary execution – yet the loss in cash still remains:
       you'll never get back your deposit. All the blood from a headless
       trunk will satisfy nothing but pure vindictiveness.[21]
180   'Ah, vengeance is good, though, sweeter than life itself –'
       that's how the ignorant talk, you'll see their passions
       flare up for the flimsiest reason, or maybe for none at all
       [any trifling excuse will justify loss of temper].
       But Chrysippus wouldn't say that, nor would kind-hearted
185   Thales, nor the old man who dwelt by sweet Hymettus
       (who'd never have made his accuser drink one drop of the
                   hemlock
       forced on him during his cruel bondage). Benign
       Philosophy, by degrees, peels off most of our follies
       and vices, first shows us what's right.[22] It's always a petty, mean,
190   and feeble mind that takes the greatest pleasure
       in paying off scores, and here's the proof: there's no one
       enjoys revenge like a woman.[23] But why should you suppose
       such people *do* escape justice? Their guilty conscience keeps them
       in a lather of fear; the mind's its own best torturer,
195   lays on with invisible whips, silently flays them alive.
       it's a fearful retribution – more cruel than any devised by
       our early Republican judges, or Hades' Rhadamanthus[24] –
       to be stuck, day and night, with this witness in one's breast.
           The Pythian prophetess once replied to a certain Spartan
200   that the notion he had in mind, of embezzling a deposit
       and backing his fraud with perjury, would not, in the end,
       go unpunished. (He wanted to know the God's reaction,
       did Apollo advise him to perpetrate such an offence?)
       So he gave the funds back – but from fear, not honesty. Yet
205   the oracle was proved true, and worthy of that great shrine:

he perished, he and his family, the whole house, root and branch,
down to the last relation, however far removed[25] –
such are the penalties for the mere *intention* of sinning,
for he who secretly meditates any crime is as guilty
as if he'd committed the deed. But suppose he *does* commit it: 210
then he's plagued by endless anxiety, even at meal-times –
his throat is fever-dry, he grinds away with his molars
on hard lumps of food that half-choke him, and in his misery
he spits back vintage wines, the expensive cobwebbed bottle's
not to his taste: bring out | something finer still, and his face   215
will screw up, just as though he were drinking vinegar.
At night, if his worries allow him | brief respite, a little sleep,
and his thrashing limbs are still, he'll start having nightmares
about the temple, the altar, the deity he's outraged;
what's more – and this brings him out in a proper sweat of
      terror –   220
he dreams about *you*, you're looming over him, larger
than lifesize, a fearful figure, he's quaking with fright, *he's*
      confessing –!
Such men blanch and tremble at every lightning-flash;
when it thunders, they just about swoon at the first faint rumble,
as if it weren't mere chance, or a furious gale, but rather   225
fire striking earth from heaven in wrathful judgment.
If that storm does no damage, their anxiety's even greater
as they wait for the next: this calm's a deceptive reprieve.
What's more, if they get any illness – a pain in the side, a fever
that keeps them awake at night – they're convinced it's a visitation   230
from the God they've offended: such, they suppose, are the arrows
and slingstones divinity wields. They dare not offer a bleating
lamb in the shrine, not so much as a crested cockerel
to their household gods: when the guilty fall sick, what hope
is allowed them? Have not their victims a better title to life?   235

    Bad men, by and large, display shifty, capricious natures:
when committing a crime, they've boldness to spare: it's later,
after the crime's accomplished, that notions of right and wrong
begin to assail them. And yet | their nature – immutable, fixed –
reverts to the ways they've abjured. Has anyone ever   240
set a term on his programme of crime, or seen his hardened

brow recover, once lost, its capacity for blushing?
What man have you ever seen satisfied by a single
villainous action? This forsworn scoundrel will one day
245 catch his foot in a snare, face the hook | in some dark oubliette,
or languish on one of those craggy Aegean islets, packed
with distinguished exiles.[26] Your hated foe's bitter sentence
will delight you: at long last you'll happily agree
that the Gods aren't deaf after all, or blind, like Tiresias.[27]

SATIRE XIV

A great many things, Fuscinus,[1] of deservedly ill repute,
things that would leave an indelible stain on the brightest fortune,
parents themselves display and pass on to their children.
If Papa's a ruinous gambler, then his son and heir is bound
to be rattling a little dice-box by early adolescence;   5
nor need the family expect better things from any youngster
whose spendthrift father, a hoary old glutton, has taught him
to appreciate peeled truffles, and the proper sort of relish
on mushrooms; who's learnt to tuck into quails and plovers[2]
served up with their natural juices. By the time that he's seven,   10
with quite a few milk-teeth left still, a boy like this has got
his character fixed for life. Set a thousand bearded tutors
on either side of him, he'll never give up his passion
for luxurious meals, or lower his standards of *haute cuisine*.[3]

    Does Rutilus'[4] conduct promote | a mild temper, restraint
        when dealing   15
with peccadilloes? For him, are the souls of slaves, and our bodies,
made up from the same material, identical elements?[5]
No: sadism's what he teaches. He revels in the bitter
sound of a flogging, knows | no siren song like that of the lash.
To his quaking household he's a monster, an ogre,   20
happiest when the torturer's there with his red-hot irons
ready to brand some wretch for stealing a couple of napkins.
What effect on the young must he have, with his yen for clanking
    fetters,
for dungeons, and seared flesh, and field-gang labour camps?[6]
    How can you hope, you bumpkin, that the daughter won't
        sleep around   25

when however fast she reels off the list of her mother's lovers,
gabbling their names, she must stop to get her breath back
a score of times and more? As a schoolgirl she was Mummy's
accomplice; now she composes her own billets-doux – at
              Mummy's
30   dictation – which go to her lover by the same fag go-between.
Thus Nature ordains: we're sooner, more swiftly corrupted
by examples of vice in the home, since they enter our minds
with high authority's sanction. Perhaps you'll find one or two
youths who despise such conduct, whose spirits have been formed
35   from finer clay, with a kindlier touch in the firing;
but the rest trail in Daddy's most undesirable footsteps,
and are dragged through the ruts of all-too-familiar vice.
So avoid what should be condemned. There's at least one
              compelling
motive for doing so – to stop the next generation
40   from imitating our crimes, since we're all more than willing
to take models from vice and depravity. You'll discover rebels
and traitors wherever you look, in every clime and country;
but a patriot – much less a family of patriots – nowhere.

      Let no foul sight or utterance ever approach the threshold
of a father's dwelling-place: may this house be free from
45   call-girls –
and freeloaders' noisy all-night parties. If you're
up to no good, remember: a child has the greatest claim
on your respect. Don't ignore him simply because he's young,
but from infancy let him restrain you, prevent your urge to sin!
50   For if, in time to come, he earns officialdom's censure,
and proves himself your son in more than physical build
and features, if he's the child of your moral actions,
and by following your footsteps sinks deeper still in crime –
then, I don't doubt, you'll revile him, read him a bitter
55   and furious lecture, get ready to alter your will.
Yet how can you assume the mien, and rights, of a father
when your conduct is worse than his, and your vacuous noddle
has been needing cupping-glass suction since heaven knows
              when?[7]
If a visitor is expected, then none of your household's idle.

'Get the floors swept,' you shout, 'polish up those columns!   60
Fetch down that dried-up spider, and every bit of its web!
You, clean the silver plate, and you, the embossed vessels –'
thus the voice of their master, all urgency, stick in hand.
The worries you've got, poor fellow! The lobby might harbour
a dog's turd to offend your friend's eye on arrival,   65
the vestibule might be muddy – yet these are problems
that one small slave-boy could fix with a bucket of sawdust.
Then why take no trouble to ensure that your son will enjoy
the sanctity of the home, unmarred and free from blemish?
You've given country and people one new citizen – that's fine   70
if you make him fit for his country, a competent farmer,
competent, too, at handling the business of peace and war.
It'll makes a great difference, then, what moral, what practical
training you give your son. The stork scours the countryside
for snakes and lizards with which to feed its young ones;   75
and these, when they've learnt to fly, seek out the same prey
          themselves.
The vulture, leaving behind dead cattle and dogs, or the gibbet,
hastens back to its chicks with bits of the cadaver:
so when the grown chick has constructed | a nest in its own tree,[8]
and provides its own sustenance, it feeds on carrion still.   80
But Jupiter's noble eagle goes hunting hare and roe-deer
over the upland pastures: this is the prey it brings home
to its eyrie: so when the eaglets reach full maturity
and leave the nest, at the dictates of hunger they'll swoop
on the same prey that they ate when first they burst the eggshell.   85
X had a passion for building: he ran up multi-storeyed
mansions all over the place – at the seaside, in mountain resorts
like Praeneste, on Tivoli's hillsides – adorned with marble brought
          in
from Greece, or still further afield, great piles[9] that eclipsed the
          local
temples in splendour (just like | that eunuch nabob, freedman   90
of Claudius,[10] whose town house far outshone our Capitol).
Such grandiose schemes diminished his assets, frittered away
his ready cash; yet somehow he kept a quite substantial
percentage intact – all of which his crazy son then squandered

95   on building more stately homes with even costlier marble.
Some, whose lot it's been to have Sabbath-fearing fathers,
worship nothing but clouds and the *numen* of the heavens,
and see no difference between the flesh of swine and humans
since their fathers abstained from pork. They get themselves
      circumcised,
100 and are wont to condemn our Roman laws, preferring
to learn and honour and fear the Jewish commandments,
all that Moses handed down in that arcane tome of his –
never to show the way to any but fellow-believers
(if they ask where to get water, find out if they're foreskinless).
105 But their fathers were the culprits: they made every seventh day
taboo for all life's business, dedicated to idleness.[11]
Most faults the young pick up instinctively: one only,
avarice, has to be taught them, against their natural instincts.
A deceptive vice, this, with the shadow and semblance of virtue:
110 dour-faced, gloomy of mien, always dressed like an undertaker,
the miser's strongly commended for his frugal way of life –
a thrifty fellow, they say, a man who keeps closer watch
over his wealth than the dragons of the Hesperides or Colchis[12]
could, if put on the job. What's more, the type I speak of
115 is thought by the public at large to be an expert craftsman
at moneymaking: such workers forge ever-larger fortunes,
by any and every method. The anvil rings ceaselessly,
the furnace is always glowing: that's how the pile mounts up.
So Daddy's convinced that the miser enjoys true happiness:
120 the man who goggles at wealth, who can't credit any instance
of poverty plus contentment, is bound to advise his sons
to tread in the skinflint's footsteps, to follow the same way of life.
Each vice has its rudiments: these he drums into their heads
from the start, they're grounded in all the pettier meannesses.
125 But soon he's teaching them the insatiable lust for profit:
he'll pinch his slaves' lean bellies by giving them short rations,
but himself goes hungry too – those crusts of hard stale bread,
all blue with mould, are something even *he* baulks at.
He'll rehash yesterday's mince in the middle of a September
130 heatwave, hold over for tomorrow's summer dinner
an assortment of left-overs – beans, a tail-end of mackerel,

half a catfish, already stinking – all under lock and key:
he'll even count the chopped leeks before he stores them.
If offered such food, a professional beggar would spurn it.
But why suffer such tortures in pursuit of riches?   135
It's craziness, no doubt about it, plain lunatic folly,
spending your life in squalor just to die a millionaire.
What's more, with your money-bags crammed to the top, you'll
        find
your love of cash will grow in proportion to your assets:
you don't have it, you want it less. So just one country house   140
won't be enough – you'll have to purchase a second,
you'll enjoy extending your boundaries, that neighbour's
        wheatfield
looks bigger and better than yours, so you buy it up, plus his
        vineyard,
and that hillside thickly planted with its grey-green olive-trees.
But if no figure you offer will tempt the owner to sell,   145
then a herd of famished cattle, lean work-weary oxen,
will be driven, at night, in among his green standing wheat,
and not go home till the whole new crop's found its way
into their bellies: you'd think the field had been scythed.
Complaints of this sort are so common it's hard to count them –   150
or the farms that come on the market through such outrageous
        acts.
    But what gossip there'll be, what nasty trumpeted rumours!
'What harm in that?' you reply. 'I don't give a row of bean-pods
for the neighbourhood's good opinion – especially if to earn it
means working some meagre holding for a chicken-feed harvest.'   155
Oh sure: you'll keep totally free of infirmity and disease,
contrive to escape all worries, and every disappointment,
live to a ripe old age, attain true happiness – *if*
you own as many acres as Rome's whole population
had under the plough in the days of the early kings.   160
Later, a battered veteran who'd campaigned for his country
against Carthage or dread Pyrrhus,[13] who'd braved the Epirots'
        swords,
would get, in the end, a bare two acres as quittance
for all his wounds. Yet no one | ever held this a niggardly

165 recompense, less than their service of blood and toil deserved;
     none charged the state with bad faith or ingratitude. This
              allotment
     was enough to support a man – not to mention his wife in labour,
     and the other four children, three his and one a house-slave's,
     playing around the cottage: and when their big brothers returned
     from the day's work, ditching or ploughing, a second, ampler
170   supper
     of porridge awaited them, steaming hot in the stewpan –
     yet today the same holding's too small for our kitchen-garden.
     Here lies the root of most evil: no vice of the human heart
     is so often inclined to mix up a dose of poison,
175 or slip a knife in the ribs, as our unbridled craving
     for limitless wealth. The man who must have a fortune
     must have it quickly; yet how much respect for the laws, what
     scruples or moral compunction can such a go-getter afford?
     'Live content with these humble cottages, my boy, don't look
180 beyond these hills of ours' – that's what old mountain peasants
     used to tell their sons. 'The ploughshare should furnish men
     with sufficient bread for their needs: the gods of the countryside
     so ordained it, whose generous bounty brought us the blessing
     of wheat, and rescued us from our old, crude acorn diet.
     The man who doesn't disdain to wear kneeboots when it's
185   freezing,
     and keeps off an east wind's chill with sheepskins, fleece inside –
     he'll never be tempted by evil: it's these strange foreign garments,
     purple robes and the like, that breed wickedness and crime.'
     Such maxims the ancients gave their children; but now
190 when autumn is ending, a father will rouse his drowsy son
     soon after midnight. 'Wake up, boy!' he'll bawl, 'get out
     your notebooks! Scribble away, son, mug up your cases, study
     those red-letter legal tomes! Or apply for the vinestaff[14] at once –
     but make sure that your general notes your hairy nostrils,
195 your uncombed hair, and those broad shoulders of yours;
     destroy some Moroccan encampments or British border forts;[15]
     then at sixty you'll rank as Centurion of the Standard –
     and make your pile. But if endless chores in barracks
     aren't to your taste, if your bowels turn to water

at the sound of bugle or trumpet, then find something   200
that you can resell at a profit of fifty per cent – and don't
turn up your nose at the trade that's kept beyond the Tiber,[16]
or get the idea you should make some classy distinction
between perfume and hides: the stink of profit is pleasant
whatever its source.[17] Here's the maxim your lips should ever
      frame,   205
words worthy of the Gods, or of Jove himself as poet:
"No one asks where you get your wealth from – but have it you
      must." '
Every ancient nanny dins this saw into her toddlers,
it's the first thing little girls master, long before their ABC.
To any parent who hands out precepts of this sort   210
I'd say something like this: 'Look here, you pinhead, just who
says you have to hurry the process? Your pupil, I'm sure, will
      outdo
his teacher. Relax, don't worry: you'll be beaten, just as Ajax
overtook Telamon, and Achilles outstripped Peleus.'[18]
    Go easy on youngsters: the marrow of adult evil   215
has not yet filled their bones. Now when your boy's reached the
      age
to comb out his beard and submit it to the trimmer's knife, yes,
      then
he'll bear false witness, then he'll perjure himself for tuppence,
laying hands on Ceres' altar, or on her statue's foot.
Your daughter-in-law's as good as dead if she enters   220
your house with that fatal dowry – whose fingers, do you imagine,
will throttle her while she's asleep? He's found a quicker method
than yours of amassing riches by land and sea: great crimes
involve no hard work. 'But *I* never taught him such habits,'
you'll declare some day, 'much less forced him into them.'   225
Yet the root and cause of his downfall lies within you.
Whoever instils the passion for great riches,
and by such cack-handed advice breeds greedy sons,
is also giving him licence to double his patrimony
by fraudulent methods.[19] He's off, reins flying, full pelt: 230
if you call him back, he can't stop, his chariot whirls him
away past the turning-post, indifferent to your commands.

Delinquency knows no boundaries: what youth will not exceed
the limits you set? Don't they always indulge themselves further?
235   When you tell a young man that only fools give presents
to friends, or relieve the debts of a poverty-stricken relation,
you're simply encouraging him to rob and cheat, to acquire
riches by any crime. Wealth arouses as great a passion
in you as love of country in the breasts of the Decii;
as great – if the Greek tale's true – as the love that fired
240   Menoeceus
for his city of Thebes, where once | armed men sprang from the
                furrows,
born of the dragon's teeth, shields at the ready, prepared –
as though a bugler rose with them – for grim battle on the spot.[20]
Just so you'll see the fire – of which you yourself kindled the
                spark –
245   spread, a huge conflagration, consuming all before it.
Nor will *you* be spared, poor devil: the trembling maestro
will be gobbled up, with roaring, in the den of his trainee lion.
The astrologers may know your nativity: but it's a bore
to wait for that slow-running spindle: you'll die before your
                thread
250   is due for shearing. Already | you're an obstacle, blocking his will:
your stag-like longevity's torture for that juvenile mind.[21]
Hurry round to the doctor, have him make you up the mixture
that Mithridates employed.[22] If you hope to pick one more fig,
to continue gathering rosebuds, you must swallow a dose,
255   before meals, of the medication needed by kings – and fathers.
I present you a first-class attraction: no theatre can rival it,
no munificent praetor can match it with his Games.[23]
Just think at what hazard to life men's household fortunes
are increased, their brassbound coffers comfortably filled,
260   their cash deposits banked with the vigilant Castor
(ever since Mars the Avenger was robbed of his helmet, and failed
to safeguard the goods in his keeping[24]). So consign to oblivion
all those lavish productions put on at religious festivals:
mankind's commercial dealings offer far bigger sport.
265   What's better entertainment, the trampoline acrobat,
the funambulist showing his skill at tightrope walking –

or you, spending half a lifetime aboard your merchantman,
forever exposed to each hurricane gale that blows,
a reckless, contemptible[25] trader in stinking burlap, glad
to ship fortified muscatel at some ancient Cretan wharfside,   270
and travel with demijohns from Jove's own birthplace?
And yet that neat-stepping balancer makes a livelihood
by his footwork, the rope he descends is his prop against cold
and hunger. But you take your risks | for the sake of a thousand
          talents,
a hundred country estates. Look at the big ships crowding   275
our harbours and seas: we've more men in the merchant navy
than on dry land now. Wherever there's hope of profit
our merchant vessels will venture, will sail beyond Crete or
          Rhodes,
will pass the Moroccan coastline, leaving Gibraltar behind them,
till they hear the sun sink hissing in Ocean's western streams.   280
It's a fine return for such labours to sail back home in triumph,
purse full, money-bags bursting, with tales to tell
of the wonders of Ocean – not least those husky young mermen![26]
Delusions take various forms. Mad Orestes, cowering
in his sister's arms, had fiery visions of the Furies;   285
when Ajax slaughtered an ox, he thought it was Agamemnon
or Ulysses that bellowed.[27] And though he doesn't rend his
          clothing,
the man who loads his vessel with freight to the gunwales,
leaving only one plank above water, needs a keeper none the less,
since the cause of all his troubles and perils is – silver,   290
stamped out in tiny roundels, with portraits and superscriptions!
Storm-clouds and thunder threaten. 'Cast off!' the merchant cries,
having bought up a cargo of grain or pepper. 'This overcast
sky, these pitch-black cloud-banks, are nothing to worry about –
just summer lightning.' Poor devil, that very night he may   295
fall from his ship as it breaks up, be battered by the waves,
still clutching his money-belt in one hand or between his teeth.
Yesterday all the gold-dust washed down by the river-gravels
of Spain or Lydia[28] wouldn't have sated his ambitions:
but now he must rest content with a rag round his chilly loins,   300
and scraps of food, while he begs, a victim of shipwreck,

for coppers, displaying a picture of the storm that ruined him.
Riches so hardly come by cost still more fear and worry
to preserve: safeguarding a fortune is a wretched chore.

305   One millionaire kept a contingent of servants with water-buckets
on duty all night, so obsessed was he for the safety
of his amber, his statues, his Phrygian marble columns,
his ivory plaques, his tortoiseshell inlay.[29] The tub of the naked
Cynic[30] was fire-proof: if it broke, he could get another

310   the next day – or fix up the old one with lead clamps.
Alexander perceived, on seeing that tub and its great
inhabitant, how much happier was the man who desired
nothing than he whose ambitions encompassed the whole world,
yet would suffer perils as great as all that he'd achieved.[31]

315   [Fortune has no divinity, could we but see it: it's we,
we ourselves, who make her a goddess.][32] If anyone asks me
where we're to draw the line, how much is sufficient, I'd say:
enough to meet the requirements of cold and thirst and hunger,
as much as Epicurus derived from that little garden,[33]

320   or Socrates, earlier still, possessed in his frugal home –
Nature never says one thing and Philosophy another.[34]

    Are those over-strict examples? Am I cramping your style?
        Then add
a dash of our latterday morals: let's compound for the capital
needed to sit in the theatre's first to fourteenth rows.

325   If *that* still makes you frown and pout with resentment,
double – all right, then, *treble* – the knight's four hundred
        thousand![35]
What? Not satisfied yet? Still gaping for more? In that case
nothing will be enough, not the wealth of Croesus and all
the kings of Persia – not even that of Narcissus,

330   Claudius' favourite freedman, on whom the Emperor lavished
such favours, and at whose say-so he put his own wife to death.[36]

SATIRE XV

Who has not heard, Volusius,[1] of the portentous gods
those crazy Egyptians worship? Some adore crocodiles,
another lot quakes at the ibis, gorged on serpents.
A sacred long-tailed monkey's gold effigy gleams
where magic chords resound from Memnon's truncated statue,   5
and old Thebes, with her hundred gates, now lies in ruins.
You'll find whole cities devoted to cats, or to river-fish,
dogs, even – but not a soul who worships Diana.[2]
Eating onions or leeks is an outrage, they're strictly taboo:
how holy the nation that has such gods springing up in the   10
kitchen-garden! All households abstain from lamb and mutton,
the slaughtering of young kids is strictly forbidden –
but to make meals of human flesh is permitted.[3] When Ulysses
narrated this crime over dinner, he shocked King Alcinous –
and some others present, perhaps, who, angry or laughing,   15
thought him a braggart liar.[4] 'Won't somebody throw this fellow
back in the sea? He deserves | a real-life Charybdis, a maelstrom,
with his lying tales of Cyclopes and Laestrygonian monsters!
I'd sooner believe in Scylla, or the Clashing Rocks,
or that leather bag stuffed with every kind of storm-wind,   20
or Circe, with one light touch of her wand, transforming
Elpenor and all the rest into grunting pig-oarsmen.[5]
Did he really take us Phaeacians for such credulous numskulls?'
So might a more or less sober | guest, who'd not over-indulged
in that powerful Corfu wine, have justly complained: 25
for the Ithacan's tale was his own, he had no witnesses.
But the incident *I* shall relate, though sufficiently fantastic,
happened not long ago,[6] up-country from sunbaked

Coptos, an act of mob violence worse than any tragedy.
30   Search through the mythical canon from Pyrrha[7] onwards,
you won't find any instance of a collective crime. Now listen,
and learn what kind of atrocity *our* times can add to the ages.

Between two neighbours there smoulders an ancient vendetta,
undying hatred, a wound | that can never be healed. What fills
35   both Ombi and Tentyra[8] with such violent rancour
is the loathing their peoples feel towards each other's gods:
only the gods *they* worship, each side believes,
deserve to be recognized.[9] So on one town's feast-day,
the chiefs and leading citizens of its rival determined
40   to seize this occasion for their own profit, to wreck
all the gay merry-making, break up the fun of the party,
the tables that would be spread by every temple and crossway
for the junketing that goes on day and night non-stop
and can last for a week. (The Egyptians are peasants, of course,
but for self-indulgence there's nothing – as far as I have
45   observed[10] –
to choose between city smarties and the barbarous fellaheen.)
Besides, it would be an easy victory over these sodden
revellers, slurred of speech and lurching from booze. On one side
men danced to some blackamoor's piping, cheaply pomaded,
50   sporting garlands galore, wreaths all askew; on the other,
pure ravenous hatred. Random insults began the affray,
a trumpet kindling men's too-combustible passions.
Then both sides roared into action, battle was joined
with naked hands as weapons. Few jaws got through unscathed,
55   and by the end of the punch-up scarcely anyone had a nose
that remained intact. Throughout the ranks you saw faces
half-bashed to a jelly, features reshaped, fists bloodied
from eyes, split cheeks laid open, exposing naked bone.

Yet with no corpses to trample, they treated the whole affair
60   as the merest horseplay, a sort of children's mock-battle:
for what's the point of so many thousands brawling
if no one gets killed? So the fight grew fiercer, by now
they were looking around on the ground for stones – the rioter's
regular weapon – flexing their arms, and letting fly, though
65   such missiles couldn't match those that Turnus and Ajax wielded,

or the great rock with which Diomedes shattered the hip of
Aeneas, but such as the arms of our puny generation,
so very different from theirs, have the strength to throw.[11]
Mankind was on the decline already in Homer's lifetime;
today the earth breeds a race of degenerate weaklings,   70
who stir any god that views them to laughter and loathing.

    Digression ended: now back to my tale. One side
brought up reinforcements, dared to continue the battle
with swords, to loose off whole volleys of lethal arrows.
The faction from nearby Tentyra's shady palm-groves   75
now fled in headlong confusion before the Ombite charge.
But one of them, panic-stricken, pressed on[12] too quickly,
tripped, fell, and was captured. The victorious rabble
tore him apart into bits and pieces, so many, that this one
corpse provided a morsel for all. They wolfed him   80
bones and all, not bothering even to spit-roast
or make a stew of his carcase. Building a proper fire-pit
was a bore, and took time – so they scoffed the poor devil raw.
One should, I suppose, be grateful, Prometheus,[13] that your sacred
gift of fire to mankind, the spark from heaven, was spared   85
such an outrage: the element gets | my congratulations! You too,
I trust, are well-pleased. But those who brought themselves
to devour this corpse never ate meat with greater relish;
for in judging a crime of such magnitude, you shouldn't assume
it was only the first man's gullet relished each mouthful: 90
when the whole of the body was finished, the last in line
scraped the ground with their fingers to get a lick of the blood.
Some Spaniards, history tells us,[14] once kept themselves alive
on just such a diet: but here the circumstances were different –
an unkind Fortune had brought them war's harshest extremity,   95
the grinding famine engendered by a drawn-out investiture.
[This present wretched case that I'm now discussing
should prove no less instructive than my previous instance.][15]
Only after they'd scoffed all the grass, every living creature,
and whatever else their ravening bellies dictated, when even   100
the besiegers pitied their pallor, bony limbs, and emaciation,
did they wolf, in their hunger, the flesh of their fellows – by then
they were ready to start on their own. What man, what deity

but would pardon these famished victims, after all the horrors
105 they'd suffered, for such an act? The very souls of the dead
bodies that gave them sustenance might condone it. Zeno[16] offers
us better advice [yet some set bounds to one's actions
for the saving of human life] – but where would Iberian Stoics
have sprung from, back at the time | of the Spanish Rebellion?[17]
         Now
things are different: the whole world has its Graeco-Roman
110   culture.
Smart Gaulish professors are training the lawyers of Britain;
even in Iceland there's talk of hiring rhetoricians.
Yet the tribesmen I spoke of were noble; and those other
         Spaniards
who suffered yet worse disaster (but matched them in honour
115 and courage), share their excuse.[18] But this Egyptian shambles
out-savages Artemis' altars in the Crimea: the foundress
of that accursed cult (if you credit poetic tradition)
sacrificed strangers, yes – but nothing further, or worse,
was left for the victim to fear than the knife.[19] But what affliction
120 drove *these* men? Where was the famine, the siege severe enough
to force them into embracing so foul an abomination?
What more could they dare to shame their lax gods, had drought
parched up the land of Memphis, had Nile refused to flood?
Not even the fearsome tribesmen of Britain or Germany,
125 or the fighting Poles, or the hulking Transylvanians
ever went so berserk as this useless, unwarlike rabble,
who rig up miniature sails on their earthenware wherries
and row with diminutive oars in painted crockery skiffs.[20]
         You could never devise a fitting punishment for this crime, or
130 a penalty stiff enough for a people in whose minds
hunger and rage are alike. When Nature equipped mankind
with tears, she proclaimed that tenderness was endemic
in the human heart, the best part of our feelings.
So we're moved to pity a defendant's shabby top-coat
135 as he pleads his case – or a ward who's brought his guardian
to court for embezzlement, and whose adolescent kiss-curls
make you doubt if those tear-stained cheeks are a boy's or a girl's.
It's at Nature's behest that we weep when the funeral cortège

of a ripening virgin goes by, or the earth is heaped over
an infant too young for burning.[21] What good man, worthy to
    bear   140
the mystic's torch, and such as Ceres' priest would wish him,[22]
thinks any human ills outside his concern? It's this
that sets us apart from dumb brutes, it's why we alone possess
a brain that's worthy of homage, have divine potential,
are skilled to master and practise all civilized arts,   145
have acquired a sense, sent down from the citadel of heaven,
that's kept from creeping beasts, their eyes on the ground.[23] To
    them,
when the world was still new, our common creator granted
the breath of life alone, but on us he further bestowed
sovereign reason, the impulse to aid one another,   150
to gather our scattered groups into peoples, to abandon
the woods and forests where once | our ancestors made their
    homes;
to build houses in groups, each with the next-door hearth-gods
snug by its own, and sleep safe in the trust and knowledge
that a friendly neighbour was there; to protect, by dint of arms,   155
any comrade fallen, or reeling from fearful wounds;
to obey one common trumpet, seek refuge behind the same
ramparts, and share one gateway, locked with a single key.[24]
But now snakes agree better than men. Wild maculate
beasts spare their own species: when did the stronger lion   160
ever strike down the weaker? And was there ever a forest
in which some boar was slain by a bigger boar's tushes?
The savage Indian tigress dwells in unbroken peace with
her fellow-tigresses: bears | agree with their own kind.[25]
But for man, to have mastered the art of forging deadly steel   165
on an impious anvil's too little. Our primitive smiths were used
to turning out nothing but rakes, hoes, ploughshares and
    pruning-hooks:
these required all their labour, to beat out swords was beyond
    them.
Yet now we behold a people who need, to appease their fury,
something more than a murder, who think a man's limbs, head,
    torso,   170

are a species of food. How, I ask, would Pythagoras
react to such horrors? Surely | he'd flee to the ends of the earth,
this man who abstained from all animal flesh just as though
it was human, who even regarded some kinds of bean as taboo?[26]

SATIRE XVI

Gallius, who can count up the rewards of a successful
army career?[1] If you do well during your service
[the sky's the limit, there's nothing you can't hope for].[2]   2A
Find me a lucky star, and the barracks would welcome me in,
a trembling recruit. One moment | of Fortune's favour does us
more good with Mars than a commendation from Venus,   5
or Juno her mother, who delights in the Samian shore.[3]
Let us consider first,[4] then, common benefits: of these
not least is the fact that no civilian would dare
to give you a thrashing – indeed, if punched up himself he'll hide
        it,
would never dare show any magistrate his knocked-out teeth,   10
the blackened lumps and bruises all over his face,
that surviving eye for which the doctor offers no hope.
And if he seeks legal redress, he'll face some hobnailed
centurion plus a benchful of brawny jurors:
as ancient military law lays down in its statutes –   15
still valid – no soldier may sue or be tried except
in camp, by court-martial.[5] 'The centurion's tribunal
sticks to the rules when a soldier's charged, so if my
complaint is legitimate, I'm sure to get satisfaction.'[6]
The whole regiment, though, is against you, every platoon   20
will unite, as one man, to ensure that your 'redress' needs a doctor
and is worse than the first assault. It's the kind of stupidity
you'd expect from some mulish idiot on a soapbox,
when you've got two good shins, to provoke all those jackboots,
        all
those thousands of hobnails. Besides, what witness would venture   25

so far from the City, beyond the walls and the Embankment?[7]
Have you a friend *that* devoted? Best dry one's eyes at once, and
stop importuning friends who will only make excuses.
When the judge says, 'Call your witness,' if *one* of the onlookers
30   during that brawl should dare | to say, in court, 'I saw it,'
I'll allow his right to stand with our bearded and shaggy
forebears. You'll more easily find a perjured witness
to lie against a civilian than one who'll tell the truth,
if that truth is against a soldier's interest or honour.

35   Now let us note various further emoluments and rewards
of a life with the colours. Suppose some chiselling neighbour
has encroached on a valley or meadow that's part and parcel of my
ancestral estates, and uprooted | the mid-point boundary-stone
to which I annually offer my cake and dish of pottage;[8]
40   or if a debtor refuses to pay back the sum I lent him
(claiming his signature's forged, the document worthless), my case
will have to wait, it'll be set down for the most
crowded and popular session. And even then I'll suffer
a thousand irksome postponements: quite often the courtroom
45   has just been got ready, one lawyer's taking his cloak off,
another's gone out for a piss, when – presto! – there's an
            adjournment
and we all disperse. These bouts in the legal arena
take endless time. But the armed and belted gentry
have their cases set down for whatever date may suit them;
50   *their* substance isn't diminished by the drag of a lengthy lawsuit.
Soldiers alone, moreover, are entitled to make a will
during their father's lifetime. The law decrees that all monies
earned by military service shall be exempt
from the bulk of property held in parental jurisdiction.[9]
55   That's why some regular sergeant on active service pay
will find himself courted and honoured by his doddering Papa;
he wins promotion on merit, distinguished service brings him
his just reward. And indeed, it's in any commander's interest
to see that the bravest soldiers obtain the best recompense,
that they all have decorations | and medals to show off, that
60   all . . .[10]

NOTES

SATIRE I

Useful General Studies

Anderson	Anderson, W. S., *Essays on Roman Satire* (Princeton: 1982), ch. x, 'Studies in Book I of Juvenal', 197–254 ('Satire 1') = *YClS* 15 (1957) 33–90.
Baldwin	Baldwin, B., 'Cover-names and dead victims in Juvenal', *Athenaeum* 45 (1967) 304–12.
Braund~Cloud	Braund, S. H., Cloud, J. D., 'Juvenal, a diptych', *LCM* 6 (1981) 195–203; 'Juvenal's libellus: a farrago?', *G. & R.* 29 (1982) 77–85.
Facchini Tosi	Facchini Tosi, C., 'Arte allusiva e semiologia dell'imitationstechnik: La presenza di Orazio nella prima satira di Giovenale', *Boll. di Stud. Lat.* 6 (1976) 3–29.
Griffith	Griffith, J. G., 'The ending of Juvenal's first satire and Lucilius, Book XXX', *Hermes* 98 (1970) 56–72.
Helmbold	Helmbold, W. C., 'The structure of Juvenal I', *UCPCP* 14/2 (1951) 47–60.
Kenney	Kenney, E. J., 'The First Satire of Juvenal', *PCPhS* 8 (1962) 29–40.
La Penna	La Penna, A., 'Il programmo poetico di Giovenale (con un referimento a Prop. 1.9)', *Paideia* 45 (1990) 239–75.
Martyn	Martyn, J. R. C., 'A new approach to Juvenal's First *Satire*', *Antichthon* 4 (1970) 53–61.

1. Cordus was an unknown writer of epics: the *Theseïd* (analogous to the *Aeneid*) was the work he gave at public recitations. It would have taken several days to read. Gowers (192) suggests that J. is here emulating Callimachus' attack on inflated, verbose poetry, epic in particular, or, in elegy, the 'fat *Lyde*' of Antimachus. *Telephus* and *Orestes* are tragedies – Euripides wrote two plays with these names – composed for platform performance rather than the stage. In this whole catalogue J. is emphasizing the derivative, artificial, cliché-ridden nature of contemporary literature – a point also made by the list of hackneyed mythological references, which he takes obvious pleasure in debunking: a swipe at the allusive poets in the Alexandrian tradition, who dragged them in on every page, and were especially fond of obscure periphrasis. Fronto may have been the T. Catius Caesius Fronto mentioned by Martial (1.55), and Consul in AD 96. Ferguson (112) points out that he is mentioned, together with one Q. Fulvius Gillo Bittius Proculus (see 40–41: coincidence?), in the Acts of the Arval Brethren; and, according to the Younger Pliny (*Ep.* 2.11), he was a prominent orator.

2. The mythical examples chosen – the 'grove of Mars' is where the Golden Fleece was guarded by a giant serpent; 'old what's-his-name' is Jason – suggest that J. had an *Argonautika* in mind. But which one? Braund (*JS* I 76–7) argues that his target was Valerius Flaccus. This is highly dubious: Braund herself admits that, even if Valerius did depict the battle of Centaurs and Lapiths as being painted on *Argo* (1.145–6, cf. line 11 here), he makes no mention of Aeacus as judge of the dead (9–10).

Pupils at school were often given the task of composing declamations, either to be put in the mouth of, or directed at, some great man of history. These exercises were known as *suasoriae*: examples by the Elder Seneca have survived. L. Cornelius Sulla Felix (b. 138 BC) was Dictator from 82 to 78.

3. Gaius Lucilius (*c.* 170–*c.* 102 BC), from Suessa Aurunca in Campania, near J.'s home-town – hence 'the great Auruncan' – was one of the earliest, and most notable, Roman satirists. Protected by Scipio, he indulged in extremely outspoken social criticism, though his strictures, like J.'s, lacked moral coherence. Only fragments of his work survive. He was, for obvious reasons, extremely popular in J.'s day (Quint. 10.1.93). Horace, too, proclaimed his debt to Lucilius (*Sat.* 2.1.34–5).

4. It is quite uncertain whether the topless pig-sticking hoyden (named as 'Mevia': probably well connected, if not aristocratic, and not a tart, as often assumed) is dealing with her boar al fresco, out in the countryside, or as a gladiator in the arena. Braund (*JS* I 81) prefers the second option. Mevia would go bare-breasted for either.

Crispinus, the profligate dandy and roué, began his career as a fishmonger and was made an *eques* by Domitian. J. appears to have had some special grudge against him: see Sat. IV, *passim*. He was from Memphis or Canopus in Egypt. See B. Baldwin, *Act. Class.* 22 (1979) 109–29 for speculation as to his identity, and P. White, *AJPh* 95 (1974) 377–82, who stresses the lack of evidence for his having held any kind of official position. The 'thin gold ring' (28) indicates equestrian status. For Matho cf. Sat. XI 34. He is so bulky that he fills the whole litter, normally designed for two passengers.

5. Sexual excess was commonly supposed in antiquity to produce an anaemic, washed-out appearance. For 'Caligula's competitions' see Suet. *Gaius* 20: 'Caligula gave . . . miscellaneous Games at Lyons, where he also held a competition in Greek and Latin oratory. The loser, it appears, had to present the winners with prizes and make speeches praising them; while those who failed miserably were forced to erase their entries with either sponges or their own tongues – at the threat of being thrashed and flung into the Rhône.' The name 'Gillo' (cf. n. 1 above) was also that of a tall vase, and here carries obvious phallic connotations: see N. Horsfall, *Mnemosyne* 28 (1975) 422. Apprehension caused by treading on a snake echoes Virgil, *Aen.* 2.379–80. The exiled governor who went on with his life of luxury (49–50) was Marius Priscus (Plin. *Ep.* 2.11), prosecuted for extortion – by Pliny and Tacitus – on his return from a tour of duty in N. Africa. Even after repaying 7 million sesterces to the treasury he seems still to have been well off.

6. The reference is to the Fall of Icarus: another sneer at ancient mythology, which in J.'s day had become no more than the lifeless stock-in-trade of every third-rate poet. There are also deliberate evocations of Horace both at the beginning and at the end of this Satire. The early allusions, to *Sat.* 1.10.40 ff. and *Epist.* 2.2.90–105, are designed to emphasize the *contrasts* between the two poets: see A. J. Woodman, *G.& R.* 30 (1983) 81–4. For the significance of J.'s closing echoes of Horace, see below, n. 16. Diomedes was a popular figure for Roman epic poets, since after the Trojan War he was said, like Aeneas, to have emigrated to Italy. The mocking allusion to the Minotaur hints at yet another *Theseïd*.

7. Locusta was a famous poisoner in Nero's reign. She dispatched the Emperor Claudius at Agrippina's orders, and also poisoned Britannicus for Nero himself. She was executed by Galba. See Suet. *Nero* 33, Tac. *Ann.* 13.15, cf. 12.66, and Dio Cass. 64.3. At line 70 I read, with Griffith, *rubeta* (Par. 8072, Montpell. 125, Vind. 111/107) rather than *rubetam* (rell.), and translate accordingly.

8. It was the late Professor J. P. Sullivan who, long ago, reminded me of Harrison's argument that the removal of lines 85–6 from their present position in the MSS leaves a far more logical sentence structure behind. He was not, however, responsible for my decision to insert them after line 80, of which Martyn (54–5, n. 10) remarked: 'They would be better left as "homeless wanderers"!' Braund (*JS I* 94) argues that the transposition detracts from the momentary adoption of the grand style in order the better to deflate; in fact it has nothing to do with it. I remain unrepentant: such 'slipped-position' lines are by no means rare in Juvenal. I also accept Harrison's suggestion of *ecquando* for *et quando* in the same passage.

9. For the Flood story featuring Deucalion and Pyrrha (the stones he threw over his shoulder became men, Pyrrha's turned into women) see Ovid, *Met.* 1.253–416. Their 'ark' landed on Parnassos. At 84 Braund (*JS I* 95) argues that 'Pyrrha is portrayed as the madam of a brothel, diplaying her girls to the customers'. Loath though I am to pass up any hint of *sens. obsc.* in a Roman satirist (or elsewhere), I'm not persuaded by this one: the most J. is saying is that the minute man and woman set eyes on each other, trouble started.

When it comes to 'the mixed mash of my book' (*farrago libelli*), Gowers (192 ff.), with her strong interest in food and culinary metaphors, is as good a guide as any. Here, as elsewhere, J. is dealing in extreme contrasts: on the one hand, bloated luxury and glut; on the other, stale scraps, hunger and humiliation. The battle extends to literature. Those turgid epics, descendants of Antimachus' 'fat Lyde', offer a natural target. J. has to oppose them with something better than scraps: this is one area in which (*pace* Braund) he can't afford to subvert himself. He is, as Gowers says, a hungry poet. Rome has become, at every level, a world of eat or be eaten, and what J. describes is 'this iniquitous battle for a share of the Roman pie'. Cf. J. Powell, in *Homo Viator: Classical Essays for John Bramble* (Bristol: 1987) 253–8; and, on *indignatio*, Fruelund Jensen 155ff., Fabrini~Lami (1981) 163 ff.

Originally clients were entertained by their patrons; later there was substituted the *sportula*, or little basket of food, to carry away. Later still this was commuted to a financial dole. Braund (*JS I* 98) points out that normally the *sportula* was handed out at the end of the day, in return for services rendered.

10. The minimum property qualification for admission to the Equestrian Order was 400,000 sesterces. Originally a body of cavalry, the *equites* in Imperial times were largely identical with the rich non-senatorial business community: 'burghers' or 'magnates' would be a fair equivalent. They held important posts in the civil service: the Prefecture of Egypt, for instance, was reserved for an *eques*.

11. Foreign slaves just imported had their feet chalked white by the dealer to distinguish them from *vernae*, or home-bred slaves. According to Braund (*JS I* 100), Corvinus the impoverished nobleman, deprived of his own estates, would (107–8) lease and manage a flock of sheep. Cf. Sat. XII, n. 1.

12. The consuls held office for a year, and under the Empire, as *consul suffectus*, for a few months only. The position carried no salary (though there was an inadequate expense account) and most consuls reckoned on recouping from their subsequent appointment to a provincial governorship.

13. The Forum of Augustus contained an ivory statue of Apollo (Plin. *NH* 7.183), who, J. implies, had heard so much litigation that he'd acquired legal expertise himself. The 'Egyptian Pasha' was Tiberius Julius Alexander, a Jew who became a Roman *eques*; he rose to the rank of Prefect of Egypt, and may have become Praetorian Prefect as well (see E. G. Turner, *JHS* 44, 1954, 54 ff.). J. manages to symbolize in him both the contempt he felt for the Jews and his perennial dislike of Egyptians – a not unnatural feeling, since Egypt, if anywhere, was his place of exile.

14. Housman suggested, almost certainly correctly, that a line had dropped out of the text here, after 131, in which the clients would be taken back to their patron's house. I have translated in accordance with this suggestion. It is interesting to note, in the lines that follow, the ancient Greek and Roman disapproval (still evident today) of solitary meals (Courtney 112 with reff., cf. Braund, *JS I* 104).

15. For the unpleasant consequences of wolfing a large and indigestible meal (peacocks were regarded as especially risky fare in this respect: Courtney 113 with reff.), metabolizing plentiful alcohol, and then taking a hot bath, see J. D. Morgan, *CQ* 38 (1988) 264–5, who points out that this regimen would be most likely to

precipitate a heart-attack in an overweight man whose arteries were clogged with cholesterol. The passage echoes Persius, 3.98–106, and Virg. *Aen.* 2.697–8. Cf. W. V. Clausen, 'Juvenal and Virgil', *HSCPh* 80 (1976) 181–6.

As Courtney rightly insists (114), *intestata* ('intestate') at line 144 is illogical as an epithet for *senectus* ('old age'). There would be some point in the glutton either (a) dying young, or (b) dying before he could make his will. But what have his dietary habits to do with reaching old age intestate? The text is surely corrupt. Courtney suggests, diffidently, that what J. wrote may have been *intemptata*. My own preference would be for *interrupta*, and I have revised my translation accordingly.

The text of 155–7 also presents difficulties. I follow Housman (who supposes a line to have been lost after 156) and translate his conjectural restoration. For discussion of the crux see Ferguson 123, Courtney 116–27, and B. Baldwin, *CQ* 24 (1979) 162–4.

16. Again J. lists obvious epic themes: Aeneas' battle against Turnus, the death of Achilles, and (from the myth of the Argonauts) the episode of Hylas' abduction by an amorous water-nymph (Ap. Rhod. *Arg.* 1.1187–357, also treated by Theocritus, *Id.* 13, but only touched on by Valerius Flaccus, 3.596–7, 4.128–9), while out fetching water from the spring.

17. The Via Flaminia was, as it were, the Great North Road from Rome; the Via Latina branched off from its southern counterpart, the Via Appia. Burial within the city limits (*pomerium*) was forbidden by the Twelve Tables of the Law; thus the aristocracy often had tombs beside the major arterial roads, and the closing lines hint clearly at the main target of J.'s satire. The tomb of Paris the actor lay beside the Via Flaminia; Domitian himself was buried by the Via Latina. Yet – and coming after the reference to Lucilius this cannot but strike us as bathetic – J. is only going to attack those who are already dead. Highet (56–8) points out (a) that most of his subjects are timeless; (b) that he may have been lying in order to protect himself; and (c) that he felt the past was truly important; that he 'saw the empire as one long continuous process of degeneration'.

Baldwin (304–12) suggests that J. may in fact have been attacking contemporaries under cover-names, though his theory of an unknown 'Tigillinus' lacks plausibility. Griffith (56–72) sees a close rhetorical connection between the ending of this Satire and Book XXX of Lucilius. Facchini Tosi (3–29) stresses the way J. injects his own personality and times into his Horatian allusions. Martyn (53–61) argues that the main programme-theme, developed more specifically in the later Satires, is that of perversion (sexual anomalies, the *clientela* paradox).

Braund (*JS* I 110–21) compares the codas of Hor. *Sat.* 2.1 and Persius, *Sat.* 1, arguing that all three present a comparable 'pattern of apology': defiant challenge interrupted by a reminder of the risks, an appeal to Lucilius as precedent, renewed warnings, final evasion of the issue. The persona thus presented emphasizes the gap between aspiration and reality, and is drawn as 'a spineless and petty bigot'. Braund feels that this interpretation rescues J.'s narrator 'from the biographical fallacy prevalent in earlier readerships and scholarship'. Well, perhaps; but at the cost of eviscerating the satire. It's not that poets don't create such despicable narrators: think of Browning's Mr Sludge the Medium. But what would J. create his 'spineless bigot' *for*? To mock satirists along with the gluttons and mean patrons they attack? But this would undermine any thought of satirical seriousness; and J. can hardly (if Braund is right) have made his purpose clear, since no one before her ever tumbled to the idea, which certainly wasn't what saw to all that multiplication of J.'s MSS in the Middle Ages. As a programme-piece, Satire I remains as elusive as ever.

SATIRE II

Useful General Studies

Anderson	Anderson, W. S., *Essays on Roman Satire* (Princeton: 1982), ch. x, 'Studies in Book I of Juvenal' 209–10 ('Satire 2') = *YClS* 15 (1957) 33–90.
Braund~Cloud	Braund, S. H., Cloud, J. D., 'Juvenal: a diptych', *LCM* 6 (1981) 203–8 (section on Sat. II).
Konstan	Konstan, D., 'Sexuality and power in Juvenal's second satire', *LCM* 18 (1993) 12–14.
Stewart	Stewart, R., 'Domitian and Roman religion: Juvenal satires 2 and 4', *TAPhA* (1994) 309–32 (310–21 specifically on Sat. II).
Wiesen	Wiesen, D. S., 'The verbal basis of Juvenal's satiric vision, II: Satire Two', *ANRW* II, 33.1 (Berlin/New York: 1989) 714–23.
Willis	Willis, J. A., 'Ad Iuuenalis saturam alteram', *Mnemosyne* 45 (1992) 376–80.
Winkler	Winkler, M. M., *The persona in three satires of Juvenal* (Hildesheim: 1983) ch. iv, 90 ff. (and elsewhere).

1. J. is working a variant on the classic gibe of antiquity (derived largely from Plato's *Symposium* and Aristophanes' *Clouds*) which assumes that all 'philosophers' are closet homosexuals. Juvenal inverts the cliché: in his day many homosexuals pretended to be philosophers. Cf. Mart. 1.24 for a similar gibe at the pretence of ultra-masculinity. 'Intellectual perfection' is a glancing blow at the Stoics, who argued (Ferguson 127) that you were either completely wise or completely ignorant. Philosophers were also 'serious-looking' or 'solemn-faced' (9: *tristibus*); the paradox, and hypocrisy, consisted in 'humbuggers' (9: *obscenis*) assuming the same mien.

The 'fierce spirit' (12: *atrocem animum*) is a phrase lifted from Horace, *Odes* 2.1.24, who applied it, in all seriousness, to Cato. Konstan (12–14) gets to the heart of this Satire with the insight that what it pillories is not homosexuality as such, but *the passive role* (i.e., in Roman thought, effeminacy) not only in sexual matters, but also as evidenced by slavishness, lower-class habits, or the behaviour of conquered foreign barbarians: '. . . by the implicit logic of the satire (and to a great extent of Roman ideology as a whole) effeminacy has as its correlate inferiority on all the other axes of power or authority . . .' For Braund (*JS I* 121) 'the speaker is immediately established as the raging, indignant, narrow-minded, chauvinistic bigot of Satire I': this, when you come to think of it, is a nice way of reverting to the old-fashioned view of J. while neatly severing one's moral judgements from any overt application to the satirist himself. J., we are to assure ourselves, did not possess these characteristics (or if he did, the fact is irrelevant): he simply projected a narrator who was a parodic compound of them all, and gave him his head. This persona could then be deconstructed along with everything else. Something tells me that in a decade or so such a view is going to look not only dated but thoroughly illogical.

2. The unnamed adulterer was the Emperor Domitian, who *c.* AD 89 seduced his niece Julia, got her with child, and then forced her to have an abortion as a result of which she died (Suet., *Dom.* 22, Dio Cass. 67.3, Plin. *Ep.* 4.11.6). Cf. Stewart 210 ff. As Homer tells us, Aphrodite (Venus) cuckolded Hephaestus (Vulcan) with Ares (Mars): see *Odyssey* 8.266–366. Ares, in Greek mythology, had Eos, Dawn, as mistress – Venus, in revenge, made her permanently in love with someone else – besides fathering children on Aglauros and other favoured heroines and maidens. Aphrodite also had an affair with Anchises (which resulted in Aeneas) and an Argonaut, Butes.

3. For Laronia see Mart. 2.32.5–6, where she is portrayed as a wealthy and influential widow. She is to be thought of as a smart upper-crust adulteress rather than a professional prostitute. One Q. Laronius was suffect consul in 33 BC.

4. In line 45 I accept Buccheler's emendation *faciunt peiora*. The 'marriage laws' referred to in line 37 must be the *Lex Iulia de adulteriis et stupro vel pudicitia* passed by Augustus in 18 BC and revived by Domitian (as Censor!) in AD 90, a year or so after Julia's death. The use of military metaphors rubs in the contrast between 'masculine virtue' and 'effeminacy'. As Anderson says (211), the pseudo-moralist's 'martial appearance serves only to disguise his effeminate characteristics. Put to the test in battle with a woman, he is utterly routed.' The Sodomy Act, the *Lex Scantinia de nefanda venere*, of uncertain date, was sternly enforced by Domitian. See Suet., *Dom.* 8. Line 37 more than hints that the laws themselves are adulterous (so Braund, *JS I* 129). Both Martial (6.7) and, later, Pliny (*Ep.* 6.31.4–6) refer to the 'Julian Law' strict enforcement as something of a novelty.

5. For this 'double anaemia' see n. 5 to Satire I. The scholiast attributes Hispo's pallor to his habit *inguina lambentis et stuprum patientis* (Wessner 21): the passivity in this case is oral as well as anal. The argument that Roman women eschewed lesbian practices was a cheerful (and barefaced) lie designed to bolster Laronia's argument: cf. (e.g.) Mart. 7.57, and J. himself at 6.307–13. The name Hispo ('Shag') may have been chosen for purely associative reasons; but a T. Caepio Hispo was proconsul of Asia in 117/8, and J. has it in for one Hispulla (the name's feminine form) who is both fat (Sat. XII 11) and promiscuous (Sat. VI 74).

6. The term for the athlete's meat-ration, *colyphium*, may also be slang for the penis (doubted by Adams, 49–50, cf. Braund, *JS I* 135, but unconvincingly): there were phallic-shaped bread rolls similarly called *colyphia* (cf. Mart. 7.67.12). This whole passage is packed with sexual *double entendre*: it is a fair presumption that any reference to meat-eating in J. will also hint at *fellatio*. Arachne, the 'spider-girl', was a mythical Lydian who challenged Athena to a spinning competition, and was turned into a spider for her presumption. The 'drab astride her block' is Antiope, in a play by Pacuvius: she was brought on-stage in chains, bedraggled and unkempt, and shown performing menial domestic tasks at the bidding of her cruel captress Dirce, wife of Lycus of Thebes. Braund (*JS I* 136) cites Plautus and Propertius (4.7.44) to show that this block (*codex*) was part of her punishment. See further Propertius 3.15.11 ff. and T. Gantz, *Early Greek Myth: A Guide to Literary and Artistic Sources* (Baltimore: 1993) 485. The usurpation of women's tasks (spinning, weaving) by men was associated with passive homosexuality, and therefore despised.

7. This aphorism about ravens and doves contains an appropriately obscene allusion, since ravens were popularly supposed to both copulate and bring forth their young by the mouth. In his *Natural History* Pliny takes this notion one step further, and suggests (10.32) that a woman who eats a raven's egg will likewise enjoy an oral birth. But the formulation also involves a whole set of contrasts: black/white, male/female, predator/victim, pure/impure (Braund, *JS I* 138).

8. J.'s description of the spread of homosexuality parodies Virgil's references (*Georg.* 3.441, 449; *Ecl.* 1.50) to the spread of disease among sheep. At line 81, though with some misgivings, I accept the reading of the main MSS, *conspecta*. Martyn opts for *contacta*, which he supports by the argument that J. was deliberately echoing, with satirical intent, the plague-imagery in Virgil's *Georgics* (3.440–566). He could just be right, though the proverbial *uva uvam videndo varia fit* militates against him, and in favour of the traditional reading. Braund~Cloud (78–81) argue that we have the core of the poem here: the narrator's desire to flee from Rome is countered by Rome's conquest of the world: there are no refuges left – only an ever-spreading contagion.

9. As opposed to the Roman rites of the Bona Dea – a fertility goddess – where it was men who were debarred from participation. What we have here is a close, but parodic, homosexual imitation. Alcibiades' parody of the Eleusinian Mysteries comes to mind. In 62 BC Clodius similarly caused a great scandal by attending this goddess's rites disguised as a woman. See Sat.VI 335–41.

10. Women swore by Juno. Though the scene is parodic, and J. throughout is harping solely on sexual implications, this passage gives a fairly precise description of the ritual involved in the worship of the Asiatic Great Mother-Goddess, Ma or Cybele. In Imperial times her cult was assimilated to that of the Roman war-goddess Bellona. The Thracian goddess Cotys or Cotytto was worshipped in Athens as early as the 5th c. BC: her cult was orgiastic and included effeminate elements. There is a striking parallel in Josephus' *Jewish Wars* (4.9.10), where similar practices – transvestism, elaborate make-up, perverse eroticism – are described as characterisitic of certain Galilaeans in Jerusalem. See Colin (1955/6), and for phallic-shaped drinking-vessels, cakes, lamps, etc., and their popularity in Rome, G. R. Scott, *Phallic Worship* (London: 1941) 154 ff., with pls. xii, xxi and xxiv. Courtney (138) nicely observes: 'The special point of these vessels is that by drinking through the phallus the appearance of *fellatio* would be presented; but it must be remembered that many extant specimens are of apotropaic feeding-bottles for children.' Cf. Plin. *NH* 33.4.

11. Marcus Salvius Otho (AD 32–69) was married to Nero's mistress Poppaea; he also appears to have been an active homosexual who had unnatural relations with Nero himself (Mart. 6.32.2; Suet.*Otho* 2). Lines 99–100 parody Virgil's *Aeneid* (3.286 and 12.93–4): Otho bears the mirror as the heroic Abas bore his shield. After a very short period as emperor, he was defeated in April AD 69 by the legions of Vitellius, and committed suicide. It is very probable that the phrase *novis annalibus atque recenti / historia* ('new annals and recent histories', as I now translate) carries a not-too-covert allusion to the *Annals* and *Histories* of J.'s friend Tacitus – that it formed, in fact, a literary puff, private joke or advertisement (and a query as to why such juicy material hadn't been utilized). The 'imperial rival' whom Otho killed (in Jan. AD 69) was Galba.

12. Samiramis (more often Semiramis) was a semi-legendary queen of Assyria, believed to have built Babylon. Cleopatra was defeated, with Antony, at the naval battle of Actium in 31 BC, and committed suicide soon afterwards.

13. The Salii, or priests of Mars, had to be of patrician birth, with both parents living: this Gracchus (not, of course, one of the famous reformers) was a member of the *gens Sempronia*, perhaps from Domitian's reign (Ferguson 1987, 105–6). He is attacked again at 8.207–8 (a similar all-male 'marriage' was performed between Nero and Sporus). On certain days in March and October the Salii went through the City, performing ritual dances and singing traditional hymns. The 'figure-of-eight' shields they carried were supposedly modelled on the *ancile* (in all likelihood a meteorite) which Jupiter threw down from heaven as a gift to King Numa. The reference to 'straight trumpet' probably embodies a sexual *double entendre* (Braund, *JS I* 154). Also, public displays of affection (119) were regarded as highly improper.

14. i.e. the Campus Martius, or Field of Mars, once used for army parades and exercises, but also (which lends irony to J.'s peroration) for the celebration of foreign cult rituals. By J.'s own time it was almost entirely covered with public buildings. In point of religious protocol there was no reason why the Salii should not worship Bellona; the two cults had many links (see Colin, op. cit. in n. 10 above). But J. identifies foreign cults with sexual licence amongst the aristocracy – just as Livy, somewhat earlier, had associated the introduction of the Bacchanalia into Rome, not only with promiscuity, but also with perjury, forgery and murder! See Bk 39.8–18.

15. The festival of the Lupercalia, or 'Wolf-feast', was held annually on 15 February, and clearly dated back to the fertility magic of a small primitive agricultural community. Youths ran round the city limits, striking any woman they met with strips of sacrificial goatskin to promote conception. Both J. (134) and Martial (12.42) exploit the verb *nubo*, normally used of women marrying men, by applying it to passive homosexuals doing the same thing. Martial adds to the paradox by making his philosopher-bride bearded (*barbatus*: 'Our bearded philosopher's bride to an African stiffcock'). Few readers seem to have noticed the literary joke presented by 'fat Greek Lyde' (cf. notes 1 and 8 to Sat. I). Antimachus of Colophon (*fl. c.* 400 BC) composed an elegy to his late mistress of that name, which Callimachus, because of its prolixity, ridiculed as 'fat *Lyde*'. I prefer this explanation to Braund's (*JS I* 158), that Lyde was pregnant, and using the fact as an advertisement for the efficacy of her nostrums.

16. To a modern reader this final indictment may come as a crashing anticlimax, and it is possible that J. (like De Quincey in his famous essay 'On Murder as One of the Fine Arts') was deliberately aiming at unexpected bathos. But for an aristocrat to appear in the arena clearly *was* a peculiar disgrace. See Sat. VIII 199–210, and, for a detailed discussion, Braund, *JS I* 159–60. Both Juvenal and Seneca make a close connection between homosexuality and the arena. The net-fighter was despised by his more orthodox fellow-gladiators. Cf. Sat. VI O[xford passage] 7–12.

17. Below a certain age children were admitted free to the public baths: the normal fee was a *quadrans*, the rough equivalent of a farthing. For some reason women were charged more than men. See Carcopino, 253 ff. and 316–17. It is characteristic of J. that this picture of heroic ghosts in the underworld, with its Virgilian (and Aristophanic) echoes, should be prefaced by a disclaimer: only little children still believe in Hades. Similarly its opening phrase, 'That ghosts exist' (*esse aliquid manes*) recalls a haunting line of Propertius (4.7.1: *sunt aliquid manes*). See Winkler, 26–7.

18. The Orkneys were captured by Agricola (Tac. *Agric.* 10.4). Despite a recent flurry of speculation, it seems clear that though Agricola planned an expedition against Ireland, it never in fact took place (*Agric.* 24). For the short nights of the northern British Isles (in fact not all that short) see Caes. *Bell. Gall.* 5.13.2–4, Tac. *Agric.* 12.3, Plin. *NH* 2.186–7. The moral cult of the Noble Savage was by no means new in antiquity when J. wrote, as the 3rd-c. BC Pergamene sculptures of Gauls erected by Attalos I – the dying trumpeter, the suicidal Ludovisi group – amply testify.

19. Ardaschan, the ancient Artaxata, was the capital of Armenia: it stood on a tongue of land on the R. Araxes. Hannibal, as an exile at the court of King Artaxias, helped to supervise its construction (see Sat. X 160 ff.); in AD 58 it was destroyed by Corbulo, and rebuilt by Tiridates, who renamed it Neronia in honour of the Emperor who had ceded it to him. Juvenal may have in mind the 'exchange-visits' which took place on this occasion.

At 168 *indulsit*, the reading of all MSS, is not only a solecism (as Housman pointed out: the future perfect *indulserit* is required) but not particularly appropriate as a verb: Clausen was wise to withdraw his suggestion of *indulget*, and repunctuation (Courtney 149) is no improvement. Nisbet suggested *induerit*, which is strained: surely the most probable solution is *intulerit*? A long stay certainly introduced Rome to the boys as a new feature (*OLD* s.v. *infero* §6) and ended by inducing an unpleasant condition (ibid. §9).

SATIRE III

Useful General Studies

Anderson	Anderson, W. S., *Essays in Roman Satire* (Princeton: 1982), ch. x, 'Studies in Book I of Juvenal', 219–32 ('Satire 3') = *YClS* 15 (1957) 55–68.
Fredericks	Fredericks, S. C., 'The function of the prologue (1–20) in the organization of Juvenal's third satire', *Phoenix* 27 (1973) 62–7.
Fruelund Jensen	Fruelund Jensen, B., 'Martyred and beleaguered virtue: Juvenal's portrait of Umbricius', *Class. & Med.* 37 (1986) 185–97.
Lafleur	Lafleur, R. A., 'Umbricius and Juvenal three', *Ziva Antika* 26 (1976) 383–431.
Lelièvre	Lelièvre, F. J., 'Virgil and Juvenal's third satire', *Euphrosyne* 5 (1972) 457–62.
Motto~Clark	Motto, A. L., Clark, J. R. '*Per iter tenebricosum*: The Mythos of Juvenal 3', *TAPhA* 96 (1965) 267–76.
Parmer	Parmer, J. H., A new interpretation of Juvenal III, diss. Ohio State University (Columbus: 1988).
Reinmuth	Reinmuth, O. W., 'The meaning of *ceroma* in Juvenal and Martial', *Phoenix* 21 (1967) 101–5.
Rudd~Courtney	Rudd, N., Courtney, E. *Juvenal: Satires I, III, X* (Bristol: 1977).
Witke	Witke, E. C., 'Juvenal 3, an Eclogue for the Urban Poor', *Hermes* 90 (1962) 244–8.

1. The main point is made at once: 'the only way to be a Roman is to leave Rome' (Ferguson 136, cf. Motto~Clark 269). Cumae was the oldest (8th c. BC) Greek colony in Italy; it lay on the coast of Campania, six miles north of Cape Misenum. The rise of nearby Puteoli had turned it into a backwater. Baiae, a fashionable – and notorious – watering-spot, lay on the east coast of the Misenum peninsula, in J.'s day dotted with the villas of wealthy Romans. It was the Sibyl of Cumae who (as Petronius and T. S. Eliot remind us) hung in a bottle and, when asked her wishes, replied that she wanted to die. Virgil (*Aen.* 6.77–102) has a famous description of a consultation with this Sibyl, whose grotto (which still exists) is indeed, in

Ferguson's words, 'numinous and awesome'. The inhabitants of Cumae were known as her 'citizens' – perhaps because she gave her oracles from a high, throne-like seat.

2. The Porta Capena (now the Porta S. Sebastiana) stood close to the public fishmarket on the Appian Way: an aqueduct passed over it, hence the 'dripping arches'. Numa, the semi-mythical early King of Rome, was supposed to have got his laws through the divine inspiration of the nymph Egeria. J., following Livy, suggests that this was simply a cover for illicit intercourse. The Jews were evicted from Rome by Claudius, but after the sack of Jerusalem by Titus in AD 70, many made their way back, and eked out a scanty living as fortune-tellers or beggars. The 'Sabbath haybox' was for keeping food hot on a day when cooking was forbidden. Umbricius' waggon had to be loaded (by hand) at the city-boundary, since most wheeled traffic was banned inside the *pomerium* during daylight hours (see below, n. 24).

This 'prologue' (1–20) sums up all the main themes to come: the devaluation of honesty, the invasion of Rome by foreigners (with its consequent social upheaval, including the impoverishment of the 'worthy'), and the dangers, in an over-populated city, of heavy traffic, fires, and crime. See Fredericks, 62 ff.

3. The name Umbricius is Etruscan, and not known elsewhere from our literary sources; but a tombstone has been found, in nearby Puteoli, commemorating the daughter of one A. Umbricius Magnus, who *may* have been J.'s friend. A great deal has been written about this (in every sense) shadowy character (Umbricius, *umbra*): real person (and if so, who?) or fictional *alter ego*? The most cogent argument in favour of the latter is used both by Ferguson (136) and by Courtney (151): J. himself could hardly advance compelling arguments for retreating to the country – and then stay in town himself. (Johnson said that the man who was tired of London was tired of life; I suspect that a country existence would have bored J. stiff.) But most recent scholarship has leaned towards an Umbricius who was probably real (though not the *haruspex* mentioned by Pliny, *NH* 10.19, and Tacitus, *Hist.* 1.27), and in any case distinct from J. himself. J. Sarkissian, *Class. & Med.* 42 (1991) 247–58, finds U.'s arguments emotional rather than intellectual. F. Williams, in *Liverpool Latin Seminar 4* (Liverpool: 1983) 121–7, points out that J. in fact satirizes U.'s own foibles as well as the perils of the City. Lafleur (383 ff.) emphasizes U.'s separateness from the satirist's persona. All these factors are subsumed in Fruelund's detailed analysis (185 ff.). I see no reason why a real-life friend should not also have been made the mouthpiece for many of J.'s complaints about Rome.

4. Courtney offers a telling analysis (151–5) of U.'s character. The snobbish *rentier* he presents to us – anti-freedmen, anti-immigration, generally xenophobic – whose 'only idea is to hang on to the coat-tails of some wealthy man' (152) rather than find a job of work, arouses distaste today, but in Imperial Rome was the norm (cf. Cic. *De Offic.* 1.150). (It is worth pondering the fact that not so very long ago a similar principle was popular among the upper classes in England: I vividly recall a short story of Somerset Maugham's which depended entirely for its point on an expatriate's failure to commit suicide when his annuity ran out. The idea of his *working* was never entertained for a single moment.) The Romans made a firm distinction between the 'liberal arts and professions' which a free citizen might practise, and those 'sordid' or 'illiberal' occupations reserved for slaves, foreigners and the lower orders generally. J. might complain that the client-patron system had degenerated, but the last thing he wanted to do was abolish it.

5. Daedalus, as we learn from Virgil, ended his flight at Cumae. (His overreaching son Icarus was not so lucky.) The periphrastic description is typical not only of J. – who has, as Duff observes, 'a great liking for describing places and persons by a periphrasis giving some historical or mythological details about them' – but of Augustan and post-Augustan poets in general: it is an inheritance from the Alexandrian tradition. Braund (*JS I* 178) suggests that, just as Daedalus was fleeing the Minotaur, 'so the periphrasis suggests that Rome is like a labyrinth full of unnatural monsters from which Umbricius is fleeing'.

6. *Promittere* can mean either 'guarantee' or 'predict', and the ambiguity is here very much to the point, since in the climate of belief then prevalent, to *predict* the death of a relative would go a long way, if known, towards *guaranteeing* it. Such fortune-telling was illegal, and small wonder. Similarly with frogs' guts: the reference could be either to divination, or to maleficent magic and poisoning. The frog was commonly employed in magical formulae, perhaps on account of its uncanny squamousness; the parts most commonly utilized were the tongue and the gut.

7. The Governor of Sicily (73–71 BC) against whom Cicero delivered his famous prosecution speeches on charges of embezzlement and extortion. The name passed into the language: Verres became the type and emblem of the rapacious provincial administrator. He fled into exile at Massilia (Marseilles), where he was later proscribed by Antony, who coveted his art treasures.

8. J.'s violent dislike for the Greeks had good literary antecedents. Cato and the Elder Pliny, among others, detested them: in particular they were prejudiced against Greek doctors, whom they regarded as quacks and profiteers. Lucilius, Horace and Persius all shared to some degree in this stereotyped Hellenophobia. Nevertheless, in actual fact Greeks generally were very well integrated into Roman society: this, of course, is what J. finds particularly annoying. Cf. Sat. VI 187–93, 295 ff. The Greek freedmen who had risen to positions of immense administrative and political power under Claudius (e.g. Narcissus and Pallas) only reinforced the stereotype.

9. The Orontes, now the Nahr el-Asi, was the largest river in ancient Syria; it rose in the hills near Damascus and flowed northwards by Epiphania and Apamea, turning sharply south-west by Antioch to the sea. Syrian slaves were at a premium; Syrian girl-harpists and timbrel-players were known in Rome as early as 189 BC. Inevitably, they also became prostitutes. For the racecourse or Circus Maximus as a whores' beat see Sat. VI 582–91. Callimachus had earlier used the Euphrates (*Hymn* 2.108–9) to symbolize the vast waste effluence of inferior epic poetry.

10. At 67–8 J. satirizes the affectation of Greek nomenclature in some Roman circles (cf. the modern passion for French dinner-menus). Reinmuth refers *ceroma* to the mud that became popular under the Empire for wrestling in. The locations chosen by J. as sources of the Greek influx range from northern Greece (Macedonia) and the Peloponnese (Sicyon) by way of the Aegean islands (Andros, Samos) to western Asia Minor (Tralles, Alabanda). Daedalus was traditionally supposed to have been a well-born Athenian, in fact the great-grandson of Erechtheus (Diod. Sic. 4.76): J.'s main objection to him (apart from his nationality) seems to have been that he was, in every sense of the phrase, flying in the face of nature.

11. Purple robes were only worn by certain senators on specific official occasions, under both Caesar and Augustus. Nero forbade the sale of Tyrian purple altogether. Romans asked their friends to witness such documents as wills, marriage-contracts and slave-manumissions. The order of witnessing was dictated by social status.

12. The 'giant Antaeus' lived (so myth related) in N. Africa, and, as a champion wrestler, challenged all comers to a bout, killing his opponents when he'd defeated them. His secret lay in the fact that his mother (by Neptune) was Earth herself, so that contact with her strengthened rather than weakened him (as those wrestlers who succeeded in throwing him found to their cost). Hercules finally defeated him by heaving him up and crushing or throttling him in mid-air. At 90–91 there is an untranslatable pun: the singer's shrill voice resembles that of a cock (*gallus*), but *gallus* is also the word for a eunuch priest. 'Cockless cock', perhaps? The three types of feminine role in Greek-style comedies (*palliatae*) at Rome were (a) courtesans, e.g. Thais in Terence's *Eunuch*; (b) *matrones*, i.e. ladies of a household; (c) maids or slave-girls, *ancillae*. These parts were played by men: Columella also comments on the homosexual's ability to imitate women.

13. The two most common explanations of line 108 have to assume (a) that a drinking-cup gurgles as the last drop leaves it; or (b) that most chamber-pots have false bottoms. It is, surely, easier to take lines 107–8 in conjunction: the basin or ladle (*trulla*) was placed upside-down on the floor, and the dinner-guests urinated at it in competition. The Greek applauds when his Roman patron hits the target squarely, 'with a splendid drumming sound'. Courtney (171) argues that 107 and 108 should be kept separate; but it is hard to see how, in that case, we are to extract from 108 'a commonplace [*sic*] activity which the patron does particularly well'.

14. I follow Jacoby in reading *nihil huic* here, but substitute *uel* for his *et*: most MSS read *nihil aut*. I assume *huic* to have dropped out by false reading and haplography after *nihil*, and *aut* then to have been substituted for *uel* by a stupid scribe trying to mend matters.

15. Most editors take the words within brackets as an interpolation. I believe they are genuine: the unexplained change from singular to plural suggests rather that a line has been lost after 112, the sense of which would be: 'But such creatures do not even desire sexual pleasure for its own sake', etc.

16. The Stoic informer was Publius Egnatius Celer; Tacitus gives a graphic account *(Ann.* 16.23.33) of how his victim, Barea Soranus, was accused and met his death at Nero's hands. According to the scholiast (on 6.552) Celer in AD 66 denounced not only Soranus but also his daughter Servilia for treason and sorcery. Celer's birthplace is here identified as Tarsus on the R. Cydnus; Dio Cassius claimed that he was born in Beirut and only educated at Tarsus, where Bellerophon's fall from Pegasus was supposed to have taken place. *Pinna (tarsos* in Greek) is either a feather or a hoof: hence the town's name. Pegasus was traditionally supposed to have sprung from the Gorgon Medusa's blood after decapitation by Perseus. 'Nag' is a deliberately derogatory, debunking term for the mythical flying steed.

17. In 205 BC a Sibylline prophecy foretold that foreign invasion could only be averted by bringing to Rome the cult-image of the Idaean Mother from Pessinus in Phrygia. The following year P. Cornelius Scipio Nasica – though not yet even a quaestor – was chosen, on account of his purity and virtue, to convey the image from the ship to the matrons who were to guard it. In 241 BC the temple of Minerva was burnt, and L. Caecilius Metellus, the Pontifex Maximus, was blinded while rescuing the Palladium, or statue of Minerva, from the flames. For Numa see above, n. 2. His wisdom and virtue (despite the Egeria episode, and an interesting weakness for primitive electrical experiments) were proverbial.

18. The first fourteen rows of seats behind the *orchestra* in a Roman theatre were reserved for the *equites,* or 'knights': this privilege was established by the tribune L. Roscius Otho in 67 BC, and renewed by Domitian. As the rank of *eques* carried a property qualification of 400,000 sesterces, poor men were automatically excluded from good seats. Technically, the *eques* also had to prove free birth for two generations on his father's side – which clearly does not apply in these instances. J.'s point is that the rich can flout the law with impunity, whereas the poor can't. The wealth of auctioneers was proverbial; but the profession was despised. Cf. Sat. VII 5–12.

19. The name Cossus (a very ancient and distinguished one) is used to symbolize the aristocracy; cf. Sat.VIII 21. Our Cossus was an advocate (VII 144) and a legacy-hunter (X 202). Veiento we shall meet again: see Sat. IV 113 ff. and VI 82–113. An honours-broker (and praetor) under Nero, he was expelled from Italy in AD 62 for perpetrating a libellous mock-will (Tac. *Ann.* 19.50). Under Domitian he was an informer, but (to many people's disgust) contrived to remain on good terms with Domitian's successor Nerva, even occupying a prominent position in the Senate, and becoming consul three times. He had a curious hobby of training dogs to pull go-carts, like horses: apparently this was to break the monopoly of the contractors in the Circus (Dio Cass. 61.6, cf. Ferguson 148–9).

20. At line 187 for *libis* of the MSS, which makes no satisfactory sense (witness the number of explanations it has elicited, including, now, Ferguson 149, Courtney 180, and J. T. Killeen, *LCM* 5, 1980, 105, none of whom resolves the crux satisfactorily), I maintain my original conjecture *Licinis.* Some kind of *venal person* (rather than a cake for sale) is demanded by the context: Licinus was a celebrated freedman of Augustus, a barber – peculiarly apt in this context – famous for the wealth he amassed. J. refers to him at Sat. I 109.

21. Praeneste (the modern Palestrina), Gabii (Castiglione) and Tibur (Tivoli) are all in J.'s part of Latium, between 10 and 30 miles from Rome. Volsinii (Bolsena) lies about 80 miles north-west of Rome, in Etruria, on the lake of the same name. All were quiet rural retreats: Gabii (cf. below Sat. X 100) was almost deserted.

22. The double danger of fire and collapsing houses became almost proverbial under the Empire. Jerry-built apartment blocks were run up to considerable heights in an effort to combat over-crowding: the upper storeys were usually constructed of wood. Fires were frequent and (since both water-supplies and fire-services were ill-regulated) tended to be devastating. See Carcopino 34 ff. Before the famous Neronian conflagration of AD 64 there had already been a number of previous serious fires: that of 23 BC led Augustus, eventually, to organize a fire-service of 7,000 freedmen [!] under the Prefect of the Watch (*praefectus vigilum*). This did not stop further major outbreaks in AD 6, 27 and 37. The 'heroic downstairs neighbour' of 198–9 is given by J. the Trojan name of Ucalegon. In Virgil's *Aeneid* (2.311), as Troy burns, Aeneas sees the nearby house of Ucalegon go up in flames (*iam proximus ardet Ucalegon*): but by now (J. seems to be saying) the Trojan (or his descendant) has learned by experience – *been there, done that* – and has the sense both to occupy a ground-floor apartment and to shift his stuff to safety in good time (*iam friuola transfert Ucalegon*). Roman listeners, who knew the *Aeneid* more or less by heart, would appreciate the parody.

23. Lines 217–18: I read *praedarum* and *aera* with Housman. Giangrande retains the reading *phaecasianorum*, rather than *haec Asianorum*, and suggests (on the principle of *lectio difficilior*) that J. was referring to the gods of local *Greek* officialdom, the *phaecasium* being a special white shoe affected by, among others, Athenian gymnasiarchs.

Euphranor of Corinth (mid-4th c. BC) was a sculptor and painter who seems to have specialized in public commissions: in the Royal Stoa of Athens he painted a work entitled 'Theseus with Democracy and Demos', and also the cavalry engagement at Mantinea (362 BC). Pausanias mentions his statue of Apollo Patroös. Polyclitus (5th c. BC) was an Argive sculptor in bronze and marble, best known for his Doryphoros ('Man with a Spear'), copies of which survive, and which was known as 'The Canon' because it exemplified the ideal proportions of the human male figure. The whole episode is also treated by Martial (3.52): the 'dandified bachelor' was named Tongilianus, and recouped his losses five times over.

24. No wheeled traffic was permitted in the streets of Rome for ten hours after dawn: the night, as many writers from Horace to Martial testify, was constantly disturbed by rumbling carts and shouting drovers. The worst sufferers were the poor, who lived in tenements above the main thoroughfares. The 'dozing seal – or an Emperor' was probably Claudius, who had a habit of cat-napping in public: see Suet. *Claud.* 8. The connection with sea-cows or seals is explained by Seneca, *Apoc.* 5, where Claudius' voice is described as 'a kind of hoarse inarticulate bark, like a sea-beast'. Seals were also believed – as Pliny's *Natural History* shows – to have curious sleepy habits: so the joke was doubly appropriate.

25. Cf. above, n. 22. Even after the Great Fire of AD 64, and despite repeated legislation on the subject (Trajan, for instance, imposed a limit of 60 feet on the height of frontages), 'skyscrapers' continued to be built well above the safety margin. Only the upper storeys had windows looking out on the road.

26. To rub the epic comparison in, J. at 279–80 virtually translates Hom. *Il.* 24.10–11. If the mugger is given spurious heroic status, Achilles' own position is subtly called in question: is the great warrior a mere bully after all?

27. 'The swamps and forests': in particular, the Pomptine marshes, south-east of Rome and close to the Appian Way, between the mountains and the sea; and the Gallinarian pine-forest, on the road to Cumae (a not entirely peaceful retreat after all, it would seem), Sextus Pompeius' pirate headquarters towards the end of the Civil Wars (Strabo 5.4.4, C.243). Both areas were ideal for brigands, being desolate (though also, in the case of the marshes, malarial), besides offering excellent safe refuge and concealment.

28. Traditionally the 'Mamertine jail' (*carcer Mamertinum*) at the foot of the Capitol, the provision of which was ascribed to Ancus Martius, the fourth of the early kings (Livy 1.33). An extra wing, the Tullianum, was added by Servius Tullius: this was where the Catilinarian conspirators – and Jugurtha – were executed.

29. What I have translated as 'fields and coverts' J. in fact personalizes, by reference to Ceres and Diana, the two country goddesses of agriculture and hunting respectively. Ceres here is described as 'Helvine', thus probably indicating (Ferguson 156) 'that she was the patron-goddess of the wealthy Helvii, a well-known family in the locality'. It is thus of considerable interest that Aquinum should have yielded a fragmentary inscription of a dedication to Ceres by one [Iu]nius Iuuenalis who, though not the satirist himself (see Introduction pp. xxiii–iv), must have been a relative or descendant.

30. Braund (*JS I* 234–5) once again subverts J.'s narrator in this satire, suggesting 'an alternative symbolic interpretation of Umbricius' name as "Mr Shady" in a less than favourable sense: he is a manifestation of the petty greed and jealousy which haunts the city of Rome'. But if this is true – quite apart from the truth having eluded everyone for almost two millennia – we are left with a satire based on no clear standpoint. Fashionable though such a view may now be, it is hardly the reason why Juvenal not only survived, but was imitated by writers such as Boileau, Pope or Byron.

SATIRE IV

Useful General Studies

Adamietz   Adamietz, J., 'Zur Frage der Parodie in Juvenals 4. Satire',
Würzburger Jahrbucher für die Altertumswissenschaft n.f. 19 (1993)
185–200.

Anderson   Anderson, W. S., *Essays on Roman Satire* (Princeton: 1982) ch.
x, 'Studies in Book I of Juvenal', 232–44 ('Satire 4') = *YClS*
15 (1957) 68–80.

Crook   Crook, J. A., *Consilium Principis: Imperial Councils and
Counsellors from Augustus to Diocletian* (Cambridge: 1955) 50 ff.

Flintoff   Flintoff, T. S., 'Juvenal's Fourth Satire', *Papers of the Leeds
International Latin Seminar*, vol. 6 (Leeds: 1990) 121–37.

Griffith   Griffith, J. G., 'Juvenal, Statius, and the Flavian Establishment',
G. & R. 16 (1969) 134–50.

Jones   Jones, F. M. A., 'The persona and the dramatis personae in
Juvenal Satire 4', *Eranos* 88 (1990) 47–59.

Kilpatrick   Kilpatrick, R. S., 'Juvenal's patchwork satires, 4 and 7', *YClS* 23
(1973) 229–35.

Luisi   Luisi, A., 'Struttura e composizione della quarta satira di
Giovenale', *Invigilata Lucernis* 17 (1995) 77–95.

Stewart   Stewart, R., 'Domitian and Roman Religion: Juvenal Satires 2
and 4', *TAPhA* 124 (1994) 322–32.

Sweet   Sweet, D., 'Juvenal's Satire IV: Poetic Use of Indirection',
CSCA 12 (1979) 283–303.

Thomson   Thomson, J. O., 'Juvenal's Big Fish Satire', *G. & R.* 21 (1952)
86–7.

Waters   Waters, K. H., 'Juvenal and the reign of Trajan', *Antichthon* 4
(1970) 62–77.

Winkler   Winkler, M. M., 'Alogia and Emphasis in Juvenal's fourth
satire', *Ramus* 24 (1995) 59–81.

1. See Sat. I 26 with n. 4: he is clearly the dandy of Sat. I and Martial (8.48). Griffith
(145) points out the oddity of so prominent a figure in Roman society leaving no
epigraphical trail behind; though if White (377 ff.) is right that he never held an
official post, this would not be so surprising. White's arguments dampen what would
otherwise be a highly tempting speculation on Griffith's part (145–6): that this
(supposed) former Alexandrian fish-hawker rose to be Prefect of Egypt (32: 'iam
princeps equitum', a debated title which I translate as 'Senior Knight, no less'). As
Griffith says, this would certainly lend point to J.'s animadversions. What seems

quite certain is that J. (like Aristophanes with Kleon) deliberately downplays his victim's social status (Flintoff §3, 125–9: a sharp and compelling analysis). The name Crispinus is *echt* Roman, and indeed many holders of it were aristocratic. C. was clearly no Egyptian, but a Roman domiciled in Egypt: Flintoff rightly stresses the virtual impossibility of a native Egyptian acquiring Roman citizenship. The 'fishmonger' may well have been a successful Roman entrepreneur who made a fortune by trading fish: again, the parallel with Kleon 'the tanner' at once suggests itself. His dandyism (the purple cloak, the rings and pomade, etc.) would thus have a far more plausible basis than the upward aspirations of a native peasant on the make. Cf. W. C. McDermott, *Riv. Stor. dell'Ant.* 8 (1978) 117–22. Vassileiou's assumption, *Latomus* 43 (1984) 27–68, that Crispinus really *was* Domitian's 'Palace buffoon' (*scurra Palati,* 31) has little to commend it. 'I shall have frequent occasion to bring him on stage': Satires I and IV are, in fact, the only two where Crispinus is mentioned; so either J. changed his mind, or some of his work is lost.

2. It seems clear that at least one line, and possibly much more, has fallen out between lines 4 and 5. The whole passage from 5 to 10 clearly refers to a previous description of Crispinus' downfall, or mortality, or both, and comes as a complete *non sequitur* after the introductory sketch. Neither emendation (e.g. Housman's desperate *cum sit* for *minime*) nor the removal of line 8 as an 'interpolation' will really do. There are, I believe, many more sins of omission than commission in J.'s text (the 'O Passage' in Sat. VI is only the best-known example); and though – as the scholiast reveals – that text has, on occasion, been tampered with, most of the more obvious alterations seem to have been made in an attempt to cobble together broken fragments where something had been lost. This however does not justify Willis's condemnation of the entire opening section (1–36): Ribbeck's ghost still walks in odd places.

3. These enormous covered colonnades, in which the wealthy could ride or drive protected from the weather, are referred to again in Satire VII 178 ff., and also by Martial (1.42, 12.50). There were no fewer than three of them in Nero's Golden House, each 1,000 feet long (Suet., *Nero* 31).

4. Domitian revived the ancient punishment of burying unchaste Vestal Virgins alive: this allusion is almost certainly to the death of the Virgin Cornelia in AD 93 for intercourse with various lovers – including an unnamed Roman *eques* who may, but need not, have been Crispinus. See Suet. *Dom.* 8, Plin. *Ep.* 4.11.6–10. The words I have translated as 'virgin . . . , lately' are *nuper uittata*, more literally 'lately wearing her [sacred] headband'. But the syntax is ambiguous: it could also simply mean 'lately a headbanded priestess'. Ferguson (160) acutely points out that if we take *nuper* with *uittata*, the implication is that she took the headband off to have sex. It also thus clearly indicates the loss of that virginity which defined a Vestal's status. Stewart (321) translates *uittata* as 'filleted'; but despite the economy and accuracy, there remains the fear that some unwary readers may suppose the unlucky

Vestal to have been not only starved but also degutted. It is true, however, that the *uittae* were stripped from peccant Vestals (Courtney 202 with reff.), in the same manner as badges of rank were once cut off the uniforms of military personnel convicted by court-martial of certain heinous offences.

5. M. Gavius Apicius lived in the reigns of Augustus and Tiberius, and was renowned both for his gourmandise and his extravagance (Plin. *NH* 10.13, Tac. *Ann.* 4.1). It is said that after he had spent the rough equivalent of £1,000,000 he balanced his books, found he had no more than 100,000 gold pieces left, and poisoned himself (Mart. 3.22, Sen. *Cons. Helv.* 10.8–9), on the grounds that no gourmet could be expected to live on such a pittance. The cookery-book associated with his name is a late compilation, though tradition maintains that he did in fact write one (Sen. ibid. 10.3).

6. The first Flavian was Vespasian (T. Flauius Vespasianus), the final victor (supported by his Eastern legions) in the 'Year of the Four Emperors' (AD 69). He was succeeded ten years later by his elder son Titus (79–81), and Titus by his younger brother Domitian, the last of the line, assassinated in AD 96. Domitian is here described as the 'hairless Nero' because he went bald in middle age and 'took as a personal insult any reference, joking or otherwise, to bald men, being extremely sensitive about his own appearance' (Suet. *Dom.* 18). The whole passage, including the invocation, is a deliberate parody of epic convention (and an attack on imperial epic as gross flattery: Jones 47 ff.), in particular of a lost poem by Statius on Domitian's German wars. (On this, and the *consilium Principis* of Domitian in general, with a useful prosopographical analysis, see Crook 50 ff., Griffith 134 ff.) Four lines of Statius' poem survive: it is interesting that they mention no fewer than three of the *amici Principis* (Privy Councillors) whom J. goes on to satirize by name.

Note the length of the sentence here (37–44): Braund (*JS I* 244) suggests that J. means it to evoke the size of the turbot. This whole extended third-person narrative, by turns mock-heroic and deflationary, is something quite new in Roman satire (ibid. 271). What is more, J. appears to be attacking an epic now lost, the *De Bello Germanico* of Statius, describing Domitian's over-hyped European campaign. There remains the much-debated question of what function is served by the introductory section featuring Crispinus. Gowers (206, cf. Braund *JS I* 274) argues that Crispinus' nastiness 'is a mere hors d'oeuvre to Domitian's cruelty', and that Crispinus himself, with his viciousness, frivolity and gourmet taste in outsize fish, is a kind of small-scale Domitian. As Braund notes, the two men are linked also by the word *monstrum* ('portent' or 'monstrosity'), the implication being that Domitian's reign 'is marked by the extraordinary, the portentous, and the ominous' (274).

7. All the Emperors, from Augustus onwards, assumed the title of Pontifex Maximus. Apropos this 'fish story' in general, Flintoff (132) reminds us that J.'s account borrows heavily from a very similar story told by Herodotus (3.41–2) of the tyrant Polykrates. There was, of course, another and nearer precedent: Tiberius (whose legislation and life Domitian studied, Suet. *Dom.* 20) was presented with a large mullet on

Capri from the fisherman who had caught it (Suet. *Tib.* 60), with nasty consequences for the donor. Cf. Courtney 198.

Winkler, ingeniously (75-7) links the size and roundness of the fish, not only with the girth of Domitian himself (both are *monstra*, Anderson 242), but also with the Roman world (*orbis* used of both), arguing that both fish and Emperor end by being cut up, just as the latter had earlier (37) been portrayed as 'flaying a half-dead world' he ruled. This world (Sweet 288) J. portrays in terms of fish and oysters, a huge breeding-pond extending from the Crimea to Britain: 'Whether or not Domitian himself was an actual glutton, the story demonstrates that in his megalomania he treated the world as if it were a piece of food meant to please his palate.' At 56, *ne pereat* is ambiguous: is it fish or fisherman that must not perish? I have tried to preserve the ambiguity in my translation. Cf. Ferguson 153.

8. The two lakes were the *lacus Albanus* and the *lacus Nemorensis*. Alba Longa was supposedly founded by Ascanius son of Aeneas, who removed his seat of government thither from Lavinium. Its destruction was due to the Roman king Tullus Hostilius, but the temples were spared (some were still standing in Augustus' day) and a sacred flame alleged to have been brought from Troy still burnt there. (J.'s reference to this suggests that in his opinion, as in that of the Younger Pliny, *Ep.* 4.11.6, Cornelia the Vestal was wrongly accused.) Domitian resided permanently at his huge villa on the site (as the Popes have done in summer ever since it became Castel Gondolfo); the fisherman must have brought the turbot to Rome from Ancona, and thence along the Via Appia to Alba – a total journey of about 150 miles.

9. The Imperial *consilium Principis*, or Privy Council, was instituted by Augustus, more formally established by Tiberius and continued by subsequent Emperors. This quasi-Cabinet seems to have consisted of leading senators, such as the Consuls and City Prefect, and those Equestrians with key posts – e.g. the Prefect of Egypt and the Commander of the Praetorian Guard. A member of the Council was known as *amicus Caesaris*, or 'Friend of Caesar'. Other writers beside J. (such as Plin. *Pan.* 85, and Dio Cass. 67.1.3-4) allude to the irony of this term under Domitian, and the terror which such an Imperial summons might induce. Certain *amici* had the additional and still more honourable title of *comes*, 'companion' (hence 'Count') – just as some of their modern equivalents are Privy Counsellors.

10. Plotius Pegasus was made *consul suffectus* and City Prefect (hence J.'s contemptuous 'bailiff') in Vespasian's reign (Just. *Dig.* 1.2.2, 47). This sets the dramatic date of the satire at a point soon after Domitian's accession in 81 (Griffith 137). Yet 153-4 clearly alludes to the Emperor's assassination in AD 96. This, like most of the Satires, seems, on the basis of internal evidence, to have been worked at over a long period, which may answer Courtney's complaint (199) that Domitian's paranoid cruelty is retrojected, unhistorically, from the revolt of Saturninus in 89 to the opening years of his reign. Afterwards Pegasus served as governor of several provinces, including Dalmatia. He acquired great fame as a jurist: his learning was such, we are told, that men thought him a walking book rather than a human being.

He was the son of a trireme-commander, and derived his name from the figurehead on his father's pinnace. As Griffith says (144), his description as Rome's 'bailiff' stresses not only Domitian's authoritarian rule, but also the emperor's habit of exercising his power from the Alban Mount, by remote control, through delegated subordinates.

11. At line 79 I read, and punctuate, *sanctissimus – omnia quamquam*.

12. Q. Vibius Crispus was from Vercellae (b. *c*. AD 10); three times consul, including a spell as *consul suffectus* under Nero in 61, and probably for the last time in 83, with Veiento as his colleague. He held a proconsulship in Africa between 71 and 75, and was also Inspector of Aqueducts. He was a drinking companion of Vitellius (Dio Cass. 65.2.3), and Quintilian describes him as a witty man: his standard of wit may be judged from an anecdote in Suetonius (*Dom*. 3): 'At the beginning of his reign Domitian would spend hours alone every day catching flies – believe it or not ! – and stabbing them with a needle-sharp pen. Once, on being asked whether anyone was closeted with the Emperor, Vibius Crispus answered wittily: "No, not even a fly." ' A regular Vicar of Bray, he survived several changes of emperor by making himself useful and through calculated charm (Quint. 5.13.48); Vespasian found it impossible to dispense with his services (Tac. *Dial*. 8). He also, not surprisingly, amassed enough wealth to be used by Martial (4.54.7) as a benchmark for millionaire status. The picture of a successful, diplomatic yes-man who lived to a ripe old age is confirmed by Tacitus (*Dial*. 13). There is remarkable, and unusual, unanimity on him in our sources. See Griffith 139–40.

13. Acilius Glabrio the Elder is only mentioned here: he would be about eighty at the time, and we can place his *floruit* under Claudius or Nero (P. Gallivan, *Historia* 27, 1978, 621–5, who posits a consulship – several blank dates are available – under the latter). His son M.' Acilius Glabrio was consul, together with the future Emperor Trajan, in AD 91. Why he was made to fight bears (and a huge lion too, it seems) in Domitian's private arena at some point after the April of that same year is unclear. Domitian apparently suspected him of treason, but could not prove his suspicions. At all events, despite (or perhaps because of) his triumph over the assorted wild beasts put up against him, he was afterwards exiled as a revolutionary, and in 95 executed, the charge being augmented with one of 'atheism and . . . Jewish customs' (Suet. *Dom*. 10, Dio Cass. 67.14.3, cf. Gallivan 621–2). The name Acilius Glabrio is found in the catacomb of Priscilla, so it seems possible that this Acilius was in fact a Christian convert (Highet 259–60 n. 14).

14. All giants were supposed to be 'earth-born', like Antaeus; but the Latin term *terrae filius* also meant 'a son of the soil' in the sense of 'a nobody'. The point (Ferguson 167) is that when the Giants challenged Olympus and were fulminated, the small fry escaped. No such luck attended those confronting Domitian: thus, safer with Jupiter!

15. The reference is to L. Junius Brutus, who by feigning feeble-mindedness persuaded his uncle, Tarquinius Superbus, that he did not constitute a threat to the

throne (Livy 1.56.7–8). A 'bearded king' symbolizes old-fashioned simplicity. Africanus Minor first set the fashion for daily shaving – Varro (*RR* 2.11.10, cf. Plin. *NH* 7.211) claims that barbers first came to Rome from Sicily *c.* 300 BC – and it was not till Hadrian's day that the beard returned. I have sometimes wondered whether the whole passage may not contain a sly reference to Hadrian's weakness for 'advanced' literature, and his consequent gullibility where fraudulent *avant-gardisme* was concerned; there is, similarly, something very ambiguous about the opening of Satire VII, on Imperial patronage for the arts.

16. Rubrius Gallus was a veteran military commander: he fought for Nero against Galba and Verginius Rufus in AD 68, subsequently switching sides with diplomatic panache, and later for Otho against Vitellius, perhaps as commander of the Praetorian Guard. He sided with Vespasian, who in 70 appointed him governor of Moesia (Tac. *Hist.* 2.51, 99). According to the scholiast, his 'unspeakable crime' was the seduction of either Domitia Longina or Titus' daughter Julia, in either case while the girl was still a minor.

17. Perhaps T. Junius Montanus, *consul suffectus* in AD 81 and a friend of Nero's. The Curtius Montanus expelled from the Senate in 66 for lampooning Nero (and afterwards rehabilitated under Vespasian) may have been his son (Tac. *Ann.* 16.33).

18. This unpleasant character is otherwise unknown. He has been tentatively identified with M. Pompeius Siluanus Staterius Flauinus, Consul in AD 45 and possibly again in 76 (Gallivan, above, n. 13, 621 with further reff.).

19. Cornelius Fuscus, a man of distinguished ancestry, supported Vespasian against Vitellius in 69, and is highly praised by Tacitus for his qualities of leadership. (He had, wisely, lived in retirement on his estate during Nero's reign.) He was appointed procurator of Pannonia by Galba. The fleet at Ravenna elected him commander in the campaign against Vitellius, and Vespasian rewarded him with the rank of praetor (Tac. *Hist.* 3.4, 42). Domitian appointed him Praetorian Prefect, and (some fifteen years later) sent him out as general in the second Dacian War of AD 86/7, during which his army was annihilated and he himself killed. Dacia was roughly equivalent to modern Romania. This event offers a firm *terminus ante quem* for the dramatic date of the satire.

20. Aulus Didius Gallus Fabricius Veiento belonged to a family known in Republican times (cf. Cic. *Att.* 4.17.3, 7.3.5). In AD 62 he was prosecuted (Tac. *Ann.* 14.50) for, as Griffith (141) nicely puts it, 'uttering scandalous literature against persons prominent in political and religious circles at the time': the fact that he was still very much alive, however, does not (*pace* Griffith) militate against the idea that his squibs took the form of mock-wills (*codicilli*), which could quite easily celebrate a mock-death. He also seems to have traded in honours and appointments. Nero exiled him and ordered his *feuilletons* burned (they continued to circulate as *samizdat* literature). He was recalled by Vespasian, and by 83 had held three consulships; he served as a privy councillor under Domitian, Nerva and Trajan as well as Nero. In old age he discharged several honorary priestly offices. He and the blind informer

Catullus were close friends (Plin. *Ep.* 4.22.4–5). See also Sat. III 185 and n. 19. His wife may have been the Eppia who ran off with a gladiator: see Sat. VI 113.

21. The blind informer Catullus – L. Valerius Catullus Messalinus – was Consul in AD 73 and 85 with Domitian, and did not outlive him, though he seems to have been active and influential as late as 93 (Tac. *Agric.* 45, Plin. *Ep.* 4.22.5). Lines 116–19: beggars traditionally had their 'stands' or 'pitches' on bridges or at the bottom of hills, to catch the traffic as it slowed down. Ariccia – a favourite haunt of beggars in Martial's and Juvenal's day – is in a hollow on the Via Appia, about twenty miles south of Rome. The phrase *a ponte* (116) perhaps parodies the titles of the Imperial Secretaries: *ab epistulis, a secretis*, etc. Courtney's arguments (222–3) for line 116 being spurious do not convince. J., who dearly loved a literary in-joke, couldn't resist playing on the fact that this malevolent character shared a name with the earlier, more famous, lyric poet. Ferguson (169) picks up the stylistic echoes, including the Catullan adoption of the word *basia* for 'kisses'.

22. I accept Hirschfeld's emendation of *pugnos* for *pugnas*.

23. According to Caesar, the British in battle habitually ran out along the poles of their chariots and fought from the yoke. The name Arviragus is mentioned by Geoffrey of Monmouth: Shakespeare borrowed it for *Cymbeline*. But nothing substantial is known of him. Stewart (329) remarks that 'at Domitian's Alba, the prophecy for the military campaign came not from Jupiter's bull, but from an extravagant fish, and was given not by a Roman priest but by the oriental priest of a foreign, Eastern Bellona' (123–7). Bellona, originally a Roman war-goddess, had her name transferred to the Cappadocian Ma, an orgiastic deity akin to Cybele, whose cult 'involved noise, ecstasy, and self-mutilation' (Braund, *JS* I 263).

24. 'Prometheus' is used here, with grandiose pretentiousness, to denote an especially skilled potter, since there was a creation myth (Paus. 10.4.4) in which he had fashioned the human race from clay.

25. K. Coleman's ingenious emendation *stagnum* ('pond', 'pool', 'stews') for the meaningless *saxum* ('stone' or 'rock') of the MSS carries instant conviction, and I have gratefully utilized it in my translation. See 'The Lucrine Lake at Juvenal 4.141', *CQ* 44 (1994) 554–7.

26. The ancient names of the tribes I have (roughly) equated with Prussians and Rhinelanders were the Chatti and the Sygambri (so named by J.). Domitian campaigned against the Chatti in AD 83, and was given a triumph (Suet. *Dom.* 6), as well as the honourable title of Germanicus; but the general belief was that he did not deserve it (Tac. *Agric.* 39). See Courtney 227–8 (with further reff.), who observes that 'the Sygambri had been completely subdued since the time of Augustus … and if Juvenal is not simply mentioning them as a Germanic-sounding name he may be hinting at the fictitious nature of Domitian's triumph.'

27. Domitian's murderers were his niece Domitilla's steward Stephanus, a junior officer called Clodianus, a freedman named Maximus, a chamberlain, Satur, and an unnamed Imperial gladiator (Suet. *Dom.* 17). So far some sort of justification for

J.'s gibe about 'the commons' can be made out. But in fact all these were Palace retainers, and the plot was a Palace conspiracy instigated by Domitian's wife, with the support of the Praetorian Prefect Norbanus. The working classes had no more to fear from him than from any other Emperor. J.'s knowledge of the proletariat is almost as deficient as his sympathies for them.

The Lamiae were a well-to-do family – Domitian executed L. Aelius Lamia Aelianus, Consul in AD 80, and first husband of Domitian's wife Domitia, for mocking him (Suet. *Dom.* 10): one would like to know how – but the name, of course, was also that of some peculiarly nasty quasi-vampiric bloodsucking bogeys of Greek myth (Flintoff 134–5). J. suggests, mischievously, that the victims were no better than the monster at whose hands they perished.

SATIRE V

Useful General Studies

Adamietz	Adamietz, J., *Untersuchungen zu Juvenal* (*Hermes Einzelschriften* 26) (Wiesbaden: 1972) 78–116 ('Satire 5').
Anderson	Anderson, W. S., *Essays on Roman Satire* (Princeton: 1982) ch. x, 'Studies Book in I of Juvenal', 244–50 ('Satire 5') =*YClS* 15 (1957) 80–86.
Cuccioli	Cuccioli, R., 'The "banquet" in Juvenal Satire 5', *Papers of the Leeds International Latin Seminar*, vol. 6 (Leeds: 1990) 139–43.
Highet	Highet, G., *Juvenal the Satirist* (Oxford: 1954) 83–8 ch. xi ('Satire Five: Snobs and Snubs').
Jones	Jones, F. M. A., 'Trebius and Virro in Juvenal 5', *LCM* 12 (1987) 148–54.
Morford	Morford, M. P. O., 'Juvenal's 5th Satire', *AJPh* 98 (1977) 219–45.
Shero	Shero, L. S., 'The *cena* in Roman satire', *CPh* 18 (1923) 126–43.

1. A Trebius Sergianus was Consul in AD 132, under Hadrian; it is pleasant to think that this might conceivably be the same man, and that Fortune, after his early humiliations, smiled on him in his later years. The name also occurs in inscriptions from J.'s birthplace, Aquinum (*CIL* 10, 5528–9).
2. See Satire IV, n. 21.
3. The name Virro is uncommon. J. uses it once again, in Satire IX, to portray a homosexual, who may possibly be the person referred to here (the name, with its *uir*-component, carries ironic connotations of 'manliness'). The best-known historical holder of the name, Vibidius Virro, was in AD 17 expelled from the Senate

by Tiberius for dissolute behaviour. Syme suggested (*JRS* 39, 1949, 17) that the family was Paelignian: if so, it came from within forty miles of Aquinum.

From line 30 onwards we get a long series of sharp contrasts between the luxury dishes reserved for Virro himself and his close associates, and the cheap food served to 'inferior' guests. As Anderson says (250: cf. Highet 88) 'a series of antithetic dishes, enhanced by appropriate association, have formed the heart of the Satire, confirming the fundamental theme of slave and king'. J. did not invent this sorting of dinner-guests into classes. Morford (221–3) culls evidence from the Younger Pliny (*Ep*. 2.6) and Martial (3.60) to show that what we read in Sat. V has its roots in nasty social reality. Martial recites a list of contrasts (oysters/mussels, mushrooms / toadstools, turbot/bream, pigeon/magpie [!]) very like J.'s. Pliny has to go out of his way to assure an acquaintance that he, Pliny, treats his guests as he does himself. 'What?' his friend exclaims, 'even the *freedmen*?'.

4. The 'Social Wars' – perhaps 'Wars with the Allies' would be a better translation, but 'Social Wars' has been canonized by long usage – lasted from 91 to 88 BC. They were, essentially, a general rebellion against Rome by her Italian allies, who, after the assassination of their champion, the tribune Livius Drusus, saw no hope of obtaining full Roman enfranchisement by peaceful means. Wine bottled then would be nearly 200 years old by J.'s day, and quite undrinkable: J.'s point would seem to be either that Virro lied about the vintages in his cellar, or else that he lacked the discrimination to tell wine from vinegar. Cf. Plin. *NH* 14.55.

The Albine and Setine hills were two famous wine-growing districts of Latium. Some regarded Alban wine as second only to Falernian (Dion. Hal. *RA* 1.66.3); others (e.g. Plin. *NH* 14.59 ff.) ranked Setine (a favourite of Augustus) first, Falernian second, Alban and Surrentine third, and Mamertine (from Sicily) fourth. Wine (surprising though we may find this) was the only cure known for serious cases of dyspepsia (which, one might suppose, it would exacerbate rather than alleviate): Plin. *NH* 23.35–6, 50, cf. Braund, *JS I* 282.

5. The 'Stoic martyrs' were P. Clodius Thrasea Paetus (suffect consul AD 56) and his son-in-law, Helvidius Priscus, who both lost their lives as a result of aggressive Republicanism under Emperors who did not care overmuch for the memory of the Republic. Thrasea was forced to commit suicide by Nero in AD 66, and Helvidius, after a spell in exile, was executed by Vespasian, probably in 75. Observing the birthdays of Brutus and Cassius, Caesar's assassins in 44 BC, was only one among many ways in which they proclaimed their attitude; another was by 'offering bitterly satirical vows to Jupiter Liberator at their deaths' (Ferguson 176 with reff.).

6. The youth preferred – by Dido – to Iarbas was Aeneas. For his jewelled scabbard see *Aen*. 4.261. J. here indulges in a neat sexual ambiguity which defies translation. The Latin for 'scabbard' is *uagina*, and Aeneas displays his jewellery *in uaginae fronte*, which can mean either 'on the outside of his scabbard' or, by obscene synecdoche, 'on his mistress's person' (one thinks of the current fashion for pierced labia, which would give the pun even greater force). I also wonder whether 'gems' here in

connection with 'fingers', 'cups', and *uagina*, may not have been a slang term for 'testicles', akin to our semi-euphemistic phrase 'crown jewels' (even though Adams, 66–71 s.v. 'testicle', offers no parallel): Aeneas would then be servicing Dido as well as showing off his wealth.

The 'long-nosed cobbler from Beneventum' was a deformed shoemaker's apprentice, one Vatinius (Tac. *Ann.* 15.34), who rose to power and wealth under Nero – having by AD 62 amassed enough of the latter to give a gladiatorial show – first as court buffoon, then as a professional informer against the great (Mart. 14.96). J. might almost have put in the reference to him here as a contrast to the 'Stoic martyrs', since he made his unsavoury career at the expense of the Senatorial opposition. The cheap cup with its four long nozzles was named after him, not, one suspects, in a friendly spirit.

7. The 'Saharan groom' has clearly been brought in from the stables to wait on socially inferior guests (for the use of African slaves as drivers or carriage-runners see Sen. *Ep.* 123.7). But what was there about this Moor that might particularly scare a traveller on the Latin Way? The prospect of being beaten up or robbed? A generally villainous appearance? Possibly; but Jennifer Hall, in a fascinating article (*PACA* 17, 1983, 108–13) shows (a) that blacks were regarded as unlucky omens of doom in antiquity, probably because (b) ancient ghosts, in striking contrast to the modern white ectoplasmic variety, were also thought of as black. No wonder J. figured on Trebius being scared.

Tullus Hostilius was Numa's successor as King of Rome, about 670 BC; he embarked on a series of wars which fully justify his epithet here. Ancus Marcius, the fourth of the kings, came to the throne about 638: he is supposed, among other achievements, to have founded the port of Ostia and built the first prison in Rome. 8. The Esquiline Hill was the richest and most fashionable residential quarter of the city.

9. Nine days after a funeral offerings of eggs, salt and lentils were left on the grave of the deceased.

10. Lampreys, as the context implies, were great delicacies: some wealthy citizens kept a live supply of them in salt-water tanks. Sicilian lampreys (in particular those from Messina) were reckoned among the best: see Plin. *NH* 9.169, Varro *RR* 2.6.2, Mart. 13.80. The description of the south wind drying wings in his cell is a mock-epic spoof of similar pseudo-anthropomorphic fancies (cf. Ovid *Met.* 11.432 and Virg. *Georg.* 1.462).

Lines 103–6 have always presented a puzzle, both textual and interpretative. What kind of fish was the *Tiberinus*? How was it spotted, and what was its connection with ice (*glacie*)? Professor D. S. Robertson's attractive theory was that the fish is rotten, and the marks of putrefaction are hidden by lumps of ice. For long I accepted this theory; now I am not so sure. The context deals with the live fish in its natural habitat; then, by transition, with the cooked fish served up to the guests. A fish on its slab in the shop would be out of place here. Hesitantly I accept Clausen's emendation, *glaucis* for *glacie*, which gives us a 'grey-spotted' *Tiberinus*: but this can scarcely be – as he supposes – the sea-bass (*lupus*), which was a noted delicacy. The river-pike, a habitual foul feeder, fits the context far better, and I have translated accordingly. However, the latest critic to tackle this crux, Bradshaw, keeps the text as it stands, arguing ingeniously that the *Tiberinus was* the sea-bass (*lupus*), which came up-river and contracted the disease known as saprolegnia: this both produced the patches on its skin – wrongly attributed to the effect of ice – and made the fish sluggish and easily caught. Giangrande similarly upholds the reading of the MSS. He cites Galen and Macrobius to show that the Romans avoided – if they could afford to – any fish that fed in the tainted waters of the Tiber, and specifically the *lupus*. But his attempt to justify *glacie* by a reference to Satire IV 41–4 is less convincing.

11. The 'old Republican gentry' once again refers to the Republican-minded senatorial opposition group under the early empire: J. names Gaius Calpurnius Piso and Seneca (both of whom lost their lives as the result of the famous 'Conspiracy of Piso' against Nero in AD 65), together with Cotta, who was a patron of the poet Ovid.

As Cuccioli (140) rightly observes, J.'s main points 'are made in lines 107–113 . . . All that is asked of Virro and similar *patroni* is that they should have some table manners and that they should treat their *clientes* as their equals and fellow-citizens'. J. is nostalgic for the supposed 'civilized, courteous relationship between *cliens* and *patronus* that once existed', etc. I am less sanguine about this lost relationship than either Cuccioli or J. himself seems to be: what comes to *my* mind is the old adage about slavery not being justified by kindness to slaves. J. never for one moment challenges the relationship as such, nor its social implications. He reminds me, in this context, of Dickens, who (as George Orwell pointed out) had no desire to abolish the Bumbles of this world, but just wanted better, nicer Bumbles, with a proper sense of their own responsibilities (cf. Introduction p. xxxiii).

12. Meleager, son of Oeneus and Althaea, neglected to sacrifice to Artemis, who therefore sent a huge boar to ravage his homeland of Calydon. Meleager assembled a great meet of heroic hunters – including Atalanta – and killed the boar. J. here picks up the gastronomic myth, popular in antiquity, that truffles grew sweetest in springtime, and fastest during a thunderstorm (Plin. *NH* 19.37).

13. The story of the monster Cacus is told by Virgil in Bk VIII of the *Aeneid* (193–270).

14. i.e. provided the minimum sum of 400,000 sesterces needed to qualify for the Equestrian Order.

15. The allusion is to the eternally productive orchard of Alcinous, the King of Phaeacia who figures in Homer's *Odyssey* (Bk VII 114–21).

16. The 'Embankment' was originally a defensive earthwork constructed by Servius Tullius to protect the eastern side of Rome: it stretched from the Esquiline Hill to the Colline Gate, and later became a favourite spot for citizens to take a constitutional,

being both high and breezy, and very like the modern promenade. Not only performing animals, but also fortune-tellers were often found there: see Sat. VI 588.

17. Morford (232) tellingly assembles other examples of selfish greed from Satires I and IV: the patron dining alone while his 'clients' collect their hand-out, and then dying of a surfeit of peacock (I 132–46); Crispinus scoffing his huge mullet solo (IV 15–33, esp. 22). Repeated themes are several times emphasized 'by grafting them onto the stock of the satirical *cena*'. As Braund says (*JS I* 305), 'it is difficult, and would be rash, to attempt to reconstruct real Roman feasts from the pictures provided by satire'.

18. A certain type of professional buffoon – the 'fall-man', the eternal he-who-gets-kicked – always had his head shaved: this applies equally to the *stupidus* of the mimes and the idiot clown (*morio*) who performed at private parties. Highet (as so often) has the perfect modern parallel: 'A clown act called "The Three Stooges", which used to appear in short film farces during the 1940s, had a perfect *stupidus* in it, a burly man with a head clipped or shaven smooth, who was always being slapped on it by his quicker and cleverer fellow stooges.' There is also sexual innuendo in the mime here. From Mart. 2.72 it seems clear that the *stupidus* was not only 'banged' in the sense of being cuffed, but also subjected to *irrumatio* by his wife's lover. See J. Y. Nadeau in his review of Adamietz, *Untersuchungen*, *Latomus* 35 (1976) 908. I have tried to bring out the *double entendre* in my translation. It is undeniable (and goes some way to support Braund's view of these satires as being as scornful of victims as they are angry with bullies) that J.'s attack is not only against Virro, but equally against Trebius himself for his readiness to put up with such humiliations.

SATIRE VI

Useful General Studies

Anderson	Anderson, W. S., *Essays on Roman Satire* (Princeton: 1982) ch. xi, 'Juvenal 6: A Problem in Structure', 255–76 = *CPh* 51 (1956) 73–94.
Braund	Braund, S., 'Juvenal – misogynist or misogamist?' *JRS* 82 (1992) 71–86
Cecchin	Cecchin, S. A., 'Letteratura e realtà. La donna in Giovenale (analisi della VI satira)' in *Atti del II Convegno nazionale di studi su la donna nel mondo antico. Torino 18–19–20 aprile 1988*, ed. R. Uglione (Turin: 1989) 141–64.
Griffith	Griffith, J. G., 'The Oxford Fragments of Juvenal's Sixth Satire', *Hermes* 91 (1963) 104–14.

Luck   Luck, G., 'The textual history of Juvenal and the Oxford lines',
              HSCPh 76 (1972) 217–32.

Nardo   Nardo, D., *La sesta satira di Giovenale e la tradizione erotico-elegiaca
              latina* (Padua: 1973).

Perelli   Perelli, A., 'Il paradigma di Elena e un'allusione in Giovenale',
              Euphrosyne 20 (1992) 187–210.

Reinmuth   Reinmuth, O. W., 'The meaning of *ceroma* in Juvenal and
              Martial', *Phoenix* 21 (1967) 191–5.

Singleton   Singleton, D., 'Juvenal 6.1–20 and some ancient attitudes to the
              golden age', *G. & R.* 19 (1972) 151–64.

Smith   Smith, W. S., 'Husband and wife in Juvenal's sixth satire', *CW*
              73 (1980) 323–32.

Vianello   Vianello, N., 'La sesta satira di Giovenale', *Historia* 4 (1930)
              747–75.

Wiesen   Wiesen, D. S., 'The verbal basis of Juvenal's satiric vision: III,
              Satire Six', *ANRW* II, 33.1 (Berlin/New York: 1989) 723–33.

Winkler   Winkler, M. M., *The persona in three satires of Juvenal*
              (Hildesheim: 1983) ch. v, 146 ff. (and elsewhere).

1. 'Cynthia' was the pseudonym which Propertius used to describe his mistress Hostia in the poems he wrote about her; the girl who wept for her sparrow (Catull. 3, esp. 16–18) was 'Lesbia', Catullus' mistress: her real name was Clodia, and she was the sister of Publius Clodius, referred to in lines 335–45. The point, of course, is that both these women were neurotic, sophisticated creatures with the loosest of sexual habits. Hostia was chronically unfaithful. Cicero accused Clodia of incest with her brother (*Pro Caelio* 14–20, 32); one of her later lovers described her as a 'two-bit [*quadrantaria*] Clytemnestra' (Cic. ibid. 26, Quint. 8.6.53). As Ferguson (186) nicely puts it, 'in Saturn's reign the women had less style, but more morality'.

2. At line 12 I accept Scholte's emendation *rupe et robore*, a proverbial expression as old as Homer (*Od.* 19.163; cf. Virg. *Aen.* 8.315). For the 'living clay' theory (with Prometheus as artist) see Ovid, *Met.* 1.82–3, cf. Sat. XIV 35. J.'s literary echoes are hard to track, and often impossible to convey in a translation. At 14, for instance, the 'traces of ancient' X – in this case 'presence' – slily pick up a phrase, *ueteris uestigia*, best known from Virgil (*Aen.* 4.23), where it refers to the flame of old passion in Dido, but also found in Catullus (64.295) and Ovid (*Am.* 3.8.19).

3. Justice, Astraea, daughter of Zeus, was the last of the immortals to leave earth (Ovid, *Met.* 1.150, cf. Arat. *Phaen.* 101–36): she was catasterized into the constellation Virgo. Chastity (or Modesty: *Pudicitia*, Greek *Aidôs*), together with Nemesis (an earlier version of Justice) supposedly abandoned mankind in the Iron Age (Hes. *WD* 199–201). Hesiod listed five ages: gold, silver, bronze, heroic, and iron (cf. 23–4). A good analysis of J.'s mocking send-up of the so-called 'Golden Age' is in Winkler, 27–32.

4. Nothing is known about either J.'s dedicatee Postumus, or the Ursidius mentioned at 38 ff. Indeed, our ignorance is so profound that some scholars (e.g. Ferguson 187) assume them to be the same person, Postumus Ursidius; but the thrust of J.'s rhetoric militates against this interpretation.

J. is referring at 32 to the Pons Aemilius, dating from 179 BC. It became known to Italians, after its partial collapse, as the Ponte Rotto. One arch still survives. Ferguson (187) points out the clever onomatopoeia in the Latin line: the unusual monosyllabic end 'expresses the thud of the body on the water'. Virgil (*Aen.* 5.481) had earlier used the same device to suggest the fall of a slaughtered ox. I have tried to duplicate the effect in my translation.

5. This may (so Courtney 266) be a literary topos (Lucilius fr. 866 said much the same; so did Propertius, 2.4.17–18); it may also (Ferguson 187) hint at antipathy towards women on J.'s part, and a corresponding taste for pederasty; but few, I think, would accept it as an accurate description of real-life behaviour by the Gitons of this world.

6. There are two ordinances alluded to here. The 'Julian Law' (*Lex Iulia*) for regulating marital affairs was promulgated by Augustus in 18 BC. This is the law to which J. specifically refers at 38. But this was both amended and extended by the *Lex Papia Poppaea* of AD 9, which gave special privileges to those with three or more children, and restricted the rights of bachelors, spinsters or childless couples to inherit property.

7. The 'feast of the Corn-Goddess' (Ceres) took place in August, and somewhat resembled a Harvest Festival: it included a ceremonial procession of white-clad women bearing first-fruits. One condition of participation in this ceremony was nine days' previous abstention from sexual intercourse. The scholiast, with typical blunt accuracy, explains the point about fathers fearing their daughters' kisses in terms of oral sex: *quia et irrumantur mulieres, dicit.*

8. Bathyllus seems to have been a *pantomimus*, or ballet-dancer, under Domitian. The most famous Bathyllus, however, who was, broadly speaking, the Diaghilev of the Imperial ballet, lived much earlier, under Augustus, and was a favourite of Maecenas: it was customary to repeat the names of 'stars' in successive generations: we shall find the same thing happening with Paris the actor. It is hard to realize the influence which the Roman ballet exerted on Roman citizens. It was not only immensely popular, but formed a centre for violent factions like those of the various racing-colours (there were two rival schools of ballet), and was sometimes the cause of riots and bloodshed.

9. The question is not (as might be supposed) entirely rhetorical. The rhetorician J. chooses as an example is Quintilian (M. Fabius Quintilianus: possibly his teacher, undoubtedly his acquaintance); and one thing we know about Quintilian is that *c.* AD 85, when about fifty, he married a young girl, who bore him two children before her premature death at the age of nineteen. Rudd (1986: 171) assumes that he was a 'boring old husband'. Was he? On his own account (*Inst. Orat.* 6 pref. §6)

he was very much in love with his bride, and two children in two years are poor evidence for a *mariage blanc*. It looks very much as though the young lady *did* prefer a professor of rhetoric, and a quinquagenarian one at that.

10. At line 107 I accept Nisbet's ingenious emendation *sulcus* (for *sicut*): the only way so far suggested of making this passage into tolerable Latin. At 113 the name of Veiento comes as a surprise. We know that the name of the woman he married (c. 83–5) was Attica. Why would J. have given her a metrically identical pseudonym? All danger from that era was long past. Or was he (cf. Sat. IV 113, with note ad loc.) simply using Veiento's name to typify a particularly revolting kind of man? Perelli (187 ff.) suggests that J. is using Eppia to parody the myth of Paris and Helen, in terms which also recall Virgil (*Aen.* 2.567 ff.).

11. Lines 114–24 are a textual nightmare. The general sense is clear: the Latin is in many places quite hopeless. I do not agree with attempts by various editors to solve the problem on a basis of wholesale linear transposition (for the latest attempt see Courtney 39) and have kept the text in the line-order given by the MSS. Again, it seems clear that several lines must have fallen out: possibly after 117, certainly after 118. To avoid the first loss we must take *meretrix augusta* in apposition to *uxor*, which is awkward, but just possible. To make 119 follow on 118 we have to get rid of *linquebat*, which, despite editorial claims, cannot be anything but a transitive verb. I have sometimes wondered whether *linquebat* was not a corruption of something like *iam properat*; but it seems more sensible to assume a lacuna after 118, perhaps of one line only, something such as *iussit, et amplexus subito cubitusque seniles* . . . etc.

12. The 'prince of the blood' was Britannicus, Messalina's son by Claudius. The boy's stepmother, Agrippina, persuaded Claudius to adopt her own son Lucius Domitius (Nero), who thus succeeded to the throne after Claudius' death by poisoning in AD 54. Britannicus himself was also murdered a year later, presumably as a potential rival to Nero. See lines 615–26.

13. Reading *nimium*, Martyn's excellent conjecture for the contradictory *minimum* of the MSS.

14. During the Saturnalia (17–19 December) a fair and market were held in the Campus Martius, and the canvas stalls erected for this purpose made it impossible to see the frescoes in the Portico of Agrippa. One of the more famous of these frescoes depicted Jason and the Argonauts. Once again J. belittles a mythological theme here by reducing the voyage of the Argonauts to a mere trading venture.

15. Berenice and Agrippa II are perhaps best known for St Paul's appearance before them at Caesarea in AD 62. Berenice, after two marriages, the second to her uncle, lived for many years with Agrippa, her brother, incestuously according to general belief. The Emperor Titus fell in love with her during his Jewish campaign (67–70), and had her as his mistress in 75, when she visited Rome. It is quite possible that she sold some famous ring during this visit.

At 158 I now accept Housman's brilliant emendation *gestare* for the otiose and repetitive *dedit hunc* of the MS tradition.

Apropos Bibula and Sertorius, Braund (71 ff.) makes an excellent case for J.'s attack being directed against marriage, and the behaviour of wives, rather than women generally. Smith (330–32) adds to this the shrewd observation that J.'s secondary aim is to upbraid husbands for their *submissiveness*. This picture at once aligns itself with predominant (in every sense) ancient sexual attitudes, which upheld male aggressiveness (whether against women or boys), but castigated, in the strongest terms, any male sexual passivity (e.g. as catamite or *cinaedus*). The role of an adult male was to penetrate; to suffer penetration himself – worse, to *enjoy* it – was regarded as moral turpitude of the first order. This clearly extended to social and domestic relations. Smith argues that J.'s sympathy is not for Bibula (the shameless gold-digger), but for Sertorius, who has at last put his foot down and thrown her out. 'Love is condoned in a man only when it is used as a pretense in order to achieve some material gain.'

16. Sabine women had a high reputation for chastity. Their role as peacemakers is described by Livy (1.13). After their 'rape', Sabine troops urnder Mettius Curtius irnvaded Rome, and came very close to capturing the Palatine Hill. As the battle raged in the valley between the Palatine and the Capitol, the women (for whatever motive) decided to intervene. 'With loosened hair and rent garments they braved the flying spears and ·thrust their way in a body between the embattled armies', etc. The whole passage makes me wonder whether scholars do not seriously underestimate Livy's deadpan sense of humour.

17. Reading *Venustina*, which I take to be a piece of contemporary argot for a prostitute.

18. Cornelia was the second daughter of Scipio Africanus, who conquered the Numidian prince Syphax in 203 BC and defeated Hannibal at the Battle of Zama in 202. She had twelve children (though only three survived to adult life, and of these three the two boys, Gaius and Tiberius Gracchus, both suffered political assassination) – a fact which suggests that the next few lines, describing the fate of Niobe, may have something of a back-kick at Cornelia herself. 'CORNELIA MATER GRACCHORUM' (hence, 'Mother of Statesmen') was inscribed on at least one of her statues. J. picks up this proud title for deflation.

19. Niobe was the daughter of Tantalus and wife of Amphion. She went two better than Cornelia by bearing no fewer than fourteen children, equally divided as to sex. She then courted disaster by boasting that she was at least the equal of Leto, who had borne two children only, Apollo and Artemis. (Ovid tells us that she also disparaged Leto's ancestral connections.) The two, thus slighted, proceeded to kill all Niobe's offspring; Amphion hanged himself; and Niobe, after one tearful meal, was turned to stone. The 'white Alban sow' may be found in the *Aeneid*, together with its farrow of thirty young: it marked the future site of Alba Longa (*Aeneid* 3.390 ff.).

20. Reading, with Housman, *ferendis* for relictis: Nisbet suggested *loquendis*, which would fit equally well. Neither emendation, however, is entirely convincing.

21. The coins were *aurei* (almost the equivalent of the British guinea); the 'victory issues' were for Trajan's conquests in Germany (AD 97) and Dacia (AD 102/3). This detail provides a *terminus post quem* for the composition-date of Satire VI. We have no other reference to such a marriage-custom, but we know from Martial (*Epigr.* [*Lib.*] 29.6) that successful gladiators in the arena were so rewarded: J. may simply be making a not uncommon joke, the transference of battle-imagery to the bedroom.

22. The scholiast points out, very sensibly, that the mother-in-law fakes illness in order to give her daughter a good excuse for frequent visits: the adulterous meetings take place in the mother-in-law's house. This passage would not require a note were it not for the fact that some modern scholars seem to believe that it is the *daughter* who feigns illness: a Kaufman and Hart notion hardly (one would have thought) conducive to peaceful infidelity. For a sensible examination of the evidence see Courtney 288.

23. Courtney (289) finds this passage difficult and its sense hard to grasp, arguing that 'the most obvious interpretation is that a woman is behind every case that comes to court'. But more obvious, surely, is J.'s ultra-masculine distaste, exhibited again and again (see n. 15 above, ad fin.), for women who in any way (as here) move into a men's preserve, or (in his opinion) usurp proper male prerogatives, putting husbands (in particular) at a disadvantage.

24. On female mud-wrestling see Reinmuth. The Floralia, or Festival of Flowers, took place between 28 April and 3 May. Games were held and farces performed: as Duff delicately puts it, 'custom sanctioned unusual freedoms on the part of the actresses'. Prostitutes played a large part in the proceedings, and some of the ritual – clearly of the old ithyphallic fertility-cult variety – was described as 'most improper'. Trumpets were blown at the beginning of all public shows.

25. Two types of gladiatorial equipment are described here: (i) the armour of those fighters known as 'Samnites': sword-belt or baldric, metal armlets, plumed or crested helmet, a greave on the left leg only; and (ii) Thracian: full armour, with greaves on both legs. See Ferguson 195, Courtney 291.

26. For Metellus see n. 17 to Sat. III. The Aemilii Lepidi were a most distinguished Roman family who produced numbers of statesmen (including the Triumvir). The Fabii were one of the most ancient patrician *gentes*, tracing their ancestry back to Hercules and the Arcadian Evander: 'Gut' Fabius, so named because of his youthful gourmandizing, was Q. Fabius Maximus Gurges, Consul in 292 and 276 BC, and Leader of the Senate (*princeps senatus*). Courtney (292) notes that in J.'s day both Fabii and Metelli were extinct.

27. Quintilian – M. Fabius Quintilianus (AD *c.* 35–*c.* 100) – was a Spanish rhetorician, educated in Rome, and appointed Professor of Latin Rhetoric by Vespasian (cf. n. 9 above). He is best known from his surviving work, the *Institutio Oratoria*, composed after his retirement in AD 90. The 'pat excuse' is the *color*, a frequent technical term among the rhetoricians for any approach that would present an action in the most favourable possible light.

Smith (332) remarks that at 275–6 'love and trust are . . . considered ignoble; a trusting husband is a miserable worm'. Cf. n. 15 above, ad fin.

28. There is a highly obscure allusion here. In 281 BC the Romans sent an embassy to Tarentum, the rich Greek foundation in S. Italy, to complain of various outrages the Tarentines had been guilty of; the ambassador was insulted during a Dionysiac festival (hence 'wine-flown and garlanded') by a drunk in the theatre, who befouled his robe. 'It will,' said the ambassador, 'take much blood to clean'; and since the Tarentines called in King Pyrrhus of Epiros to help them, it did. The other cities mentioned all, like Tarentum itself, were, or had been, famous for wealth and luxury: Sybaris (hence 'sybaritic') in the instep of Italy; Rhodes, the powerful maritime island republic of the E. Mediterranean; Miletus, the chief port of Ionia and at the head of a caravan route into Asia.

29. The Bona Dea, or 'Good Goddess', was said to be either the daughter or wife of the Roman deity Faunus. Her worship, which appears to have been a mystic and orgiastic fertility cult, was strictly reserved for women. Men were not even supposed to know her real name. Her sanctuary – alluded to here – was a grotto on the Aventine. Her festival was celebrated annually on 4 December in the house of the consul or praetor, since the offerings made then were on behalf of the Roman people as a whole, and (theoretically at least) promoted their welfare. During the ceremony no male could enter the building, and all male images had to be covered. It began with a sacrifice, and included dancing and the drinking of wine (which was referred to throughout as 'honey'). It generally took place at night.

30. 'Saufeia' and 'Medullina' are names carefully chosen as representative of ancient Roman families. The latter was a family name of the Gens Furia; Claudius' first fiancée was called Livia Medullina Camilla.

31. It is hard to tell throughout this passage how far J. is giving a slanted and prejudiced account of a genuine – if by his day somewhat debased – ceremony, and how far what he says is mere malicious invention. But the details seem genuine enough: we may also note that women were required to prepare for the occasion by a period of sexual abstinence, which gives more point to J.'s climax.

Cato of Utica (M. Porcius Cato Uticensis) nursed an implacable hostility to Julius Caesar, culminating in his characteristically Stoic-style suicide after the battle of Thapsus in 46 BC. Cicero's pamphlet in his praise was countered by not one, but two, protracted rebuttals by Caesar, the 'anti-Catonian pamphlets'. See Ferguson 199. Courtney (300–301) points out that J.'s animadversions on the supposed length of Clodius' penis could mean either that it was twice the size of Caesar's text, or (an interpretation I prefer) that the text itself took up two whole rolls (*volumina*), and 'that the penis was longer than these placed end to end'.

32. Publius Clodius profaned the ceremony of the Bona Dea in December 62 BC, when it was being held in Caesar's house. Caesar's wife Pompeia (to complicate matters) was Clodius' current mistress. This triggered off a sizable political crisis; it also adds to J.'s image of the 'two anti-Catonian pamphlets'. Clodius was brought to trial, but got off by bribing the jurors.

The following 34 lines, the so-called 'O[xford] Passage', were first discovered in a unique Bodleian MS in 1899, and have been much discussed since (see Introduction, pp. lxi–lxiii ff.). They were inserted after line 365, where they seem singularly out of place. For many years I had thought that the logical point for their introduction was after line 345, and was therefore encouraged, when Griffith (104–14) made precisely the same recommendation, to transfer them in my translation. Since then Luck (217 ff.) has also come out in favour of this repositioning.

This is not the place to discuss, yet again, the problem of their authenticity. Like Ferguson, however, I feel strongly that 'if J. did not write them we have to posit another satirist of like temper and equal genius'. Courtney (304) also finds them genuine. For general discussion since Griffith, see G. Laudizi, *Il Frammento Winstedt* (Lecce: 1982), and G. Mohilla, *Juvenals Oxford-Verse 6, O1–34: Neu-Interpretation im Rahmen von Studien zur Kompositionstechnik seiner Satiren* (diss. Vienna: 1990). The best-articulated arguments against authenticity are to be found in Anderson (266–8) and Willis (1997: 441 ff.).

33. Courtney (305–6) makes surprisingly heavy weather of the sexual allusions here. References to anything suggestive of an unclean mouth (*os impurum*) by definition are based on the assumption of oral sex, *fellatio*. The nicknames given these two *cinaedi* indicate which gender they prefer: women for 'La Courgette' (*colocyntha*, an obvious symbol for the erect penis); men for 'The Bearded Cowrie' (*barbata chelidon*, the vagina and surrounding pubic hair). The first uses his tongue for penetration; the second offers his mouth in lieu of a cunt.

34. The *lanista* was the director and trainer of a gladiatorial school. There is no precise equivalent in English without a cumbersome periphrasis.

35. Thaïs was the famous Athenian courtesan, mistress of Ptolemy I; Triphallus (as the name suggests: 'Triplecock' would be an approximation) was a title of Priapus, and also the name of a play by Naevius. This passage introduces (O 27 ff.) a sudden apostrophe of the crypto-adulterer, the king in queen's robes. But who makes it? Courtney (308–9) thinks that the entire passage, down to O 34, is spoken by the (unintroduced) husband. Others take the lines to be spoken by the poet, *in propria persona*. But this has difficulties. The sense of the passage makes it far more likely that the husband's speech ends in line O 29, and I punctuate accordingly.

36. J.'s belief in this section, clearly, is that eunuchs castrated when full grown can enjoy a normal sex-life, minus the risk of impregnation. Courtney, however (309), cites evidence indicating that this is true, at most, for a year or eighteen months after the operation, after which the ability to achieve erection is largely lost. But since the thrust of J.'s argument (not least at 376–7) depends on penetration, one has to ask just how invariable such caveats in fact are (or, *per contra*, how far J. believed popular fantasies).

37. In AD 86 Domitian restored the great temple on the Capitol. To celebrate this he founded 'a festival of music, horsemanship and gymnastics, to be held every five years, and awarded far more prizes than is customary nowadays. The festival included Latin and Greek public-speaking contests, competitions for choral singing to the lyre and for lyre-playing alone, besides the usual solo singing to lyre accompaniment . . .' (Suet. *Dom.* 4). The prizes were oakleaf wreaths, and the competition lasted without interruption until the 5th c. AD.

38. Janus is here appealed to as the oldest indigenous Italian deity, in some sense senior even to Jupiter. He was variously regarded as a sky-god or a door-spirit (Ferguson 202–3), and hence of the year's opening. He was portrayed as looking both forward and back.

39. Trajan invaded Armenia in AD 113 and Parthia, probably, in 116. In November 115 a bright comet was visible in Rome, and a month later there was a great earthquake at Antioch (Dio Cass. 68.24–5). Highet (12–13) concludes from this that Satire VI was composed and published at some time fairly soon after 116, and that these are the events which J. makes his gossip allude to.

40. The whole point is that Niphates was a mountain, not a river: in fact, the highest range in the Taurus, rising to over 10,000 feet, and the source of the R. Tigris (Strabo 11.12.4, C.522, 11.14.8, C.529). The lady, with typical (J. alleges) feminine inaccuracy, fails to get her geography right. (On the other hand both Lucan, 3.245, and Silius Italicus, 13.765, make the same mistake, so perhaps J.'s pleasant effect here is unintentional.)

41. At line 415 I accept Duff's ingenious emendation *experrecta*, based on the scholium to line 417: this suggests that the true reading was ousted by a gloss, *exorta*, which was then changed, for metrical reasons, to *exortata*.

42. Till I read Courtney's note (317) I assumed that J. here was simply presenting a picture of vulgar excess and lack of self-restraint. I still think that this element predominates. But Courtney cites evidence to show, not only that hot baths were take specifically in order to sharpen the appetite (Columella 1 *praef.* 16, Sen. *Ep.* 15.3, 122.6, Plut. *Moral.* 734a), but also that large quantities of wine were drunk – *and then regurgitated* – with the same object (Plin. *NH* 14.139, 29.26; Athen. 15.665e; Sen. *Dial.* 1.3.13, 12.10.3, *Ep.* 95.21).

43. Eclipses of the moon were supposed to be caused by witchcraft: the witch's incantations, perhaps reinforced by the magic bird-wheel, or *iynx*, would torture and diminish the moon unless such a din was created that the spells were inaudible. The moon's waxing was not only connected in the popular mind with menstruation, but also regarded in itself as a kind of pregnancy. The beating on pots and pans (cf. Livy 26.5.9) also acted as an apotropaic against evil spirits. Witches were supposed to be able to 'call down' the moon, and obtain a curious magical foam from it.

44. Both these activities symbolize masculine status. Silvanus, a vague and numinous deity of all wild land beyond the tillage, was exclusively worshipped by men. The 'penny baths' were where men went; it is not certain whether women merely paid more (or less, or nothing). When there was only one bath-house, women used it in the morning; in some cases (Vitruv. 5.10.1) they had an adjacent establishment heated by the same system. Mixed bathing was known, but banned by Hadrian: see Ferguson 204.

45. At lines 454–5 I read, and punctuate, as follows: . . . *antiquaria versus:* / *haec curanda uiris. opicae*, etc. Housman is responsible for the full stop after *uiris; haec* (in my opinion an almost certain emendation for *nec*) was picked up by Postgate from one of Ruperti's MSS. See now Courtney 321.

46. Reading *educat* with Housman and Courtney for the MSS's *educit*.

47. Sicilian tyrants had a reputation for arbitrary despotism and outlandish cruelty: the most notorious was Phalaris of Acragas (6th c. BC), on whom see Sat. VIII 81–2 and note ad loc. For the habitual cruelty of Roman ladies to their maids, see Ovid *Am.* 1.14.16, *AA* 3.239, Mart. 2.66.

48. Temples, that of Isis in particular, were notorious for the assignations arranged in their precincts: cf. Sat. IX 22–4.

49. The description makes clear (what line 492 had already suggested) that the hairstyle is that (somewhat grotesque) arrangement of curls on a tall wire frame briefly popular under the Flavians, but obsolete by J.'s own day: several surviving statues reproduce it faithfully.

50. I strongly suspect that line 511 has been cobbled together, and covers a considerable omission. The break in the sense is violent; we pass, with no real or logical transition, from the portrait of the sadistic mistress to that of a superstitious lady, rather akin to the *Superstitious Man* of Theophrastus. What is more, we appear to come in on it in the middle, where she is being visited by a series of quacks and diviners such as turn up in Aristophanes' Cloud-Cuckooland.

51. Bellona (cf. Sat. IV 124 and note ad loc.) was originally a native Roman war-goddess; but by Imperial times her worship had been syncretized with that of the Cappadocian mother-goddess Ma. Cybele, the great mother-goddess of Anatolia, whose main shrine was at Pessinus in Phrygia, was also known as the Idaean or Dindymenian Mother; her cult was officially brought to Rome in 205/4 BC (see n. 17 to Sat. III), together with that of her young consort Attis. The great spring festival, from 15–28 March, was probably developed after Claudius' day, and it seems to be this which is alluded to here.

52. The scholiast points out that this descent into the river took place after intercourse with a man. Courtney 328: 'Bathing in flowing water in the morning to wash away the pollutions of the night . . . was one of the normal purifications even in Roman ritual before prayer and sacrifice.'

53. Io was originally the daughter of a river-god, and (like many such) impregnated by Zeus, who turned her into a white cow to protect her from the wrath of Hera: in this guise she wandered to Egypt. As early as Herodotus' day she was identified with Isis (Hdt. 2.41). Isis too had wandered after the death of Osiris, and, as a

moon-goddess, was depicted with cow-like crescent horns. The assimilation is understandable.

54. The site of the Isaeum in the Campus Martius has been identified. So, more strikingly still, has the great temple of Isis on the Ethiopian island of Meroë, far up the Nile: it is clear, then, that what J. says here is no rhetorical exaggeration. For evidence of Greek and Roman pilgrimages to Meroë see Highet, 242–3. Sleeping in shrines (*incubatio*) in the hope of being vouchsafed a divine epiphany as a dream (530–31) was a regular feature of the worship of Isis (Diod. Sic. 1.25; Courtney 329 with further reff.; Ferguson 208). The use of lustral water (528–9) is also well attested: Apul. *Met.* 11.20, Vitruv. 8 *praef.* 4.

55. The priests of Isis shaved their heads and wore white linen robes: a famous wall-painting from Herculaneum illustrates this. The dog-headed (or sometimes jackal-headed) Egyptian minor deity Anubis was an attendant of Isis who helped her embalm the dead Osiris. He was often identified, as Guide of the Dead (*psychopompos*), with Hermes or Mercury. The lament for Osiris celebrated his death at the hands of Set, and his subsequent resurrection: the *mythos* carried a powerful eschatological message.

56. Abstention from intercourse was another regular feature of Isis-worship: Courtney 331 with reff. The goose was sacred to both Isis and Priapus: perhaps, given the nature of the offence, J. also had this second connection in mind.

57. On the Jewish squatters in Egeria's grove, see Sat. III 14–16 and note ad loc. This could be enough (*pace* Courtney) to explain 'the tree's high priestess'; but D. S. Wiesen, *CJ* 76 (1980) 4–20, ingeniously suggests that what, in representation, was misinterpreted as a background tree was in fact the seven-branched menorah. Other (less cogent) speculations in Courtney (332–3).

58. Ammon was originally the god of Thebes in Egypt. His fame in Hellenistic and Roman times was almost entirely bound up with his oracle in the oasis at Siwah, in Cyrene, which came to rival the oracles of Delphi or Dodona – especially after it was consulted by Alexander, who may have gone there in the hope of being acknowledged as a god. Delphi, in fact, was enjoying something of a revival in J.'s day, though primarily through private rather than official consultations. Its final end seems only to have come in the time of Julian the Apostate.

59. Lines 558–9 are omitted by several of the best MSS and not commented on by the scholiast; they are certainly J.'s, but seem out of place here, where the sense would run more smoothly if the text read '. . . more than once. Nothing . . .' etc. The astrologer in question was called either Ptolemaeus or Seleucus; the 'great citizen' whom Otho feared was the future brief-lived Emperor Galba. It seems that Ptolemaeus switched allegiance from one to the other with considerable dexterity – as anyone of his calling must have needed to do, not once but several times, in the 'Year of the Four Emperors' (AD 69).

60. The wife is given the sobriquet 'Tanaquil' (an Etruscan name) after the wife of Tarquinius Priscus, whose skill in magic and fortune-telling enabled her to learn the destiny of Servius Tullius. She was also (and this point will not have been lost on J.) 'an aristocratic young woman who was not of a sort to put up with humbler circumstances in her married life than those she had been previously accustomed to' (Livy 1.34). Courtney (336, citing Sen. fr. 79) argues that Tanaquil is mentioned, ironically, 'as the pattern of a good wife'.

61. Petosiris was joint author, with Nechepso, of an astrological teatise composed about 150 BC or a little later. The two names may be a double pseudonym for one author. The treatise is supposed to have been the first to give the signs of the zodiac their astrological significance. See Plin. *NH* 2.88, 7.60.

62. The *poppysma* ('much smacking of lips') was a sound made with the lips to avert the evil eye or similar maleficent influences (Plin. *NH* 28.25, Mart. 7.18.11): it may still be heard today in the '*po-po-po*' of a Greek peasant woman when she is told bad news. Perhaps the implication here is that the fortunes given were, on the whole, far from flattering. For the Circus Maximus as a haunt of fortune-tellers see Livy 39.16.8, Cic. *De Div.* 1.132. It was also a prostitutes' beat: see Sat. III 64–5 and note ad loc. On the Embankment, that 'defensive earthwork between the Esquiline and Colline Gates' (Ferguson 211), see Sat. V 153. The 'dolphin columns' were used to indicate the number of laps run in a chariot-race (Dio Cass. 49.43.2).

63. Courtney (342) adduces evidence (Lucretius 4.1026 and several papyrological texts) to demonstrate that it was at latrines or on dunghills that these children were abandoned; but the evidence favouring cisterns is also considerable (Sen. *Ep.* 36.2, Prop. 2.23.2; other reff. in Courtney ad loc.) and on balance I prefer it. The Latin term *lacus* is ambiguous.

64. Thessalian women had a notorious reputation throughout antiquity for skill in magical arts of every sort: authors from Euripides to Lucian mention their uncanny powers. See in particular Plin. *NH* 30.6, Lucan 6.420 ff., Lucian *Dial. Mer.* 4.

65. My translation omits 614A–C, lines not in most MSS (including the most reliable). As Ferguson reminds us (212), even when 'they do appear, they are in different places and twice in the margin'. While not as convinced as Courtney (343) that they are non-Juvenalian, I agree that they are quite out of place here. For the reader's convenience I append a translation of them:

> . . . you aren't forever carrying water to cracked jars, forever
> > lugging that burden in pitchers that are leaky themselves,
> > > maddened by which you [Caligula] proved not our king, but a Phalaris.

As Housman saw, *CR* 15 (1901) 265–6, there is a *non sequitur* here: why should water, however leaky, madden? He substituted *peius* for *istud*, a makeshift way of getting the phrase to apply to the lethal aphrodisiac mixed by Caesonia (616–17). Even so, the passage remains unsatisfactory (though I am not so bothered as some by J., or whoever wrote these lines, sardonically referring to Caligula as 'our king').

66. Nero's uncle was the emperor Caligula. 'He was well aware,' Suetonius tells us

(*Cal.* 50) 'that he had mental trouble . . . Caesonia [his wife] is reputed to have given him an aphrodisiac which drove him mad.'

67. Claudius was poisoned with a dish of mushrooms prepared by his wife Agrippina, though the details of his death are confused, and Suetonius (*Claud.* 44) lists several variant accounts. For his physical peculiarities see *Claud.* 30 and Sen. *Apoc.* 5. After his posthumous deification, Nero, with more wit than he usually displayed, made a habit of describing mushrooms as the food of the gods (Suet. *Claud.* 44, *Nero* 33, Dio Cass. 60.35; cf. Ferguson 212).

68. Pontia's case was something of a *cause célèbre* during Nero's reign. According to the scholiast she was Petronius' daughter, and poisoned her children after her father had lost his life as a result of the 'Conspiracy of Piso'; on conviction she committed suicide by opening her veins after a sumptuous banquet – exactly as Petronius himself had done. Father-fixation, Freudians might say, could scarcely go further. See Mart. 2.34.6, 4.43.5, 6.75. Her identity has been disputed (see Courtney 346); but Gilbert Bagnani, *Arbiter of Elegance* (Toronto: 1954), Excursus vi, 'Pontia the Poisoner', while facing the considerable problems involved, concludes that a daughter of the Arbiter, born *c.* AD 60, is still the likeliest candidate (86–8). I would agree.

69. Medea and Procne were both familiar instances from mythology of mothers who killed their children – but both, as J. emphasizes, acted out of passion: Medea to avenge Jason's desertion, Procne because her husband Tereus had raped her sister Philomela, and then cut out her tongue to prevent her telling. In each case, interestingly, we see what we would think of as psychological displacement: why go for the children rather than the erring adults themselves?

70. Alcestis is familiar to us from Euripides' play of that name; she was the wife of Admetus of Pherae in Thessaly, and volunteered to die on his behalf, an offer which he willingly accepted. Later Heracles found Admetus grieving for his dead wife, and successfully forced either Hades or the incarnation of Death, Thanatos, to give Alcestis back. J.'s scepticism notwithstanding, some real-life wives *did* vow their own life in return for that of their husbands: Courtney 347 with reff., including epitaphs.

71. The Danaïds, daughters of Danaüs, killed their husbands; so did Eriphyle; so did Clytemnestra. This is the only reason J. has for bracketing their names together in this context. Clodia (see line 8 and n. 1) was described, we recall, as a 'two-bit Clytemnestra': this was for murdering her husband Metellus. The reference provides a satisfying top-and-tail to a poem not otherwise notable (*pace* Anderson) for tightly organized structure.

72. The anecdote by which Mithridates VI, King of Pontus (*c.* 120–63 BC) is best known – his diet of prophylactics which made him immune to poison – has been immortalized in a poem by A. E. Housman (*A Shropshire Lad*, lxii). See App. *Mithr.* 111–12, Dio Cass. 37.14, Plin. *NH* 25.5.

I have some sympathy, apropos this final tirade against murderous spouses, with

Braund's comment (84): 'The inconsistency of his argument betrays a man desperately seeking to make a case . . . [I]t is evident that the only person out of control here is the speaker himself.'

SATIRE VII

Useful General Studies

Anderson	Anderson, W. S., *Essays on Roman Satire* (Princeton: 1982) ch. xii, 'The programs of Juvenal's later books', 285–8.
Bellandi	Bellandi, F., 'Giovenale e la degradazione della clientela (interpretazione della sat. VII), *Dial. di Arch.* 8 (1974/5) 384–437.
Braund	Braund, S., *Beyond Anger: A Study of Juvenal's Third Book of Satires* (Cambridge: 1988) ch. 2, 'Satire 7: Irony, a double-edged sword', 24–68.
Hardie	Hardie, A., 'Juvenal and the condition of letters: the seventh satire', *Papers of the Leeds International Latin Seminar*, vol. 6 (Leeds: 1990) 145–209.
Jones	Jones, F. M. A., 'Juvenal Satire VII' in *Studies in Latin Literature and Roman History* V, ed. C. Deroux (Brussels: 1989) 444–64.
Kilpatrick	Kilpatrick, R. S., 'Juvenal's patchwork satires, 4 and 7', *YClS* 23 (1973) 235–41.
Rudd	Rudd, N., *Lines of Enquiry: Studies in Latin Poetry* (Cambridge: 1976) ch. 4, 'Tone: Poets and patrons in Juvenal's seventh satire', 84–118.
Vioni	Vioni, G., 'Considerazioni sulla settima satira di Giovenale', *RASB* 61 (1972/3) 240–71.
Wiesen	Wiesen, D. S., 'Juvenal and the Intellectuals', *Hermes* 101 (1973) 464–83.

1. There has been much argument as to the identity of this emperor, whom J. does not address by name. It is now generally, and plausibly, agreed that it must have been Hadrian (for a conspectus of alternative theories see Rudd 84–7). The occasion could have been either his accession in AD 117 (each new ruler, it was hoped, would prove a generous patron of the arts), his first appearance in Rome as Emperor (August 118), or, as Highet (236–7) suggests, his subsequent refoundation of the Athenaeum as a literary centre (Aur. Vict. *Caes.* 14.3). This last event will have taken place before 121, when Hadrian left Rome for a lengthy tour of the provinces. Highet also points out that Satire VII 'contains J.'s first dedication to any individual, and his first complimentary reference to any emperor'. J. also has in mind throughout

the example of Horace and *his* patrons, Maecenas and Augustus, the latter idealized in retrospect: Vioni 240 ff. Having in due form named his own emperor as the shining exception to a generally depressing trend – without specifying his acts of largesse, and ignoring him thereafter – J. then moves on to the more satisfying task of lambasting Rome's 'patrons' as a group, for crass and stingy philistinism.

2. The *gallica* was some kind of Gaulish shoe or slipper which left the ankle bare, thus revealing the tell-tale scars imprinted on one of them (*altera*), by the slave-dealer's shackles. In theory (the law had been enacted by Tiberius) three generations of free birth were needed to expunge the stain of prior servile status before aspirations to knighthood ('equestrian' rank) could be entertained; but this requirement was frequently ignored or circumvented (Ferguson 219, Courtney 352). Knighthood and its gold ring could, clearly, be bought by those with enough cash and determination. Cf. Mart. 7.64.2, 10.76.

With all modern editors I omit line 15 ('Although Cappadocian burghers and Bithynians do such things . . .'), since it is clearly out of place here: it may have formed part of an alternative version of the passage, later discarded. Courtney dismisses it as spurious on the grounds of 'clumsy verbosity'; but as Ferguson points out, 'postponed *quamquam* is in J.'s style'.

3. 'Indulgence' (*indulgentia*) had become a technical term for Imperial favour: it occurs regularly in the younger Pliny's letters to Trajan. Hadrian (R. Syme, *Tacitus*, Oxford: 1958, 755–6) was the first to put it on his coins, so the allusion has immediate and topical application. Note, however, that the Emperor's address is represented as being to the young, probably (27) with military epic in mind as good propaganda, whereas the narrator is clearly an older man, with no interest in epic, and therefore on both accounts a bad imperial bet: Braund 24–5.

4. i.e., burn them. The literary periphrasis, in this context, cuts to the bone. (J. in fact gives us a periphrasis within a periphrasis, referring to Vulcan as *Veneris marito*, 'Venus' husband'.)

5. There seems to be an allusion here to the libraries which Augustus and his wife Livia established, respectively, in the temples of Apollo and the Muses on the Palatine. Tiberius and Livia began a third in a 'new temple' dedicated to Augustus: this was formally opened by Caligula (Courtney 355). Hardie (186 ff.) speculates whether J. may not have been alluding to the *Aedes Herculis Musarum*, 'Hercules' shrine of the Muses', founded (?179 BC) by M. Fulvius Nobilior, which united an Ambraciot Greek cult with that of the Italian Muses, the Camenae. Though this shrine was known to have been used for recitations of poetry, and perhaps formed a centre for the College of Poets, testimony is minimal (Hardie has to concede that there is 'no evidence for any benefaction of the Aedes Herculis Musarum by Hadrian'), and Courtney may well be right in his suggestion (355) that J. is simply referring to the poet's renunciation of Apollo and the Muses (i.e. poetry) in favour of a new god in the form of a generous patron.

6. Tacitus *Dial*. 9 contains a slamming attack, put in the mouth of one Marcus Aper

('Mark the Boar'), otherwise unknown, on the whole business of poetry-writing as a full-time occupation. In the course of this he, like J., describes the demeaning details of scraping up an audience, and the expenses involved, since (§§3−4) 'he has to get the loan of a house, to fit up a recital-hall, to hire chairs, and to distribute programmes. And even supposing his reading is a superlative success, in a day or two all the glory of it passes away . . .' (tr. W. Peterson).

At line 42 I accept Jessen's ingenious emendation *porcas* (perhaps *porcos*?) for *portas*.

7. 'Euhoe!' in Latin. The allusion is to Horace's *Odes*, 2.19.5, where he describes the excited cries of the Bacchanals. Horace, having a generous patron, could write poetry under ideal conditions: certainly he never went hungry. Ferguson (221) suggests that the transition to Virgil (below) was via that poet's one use of 'euhoe!' (*Aen*. 7.389), where a Fury drives Amata into the mountains in a state of Bacchic frenzy.

8. See Virgil, *Aen*. 7.445−6: for this episode, the Fury Allecto appeared in a dream to Turnus, and when he mocked her prophecies she 'exploded into blazing anger. And even as he spoke the young prince found his limbs suddenly possessed by a trembling, and his eyes became fixed in a stare; so countless were the snakes which uttered the Fury's hiss, and so horrifying was the apparition which stood revealed . . .' etc.

9. There is a sly allusion here to the story (Suet. *Verg.* 9) that Asinius Pollio, knowing Virgil's tastes, made him a present of a beautiful slave-boy named Alexander, who figures in *Ecl.* 2 as 'Alexis'. See Mart. 8.55 (56).11−16, 5.16.11−12. Courtney (358−9), no reason given, states that J. is 'probably not thinking specially of Alexis'. Cf. Rudd 98−9, Ferguson 221.

10. We expect the indigent playwright to pawn his possessions to continue writing his *Atreus*: instead, J. makes 'Atreus' himself visit the pawnshop. Nothing is known of Numitor or his mistress Quartilla; but Numitor was also the name of an ancient king of Alba (Livy 1.3.10), while Quartilla is best known as the priestess of Priapus in Petronius' *Satyricon* (16 ff.). Domitian, improbably, owned a tame lion (Stat. *Silv.* 2.5).

11. The poet Lucan (Marcus Annaeus Lucanus) was born in Cordoba, Spain, on 3 November AD 39, but spent most of his short life in Rome. His uncle was Seneca, the philosopher: the family had considerable wealth, which is the point of the reference here: 'marbled park' suggests (Courtney 359) that the grass was virtually obliterated by statues. At first an intimate of Nero's, Lucan latterly passed out of Imperial favour: it may have been the veto on his literary activities which led him, in 65, to join the ill-fated 'Conspiracy of Piso', as a result of which he, his father, and both his uncles were forced to commit suicide. He left his epic poem *Pharsalia* (Penguin Classic, tr. Robert Graves) unfinished at the time of his death. J.'s phrasing is cleverly ambiguous: L. is *resting in peace* in his park, but he is also (RIP!) *dead*, a suicidal victim of imperial wrath.

12. Publius Papinius Statius (AD 45−96) was a Neapolitan who settled in Rome, and seems to have been on reasonably friendly terms with Domitian. His 'darling Theban epic', the twelve-book *Thebaid*, took twelve years to compose (AD 82–94), and during this period Statius – like modern writers – gave occasional public recitals of 'work in progress'. He does not appear to have ever been anything like as hard up as J. would have us believe: see A. E. Orentzel, *CB* 52 (1976) 61–2. J., as Ferguson detected (222), deliberately placed the word 'darling' (*amica*, even more ambiguous) at the end of a line, thus leading us to expect an elegy to Statius' mistress rather than an epic. Taking this line further, some critics (notably Braund 60) argue that J. presents Statius, in sub-text, as a literary pimp, selling his 'virgin [*intactam*] libretto' on Agave to Paris as whoremaster.

13. The Paris referred to here was a well-known *pantomimus*, or ballet-dancer, of Domitian's reign, executed in AD 83 for a suspected liaison with Domitian's wife, the empress Domitia. He seems to have been surprisingly popular: Mart. 11.13, Dio Cass. 67.3, Suet. *Dom.* 3.1; cf. Sat. VI, n. 8. 'Paris' was probably a stage-name, since it belonged to another *pantomimus* under Nero (this one too was executed, in 67), and recurs again in the following century (cf. n. 8 to Sat.VI). Military tribunes automatically became equestrians, or 'knights', after six months' service; the practice of appointing honorary tribunes, who were elevated without in fact holding a command, began with Claudius (see Suet. *Claud.* 25, and Plin. *Ep.* 4.4). Martial obtained equestrian status in this manner, perhaps from Titus (3.95.9).

14. The 'December vacation' was the Saturnalia (17–23 December), a riotous carnival during which slaves had temporary licence to act as they pleased, and governed by a kind of 'Lord of Misrule', the *Saturnalicius princeps*.

15. Perhaps not; but as Courtney observes in a shrewd note (362), since historians were more often than not 'aristocratic, retired politicians and the like', this tended not to matter. Livy was the exception that proved the rule. 'J.'s case is weak here.' If his 'thousand pages' is more than a random round figure, he is talking in terms of five 'books' (papyrus rolls), since these ran to about 200 'pages' (*paginae* = columns) each. Livy's *Ab Urbe Condita* contained 142 of these 'books', so the claim is by no means exaggerated.

16. The meaning here might seem straightforward: the speaker is spluttering in his emotional excitement and zeal to make a good case. The scholiast, however, while noting this, also suggests a second possibility: that he is deliberately 'spitting into his bosom' (i.e. the fold of his robe) as an apotropaic gesture against the evil eye, or to avert the jealous attention of Nemesis (perhaps because of his boasting and audacity: cf. Plin. *NH* 28.36). Further evidence in Courtney (364).

17. As both Martial (7.28.6) and Lucian (*Rhet. Praec.* 25) tell us, a lawyer who won a case was entitled to advertise the fact by hanging up palm-branches outside his door. J.'s example, despite his success, still lives in a garret.

18. I now agree with Courtney (366) that the idea of a Roman lawyer represented as a horse-archer (Griffith, 1969 382–3) must be regarded as highly improbable. Not too confidently, I adopt instead the view that both he and Ferguson (224) propose: the statue is in poor repair (one coloured stone eye has fallen out), and the spear, being made of inferior material, but with a heavy head, is sagging.

19. See (Griffith, ibid. 381–2) for the explanation of *slattaria* as 'pirate-style', 'extorted by piracy', on which my translation depends. The gown is indeed obtained by piratical extortion, through bargaining with a desperate prospective client before taking on his case. This practice was well known in Rome, and frowned on by respectable jurists: see Quint. 12.7.11.

Griffith's suggestions can sometimes be highly idiosyncratic. At 129–31, he argues (*Festinat Senex*, Oxford: 1988, 75–7) that what Tongilius took with him to the baths was not a rhino-horn flask, but the beast itself. He does not appear to have been joking. Here, it seems to me, we would be more profitably occupied in looking for one of J.'s characteristic exercises in sexual *double entendre*. The association of horns with erections and cuckoldry was notorious; so was the belief (then as now) that ground-up rhino-horn was a highly potent aphrodisiac.

Line 135 is missing from at least one MS, and bracketed by some scholars: it is certainly both flat and, more to the point, pleonastic.

20. For oratorical contests at Lyons in Gaul see Sat. I 44 and note ad loc.; other reff. to Gallic forensic eloquence collected by Courtney 368 (add Lucian *Apol*. 15), and see esp. Strabo 4.4.2, C.195. Both Gallic and N. African orators are discussed by M. L. Clarke, *Rhetoric at Rome* (London: 1953) 145–6. Both Apuleius and Marcus Aurelius' tutor Fronto were African lawyers.

21. Hannibal's failure to march on Rome after his great victory at Cannae in 216 BC marked a turning-point in the campaign. In fact he did come within sight of Rome five years later (211); but the City legions were waiting for him at the Colline Gate, and after the providential storm J. describes, he retreated (Livy 26.10).

22. The Roman passion for rhetoric is perhaps, more than any other characteristic, calculated to bewilder a modern reader. Public speaking was not only a practical skill but also an art practised for its own sake in the schools, and often kept up afterwards. Many satirists, from Petronius to Juvenal, mock the unreality of the set themes traditionally employed. As Duff remarks, one of the stock exercises was to make attacks on tyrants or panegyrics on tyrannicides: 'It might be supposed that the imperial government would not approve of this practice as a regular part of education; but the tyrant of the schools was too fantastic and unreal a creation to be taken seriously.'

There were two types of stock declamation: (i) the *suasoria*, which, as its name suggests, was an exercise in rhetorical persuasion: how should some famous historical character act in a particular, and generally well-known, crisis? (cf. the example of Sulla given in Sat. I 15–17); and (ii) the *controversia*, where the speaker was given an imaginary narrative situation, reminiscent of Hellenistic fiction – as Ferguson says (225), 'full of adventure, piracy, love and murder' – and had to sort out the rights and wrongs of the case extempore. J.'s examples are typical.

23. For Quintilian see nn. 9 and 27 to Sat. VI. His official salary as Professor of

Rhetoric under Vespasian (Suet. *Vesp.* 18) was 100,000 sesterces per annum, and this was further augmented by a large and lucrative practice at the Bar.

24. J. has an actual case in mind: an ex-praetor and senator, Valerius Licinianus, who was also an excellent rhetorician, but found himself sent into exile after an alleged liaison with a Vestal Virgin. He accepted a Chair of Rhetoric in Sicily under Trajan, and, so Pliny tells us in *Ep.* 4.11.1, began his inaugural lecture with the words: 'What sport you make with men, Fortune: you turn senators into professors, and professors into senators!' The second translation applied, in a sense, to Quintilian, since he received consular honours through the good offices of Domitian's brother-in-law.

25. P. Ventidius [Bassus] was the stock example of the upstart who triumphed over both low birth and adverse circumstances. As a child he was captured at Asculum and exhibited in the triumph of Cn. Pompeius Strabo. He is contemptuously referred to as a 'muleteer' (Aul. Gell. 15.4), but may have been an army contractor. In 43 BC he attained the consulship (see Sat. VIII 148, for another 'muleteer consul'), and in 38 himself celebrated a triumph over the Parthians. He died shortly afterwards.

26. Thrasimachus (or possibly Lysimachus) was, says the scholiast, an Athenian rhetorician who died by hanging. Secundus Carrinas was exiled by Caligula, according to Dio Cassius (59.20.6), for 'making derogatory remarks about tyrants in the gymnasium'; so the practice did have its risks, after all. But Knoche thinks, and I am inclined to agree with him, that something has fallen out of the text after 205, and that the man to whom Athens gave 'nothing but the cup of cold hemlock' must, surely, be Socrates.

27. Line 212 is another of J.'s debunking side-swipes at mythological figures: Achilles' music-master was Chiron, the Centaur, half-man and half-horse. Rufus is unknown, but apparently either a Gaul himself or resident in the province. His 'backwoods' fame was specifically linked with the Allobroges, a tribe that had, notoriously, lent support to Catiline.

28. 'What Songs the Syrens sang,' wrote Sir Thomas Browne, 'or what name Achilles assumed when he hid himself among women, though puzzling questions are not beyond all conjecture.' Another surprising thing about educated Romans is the habit, which they seem to have inherited from Greek Alexandria, of intense fascination with such *recherché* scraps of knowledge. The questions Browne lists are those which Tiberius asked his savants: see Suet. *Tib.* 70. Those who answered such *quaestiones* (ζητήματα in Greek) were known as 'solvers', λυτικοί (Athen. 11.493e, 494a). Courtney (379) proves himself an admirable λυτικός, answering the first two straight off: Anchises' nurse was Tisiphone (schol. ad loc.), and Anchémolus' stepmother a Greek called Casperia (Serv. on *Aen.* 10.388–9). All the questions refer to the *Aeneid*. For Acestes see *Aen.* 1.195 (the gift of wine: quantity not stated) and 5.73 (a mature person: no specific age). One wonders whether J. himself knew the answers, or even, perhaps, assumed that all of them were unanswerable.

29. Rudd (106) puts J.'s final peroration into nice perspective: 'Excellent, but what does this high parental role involve? Simply preventing the little brats from masturbating.' There has been some debate as to the identity of the *uictori* (not specified by J.). One theory is that a gladiator is meant (who received 4–500 sesterces per victory according to his status: Courtney 380 with reff.). For a less plausible solution see F. Davey, *CR* 85 (1971) 11, which has the teacher victorious, by way of the lawcourts (!). But as Ferguson says (230), 'the most obvious reference is to the races'. The teacher will receive per annum what a charioteer – or a gladiator: M. L. Clarke, *CR* 23 (1973) 12 – makes off a single engagement, i.e. 5 *aurei* (gold pieces) or 500 sesterces. On the discrepancy between the expertise of *grammaticus* and his salary, see L. Perelli, *Maia* 25 (1973) 107–12.

Rudd (117–18) also makes a general point of some importance when discussing the causes of the unsatisfactory climate J. describes. There is a shortage of backing for the arts (which in the ancient world were not paying professions). Why should this be so? Rudd lists the vanishing of the old republican aristocracy, the lack of 'rich men with a tradition of patronage behind them'. Hadrian's restrictive foreign policy had reduced the number of careers available in the army. And the punch line: 'At home, security and prosperity had produced too many educated men. Even if they had been willing to take up other, less intellectual, work, there was no guarantee that commerce would absorb them. And so they spent their time in an undignified and often futile quest for patronage.' Rudd claims (n. 57) that this situation 'offers some parallels to that which existed in the seventeenth century'. It surely strikes more nearly home today?

With Sat. VII, as readers will have noted, there comes a change of tone: J.'s savage indignation (*saeua indignatio*) is replaced by ambivalent irony. He is cooler, more dispassionate; as Braund (25) shrewdly points out, even the strike-rate of his angry rhetorical questions is cut right back. The subject-matter – intellectuals, the patron-client relationship – remains much the same: what *has* changed, radically, is the treatment. We sympathize, inevitably, with the maltreated schoolmaster (*grammaticus*); yet at the same time J. contrives to make him look small-minded, pedantic and prurient. Could it be that in this case patron and client deserve each other?

SATIRE VIII

Useful General Studies

Braund	Braund, S., *Beyond Anger: A Study of Juvenal's Third Book of Satires* (Cambridge: 1988) ch. 3, 'Satire 8: moralist or nihilist?', 69–122 (also Appendix, 'The Theme of true Nobility', 122–9).
Fredericks	Fredericks, S. C., 'Rhetoric and Morality in Juvenal's 8th satire', *TAPhA* 102 (1971) 111–32.

1. The only person of this name we can identify from the period is Valerius Ponticus, who was banished during Nero's reign for complicated legal collusion and chicanery in the courts: see Tac. *Ann.* 14.41. It has been supposed that J.'s 'Ponticus' may be fictitious, a mere imaginary recipient of the author's lecture on titled snobbery. I rather doubt this; almost all J.'s characters can be run to earth somewhere, and the fact that we cannot trace some of them is no guarantee (in the fragmentary state of our evidence) that they did not exist. Martial refers several times (3.60, 4.85, 9.19) to a Ponticus, mostly in unflattering terms. Perhaps the unremarkable descendant of 'a noble ancestor who had conquered Pontus' (Courtney 386)? But no specific historical occasion suggests itself, and, as Ferguson (233) says, it's odd that the name does not show up in the old Republican aristocracy (see n. 2 below).

2. During the course of this satire J. brings in the name of almost every distinguished Roman family, including such *gentes* as the Aemilia, Curia, Sulpicia, Valeria, Fabia, Cornelia, Claudia, Junia, Antonia, Sergia and Julia. The Emperor Galba, of the *gens* Sulpicia, boasted that he could trace his family back to Jupiter (Suet. *Galba* 2) and Pasiphaë (a relationship, one might have thought, better hushed up). The Corvini, a branch of the *gens* Valeria, were distinguished nobles under the Empire: see Friedländer's note (1905/1962) 401. J. is not the only writer to lament the falling off of the great aristocratic families: see, e.g., Dio Cass. *Epit.* 62.17.4–5, targeting the Furii, Horatii, Fabii, and others. Most of them in fact, what with the Civil Wars, military service, and random Imperial purges (not to mention homosexuality and other anti-familial trends) were extinct by J.'s day.

At line 7 I read *pontifices posse ac* with Housman: Clausen retains *Coruinum, posthac* and prints lines 6–8 in square brackets as an interpolation.

3. The Fabian *gens* was supposedly descended from Hercules and Vinduna, Evander's daughter. The 'Great Altar' was the *ara maxima* of Hercules, an extremely ancient shrine, between the Circus Maximus and the Tiber, close to the Aemilian Bridge. The title 'Of the Rhône' (*Allobrogicus*) was conferred in 121 BC upon Quintus Fabius Maximus after his defeat of the Allobroges, a Gallic tribe that dwelt between the Rhône and the Isère: cf. Sat. VII 213–14 and note ad loc.

4. L. Aemilius Paulus Macedonicus concluded the Third Macedonian War in 168 BC with the defeat of Perseus: he was responsible for the settlement of Greece. The Cossus here referred to is probably Cn. Cornelius Lentulus Cossus, who in AD 6 defeated the Gaetuli in Africa, earning himself the title 'Gaetulicus'. On Tiberius' accession he was sent to deal with the mutineers in Pannonia: Tacitus says of him that he 'was honoured for poverty patiently endured, followed by great wealth respectably acquired and modestly employed' (*Ann.* 4.44). His colleague in Pannonia was the Drusus referred to here, Tiberius' brother, and the father of both Germanicus and Claudius. All three examples are chosen for combining an illustrious military career with high moral character. Lentulus Cossus was about the only man of distinction to survive friendship with Sejanus (Tac. *Ann.* 6.30; and cf. Sat. X 58 ff.).

5. The joy is for the reintegration and resurrection of Osiris after his murder and dismemberment by the dark god Set: cf. Sat. VI 532–4 with note ad loc. An annual feast in November called Euresis ('Discovery') commemorated both 'the grief of Isis at the loss of the body of Isis and her joy at its recovery' (Courtney 390).

6. Tiberius' son Drusus Caesar had a daughter, Julia, who in AD 33 married a C. Rubellius Blandus. Their son, C. Rubellius Plautus, the great-great-grandson of Augustus, was a man of Stoic principles and considerable moral courage, who could have led a successful revolt against Nero, but preferred to live in loyal retirement. Yet this did not safeguard him: he was finally executed, on Nero's orders, in AD 62. It is generally, and most improbably, supposed that one of these two is under discussion here: for some choice vagaries of interpretation see Highet, 273 n. 7. But J.'s whole point is that the man whom he is addressing is a nobody, whose blood is his one claim to distinction. Duff (293), as so often, hits the mark exactly when he writes: 'Rubellius Blandus is taken as a type of noble birth and nothing more . . . Juvenal must mean one of this family, possibly a son or brother of Rubellius Plautus.' In any case, we have here 'a remarkable instance of the way in which Juvenal represents long-dead . . . characters as alive' (Courtney 391).

7. For the 'Embankment' see n. 16 to Sat. V: the weaving-women, we recall, had fortune-tellers and performing monkeys as their companions. Cf. Sat. VI 588 and n. 62 ad loc.

8. i.e. on the eastern and western frontiers of the Empire, the Euphrates and the Rhine.

9. A Herm was a quadrangular pillar of stone, topped by the head of the god Hermes: such pillars stood at most street corners and outside many private houses in Athens. Most of them (as J.'s readers would be well aware) were equipped with large erect phalluses, and the implication as regards this degenerate representative of the nobility is clear enough. The epithet 'scion of Trojans' is several times used by J., and always in the same sarcastically pejorative context: see Sat. I 100, and XI 95. It is the equivalent to our 'coming over with the Conqueror', and alludes, of course, to the settlement by Aeneas.

10. Braund, CQ 31 (1981) 221–3, points out that J. has the crowd in the Circus greet race-track victories in terms (*feruet*) which suggest a boiling cauldron.

11. Phalaris was tyrant of Acragas (Agrigento) in Sicily, *c.* 570–554 BC. He is mainly remembered today for two things: (i) the hollow brazen bull in which he is said to have roasted his victims alive, a habit reminiscent of the Moloch cult, and one, as the early 19th-c. liberal historian George Grote put it, 'better authenticated than the nature of the story would lead us to presume' (*A History of Greece*, 1888 edn, iv.65); and (ii) his supposed letters, which that great Augustan textual critic Richard Bentley, in a memorable dissertation, showed to be forgeries by some late Sophist, perhaps a contemporary of Lucian.

12. One of these was Cossutianus Capito, who in AD 57, as Tacitus tells us (*Ann.* 13.33), 'was indicted by the Cilicians . . . This vicious and disreputable man believed he could behave as outrageously in his province as in Rome.' He was, nevertheless,

condemned for extortion and went into banishment. The other is only referred to as 'Tutor', and cannot be identified with certainty, though the name is unusual.

13. There is a neat, and sinister, *double entendre* here. The wretched native's boat-fare may be his passage to Rome; but the phrase would also (*pace* Courtney 399) automatically suggest the coin due to Charon for passage across the Styx to the afterworld.

14. Cn. Cornelius Dolabella was Governor of Cilicia in 80/79 BC, with Verres as his Legate. In 78 Dolabella was prosecuted for extortion in his province, and condemned. Another Dolabella was similarly charged with extortion in Macedonia, by Julius Caesar, in 77; and in 43 yet a third, P. Cornelius Dolabella, the most vicious of them all, was murdered after wholesale extortions in Asia Minor (hence I am inclined to read *Dolabellae* in the plural at 105, and to scan the line by hiatus). The Antonius referred to here is not Mark Antony, but his uncle, C. Antonius Hybrida, whom Duff (300), scarcely exaggerating, describes as 'a monster of rapacity'. Caesar brought charges against him in 77/6 for extortion in Greece (in 84, as one of Sulla's officers); he was finally exiled in 59 for plundering Macedonia, where he had been Governor in 62. For Verres see n. 7 to Sat. III.

15. Clausen brackets lines 111−12 as an interpolation: this seems unnecessary.

16. Marius Priscus (not Gaius Marius) was prosecuted jointly by Tacitus and the Younger Pliny for extortion in North Africa, and sentenced to banishment from Rome and Italy, AD 100: see Plin. *Ep.* 2.11. He is the governor referred to in Sat. I 49.

17. Clausen brackets line 124 as an interpolation: it is, to be sure, a striking pleonasm, but here I agree once more with Duff (301), who observes acutely of J. that 'it is quite in his manner to repeat in an epigrammatic form exactly what he has just said', and who, in his note on VIII 258, has the last word on the 'interpolation theory': '. . . the line is weak in itself . . . but that Juvenal had better not have written it, is no proof that he did not.' Even a classic may nod. Cf. now Courtney 403.

18. 'Leaves from the Sibyl's book' were oracular utterance and therefore unquestioned truth. Her sayings, inscribed on palm-leaves, were preserved in the Capitol, and consulted by the Sacred College (*quindecemviri*). Cf. n. 1 to Sat. III.

19. Picus, the 'Woodpecker King', was originally a woodpecker *tout court*, sacred to Mars, but afterwards became translated into one of the early Italian kings, son of Saturn and father of Faunus. The Titans and Prometheus, though not Roman in origin, are suggested as providing a more secure genealogy. J. recurs to the dubious origins of Rome's native nobility in the last lines of this satire.

20. It is generally agreed that this was Plautius Lateranus, who narrowly escaped execution in AD 48 for adultery with Messalina, lost his senatorial rank, was restored to it by Nero in 56, and perished through his implication in the 'Conspiracy of Piso' (AD 65): Tacitus confirms that he was of 'big build'. But there are difficulties. Plautius Lateranus was executed while still consul-designate; J.'s character is clearly in office. Also, Tacitus makes it clear that Plautius Lateranus joined the plot from

patriotic motives; since J. disliked Nero intensely it is hard to see why he picked out one of that emperor's opponents for ridicule unless he considered driving one's own gig to be a worse crime – which he just conceivably may have done, or have affected to do as a paradoxical joke: see Sat. I 61 and VIII 220 ff. As Courtney says (406, cf. 29) it may have been undignified (and, one might add, a social misdemeanour) but was 'hardly the moral scandal J. considers it': the joke explanation is the most satisfying.

The alternative candidate is T. Sextius Lateranus, Consul in AD 94; he is generally excluded because of the specific reference to Nero at line 170–71. But the Emperor he served under was Domitian; and Domitian was often spoken of as a second Nero (Nero's original name was Lucius Domitius Ahenobarbus), by J. (Sat. IV 38) among others (e.g. Mart. 11.33). It is impossible to make a clear decision in favour of either Lateranus, though my own inclination, on balance, is towards the second.

We may note that J. is fond of caricaturing the decadence of latter-day aristocrats by means of arresting functional oxymora: here, 'muleteer Consul'; later (198–9) 'Emperor-harpist' and 'comic-lead nobleman'. See Fredericks 116–17.

21. Epona is called, by the scholiast, 'the goddess of muleteers': modern research suggests that she was a Gallic nature-deity specially associated with horses, asses and mules. See Highet (273 n. 4) and reff. there cited.

22. Something is clearly amiss with the text of 159–62. Line 160 looks like a doublet of 159, and is omitted by some MSS; but it makes sense of a sort as it stands. Housman thought a line had dropped out after 160. Lines 161–2 read better with 160 omitted: otherwise 161 needs the insertion of *et* after *adfectu* to make it read smoothly (see Helmbold, *Mnemosyne* 4/5, 1952, 226 f.), and there is the likelihood that more may have dropped out after 162: perhaps a line with a definite verb describing the activities of the barmaid Cyane (which even as they stand convey an obvious sexual *double entendre*). The reader should be warned that the sense here is admissible, but no more than approximate.

23. This looks like a cynical sideswipe at Stoic theories of equality.

24. The precise identity of this Damasippus (a name used by the Iunii and the Licinii) is unknown; the gentleman was probably chosen here, like Lentulus (who must have been one of the noble Lentuli Cornelii) as a typical patrician wastrel. Catullus was not the famous lyric poet, but a popular farce-writer under Nero: cf. Sat. XIII 111. The '*Ghost*' (*Phasma*) must have been very like the *Mostellaria* of Plautus, which was based on a Greek original of this name. '*The Crucified Bandit*' described the life of a famous highwayman called Laureolus, and his execution: it had become a perennial favourite as early as Caligula's reign. Suetonius (*Cal.* 57) says that 'the leading character . . . had to die while escaping, and vomit blood'; but Martial (7.4) clearly alludes to his crucifixion – while describing a real-life criminal who played the part, and at the end of the play was crucified in earnest . . .

25. Line 192 has a rare puzzle in the phrase *sua funera*, variously rendered as 'their dead selves' (Duff) or 'their (sc. distinguished) dead, i.e. ancestry, not death or moral suicide' (Quincey, in Coffey 1963/8, 193) or 'the "stage-deaths" of those who appeared in a notorious mime' (Griffith, in Coffey). The various theories are now analysed by Courtney (412−13) who suspects the text, and tentatively suggests reading *uerbera* for *funera*. I agree with Ferguson (242) that the ambiguities are almost certainly deliberate; but I believe that J. may have been primarily thinking of aristocratic degradation (or ruin, or fall). His (to us) somewhat heated feelings about well-bred persons appearing on the stage, especially in a professional capacity, is confirmed in detail by Tacitus, *Ann.* 14.20−21, *passim*. For Nero's pressurizing in this field see *Ann.* 14.14.10: '. . . he brought on to the stage members of the ancient nobility whose poverty made them corruptible. They are dead, and I feel I owe it to their ancestors not to name them' − a reticence which J. clearly did not share.

26. The descendant of the Gracchi who appeared as a *retiarius* or net-man in the arena was obviously notorious: we have already met him in Sat. II 143 ff., and previously as a homosexual 'bride'. Colin (1955/6) argues persuasively that the *galerus* worn by Gracchus was in fact the tall bonnet of a Salian priest, which, with a blasphemous flourish, he retained for his gladiatorial activities. I have translated in accordance with this interpretation. Cf. now Courtney 415−16.

27. Seneca, the wealthy Spanish Stoic *littérateur*, had been Nero's tutor, and was in a highly influential position at the outset of his reign. He committed suicide after the unmasking of the 'Conspiracy of Piso' (AD 65): some of those involved had hoped to make him emperor (Tac. *Ann.* 15.65). His public conduct, notoriously, was much at odds with his high moral precepts.

The traditional penalty for parricide was that the culprit, after scourging, should be sewn in a sack with a dog, a cock, a snake and a monkey: the sack was then thrown into the sea (*Digest* 48.9.9). Nero's victims included his mother, his aunt Domitia Lepida (Suet. *Nero* 34), his adoptive sister Antonia, Britannicus, and his wife Octavia. His epic poem on the Fall of Troy was recited at the literary festival he founded in AD 65; his tour of Greece as a concert artiste took place in 67/8, and he brought home no fewer than 1,808 crowns of victory (see below, n. 29).

28. The witty, and unexpected, *diminuendo* effect of this catalogue may well have inspired De Quincey's famous essay 'Murder considered as one of the Fine Arts', in particular the following: 'If once a man indulges himself in murder, very soon he comes to think little of robbing; and from robbing he comes next to drinking and sabbath-breaking; and from that to incivility and procrastination.'

Orestes' wife was Helen's daughter Hermione: the Neronian parallel was Octavia. The nearest equivalent to Electra was Antonia, Claudius' daughter, who was no more than Nero's half-sister, and that only by adoption: nor (Suet. *Nero* 35) is the nature of her death made clear. Claudius and Britannicus were indeed poisoned, according to general belief at the time by Agrippina and Livia respectively (on the first of these cases, see Sat. VI 619−23 and n. 67 ad loc.), but certainty is impossible. For Nero's poetry see Suet. *Nero* 52, Tac. *Ann.* 13.3, 14.16. His epic on Troy (Dio Cass. 62.29, Serv. on Virg. *Aen.* 5.770) took Paris as its hero.

Gaius Julius Vindex, of royal Aquitanian descent, but son of a Claudian senator, rebelled against Nero in AD 68 while legate of Gallia Lugdunensis. He backed Galba for the throne, but was defeated in a great battle at Vesontio. Galba (Servius Sulpicius Galba, ?AD 3–69) was in fact acclaimed Emperor after Nero's death, but was assassinated by the Praetorians, at Otho's instigation, early in 69. What is really surprising is the inclusion in this list of Verginius (L. Verginius Rufus, Consul 63, legate of Upper Germany 67), since it was he who crushed the rebellion of Vindex. He was twice offered, and twice refused, the imperial purple; served as Nerva's colleague in the consulate (97); and was commemorated by both Tacitus and the Younger Pliny (whose tutor he had been) as a figure of outstanding civic loyalty and patriotism.

29. On Nero's Greek concert tour of 67/8, see primarily Dio Cass. 62.14, 63.22, and Suet. *Nero* 19, 21.3, 22.3, 23–4 passim. For his theatricals in general: Dio Cass. 61.9, 62.9–10; Suet. *Nero* 12, 17–18, 20–21. For his colossal statues of himself see Suet. *Nero* 31, Plin. *NH* 34.45. As Fredericks says (129), he 'no longer acts like a Roman at all, but like a perverted Greek' – and we know what J. had to say about *them* (Sat. III 58 ff.).

30. Catiline was a member of the *gens Sergia* (which traced its ancestry back to the Trojans) and Cethegus belonged to a patrician branch of the *gens Cornelia*. Their famous conspiracy took place in 63 BC. The Gauls defeated Rome's armies at the Allia in 390 BC and afterwards sacked and burnt the city. The reference (234) to 'trousered Gauls' recalls that black day – and also reminds the reader of Catiline's dealings with the Allobroges (Sat. VII 214 and note ad loc.).

31. The 'shirt of pitch', or *tunica molesta*, was a punishment reserved, appropriately enough, for those guilty of arson, and probably first applied to the Christians in AD 64, when Nero convicted them of causing the Great Fire of Rome (see Tac. *Ann.* 15.44). The victim was tied to a stake, clad in a shirt impregnated with pitch, tar, resin, and similar combustibles, and turned into a kind of human torch. Cf. Sat. I 155. That some kind of actual garment was worn is also suggested by Martial (4.86.8), who applies the phrase to greaseproof paper used for frying fish in.

32. The Consul of 63 BC referred to here was, of course, Cicero, who was born in Arpinum on 3 January 106, but in fact spent most of his life from childhood onwards in Rome. He was a provincial knight, and the first of his family to hold a high office of State. In November 63 he denounced Catiline in the Senate: the conspirators were executed (a decision which afterwards caused Cicero much trouble, since his opponents never admitted the legality of this step), and Catiline's rebel forces were finally destroyed in the field on 5 January 62.

33. It was Cicero's aristocratic fellow-consul Catulus who acclaimed him 'father of his fatherland' in the Senate (App. *Bell. Civ.* 2.7, Plut. *Cic.* 23).

At line 241 I accept Jahn's emendation *sibi* for the corrupt †*int*† of the MSS, rather than the palaeographically more attractive *ui*, proposed by de Ruyt (*Revue Belge de Philologie* 23, 1944, 246–50): *sibi* balances and contrasts with *illi*, just as *abstulit* does with *contulit*. Octavius, the future Augustus, defeated Antony and Cleopatra at Actium in 31 BC, and Brutus at Philippi in 42.

34. Gaius Marius (157–86 BC) rose rather faster than J. suggests. He was tribune in 119 and praetor in 115; by 107 he held his first consulship (of seven). The invasion by two Germanic tribes, the Cimbri and Teutones, took place in 102. Marius defeated them that year at Aquae Sextiae, and again in 101, together with his colleague Q. Lutatius Catulus, at Vercellae. His acclaim during his triumph was much enhanced by the fact that he was a 'man of the people' and the prospective instrument of democratic reform, whereas Catulus was very much an aristocrat. (On the other hand it was the troops who refused to let Marius triumph unless Catulus shared the honour: Plut. *Mar.* 27.) On the size of the German corpses see Ferguson (245), who reminds us that in fact they were, on average, taller than Italians, and regarded by the Romans as giants (Tac. *Germ.* 20, Plut. *Mar.* 11).

35. P. Decius Mus and his son, of the same name, both gave up their lives in this manner to save a Roman army: the father in 340 BC, while fighting against the Latins, and the son in 295, during the Battle of Sentinum, against the Samnites: see Livy 8.9.8 and 10.28.15. This was a piece of primitive magic, known as *devotio* and accompanied by a *carmen* or spell: see Plin. *NH* 28.12. Here we have the one instance in J.'s satire of a son who actually lives up to his father's reputation.

36. The sons of Brutus, Titus and Tiberius, joined a plot for the restoration of Tarquinius Superbus: their detection (by a slave, Vindicius) and execution – the latter approved and witnessed by their father – is strikingly described by Livy 2.3–6 . Horatius Cocles, the bridge-saver against Lars Porsena, is too well known from Macaulay's *Lays of Ancient Rome* to need further explanation. Gaius Mucius entered the camp of Lars Porsena and made an unsuccessful attempt to assassinate him: on being threatened with torture unless he revealed the whole plot he thrust his right hand into the fire and let it burn, crying, 'See how cheap men hold their bodies when they care only for honour!' Afterwards he was known as 'Scaevola', or 'The Left-handed Man', a title preserved by his descendants (Livy 2.12–13). The same source tells the story of Cloelia, a girl held as hostage by the Etruscans: one day she rallied her fellow-hostages to swim the Tiber under enemy fire, and brought them all safely back to Rome. 'Porsena,' we are told, 'was furious, and sent to Rome to demand Cloelia's return – adding that the loss of the other girls did not trouble him.'

37. The 'kind of ill-famed ghetto' was the Asylum, or sanctuary, which Romulus – 'to help fill his big new town', as Livy says – threw open to every kind of slave, debtor or criminal: '. . . that mob was the first real addition to the City's strength, the first step to her future greatness' (Livy 1.8–9). In other words, a Roman noble's forebears were either shepherds (like Romulus and his first small group) or else fugitive convicts; and thus the initial question, 'What good are family trees?', gets a dusty answer. The clichés that have been paraded throughout on the theme of 'virtue the true nobility' (Braund 122–9 assembles, from Seneca, Plutarch, Pliny,

Statius and others, a quite stunning collection of lofty platitudes, all making the same point) end by being at one stroke subverted. J., in fact, having parodied just about everything else, is now taking the last logical step and parodying himself as moralist.

SATIRE IX

Useful General Studies

Bellandi	Bellandi, F., 'Naevolus Cliens', *Maia* 4 (1974) 279–99.
Braund	Braund, S., *Beyond Anger: A Study of Juvenal's Third Book of Satires* (Cambridge: 1988) ch. 4, 'Satire 9: Ironist and Victim', 130–77, 239–71.

1. Marsyas was a satyr who challenged Apollo to a musical contest on the flute, or oboe: Apollo, taking advantage of the agreement that the victor could do what he would with the loser, had Marsyas flayed alive. The scholiast suggests that 'Marsyas' here may also allude to some contemporary advocate of that name: perhaps this is no more than a guess. If so, there is probably a covert obscene allusion. The scholiast was alive to such nuances: he also points out that the name 'Ravola' was coined on etymological grounds, to suit his activity (*ravulus* means 'hoarse').

2. Highet suggests (121) that this satire was a product of J.'s earlier days, rescued from his bottom drawer later: and the context here suggests that Naevolus was a provincial, which supports such a theory.

3. On the temple of Isis as a place of assignation cf. Sat.VI 529 and, earlier, Ovid, *AA* I.77–78: the scholiast suggests, further, that both this and the shrine of Ganymede – appropriately enough – were used as a rendezvous by male homosexuals. The temples of Ceres and Cybele, being reserved for the use of women, were obvious places to watch if a man wanted a pick-up.

4. Virro is the name of Naevolus' unpleasant patron: he was, we may assume, the same person as the sadistic host of Satire V (see n. 3 to Sat. V). In both satires he is pilloried for the same vice: using his position and wealth to humiliate those over whom he can exercise control, be they clients or male prostitutes. Indeed Naevolus himself is, and refers to himself as, a client (59–60, 71–2; cf. Bellandi 279–80: the title of his article is 'Naevolus Cliens') – he simply performs somewhat unusual services for his *patronus*, and expects Virro to fulfil his part of the bargain. Instead, he is systematically insulted and sold short. Thus Sat. IX belongs not so much with II (a connection regularly made because of their common topic) but with I, III and V, which explore the decline of the client-patron relationship. Virro, like Naevolus, appears to have been a provincial, from within forty miles of J.'s home town of Aquinum: perhaps the relationship was one that J. had observed in his youth. Coarse and foul-mouthed though he is (Braund 141 talks rather prissily about his 'lack of aesthetic sensibility': she is nearer the mark in pointing out his resemblance to the popular concept of a Cynic), Naevolus cannot fail to evoke an uneasy sympathy.

5. This is a parody of Homer, *Od.* 16.294, 19.13: the original operative word was not 'a pansy' (κίναιδος) but 'cold steel' (σίδηρος).

6. It is generally assumed that from lines 40–53 Naevolus is addressing J. directly: Clausen and Knoche and Housman all punctuate thus. But this raises serious difficulties. Lines 46–7 I cannot believe were addressed to Virro: they are surely far more applicable to Naevolus, and the real problem is whether they are spoken by Virro or J. himself. The use of *tu* and *vos* throughout is puzzling. I have assumed that lines 40–46 (*ponatur calculus . . . quam dominum*) are addressed by Naevolus to Virro; that 46–7 form Virro's startled reply; that 48–9 is Naevolus' final thrust in this reported discussion, all of which is now being retailed to J., dialogue included. In 50–53 Naevolus addresses J. direct; then he resumes his apostrophe of Virro. Punctuating dialogue in a classical text is always open to error, since MSS have a bare minimum in the way of distinguishing marks. I would say no more for my rearrangement than that it makes tolerable sense.

'Ladies' Day' was the festival known as the Matronalia, celebrated on 1 March, and associated with the cult of Juno as goddess of married women and childbirth. It was a day when women received gifts from their husbands: the sexual relationship of Virro and Naevolus is defined and emphasized by this, especially by the specifically 'womanly' gifts – green parasol, amber scent-balls – that Naevolus is obliged to provide. Even the sofa (*cathedra*) on which Virro lolls is designed for ladies. Cf. Braund 140.

7. The lechery of the sparrow was proverbial in antiquity: see Plin. *NH* 10.107. Chaucer, too, had the same belief; he wrote of the Somnour: 'As hoot he was and lecherous as a sparwe'.

8. Gaurus, now Monte Barbaro, was a Campanian mountain renowned for its vineyards. The 'cymbal-bashing boy-friend' was not simply (as the context might suggest) a homosexual musician, but, more specifically, a priest of Cybele, and, therefore, a eunuch: so the scholiast, followed by Friedländer (440).

9. The reference is to the episode of the *Odyssey* in which Odysseus and his companions gouged out the Cyclops' one eye with a red-hot stake (*Od.* 9.106 ff.).

10. The exhortation 'Hold on' (*durate*) evokes the same admonition (in a very different context) in Virgil's *Aeneid* (1.207). Parodies abound in this satire: 81–3 (cf. Sat. V 137–9) offers mischievous echoes of Dido deserted (cf. *Aen.* 4. 283–6, 305, 317–19, 327–33, 366: Bellandi 297–9); while Braund (146–7) finds echoes (2, 45–6, 93–101, 105–6, 118–21, 149–50) of Alcibiades' speech in Plato's *Symposium* (215a5–22b7). This juxtaposition of elevated and degraded homosexuality is touched on more than once (see n. 15 below for another sly parody of Virgil in this connection).

11. At line 76 I accept Highet's emendation *migrabat* for *signabat:* see *CR* NS2 (1952), 70 f. Despite Braund's spirited defence (265 n. 188) of *signabat* (or Eden's even less well-founded *signabant*, with 'the appropriate parties' [*sic* !] as unexpressed subject) – '*signabat* by metonymy connotes the entire process of arranging and finalizing another marriage' – Courtney's objections (435–6) remain insuperable: if the lady 'was putting her seal . . . to a new marriage-contract with another man . . . it is hardly conceivable that she should do this while still in the patron's house'. Or in any way arrange a new marriage, even by metonymy. Braund also argues that *migrabat* would be 'a repetitive anticlimax' after *fugientem*, 'bolting'. For Courtney, *per contra* (and I agree), it forms a climax: 'she was not only herself running away from the patron, she was moving house . . . with all her property' (presumably on the grounds of non-consummation, and perhaps not to another marriage at all, but back to her parental home).

12. The 'Gazette', or *Acta Diurna*, contained a record of the acts of the Senate, the popular assemblies, and the various courts of justice, together with registrations of births, marriages, deaths, divorces and other such personal data.

13. See n. 6 to Satire VI.

14. 'Mars' Council' is J.'s Roman way of referring to the Areopagus Council in Athens (recruited from ex-archons), the meetings of which were held *in camera*.

15. Another parody: this time of Virgil, *Ecl.* 2.69, where Corydon the shepherd is recounting his more genteel homosexual passion for his master's favourite Alexis, and asks himself: 'Ah Corydon, Corydon, what madness has seized upon you?' Courtney 438: '. . . the quotation is highly ironical: the sordid reality contrasts with the stylized homosexuality of Virgil's milieu.' See Sat. VII, n. 9.

16. We last met Saufeia at Sat. VI 320, during the ritual of the Good Goddess, bumping and grinding with the call-girls. It is likely that the swigging of sacrificial wine took place on the same occasion: see notes 29 and 30 to Sat. VI.

17. Clausen follows Knoche in bracketing 120–23: I prefer, with Housman, to omit 119 (surely the intrusive gloss, if there is one, or a discarded alternative version), and, with rather less confidence, to accept his emendation *tum est his* for the impossible †*tunc est*† at 118, in default of anything better. See now Courtney 439–40.

18. The scholiast assumes that this gesture refers to their patting and fixing their hair like women: it seems more likely to have been a secret sign, easily recognized by the initiated. Ferguson (252) doubts this, arguing that the usage is more general; but the example he cites (Calvus fr. 18), when translated, supports my theory rather than his: 'Magnus, feared by all, scratches his head with one finger. What would you suppose he wants for himself? A man.'

19. At line 140 R. Saller, *PCPhS* 29 (1983) 72–6, provides evidence confirming, what I had always assumed, that *uiginti milia faenus* does indeed refer, not to annual interest, but rather to a modest capital sum placed out in interest-bearing loans: 20,000 sesterces is the sum J. specifies. Naevolus is not hopeful of climbing even to modest means (147): were the *uiginti milia faenus* interest merely (even if it could be interpreted in annual terms, which Saller convincingly rules out) then Naevolus would command, at 5%, the capital of an *eques* (400,000 sesterces). This Courtney (443) seems quite ready to believe, even though it flatly contradicts every other indication of Naevolus' poverty. But as *investable capital* 20,000 sesterces makes immediate sense for the modest competence of which Naevolus dreams.

20. In 257 BC, C. Fabricius Luscinus, as Censor, had an ex-consul named P. Cornelius Rufinus removed from the Senate on the grounds that he possessed more than ten pounds' weight of silver plate, contrary to the existing sumptuary laws: see Livy *Epit.* 14 and Friedländer 449, who collects other references.

21. Why the modest requirements of Naevolus should include a tame engraver and portraitist – especially after his strictly limited intentions in the matter of silverware – is very hard to see. Friedländer remarks that Verres had such artists as his private employees (Cicero, *In Verrem* II 4, 24, 54): we should expect Verres to, but not Naevolus. Yet he states that this will do 'for a poor man like myself'. Perhaps he hoped to establish them in a workshop and make a profit on their sales. Anything, in short, rather than work himself: the rentier mentality was too deeply ingrained to discard. Settis (1970) suggests that the 'five-minute likenesses' in fact refer to those *a macchia* designs first known from Nero's Golden House (*Domus Aurea*), and referred to by the Elder Pliny (*NH* 35.109) as *compendiariae picturae,* 'shorthand methods of painting': cf. Petr. *Sat.* 2.9. See also Plato, *Rep.* 495E, and Claude Mossé, *The Ancient World at Work* (London: 1969) 90. Courtney (444) supposes the painter to have been 'a *pictor imaginarius* . . . who would decorate room-walls with figure-scenes'.

22. This refers to the occasion on which Odysseus and his crew sailed past the Sirens' rocks, and Odysseus stopped the ears of the rest with wax to prevent them hearing the Sirens' seductive song, but himself listened, bound to the mast so that he could not jump overboard: see Hom. *Od.* 12.173 ff.

SATIRE X

Useful General Studies

Dick	Dick, B. F., 'Seneca and Juvenal 10', *HSCPh* 73 (1969) 237–46.
Eichholz	Eichholz, D. E., 'The art of Juvenal and his Tenth Satire', *G. & R.* 3 (1956) 61–9.
Lawall	Lawall, G., 'Exempla and Theme in Juvenal's Tenth Satire', *TAPhA* 89 (1958) 25–31.
Maier	Maier, B., 'Juvenal Dramatiker und Regisseur. Am Beispiel der zehnten Satire', *Der altsprachliche Unterricht* 26.4 (1983) 49–53.
Tengström	Tengström, E., *A study of Juvenal's tenth satire* (Göteborg: 1980).

1. J., as the scholiast makes clear, had a particular instance in mind here: that of the strong-man Milo of Croton, a 6th-c. BC Olympic victor, who, while out for a walk one day, found an oak-tree in a field, split down the trunk and held with wedges. Milo decided to complete the job with his bare hands: he thrust the two halves further apart, the wedges dropped out, his strength failed, and he found himself trapped as the halves snapped together again. While in this helpless position he was eaten by wolves. See Val. Max. 9.12, ext. §9.

2. C. Cassius Longinus, a famous jurist, was Governor of Syria in AD 50; in 66 he was exiled by Nero, on the trumpery excuse that he had in his house a statue of Cassius, the murderer of Caesar. His place of banishment was Sardinia: he is said to have been blind at the time. Vespasian recalled him. See Tac. *Ann.* 16.7–9; Suet. *Nero* 37. Seneca was forced to commit suicide as a result of the 'Conspiracy of Piso' in 65: there was a rumour that Piso was to be dropped, and Seneca offered the purple instead of him: Tac. *Ann.* 5.65; cf. Sat. VIII 212 and note ad loc. For Plautius Lateranus see Sat. VIII n. 20.

3. Rome's Exchange or Bourse was in the Forum: this was where the bankers operated, and where they kept their clients' deposits, in strong-boxes deposited (according to the scholiast) in the temple of Castor.

4. Democritus of Abdera (*c.* 460–*c.* 370 BC), known to later generations as the 'Laughing Philosopher', was a pupil of Leucippus, and from him inherited and developed the Atomist school of philosophy which so influenced Lucretius. Heraclitus of Ephesus (*fl. c.* 500 BC), an obscure but strikingly original thinker, conceived the world as a conflict of opposites, with fire as the agent of natural change. His Roman reputation as the 'weeping philosopher' is ill deserved: it depended partly on a misinterpretation of the famous dictum that 'all things flow' like rivers, partly on Theophrastus' attribution to him of melancholia (here not so much melancholy as impulsiveness). See Kirk~Raven~Schofield, *The Presocratic Philosophers* (Cambridge: 1983) 183.

As Ferguson (254) emphasizes, 'the digression on Democritus and Heraclitus forms a break in the structure'. It is also important. These two philosophers are presented as exemplifying two sharply contrasted ways of life: 'involvement in a spirit of satirical criticism or withdrawal in a spirit of sorrow'. The contrast (Courtney 456–7) seems to have been popularized by Seneca. See C. Lutz, 'Democritus and Heraclitus', *CJ* 49 (1953/4) 309–14. This exactly duplicates the respective positions of J. and Umbricius in Sat. III.

Ferguson also emphasizes, with good reason, the importance of Epicureanism for understanding Sat. X. The goal of the peaceful life only to be attained through virtue; the contempt for exaggerated desires – political, military or literary ambition; the targeting of superstition and the cult of Fortune; the pursuit of a sound mind in a sound body – all these are Epicurean characteristics, though J. does not (unlike Umbricius) choose withdrawal, preferring to remain ironically watchful, involved, mocking, satirical.

5. The *toga praetexta*, with purple border, was worn by senior magistrates (consuls, praetors, curule aediles), who also had the rods, or fasces, and axes borne before them as a symbol of office. The tribunal was the elevated dais or platform on which the magistrates' inlaid chairs were placed. The toga striped with purple (*trabea*) was the ceremonial attire of the Equestrian Order, or Knights, who wore it on special parades. To ride in a sedan had been at first a privilege of senators' wives, but in J.'s time, as we have seen, men also used them.

6. The occasion here described is the *pompa Circensis*, the procession which preceded the races in the Circus Maximus: it was normally presided over by a praetor (J.'s Consul in line 41 is an anomaly), and bears some resemblance to the State opening of Parliament. The president headed the procession, robed as a triumphant general in ceremonial tunics (one embroidered with palms, the other with gold embroidery on purple) and a heavy cloak: these robes were kept, except when being used, in the treasury of Jupiter Capitolinus – were, indeed, the deity's own attire, borrowed for the occasion. The point of the slave riding beside the Consul was to placate Nemesis: we are told that he was required, at intervals, to murmur in the great man's ear: 'Remember you are mortal.'

7. The ivory staff was also part of a triumphing general's insignia. The retainers, or 'clients', have received their 'dole' before the ceremony – this time in the form of a cash payment, not food. Ferguson 258: 'J. is suggesting that the aristocrat supports them simply to have his *claqueurs*, and they support him simply for the food or money.'

8. At lines 54–5 I read *aut si perniciosa petuntur, / propter quae,* etc., and (with Clausen) a mark of interrogation after *deorum*. Votive wax tablets, inscribed with petitions, were left either on the wall of a temple or else, as here, affixed to the knees of a divine image (Gnilka's explanation, cited by Courtney 460). The more commonly accepted interpretation, that ex-voto petitions or vows were inscribed on wax tablets, and these then deposited on the knees of the (seated) gods, I find less persuasive.

9. Sejanus (L. Aelius Seianus) was born at Vulsinii in Etruria (hence 'Etruscan luck' 74). His father was a Roman *eques*. On the accession of Tiberius he became joint Prefect of the Praetorian Guard with his father, and sole Prefect in AD 20. As the reign progressed his power steadily increased. He may have had a hand in the death of Tiberius' son Drusus in 23; he certainly deported Agrippina and her son Nero in 29. By 31 he was Consul, and had Tiberius (now a recluse on Capri) completely in his pocket: he judged the time had come to make a bid for the throne himself. But Tiberius, warned by his brother's widow of what was afoot, sent his 'long and wordy letter' (71) to the Senate: Sejanus was arrested, and executed on 18 October 31.

The treatment of Sejanus' statues (58 ff.) exemplifies an instructive trend throughout history. From J.'s own day we can cite Piso (Tac. *Ann.* 3.14), Nero (Dio Cass. 63.25.1) and – an event J. himself may well have witnessed – Domitian (Suet. *Dom.* 23, Plin. *Pan.* 52.4–5: again, the melting down into utensils). Similar orgies of destruction are recorded earlier, e.g. in Athens against the images, successively, of Demetrius of Phaleron and Demetrius Poliorcetes. In our own day we have seen the same treatment handed out to Nkrumah in Africa, and various communist *apparatchiks* in Russia after the dissolution of the Soviet empire.

10. Tiberius had withdrawn to Capri in AD 27: he never returned to Rome during his lifetime.

11. It was in AD 14 that Tiberius transferred the election of magistrates from the popular assemblies to the Senate – a most far-reaching constitutional change. See Tac. *Ann.* 1.15, where it is remarked that 'the public, except in trivial talk, made no objection to their deprival of this right'. On 'bread and the Games' (81): grain subsidies go back to the days of C. Gracchus; Augustus (*Res Gestae* 15, 22) reported twelve free distributions of grain in 23 BC, and also stressed the public shows he had financed. Julius Caesar found 350,000 [*sic*] citizens on a monthly 'dole', and slashed the number to 150,000. At line 82, immediately following, J.'s phrase, 'The oven's a big one' (*magna est fornacula*), expands *fornacula* (a diminutive) from its normal domestic use to the kind of sinister function which today we associate with Auschwitz, thus suggesting that Tiberius' enemies are being baked like so many loaves.

12. Bruttidius Niger ('The Black' – so calling him 'pale' would be taken as a joke) was aedile in AD 22: it is fairly certain that he is the man referred to here. Tacitus remarks of him that he 'was a highly cultured man who, if he had gone straight, would have attained great eminence' (*Ann.* 3.66). Instead he chose to curry Imperial favour as an informer: he prosecuted C. Silanus for extortion. Seneca has preserved a passage from one of his historical works describing the death of Cicero (*Suas.* 6.20 f.).

The 'slighted Ajax' out for blood is Tiberius, and J. is nothing if not ambivalent with the allusion. Ajax's 'slight' was seeing Odysseus instead of himself awarded the arms of Achilles, by chicanery: in his fury he intended to murder the Achaean army commanders, but instead went mad and slaughtered a flock of sheep. The hint that Tiberius was incapable of telling friend from foe is fairly broad.

13. After the appointment of his father as Prefect of Egypt, Sejanus concentrated the Praetorian Guard in a single barracks near the Viminal Gate, a move contrary to the original intentions of Augustus (Suet. *Aug.* 49), and the object of which was all too clear: 'Orders could reach [the battalions] simultaneously, and their visible numbers and strength would increase their self-confidence and intimidate the population' (Tac. *Ann.* 4.2).

Tiberius, like Domitian after him, (Plut. *Galba* 23) was a horoscope-addict (Suet. *Tib.* 69). Ferguson (261) points out that since the meaning of Capri was 'Goat Island', to describe the Emperor's group of astrologers as a 'herd' (*grege*) was mischievously appropriate. Given the proverbially lecherous nature of this animal, J. was probably also hinting at Tiberius' notorious sexual activities.

14. The 'other tyrant' is C. Julius Caesar (100–44 BC): together with Pompey (Cn.

Pompeius Magnus, 106–48 BC) and Crassus (M. Licinius Crassus, ?112–53 BC) he formed the so-called First Triumvirate. Here he is portrayed as reducing Roman citizens to the status of slaves. Crassus, a millionaire, was twice Consul with Pompey, and killed at Carrhae in Syria during an ill-fated campaign (55–3). Pompey, an ambitious egotist with a talent for capitalizing on other men's successes (Lucullus likened him to a vulture feeding off carrion), was not above pre-arranging his more flashy successes (e.g. clearing the Mediterranean of pirates) behind the scenes. Caesar took his measure well, and defeated him at Pharsalus (August 48 BC). For his death see below, n. 28.

15. The holiday in question was a feast of Minerva's known as the Quinquatrus, and held over the five days 19–23 March – beginning five days after the Ides, a point that would not be lost on any Roman reader fresh from Caesar's death. Since Minerva was the goddess of wisdom, this feast was particularly observed by schoolmasters and their pupils.

16. Cicero's much (and justly) derided poem *On His Consulship* was composed in 60 BC. After Caesar's murder he finally broke with Mark Antony in the late summer of 44, and delivered the First Philippic – so named after Demosthenes' speeches against Philip of Macedon – on 2 September, in reply to an attack that Antony had made on him the day before. Antony's next speech against Cicero was delivered in the Senate on 19 September, and it was this that elicited the Second Philippic here referred to. The speech seems not to have been delivered, but merely circulated in written form after Antony left Rome late in November. Cicero was executed on Antony's orders (with Octavian's connivance) 7 December 43, and his head and right hand cut off and impaled on the rostra in the Forum.

J. is somewhat cavalier with the facts of Demosthenes' life. His father was no horny-handed blacksmith but a wealthy sword-manufacturer (Plut. *Dem.* 4); and in any case he died in 377 BC, when the boy was only seven. Demosthenes himself died in 322, a year after Alexander, when Antipater had finally defeated the Athenians at Crannon. A Macedonian garrison was installed in Athens, and a warrant issued for Demosthenes' execution. He took sanctuary in the temple of Poseidon on the island of Calauria (modern Poros) in the Saronic Gulf, and there committed suicide by sucking poison from his pen: an apt end for so vituperative an orator.

17. Much heavy weather has been made of 'Juvenal's other elephants' by scholars (see, e.g., Tengström 23–32, who also summarizes earlier work): but it seems clear enough to me that J. (as at the beginning of this satire) is simply taking in another panoramic sweep – from the elephants of Morocco (which Hannibal used to cross the Alps) to those of Ethiopia. See Courtney's brief and sensible note (469).

18. At 156 J. achieves a marvellous anticlimax. Hannibal – the popular subject of stock declamation in the schools (cf. Sats. VII 161, VI 291) – is working his troops up with a fine peroration. The Alps and Italy? Nothing. Rome is the goal. Yet neither Capitol nor Senate will do: the Carthaginian standard must fly – in the middle of the red-light district! The Subura was, in effect, ancient Rome's Reeperbahn.

After his defeat at Zama in 202 BC by Scipio Africanus, Hannibal remained in Carthage till 193, a zealous and radical-minded statesman. At this point his right-wing political enemies convinced Rome that he was intriguing with the Seleucid ruler Antiochus III of Syria; and since, when a commission of inquiry arrived to investigate the matter, Hannibal fled to Syria, there may have been some truth in this charge. After Antiochus' collapse Hannibal first went to Crete, then sought refuge with King Prusias of Bithynia, the 'petty Eastern despot' here referred to. In 183/2, when his extradition was demanded by the Roman authorities, he took poison concealed in his ring.

19. J.'s phrase about one globe being too small for Alexander (*non sufficit orbis*) may be a truism, like his comparison to Hannibal (Livy 35.14.6–11): but it carries a sting in its literary tail, since the words (and their position in the hexameter) are directly borrowed from Lucan (5.356, 10.455), who used them of Julius Caesar. Alexander died of a fever at Babylon in 323 BC: the city's mud-brick walls, supposedly raised by Semiramis (Hdt. 1.178 ff.), were famous throughout antiquity.

The smaller islands of the Aegean have always been used as places of relegation or imprisonment for political opponents of the current regime – including one that J. names, Gyaros, notorious as such from Augustus' day to that of the Colonels (1967–74).

20. For Xerxes' canal through the peninsula of Mt Athos (traces of which have been discovered by modern archaeologists), and his bridging and lashing of the Hellespont, see Hdt. 7.21–5, 36–7. The hyperbolic conceit about the sea being 'paved with vessels' (175) also goes back to Herodotus (7.45), who likewise concedes (7.21) that all but the largest rivers were indeed drunk dry. The 'sweaty-drunk poet' was one Sostratus, who may have been identical with the flashy rhetorician Sosistratus who declaimed on the defeat of Xerxes (J. O. Thomson, *CR* NS1, 1951, 3 ff.): J. says his recitation was made *madidis alis*, which can mean either 'with drunken inspiration' or 'with damp armpits'. The *double entendre* is neat in Latin, but hard to reproduce in English: I assume J. intended both meanings to be taken up, and have translated accordingly. At 175 I accept Kidd's emendation *aequor* for *isdem*.

21. It is interesting to compare J.'s luridly dramatized and telescoped account of Xerxes' plight after the great sea-battle of Salamis (480 BC) with that given by Herodotus (8.97) – or even with Aeschylus' *Persians*; Aeschylus, after all, fought in the battle himself. The flogging, fettering and branding – all punishments inflicted on slaves – seem actually to have taken place (Hdt. 7.35, cf. Plut. *Moral.* 455d): all, that is, except the whipping of the winds (implausible enough in itself), for which J. is our sole surviving authority.

22. At lines 196–7 most MSS read *pulchrior ille / hoc atque †ille† alio*; P and O amongst others omit *ille* in line 197. The scholiast, interpreting this passage, remarks that all young men have different good qualities: some are handsomer than others, some *more eloquent*. Therefore we would expect, at the beginning of 197, a second comparative epithet. To my regret, I have found nothing since 1967 more convincing than my very tentative emendation *pulchrior ille / hoc aut callidior*, so I am (still tentatively) letting it stand.

There is another minor crux at 195: the baboon is clearly elderly (*uetula bucca*), but *mater* seems a very odd way of saying so, and *iam* preceding it is pointless (Courtney 473–4). Ferguson (267) emends to *Garamantis* (parodying Virg. *Aen.* 4.198), thus attaching the ape to an African tribe. I find this unconvincing. However, I would agree that what is needed is some sort of descriptive epithet: I am very tempted by *matertera*, = a great-aunt. This is just the kind of joke J. would love, and it is only too easy to see how (perhaps by haplography) one scribe might have written *mater* or *matera* for the less familiar *matertera*, and another have inserted the meaningless *iam* to repair the line's scansion.

At line 202 I accept LaFleur's emendation *Cossus* for *Cosso*.

23. The *gens Oppia* was a family of some distinction under the early Republic, but seems to have sunk into obscurity under the Empire. A Vestal Virgin named Oppia was condemned for unchastity in 483 BC (Livy 2.42): this suggests that Oppian women ran to form down the centuries, since J. is more likely to have had a contemporary in mind. Themison was a fashionable doctor in the time of Seneca and Celsus, though a more famous physician of that name from Laodicea, the founder of the Methodic School, lived under Augustus: perhaps, like the *pantomimi*, distinguished medical men assumed the names of their well-known predecessors as a form of advertisement. Fevers and other illnesses were most prevalent in autumn: cf. Sat. IV 56. For Maura's sexual activities cf. Sat. VI 307 ff. The pederastic schoolmaster Hamillus is otherwise unknown. J. seems to have borne a particular animus against his one-time barber: the line is repeated from Sat. I. 24–5.

24. Roman exaggeration went to work on Nestor, as on many other characters from Greek mythology. In the *Iliad* (1.250 ff.) he is only more than two generations old, i.e. something over sixty (cf. the scholiast here); the *Odyssey* (3.245) and Hesiod (ap. Plut. *Moral.* 415d) give him three full generations; by Ovid's day (*Met.* 12.187 ff.) he is no less than two hundred! His son Antilochus was killed while defending his father in battle: Paris had killed one of Nestor's horses, and Nestor called out to Antilochus for help: see Hom. *Od.* 3.111, Pindar, *Pyth.* 6.28 ff. J. is also parodying Propertius (2.13.47–50, cf. Ferguson 269).

25. Priam's fate is not mentioned by Homer: J.'s account is taken more or less directly from Virgil, *Aen.* 2.506–58, a moving and dramatic sequence. The myths concerning Hecuba's end are interesting. Polymestor (whom she had blinded for the murder of her son Polydorus) prophesied that she would be metamorphosed into a bitch, and leap into the sea from the headland in the Hellespont (Dardanelles) later known as Cynossema, or 'The Bitch's Grave'. Other accounts say she wandered round Thrace for a long time, in the shape of a bitch, howling and being stoned by the inhabitants; or that she was made Odysseus' slave, and either committed suicide by drowning herself, or else was put to death because of her furious invectives against the Greeks. Surely it needs a minimum of aetiologizing to deduce from this that the sack of Troy and the deaths of her husband and children were traditionally believed to have deranged her mind?

26. Croesus, the last King of Lydia, was overthrown by Cyrus in ?546 BC. His supposed encounter with Solon of Athens (there are difficulties in the chronology) is recounted by Herodotus (1.29 ff.) in a famous passage: Solon persisted in denying Croesus the accolade of splendid fortune he craved, warning him that only if he ended his life well could he be accounted truly happy. Mithridates Vl of Pontus (cf. n. 72 to Sat. VI) was driven out by Lucullus in 72 BC, finally defeated by Pompey in 67, and died in the Crimea, at the hands of a guard, when faced with rebellion by his son Pharnaces. Both men are chosen here as types of wealthy and powerful monarchs who finally lost all they had, including their lives.

27. For Marius' victory over the Teutones and Cimbri, see n. 34 to Sat. VIII. In 88 BC his undignified struggle with Sulla for appointment to the post of supreme commander in the war against Mithridates led directly to Sulla's march on Rome. Marius fled to North Africa, enduring much on the way. He was several times captured and in danger of death, once after being dragged out of the stinking Minturnae swamps at a rope's end. When he finally reached Africa he is reported to have said: 'Tell the praetor that you have Gaius Marius sitting as a fugitive on the ruins of Carthage.' The appeal fell on deaf ears. But (what it would have spoilt J.'s climax to add) in 87 Marius returned to Rome, joined forces with Cinna and the 'popular party', and captured the city. Then the bitter old man, crazed by his sufferings in exile, took a bloody revenge. His slave-bodyguard conducted an indiscriminate *putsch* of all Marius' personal enemies, whatever their rank or status. Meanwhile Marius and Cinna elected themselves Consuls for 86; but Marius died within three weeks of taking office, and his ashes were afterwards, on Sulla's orders, scattered in the R. Anio.

28. Pompey's fever was in 50 BC (Sen. *Dial.* 6.20.4, Courtney 480). After his defeat at Pharsalus (9 August 48 BC) he sailed to Egypt to seek asylum and protection, on the grounds that he had been instrumental in restoring the father of the present monarch to his throne. But Ptolemy was only a boy of thirteen, and the power lay with Theodotus of Chios, Achillas and the eunuch Pothinus, his advisers. Nervous of antagonizing Caesar, they had Pompey murdered as he stepped ashore from his boat. His head was cut off and sent to Caesar, who wept at the sight, though Pompey's death solved several awkward problems for him. The decapitated corpse was left lying on the seashore, and afterwards buried by Pompey's freedman Philippus. Pompey's murder seems to have inspired Roman writers with a special kind of horror and repugnance: the image of the deserted and headless body recurs again and again.

On Catiline, see Sat. VIII 231 ff. and note ad loc. He himself died fighting; his lieutenants, P. Cornelius Lentulus (Consul 71, praetor 63) and the senator C. Cornelius Cethegus, were executed by garrotting in the state prison, the Tullianum. Interestingly, Dio Cassius claims (against J.) that Catiline, too, like Pompey, was beheaded (37.40.2). The anxiety about mutilation seems to have derived from the belief that such disfigurement would persist in the afterlife (Courtney 481 with reff.).

29. Lucretia and Virginia were the two classical instances in early Roman history of the dangers to which feminine beauty could lead. Lucretia was the wife of L. Tarquinius Collatinus, and her rape by Sextus Tarquinius is said to have been directly responsible for the overthrow of Tarquinius Superbus and the establishment of a Republic in Rome. (See Livy 1.57–60.) Virginia, the daughter of a centurion, caught the eye of the decemvir Appius Claudius, who tried every trick to get her, including a rigged court hearing in which a retainer of his claimed the girl as his slave. In the end, amid scenes of riot, the father stabbed his daughter to prevent her falling into Appius' hands (Livy 3.44–58).

At line 295, for the meaningless *accipere* †*atque suum*† *Rutilae dare* of the MSS I originally suggested, not very hopefully, *accipere et quaestum Rutilae dare*, i.e. 'give her the advantage', 'give her best': *satis inepte*, comments Willis (rightly for once: but in that case why give it space in a crowded *apparatus criticus*?). I now regard Weidner's *osque* for *atque* as far preferable, and translate accordingly (cf. Courtney 483). Tengström reads *atque suam* and interprets *gibbum* not as a hump but as a facial wen (cf. Sat. VI 108). Rutila is otherwise unknown: presumably she was some well-known hunchback of the day. The *gens Rutila* was an ancient plebeian family.

30. The allusion is to the trick by which Hephaestus contrived to catch Ares (Mars) and Aphrodite in the act of adultery: see Hom. *Od.* 8.266 ff. At 312–13 I accept Courtney's emendation *mariti / irae debebit* (see now Courtney 483). Under the *Lex Iulia de adulteriis*, as Courtney (483) reminds us, 'both guilty parties might be killed at once by the wife's father if called in by the husband; the husband might kill the male adulterer if he were a freedman, a slave, or belonged to a disreputable profession or had been condemned in a public trial'. The mullet (in shape similar to the large radish used for the same purpose in Greece) was thrust into the adulterer's anus for two reasons: (i) to shame him by a simulation of homosexual rape, and (ii) to inflict real pain (which, especially on withdrawal, its spines would accomplish in a way that the unbarbed radish would not).

31. At 326 there is another odd textual crux: the best MSS have *erubuit* †*nempe haec*† *ceu fastidita repulso* (or *repulsa*), for which in 1967 I substituted *erubuit nam Phaedra ut fastidita repulso*, an emendation which would explain the metrically unnecessary periphrasis *Cressa* at line 327.

The late David Wiesen objected to this emendation (*Eranos* 79, 1981, 99–103) on three grounds: (i) 'It would be clumsy for J. first to introduce the wrathful reaction of Phaedra, to turn next to Sthenoboea, and then to revert to Phaedra with special reference to her place of origin.' This is pure huff-and-puff. J. lists (325) the cases of Hippolytus and Bellerophon, in that order. We then (in the text as I emend it) have the reactions of their spurned lovers, in the same order (326–7).

(ii) ' "Cressa" looks like a typically Juvenalian derogatory substitute for a heroic name . . . its pejorative force would have been lost if the heroine's proper name had been given in the previous line.' In fact the periphrasis *Cressa* ('the Cretan woman') is now justified, since Phaedra has already been named: far from being derogatory, it is mere *variatio*. (iii) '[W]hat are we to do with the last word of the verse? G[reen] chooses *repulso*, which makes no sense with his emendation.' This objection has some force, and would have more if Wiesen did not at once go on to assume (as I had done) that *repulso* could be taken as a noun, an error that would at once validate a translation such as 'sickened by rejection'. I now prefer to read *fastidita repulsam*, taking *fastidita* in its active sense (cf. Petr. *Sat.* 48) and translate 'disdaining rejection'. *Repulsa*, the reading of the lesser MSS, could easily have been read in error for the abbreviated form of *repulsam*. And what did Wiesen himself prefer instead of †*nempe haec*†? Why, *cunno*, with Sthenoboea in line 327 as subject. Great fun, except that J. *never* uses direct (as opposed to off-beat or periphrastic) Martial-style obscenities.

Phaedra was the daughter of Minos (and thus 'the Cretan woman'); she fell in love with her stepson Hippolytus, and slandered him when he rejected her advances. After his death, when Theseus, Hippolytus' father, learnt of his innocence, Phaedra committed suicide. Sthenoboea was the wife of Proetus, king of Argos, but nursed a hopeless passion for Bellerophon, and when he, similarly, refused her, she accused him of rape and, like Phaedra, killed herself.

32. This extraordinary story is confirmed, at length and in detail, by Tacitus (*Ann.* 11.12 and 26 ff.). The man in question was Gaius Silius, the consul-designate, whom Messalina forced to divorce his aristocratic wife Junia Silana. Both were subsequently executed. The only point in which the two accounts differ is that Tacitus makes Silius, rather than Messalina, the initiator and advocate of the marriage ceremony – which of course would spoil the point of J.'s rhetorical argument. (See now Maier 52.) The incident took place in AD 47/8. Also, Silius was not 'a blue-blooded sprig of the highest nobility', but came from a plebeian family.

33. What follows is a stocklist of desirable prayers, 'derived from the commonplaces of Hellenistic philosophy', both Epicurean and Stoic: health, common sense, endurance, all the alpha-privative negative virtues – freedom from anger, desire, greed, indulgence, and fear (fear of death above all) – leading to tranquillity or absence of upset (*ataraxia*). Reeve (*CR* 20, 1970, 134–6) suggests excising 356, the famous *mens sana in corpore sano* line, on the grounds of illogicality and awkward syntax: if the only thing worth praying for is virtue (which lies in your own hands anyway), what becomes of sense and morality if you are then told to pray for health instead? I admit the awkward syntax, but find the logic a trifle disingenuous. Famous tags need more to dislodge them than that (who else, in any case, could have written the line?), and J. did not, it is clear, possess the well-ordered and ruthlessly consistent mind of a professional academic.

34. Sardanapalus, more correctly known today as Assurbanipal, was King of Assyria

668–631 BC. Famous in antiquity for his luxury and effeminacy, he is now immortalized by some famous reliefs in the British Museum (a lion hunt, a garden feast) and by Layard's discovery of his palace and library.

SATIRE XI

Useful General Studies

Adamietz	Adamietz, J., *Untersuchungen zu Juvenal* (*Hermes Einzelschriften* xxvi) (Wiesbaden: 1972), ch. iv ('Satire 11'), 117–59.
Facchini Tosi	Facchini Tosi, C., 'Struttura e motivi della Sat. XI di Giovenale', *SIFC* 51 (1979) 180–99.
Felton~Lee	Felton K., Lee, K. H., 'The theme of Juvenal's 11th Satire', *Latomus* 31 (1972) 1041–6.
Jones	Jones, F. M.A., 'The persona and the addressee in Juvenal Sat. 11', *Ramus* 19 (1990) 160–68.
McDevitt	McDevitt, A. S., 'The structure of Juvenal's Eleventh *Satire*', *G. & R.* 15 (1968) 173–9.
Weisinger	Weisinger, K., 'Irony and moderation in Juvenal XI', *CSCA* 5 (1972) 227–40.

1. The Atticus here used as a symbol of wealth is probably Tiberius Claudius Atticus, father of the Athenian millionaire, rhetorician and public benefactor Herodes Atticus, and a near-contemporary of J.'s. He discovered a vast treasure on his estate in Attica, which subsequently formed the nucleus of his son's fortune. Rutilus cannot be identified with any certainty. He may or may not have been related to the humpbacked Rutila of Satire X; we cannot tell. In any case he is here no more than the type of the self-beggared spendthrift. The 'gourmand gone broke' that J. alludes to is Apicius: see n. 5 to Sat. IV.

2. If a Roman citizen of means intended to hire himself out as a gladiator he had to notify one of the Tribunes of the People (*tribuni plebis*), who could, at discretion, approve or cancel the contract (hence the reference to 'official compulsion', etc.). The gladiators' oath to the *lanista*, or trainer, virtually stripped those who took it of their individual rights. Courtney 493: 'By this the gladiator . . . became a chattel of the *lanista*, who was thus rex over him.' See Petr. *Sat.* 117: 'We swore an oath dictated by Eumolpus, that we would be burned, flogged, beaten, killed with cold steel or whatever else Eumolpus ordered. Like real gladiators we solemnly handed ourselves over, body and soul, to our master.' Cf. Hor. *Serm.* 2.7.58–9, Sen. *Ep.* 37.1–2.

3. The *macellum*, or Market, was where meat, fish, and vegetables were sold in bulk: it was like Smithfield, Billingsgate and Covent Garden rolled into one. Augustus built the Macellum Liviae on the Esquiline; Nero added another, the Macellum Magnum, on the Caelian (Ferguson 279). An exact modern equivalent is the great open market in Piraeus. It was the obvious place for a gluttonous debtor to be caught and pinned down by his creditors.

At line 13 J. brings off a bold and striking image: spendthrift and collapsing house are, by a nice syntactical ambiguity, fused into one, so that momentarily it is the man through whose cracks harsh daylight shines.

4. At line 18 the MSS have *vel matris imagine fracta*. In order to explain why the mother's likeness is broken up, we have to assume (a) that it was a statue and (b) that it was of solid silver. But the spendthrift's need is to raise quick ready money: and the value of a silver statuette is not visibly appreciated by melting it down, though *fracta* can be used in this sense: see line 102. What the wastrel does, surely, is to *pawn* this family heirloom; and therefore I suggest the emendation *pacta*, which is also palaeographically plausible, since *fr* and *p* are barely distinguishable in many hands. The *imago* may then be any kind of portrait. (This emendation, I am pleased to note, has found its way into Martyn's text; Willis briefly remarks of it, in his apparatus, 'which weakens the sense', *quo sensus debilitatur*, a comment that leaves one wondering whether he has quite grasped what the sense is.)

5. The highest point of the Atlas mountains, towards the Atlantic, is 13,665 ft.; this, the Jebel Toubkal, formed one of the 'Pillars of Hercules'. The peak with which the Romans were most familiar in this extended range, the Jebel Tidirhine, is no more than 8,058 ft. Thus the figure stipulated by J.'s pundit could plausibly be assessed at 5,607 ft. *Know Thyself* was the famous aphorism inscribed on the temple at Delphi (Xen. *Mem.* 4.2.24), and variously ascribed to Apollo himself, through the intermediary vehicle of the Seven Sages, or, more prosaically, to one of the latter (Cic. *De Fin.* 5.44). J., with a straight face, applies the saying to the proper scrutiny of one's bank-balance. Facchini Tosi (180 ff.) suggests that 'Know Yourself' is in fact the dominant theme throughout, here applied to one's appetite for luxury. This luxury is regarded by Adamietz (158–9) as a symptom of Rome's general social degeneration. Felton~Lee (1041 ff.) prefer to stress J.'s emphasis on seeing things as they really are, penetrating beyond surface appearances to the essential. All three views contain partial aspects of a highly complex reality.

6. J. is here echoing the low opinion of Odysseus as expressed, e.g., by Ovid or Seneca. It looks as though his version of the contest over Achilles' arms is that given by Ovid in *Met.* 13.1 ff. which illustrates the old and commonplace theme of the conflict between men of action and men of words: '. . . it was evident from the result what eloquence could do: for the skilful speaker carried off the hero's arms.' Not only that; but as a crafty, devious, cowardly, lying poltroon he brought dishonour on them. J. does not state just *how* he made himself ridiculous (*se traducebat*): I do not think it was simply (as sometimes seems to be assumed) through winning the arms by superior eloquence. Ferguson (280) rightly recalls an episode in Dictys Cretensis (2.3) where Odysseus, wearing Achilles' armour, is chased off the battlefield by Telephus. This, or something comparable, is surely what J. had in mind. There is also the sly joke about Thersites (30), who indeed did not claim Achilles' arms, and for a very good reason: Achilles had already killed him for mocking his, Achilles', grief over the death of the warrior queen Penthesilea. See W. B. Stanford, *The Ulysses Theme* (Oxford: 1954, 138 ff). For Matho, the pompous, wealthy, dishonest advocate, see Sat. I 32–3.

7. The fish actually in question are mullet and gudgeon; but since the whole point of the comparison is a question of price, and to English-speaking readers the contrast might be blunted by unfamiliarity, I have taken the liberty of substituting more local varieties.

8. The spendthrifts go 'down the coast' to Baiae, on the Bay of Naples: cf. Sat. III 4 and n. 1 ad loc. Lucrine oysters, from the same area, were a famous delicacy: see Sat. IV 141.

9. Jones, in an interesting analysis (160 ff.), stresses the unusual nature of so long an introduction (on proper restraint in self-indulgence) before any mention of Persicus *qua* guest. This, as Jones says, enables J. to take some covert jabs at Persicus thereafter for the benefit of his readers: if there are degrees in allowable luxury, then Persicus' (presumed) expectations are seen as exceeding them. At the same time J.'s own menu (56 ff., Jones 162–3) is not in fact all that simple or frugal. The admonition that 'a man should know, and study, his own measure' (35) has, it is clear, complex overtones.

And what about Persicus himself? What kind of dinner-guest (or friend, for that matter) is invited, by way of relaxation, to forget his wife's embarrassing habit of coming home at all hours with various signs of vigorous recent sexual activity clear upon her (186–9)? The obvious inference (not necessarily the true one) is that Persicus was some notorious glutton and cuckold – the first trait in all likelihood having been responsible for the second – probably long dead, like the occupants of those tombs along the Latin and Flaminian Ways (Sat. I 170–71 with n. 17 ad loc.) – and picked as a suitable lay figure for J.'s post-Horatian lecture on the parameters of allowable gourmandise.

But if so, his identity remains uncertain. It is generally doubted whether the man addressed here can be the rich, childless Persicus of Sat. III 222, who is suspected of firing his own house in order to collect compensation. From Persicus' own point of view this seems probable; but it implies a degree of consistency in J. himself which I do not, I fear, feel able to infer from his published work. The most likely identification is with the Paulus Fabius Persicus who was Consul in AD 34, with L. Vitellius, and achieved notoriety for his licentiousness: J.'s 'friend' could have been this man, or perhaps a descendant.

10. Evander was a king of Arcadia who, some sixty years before the Trojan War, led a colony to Italy, and built a town, Pallantium, on the Palatine Hill. This foundation was subsequently merged with Rome. Virgil, *Aen.* 8.358 ff., represents him as still being alive at the time of Aeneas' arrival, and as entertaining him, just as he had earlier entertained Hercules. Aeneas' divine descent was through his mother, Aphrodite (Venus). Both he and Hercules were deified: Aeneas died by drowning in the R. Numicius, while Hercules was burnt on Mt Oeta: 'both deaths can be regarded as purifying them for deification' (Ferguson 281). The passage which J. clearly has in mind at this point is *Aen*. 8.364–5, where Evander says: 'Guest of mine, be strong to scorn wealth and so mould yourself that you also may be fit for a God's converse. Be not exacting as you enter a poor home.'

11. M. Curius Dentatus (the 'Dentatus' is supposed to derive from the circumstance of his having been born with teeth in his mouth) defeated the Sabines during his first consulship (290 BC), Pyrrhus during his second (275), and the Lucanians, Samnites and Bruttians during his third (274). His simplicity and honesty were proverbial. After the conquest of the Sabines he took no more land than any common soldier; his only booty from the defeat of Pyrrhus was a wooden sacrificial bowl. Afterwards he retired to his farm, though he held the Censorship in 272. One Samnite embassy to him found him sitting by the fire roasting turnips: when they tried to press costly presents on him Curius remarked that he preferred ruling the wealthy to possessing wealth himself.

12. For the *gens Fabia*, see n. 3 to Sat. VIII. M. Porcius Cato Censorinus (234–149 BC) was a man of aggressive virtue, puritan instincts, and few manners, who hated foreigners, believed in traditional robust virtues, and had no hesitation about imposing his views on others. As Censor in 184 he taxed luxury, checked corruption, and, with poetic aptness, spent 1,000 talents on the sewerage system. A visit to Carthage in 157 or 153 convinced him that the city must be destroyed ('*Delenda est Carthago*'), and he lived just long enough to see war declared in 150. The Scaurus referred to here is probably M. Aemilius Scaurus, who supported Drusus' reforms in 90 BC. For Fabricius (Censor 275 BC) see n. 20 to Satire IX. The two quarrelling Censors were M. Livius Salinator and C. Claudius Nero (204 BC); see Livy 29.37, Val. Max. 2.9.6 (each forced the other to sell his horse!). The latter defeated Hasdrubal at the Battle of the Metaurus in 207.

13. J. probably has in mind scenes after Mummius' capture of Corinth (146 BC), as described by Polybius (39.2.2), of Roman soldiers playing draughts on piles of Old Masters (including, aptly enough, one of Heracles in agony, wearing the shirt of Nessus!). Mummius, ever the genial philistine, insisted that any *objets d'art* lost or destroyed in transit should be replaced by articles of equal value (Vell. Pat. 1.13.4). The 'Quirinal twins' are Romulus and Remus, and the Wolf the one that suckled them, thus by its maternal instinct setting Rome on the path of empire. The god Mars is there as their father: Duff remarks that 'in the works of art depicting this myth [Mars] is always represented as naked (except for a chlamys floating behind him), armed with shield and spear, and generally as hanging in the air, on his way to visit Rhea Silvia'. There is a similar representation on the shield of Aeneas: see Virg. *Aen*. 8.630. Cf. Friedländer 499–500. Livy (25.40.2) dates Roman appreciation

of Greek art to the capture of Syracuse in 212 BC, and the introduction of foreign luxuries to the defeat of the Asiatic Gauls in 187 (39.6.7). Sallustius also sees Asia as the source of corruption, but dates it to Sulla's campaign there, 87–83 BC (*Cat.* 11.6).

14. At line 112 (*pace* Ferguson 283) I accept Nisbet's suggestion of *tacitamque* for *mediamque* (made in his review of Clausen, *JRS* 52, 1962, 233–8).

15. The *orbis* was a table-top cut from a single tree-trunk, and roughly circular: the favourite wood was the *citrus*, or Moroccan cyprus. The curious passion which rich men had for this rather unlikely luxury, with its supporting leg of ivory or precious metal, is confirmed by Pliny, *NH* 13.91–9, where there is a detailed description of its manufacture, together with the size of particular specimens and the prices paid for them. The largest, made from two invisibly jointed semi-circular slabs, was four and a half feet in diameter and three inches thick; a single slab just under four feet in diameter is also recorded. Luxury tables could change hands for the price of a large estate, and women twitted by their husbands for excessive addiction to jewellery had an obvious retort to hand.

16. There were never any elephants in Arabia, 'but Petra was on the trade-route from India, so it was regarded as the source of the ivory which only it transmitted' (Courtney 506). It should hardly need saying, either, that there is no truth whatsoever in the belief (developed here by the scholiast) that elephants get rid of their over-heavy tusks by thrusting them into the ground, or by any other method. Perhaps ancient naturalists applied the analogy of beavers or rodents? Courtney (ibid.) argues that what led to this belief were, rather, discoveries of fossil ivory: cf. Theophr. *De Lapid.* 37, Plin. *NH* 36.134. We have here yet another of those myriad myths concerning natural history which abound in classical writers, yet which (one would have thought) even a minimal capacity for direct observation should have sufficed to dispel. The taste for them still flourishes in the Mediterranean today. On the Greek island where I used to live swallows are firmly believed to hitch lifts, during migration, on the backs of storks; and there is a local snake credited with the ability to pick up stones with its tail and sling them in cows' faces.

17. The iron ring (once generally worn) was now the mark of a plebeian nobody: Plin. *NH* 33.9–12, 17–23; Stat. *Silv.* 3.3.143–5 (cf. Courtney 506–7, Ferguson 284, with further reff.).

18. Trypherus is diabolically well named, since *trypheros* is a Greek adjective meaning both 'delicate', 'dainty' or 'soft', especially of food, and 'voluptuous' or 'effeminate' of people. As Courtney, with unwonted practicality, says (507), it is hard to imagine how a sow's paunch could be carved.

19. Reading, with the majority of MSS, *in magno* at 148, rather than *et magno* (Φ, Clausen). See Courtney 508–9.

20. The purple-bordered toga (*toga praetexta*) was worn, not only by curule magistrates (see n. 5 to Sat. X), but also by all free-born adolescents until, at about the age of sixteen, they assumed the all-white *toga uirilis* of manhood. At 157 I now prefer *raucus*, the reading of the MSS, to Calderini's emendation *draucus* (accepted by Ferguson, 285): for a good defence of the text as transmitted see Courtney 509–10.

21. It was the custom to sample the wine and then spit it out, after tasting, not into a receptacle but on the floor. Laconian or Spartan marble, especially the green marble of the Eurotas Valley (Duff 375), was much admired. Courtney revives Ribbeck's regrettable decision to excise 165–70 *in toto*. I remain, as always, highly suspicious of such wholesale discovery of 'interpolations', upheld very largely on the dubious grounds of 'feebleness' or 'irrelevance', as well as those of alleged grammatical or syntactical irregularity.

22. When the image of Cybele, the Great Mother, was brought to Rome from Pessinus in 204 BC, towards the end of the Second Punic War (see n. 17 to Sat. III and n. 51 to Sat. VI), the Megalesian Games (4–10 April) were instituted in her honour. On the last day of the festival races were held, at which the starting signal was given by the President of the Games dropping his white napkin. For the procession and ceremony on such an occasion, see n. 6 to Sat. X. The praetor had to pay the competing teams and the successful charioteers out of his own pocket: cf. Mart. 5.25.7 and 10.41.4. In J.'s day the Circus could hold about 300,000 spectators: Rome's total population then was nearer two million. But, as Ferguson says (286), 'all Rome' is 'a legitimate exaggeration'. Of the four regular *factiones*, or teams, the Red, the White, the Blue and the Green, only the last two were really important: partisan feelings ran unbelievably high. In J.'s day the Greens were firm popular favourites, though the *haut monde* seems to have supported the Blues. Ovid has a witty account of chatting up a girl at the races: *Am.* 3.2. For Nero's passionate addiction to racing see Suet. *Nero* 22. Hannibal's victory at Cannae, in Apulia, took place in 216 BC. The Consul L. Aemilius Paullus fell on the battlefield; his colleague survived. Spectators in the Circus were required to wear the toga as a mark of formality.

SATIRE XII

Useful General Studies

Helmbold	Helmbold, W. C., 'Juvenal's Twelfth Satire', *CPh* 51 (1956) 14–23.
Ramage	Ramage, E. S., 'Juvenal Satire 12. On friendship true and false', *ICS* 3 (1978) 221–37.
Ronnick	Ronnick, M. V., 'Form and Meaning in Juvenal's 12th Satire', *Maia* NS 45 (1993) 7–10.
Smith	Smith, W. S., 'Greed and sacrifice in Juvenal's 12th satire', *TAPhA* 119 (1989) 287–98.

1. Corvinus is a regular cognomen of the *gens Valeria*: see Sat. VIII 5–7, and n. 2 ad loc.; cf. Sat. I 107–8. J.'s friend was therefore a well-connected person, but nothing else is known about him. See Courtney 517 for the interesting suggestion that J. carefully selected this name (*coruus* = 'crow') 'to represent his poem as addressed to one who was himself a legacy-hunter and is quick to suspect a rival in that line (93)': legacy-hunters were often compared to carrion-eating birds, crows included (Hor. *Serm.* 2.5.56, Petr. *Sat.* 116).

Corvinus also induces reflection on the dramatics of this odd poem. J. is apostrophizing him throughout. Is he simply the poem's recipient, or is he to be thought of as part of its dramatis personae, directly involved with the narrator? We don't know. The celebration is not for him but for Catullus, whom, equally, we never meet (nor, indeed, do J. or Corvinus). Catullus' greed is mocked, but he is also represented as a likely target for legacy-hunters. Then he turns out to have three children, and J. firmly assures us that he, J. (or his persona), is no legacy-hunter himself. Something tells me that this is a private-joke poem, and that if we knew the three protagonists, much that is now obscure about their relationships with each other would become clear.

2. It looks very much as though a line has dropped out between vv. 3 and 4. It is stretching *reginae* somewhat to translate it as 'Queen of Heaven', though the scholiast explains that this was Juno (adding, significantly, that some authorities took it as Fortune). Juno was worshipped as *regina* at certain Etruscan shrines, and in at least three Roman temples: on the Capitol and the Aventine, and near the Circus Flaminius. Pallas Athene can be identified from her attributes, but, again, is not named. Perhaps there was once another line here, something such as *Iunoni, Fatisque iterum; torvaeque Minervae*, and some early copyist's eye slipped from *Minervae* to *Maura*.

Minerva, the Roman equivalent of Athena, had a shield, or aegis, (Virg. *Aen.* 2.616), decorated at its boss with an image of the snake-haired Gorgon Medusa: the latter is 'Moorish' because of the ancient tradition placing her origin in N. Africa. Jupiter is 'Tarpeian' because of the famous Tarpeian Rock on the Capitol, where the temple of Jupiter Capitolinus also housed Juno and Minerva.

3. Highet plausibly suggests that J. had some kind of feud with the Younger Pliny, and lost no opportunity of denigrating him or his relatives. Calpurnia Hispulla was Pliny's wife's aunt; there were two other ladies of this name – both known to Pliny – and one of the three may well have been the fat person described here: not to mention the Hispulla of Sat. VI 74 who had an affair with an actor.

4. At line 14 I read *iret et a grandi ceruix ferienda ministro*: see J. G. Griffith, *CR* NS 10 (1960) 189–92. This reading is also accepted by Ferguson (289). Housman's *<cui fo>ret et grandi ceruix* I find no more convincing than Courtney's arguments (519–20) in favour of it.

5. The reference to a 'storm in a poem' is ironic to the point of sarcasm: too many versifiers had tried their hands at it (e.g. Virg. *Aen.* 1.81 ff., Ovid *Met.* 11.478–565,

Petr. *Sat.* 114; other reff. in Ferguson 289), so that it had become hard to avoid platitudinous and shop-worn hyperbole when going for a *Götterdämmerung*-style dramatic impact. J. is clearly announcing that his satire will contain at least a touch of the mock-heroic (Ramage 227).

A shipwrecked person could use a painted picture of the storm he had escaped in two ways: he could hang it in the temple of a god or goddess as an ex-voto offering in gratitude for his deliverance, or display it as part of his stock-in-trade as a beggar (see *Sat.* XIV 301) to excite the sympathy of passers-by. Isis, in her avatar as Stella Maris or Isis Pelagia, 'Lady of the Deep' (further reff. in Courtney, 520–21), was supposed to be a most efficacious deity for the storm-tossed sailor to invoke: thus she provided artists with a steady source of income through the ex-voto offerings dedicated to her.

6. The 'friend' is named for the first time at line 29. Again, an unknown person: neither the famous poet, nor the informer of *Sat.* IV 113 (though the reference to blindness in those dubious lines 50–51 has sometimes made me wonder about this), nor the farce-writer of VIII 186 and XIII 111. Courtney (521) invokes line 37 as indication that Catullus was a merchant: it seems to me at least as likely that he is being satirized for his luxurious personal possessions.

7. At line 32 the reading *arbore et incerta* proposed by Kilpatrick (*CPh* 66, 1971, 114–15) strengthens the sense and should be seriously considered by editors. As both Ferguson (290) and Courtney (521) point out, at 33–4 J. uses a verb, *decidere*, = 'compound with', frequently applied in connection with bankrupts, when coming to terms with their creditors for a part-payment. I cannot, however, understand why Courtney should suppose the implication to be that Catullus 'is a money-grubber'; he's more likely to be a spendthrift. Ferguson sees exactly what's going on: Catullus, like a good businessman, is *bargaining with the winds* – which, of course (Smith 293–4) 'will listen to no compromise but demand total sacrifice'.

8. The beaver's glandular secretion, *castoreum* (no relation to castor-oil, derived from the plant), used to be much sought after as a putative medicine for nervous disorders (Plin. *NH* 8.109). There is no truth in the popular belief (Plin. ad loc.; other reff. in Courtney 521) that the beaver (*castor* in Latin) castrates itself (note the factitious verbal echo) by biting off its testicles when pursued. The probable explanation for this piece of erroneous folk-wisdom (Ael. *NA* 6.34) is that it can, in fact, retract its testicles into its abdomen; but sympathetic magic (*similia similibus*) must surely also have played a part, since the words *castor* and *castrare* were seen as possessing functional *sympathia* (cf. Tertullian, *Adversus Marcionem* 1.1). Nor can we exclude mischievous literary relish in a mildly comic pun. J. may, indeed, have slipped a discreet metrical joke on this theme into the prosody of line 36 in Latin. Many scholars have commented on the second-foot hiatus – unique in this author – of *testiculi: adeo*; but it took Ramage (228 n. 17) to suggest, convincingly, that the prosodic gap might be meant to indicate that other, anatomical, gap which the beaver had supposedly created. (This kind of joke was not without precedent. Readers of

Ennius will recall the spirited tmesis by which he managed to split a victim's head verbally as well as with the axe: *cere- comminuit -brum*.)

9. The last of these explanations seems the most likely one: there were rich iron deposits in Baetica (Guadalquivir) and a proportion of iron oxide in the water might well have produced the effect on the sheep which J. describes. Cf. Mart. 12.98.1 – 2, 9.61.3 – 4. Smith (293) notes the juxtaposition of 'eunuch beaver and effeminate Maecenas', suggestive of 'both sexual abnormality and refinement'.

10. This Fuscus may have been the Cornelius Fuscus referred to in Sat. IV 111 (cf. n. 19 ad loc.); nothing else is known of his allegedly hard-drinking wife.

11. This was Philip of Macedon, Alexander's father; and the specific occasion which J. has in mind is the capture of Olynthus in 347 BC, which was achieved by bribing the city's leaders (Dem. 19.263 – 7). Duff quotes Philip's justly famous dictum that 'no fort is impregnable into which an ass, laden with gold, could make its way' (Plut. *Moral*. 178b).

12. Lines 50 – 51 have been generally condemned by recent editors as a feeble interpolation: 'poverty of diction', 'vapid chiasmus', 'tame repetition', and now 'ridiculous anticlimax' (Courtney 523) are only some of the insults hurled at them. They seem to me no worse than many of J.'s aphorisms, and their deletion yet another instance of that odd editorial belief that an ancient author is always self-consistent, and always writes at the top of his bent – or that interpolations (at least, those recognized as such) must be by definition feeble. How many *ingenious* ones, I wonder, have escaped detection? See Ferguson 290 – 91, who observes that the lines 'seem needful to J.'s theme, for this is what Catullus was doing', and Introduction p. lxii.

13. As we might expect, white wool spun by the Fates (here at 64 – 5: cf. Mart. 6.58.4) indicated good fortune, black the reverse (Ovid, *Trist*. 4.1.64). The white sow was to be the sign by which Ascanius (or Iulus, Aeneas' son) would recognize the site of his new city. The number of piglings denoted the number of years before the founding of Alba Longa: see Virg. *Aen*. 3.389 ff. and 8.43 ff., Livy 1.3.3. Lavinium had been named after Ascanius' stepmother Lavinia, daughter of King Latinus.

14. Ostia's first artificial harbour was begun by Claudius in AD 42. It had two curving moles and enclosed an area of some 850,000 square yards. Between the moles stood an artificial island with a lighthouse on it ('Tyrrhenian' – i.e. Etruscan – because facing the sea of that name). But despite its size, this harbour was ill-protected against strong prevailing winds. In AD 62 a particularly violent storm wrecked some two hundred vessels lying at anchor there. It was not until 104 that Trajan constructed his hexagonal inner basin, with numbered berths and a right-angled channel that protected it against bad-weather hazards. There is an excellent and well-illustrated account of Ostia and its harbours in Paul Mackendrick's *The Mute Stones Speak* (London: 1962) 251 – 65; those who wish to pursue the topic in greater detail should consult Russell Meiggs' *magnum opus*, *Roman Ostia* (Oxford: 1960). J.'s description here clearly refers to Trajan's inner basin, and the Satire must, therefore, be dated after 104. The crew of Catullus' vessel shaved their heads in fulfilment of a vow made during the storm.

15. We have already had several glimpses of the legacy-hunters in action – as Highet (134–5) so well describes them, 'that strange class of schemers who would court the childless rich in the hope of being left a substantial legacy' – see Sat. V 98, VI 40; cf. Sat. V 135–45. Horace has a biting picture of them in the *Sermones* (2.5). When Eumolpus, in Petronius' *Satyricon*, makes his will, he stipulates that 'those who come into money by the terms of my will shall inherit only upon satisfaction of the following condition: they must slice up my entire body into little pieces and swallow them down in the presence of the entire city.' 'Just close your eyes,' says one determined beneficiary, 'and pretend you are eating a million sesterces, not human offal . . .' (*Sat.* 141). Ferguson notes the elegant irony at 96–7: the more fertile Catullus proves in the flesh, the more barren the legacy-hunters find him.

16. The keeping of elephants was an Imperial prerogative: the Emperor's herd, as we know from inscriptions, had its reserve at Laurentum, near Ardea (= modern Anzio), the city of the Rutuli. 'They were used to draw triumphal chariots, to pull heavy loads, for *uenationes* or to perform tricks in the circus' (Courtney 529–30). As early as 281 BC King Pyrrhus of Epiros used them on his S. Italian campaign (they were a tactical legacy from Alexander's invasion of India). The Romans themselves first employed elephants in 200 against Philip V of Macedon (Livy 31.36.4). The 'turrets' on their backs held about four combatants in addition to the mahout (H. H. Scullard, *The Elephant in the Greek and Roman World*, Ithaca, NY: 1974, 240, 243, cf. Courtney 530). J. seems in some sense to regard them as monsters, alien freaks (Adamietz 244, Ramage 233, Smith 296 with n. 19). Helmbold treats 102–10, the excursus describing them, as a (suitably large) interpolation, a view that has found few takers, least of all among elephant enthusiasts (surprisingly numerous) or those inured to displays of Hellenistic-style erudition in unlikely places (e.g. Lucan's disquisition on snakes, 9.607–937). For Turnus see the *Aeneid*, *passim*, especially Bks VII–XII.

17. The passage, as Ramage says (234), rises to a climax of 'grotesqueness and hyperbole' as the offerings pile up: elephants, choice slaves, a favourite daughter – *and it all pays off* (126–7). At 116–17 the MSS have *magna et pulcherrima quaeque / corpora*. The interpretation of this as 'the tallest and most good-looking' slaves is, *pace* Housman – who takes *magna* as adults, in contrast to *pueri* and *ancillae*, 'houseboys and chambermaids' (but neither of these need be 'young'!) – almost certainly right. Courtney (530–31) is unnecessarily put off by the rare combination of positive and superlative: his *ut* for *et* is ingenious but otiose. The substitution of a doe or hind for Iphigeneia on the sacrificial slab at Aulis has all the marks of a late 're-write' designed to purge the original myth of its more barbarous elements. Neither Pindar, Aeschylus nor Sophocles alludes to this incident: the earliest reference is that of Euripides, *IT* 28, and the version J. almost certainly had in mind is that of Lucretius (1.84–100), a passionate and powerful diatribe against religious cruelty, culminating in the famous line, sharp with contemptuous disgust, *Tantum religio potuit suadere malorum*, 'So great the tally of evils that religion could induce.'

18. A thousand ships was the traditional round number of Agamemnon's pan-Hellenic fleet (see, e.g., Varro, *RR* 2.1.26); the Homeric Catalogue of Ships in *Iliad* Bk II gives a slightly larger figure, 1,186. The trap (*nassae*, 123–4), here used metaphorically, was a wicker creel akin to our lobster-pot, which let the fish in but not out again. The applicability to legacy-hunting is self-evident. The 'Mycenaean maiden' (127) is, of course, Iphigeneia (see lines 119–20 with n. 17). For Nero's looting habits see, e.g., Dio Cass. 63.11–12, Tac. *Ann.* 15.45: many of his depredations were carried out in Greece. For Nestor's age see Sat. X 246–55 and note ad loc.

Line 130 carries a sharp moral message: even the greatest wealth is not worth the loss of friendship. Thus J. closes with an impeccably Epicurean wish: cf. Ferguson 293. The concluding couplet is given extra edge (Ramage 237 with n. 29) by being a very close paraphrase of Cicero, *De Amic.* 52: '. . . nam quis est . . . qui uelit, ut neque diligat quemquam nec ipse ab ullo diligatur, circumfluere omnibus copiis atque in omnium rerum abundantia uiuere?' ('Who would ever wish to be awash in a glut of all material things, if it meant loving no one and being oneself loved by none?').

SATIRE XIII

Useful General Studies

Adamietz   Adamietz, J., 'Juvenals 13. Gedicht als Satire', *Hermes* 112 (1984) 469–83.

Anderson   Anderson, W. S., *Essays in Roman Satire* (Princeton: 1982) 281–3 = *CPh* 57 (1962) 149–52.

Edmunds   Edmunds, L., 'Juvenal's Thirteenth Satire', *RhM* 115 (1972) 59–73.

Fredericks   Fredericks, S. C., 'Calvinus in Juvenal's Thirteenth Satire', *Arethusa* 4 (1971) 219–31.

Jones   Jones, F. M. A., 'Juvenal Satire 13', *Eranos* 91 (1993) 81–92.

Morford   Morford, M. P. O., 'Juvenal's thirteenth satire', *AJPh* 94 (1973) 26–36.

Pryor   Pryor, A. D., 'Juvenal's false consolation', *AUMLA* 18 (1962) 167–80.

1. Again, this sexagenarian friend of J.'s is otherwise unknown. Calvinus was the family name of a long-established branch of the *gens Domitia*, and occurred in other families as well. I agree with Courtney (17) that he gives evidence of being a real person. If this is so, one wonders how he felt being made the target of what was largely a *mock* consolation-poem, primarily directed against the collapse in Rome of order and morality, the rise of criminal behaviour, with a plain statement (11–18) that his fury at the loss of a comparatively small sum of money was, to say the least, disproportionate. I suspect, too, that J. regarded him as hopelessly naïve: see n. 27 ad fin.

2. Fonteius Capito, the only consul in the *Fasti* to satisfy the requirements of this context (see Duff's useful note, 394), held office in AD 67. We therefore have a *terminus post quem* of AD 127 for the composition of the satire.

3. The Nile in antiquity had seven mouths: see Stat. *Theb.* 8.353. It might be supposed that Egyptian Thebes is referred to in such a context; but Egyptian Thebes had a hundred gates, whereas Thebes in Boeotia had seven. The scholiast, correctly, ties up Thebes and the Nile mouths with the Seven Sages, which gives an extra edge to J.'s number-play: the good man is indeed a rare and wonderful phenomenon.

4. The longest list of the Ages of Mankind is that given by Hesiod in *WD* 109–210, which includes five ages only: Gold, Silver, Bronze, Heroic and Iron. Moreover, as Professor S. G. F. Brandon remarks, in *Creation Legends of the Ancient Near East* (London: 1963) 182, 'this scheme of the five races or generations is truly unique; it had not been anticipated elsewhere in the ancient Near East, and in Greek literature it appears only in the *Works and Days* and its presence there seems to have exercised little influence on subsequent Greek thought'.

McGann (*Hermes* 96, 1968, 509 ff.) has suggested that the mysterious 'ninth age' (*nona aetas*) referred to by J. may express a concept borrowed from the Sibylline Oracles – that human history evolves in *ten* ages, ending in utter ruin with the destruction of mankind at the close of the tenth. J. and his contemporaries would then be in the penultimate age, just before this final *Götterdämmerung*. Ferguson (296), who accepts McGann's interpretation – I think rightly – comments: 'The tenth is the peaceable kingdom, but it is inaugurated by apocalyptic disasters. To live in the ninth age is to face this last prospect. It is to experience it indeed, for the ninth age contains darkness at noon, wars and rumours of war, eruption and earthquake.' Another theory that has commanded some assent is that this *nona aetas* means the city of Rome's ninth century (*saeculum*, schol. Lucan 1.564), which, prophecy declared,would herald its end. Claudius had declared the eighth *saeculum* ended in AD 47; Sibylline prophecies in AD 19 and 64 also predicted Rome's end, from civil war and Sybaritic luxury (Dio Cass. 57.18.3–5, 62.18.3). Cf. Courtney 541.

5. At line 31 the Latin for 'Gods and mortals' is *hominum diuuomque* – as Ferguson (296) says, epic parody. I find it odd that the various instances cited by Courtney (541) do not include the most famous example of all (too obvious?), the opening line of Lucretius' famous invocation to Venus – '*Aeneadum genetrix, hominum diuuomque uoluptas*'. Where Lucretius found *uoluptas*, J. seeks *fidem*, 'good faith'; but surely his audience was meant to recall Venus too?

The lawyer's 'hired claque' (33) is expressed in Latin by the term *sportula*, the hand-out they receive (the effect is as though a bribe had suddenly started yapping in public), and given shock-value by being placed at the beginning of a line, but impossible to translate as is without sounding ludicrous. J. elsewhere expresses the personal by the impersonal (Ferguson cites Sat. X 95). According to the Younger Pliny (*Ep.* 2.14.4), the *sportula* was actually paid out in court when the cheers and applause had had their effect. Hebe and Ganymede were both cup-bearers to the gods: Hebe was married to Hercules ('in a kind of beauty-and-the-beast folk-tale', Ferguson 296), while Ganymede was carried up to heaven by Zeus-as-eagle, with erotic intent. This heaven (like the real Mt Olympus' summit on occasion) was 'above the clouds', and thought of as being in the realm of pure upper air (*aether*).

For an idyllic description of the Golden Age under Kronos (identified by the Romans with Saturn) see Sat. VI 1–24. In Roman myth Saturn found a home in Latium and taught the Latins farming (Virg. *Aen.* 8.319–20). Greek Kronos was originally an unpleasant enough deity; his 'country sickle' is generally supposed to have been the instrument with which he castrated Uranus, and since both Uranus and Ge had prophesied that he would be overthrown by one of his children, he ate them as soon as they were born. But his wife Rhea smuggled Zeus (Jupiter), the youngest, away to the caves of Ida, giving Kronos instead a stone wrapped in swaddling-bands. When Zeus grew up he raised the 'Hundred-handed Ones' and the Kyklopes against Kronos, and defeated him after an Armageddon-like conflict, that lasted ten years.

6. *Siccato nectare* in 44–5 is generally construed as an ablative absolute, which gives rise to some awkward and strained interpretations. I prefer to take it in the instrumental sense: *siccato* (or perhaps *saccato*, which the scholiast would seem to have read) will then mean 'distilled' or 'evaporated', and the nectar will be what Vulcan uses to clean the filth off his arms – much as a modern mechanic will sometimes use surgical spirit. See now Ferguson 296. I am less convinced by the theory that the hot smithy 'has made [Vulcan] so thirsty that he has to drain off a cup of nectar before cleaning himself' (Courtney 542–3).

7. The story of Ixion is curious. He promised a large bride-price to his prospective father-in-law, but when the poor man came to collect it, he fell into a red-hot barbecue-pit set as a trap for him by Ixion. After he had failed to persuade anyone else to purify him of his blood-guilt, Ixion sought refuge with Zeus – and promptly attempted to seduce Hera. To lull his suspicions, Zeus fashioned a cloud-double of Hera called Nephele, on whom Ixion sired the first Centaur. As a punishment Zeus bound him to a burning wheel for all eternity. The vulture is that which pecked at Tityos' liver (supposedly the seat of desire) as a retribution for his attempt to rape Leto; the punishment of Sisyphus was to roll a boulder uphill only to have it topple back to the bottom again when he was approaching the summit. For these 'great sinners' and their punishments see Courtney 544 with reff., Ferguson 297.

8. All these prodigies were (it seems) of regular occurrence in ancient Italy: see

Julius Obsequens' *Book of Prodigies* (now available in vol. XIV of the Loeb edn of Livy, tr. A. C. Schlesinger and Russell M. Geer) 238–319, where instances of each are recorded. Courtney (545) argues that J. is mocking such catalogues of traditional portents.

9. 'The translation of specific sums of money is always awkward. Sometimes it seems best to leave the original currency; sometimes, as here, to do so would jar, since the figure in sesterces would seem very inflated.' I wrote those words in 1966; today the sums can be strictly translated without any sense of unreal inflation at all: a depressing thought.

10. The point of this odd assortment as objects to swear by is that the oath-taker is inviting all of them to be turned against him as weapons (the sun's rays probably by blinding him) if he perjures himself: cf. Ovid *Am.* 3.3.27–30, Courtney 546. Ferguson (297) points out that the passage parodies Lucan (7.145–50) – until 84–5, that is, when mock-epic rhodomontade collapses in a domestic anti-climax as ridiculous as it is disgusting. J.'s mischievous subversion of the high-flown out-Ovids Ovid.

11. Ferguson (298) gets this glib generalization exactly right: 'The lines here are a garbled Epicureanism, linked to the popular idea of Tyche [chance, Fortune]'. It is true that the Epicureans did not believe in a teleological universe, but rather in creation as a random concource of atoms.

12. Housman, in the introduction to his edition of J. (xxxiv), provides a nice instance of that smart-alec pseudo-logic to which he was occasionally prone when pursuing a putative interpolation (here line 90: how come, I have often wondered, that almost all marginal glosses supposedly absorbed into the text scan correctly?) There are atheists, he says, who cheerfully perjure themselves (86–9). There are also believers, who still commit perjury regardless (91 ff.). Some dim interpolator, feeling the connection needed glossing, then (according to Housman) inserted line 90 by way of explanation, so that the division is not into atheists and theists, 'but into atheists and those who dread punishment, and it is then mentioned in passing that these latter are theists'. Great textual critics have always had their odd aberrations, mostly of an other-worldly hyper-logical nature, Bentley's rationalizing edition of Milton being perhaps the most notorious example. This is another. Courtney prints the entire passage without comment, I would like to think ironically; but something tells me it was a case of deep calling to deep. The 'rattle' (93) is the sistrum, 'which', as Lewis & Short charmingly put it, 'was used by the Egyptians in celebrating the rites of Isis, and in other lascivious festivals'. It is here envisaged as an instrument akin to Athena's aegis or the thunderbolt of Zeus. The infliction of blindness is specifically attributed to Isis by Ovid, *EP* 1.1.51–4, and explained by her anger.

13. J. reverses the traditional (Greek) aphorism: ὀψὲ θεῶν ἀλέουσι μύλοι, ἀλέουσι δὲ λεπτά, best known from Longfellow's translation (piously substituting one God for many): 'Though the mills of God grind slowly, yet they grind exceeding small.' For other variants see Courtney 549.

14. Ferguson (299) cites here an anecdote with which, I must confess, I have always had considerable sympathy: that of the brigand who reminded Alexander of Macedon that both of them were in the same business, the only difference being that Alexander practised it on a far larger scale (Aug. *Civ. Dei* 4.4).

15. For Catullus the farce-writer see Sat. VIII 186 and n. 24 ad loc. The joke is (so the scholiast) that the runaway slave greeted the master and insisted on his proving his free status (Ferguson 299). Stentor shouted as loud as fifty men (Hom. *Il.* 5.785– 6); Mars (Ares), when wounded, upped the ratio to 1:9–10,000 (*Il.* 5.850–61). The prayer that follows parodies Virg. *Aen.* 4.206 ff. Other reff.: Courtney 549–50.

16. The Cynics believed that the only good was virtue, and that pleasure, if pursued for its own sake, was a positive evil: they were thus marked by an aggressively puritanical contempt for wealth and achievement, and tended to be a 'protest group' rather than a constructive philosophical sect. A forerunner of the Cynics was Antisthenes of Athens; the more famous Diogenes of Sinope, the group's real founder, carried Cynical asceticism to bizarre lengths. The Stoic sect (founded by Zeno *c.* 308 BC) likewise believed in virtue as the supreme good, but held that action, not withdrawal or contemplation, was the highest problem for man. They thus remained in the world (many high Roman statesmen and at least one Emperor, Marcus Aurelius, were Stoics) and did not abjure material gain or luxuries: hence J.'s 'only a shirt between them'. Epicurus established a school in a garden outside Athens in 306 BC: his followers inclined towards political quietism, moderation, 'contracting out' (*cultiver notre jardin*). The differences between Stoics and Epicureans were frequently expressed in terms of Porch (Stoa, the colonnade where Zeno taught) vs. Garden. J.'s eclecticism is interesting; so is the characteristic omission of Platonic or Aristotelian philosophy, which during this period had virtually dropped out of sight.

17. What was so rare about white hens? Nothing, one would have thought. The scholiast, probably guessing, claimed the phrase as a *proverbium vulgare*, meaning 'noble'. Courtney (552, with reff.) explains that there existed a special breed of imperial white hens 'descended from one which gave an omen to Livia': the flock was extinct by the end of Nero's reign. Calvinus in that case would either have enjoyed the emperor's patronage, or else have had some putative blood-relationship with the imperial family. I do not find this explanation very satisfactory, but nobody has come up with a better one.

18. Reading *an dubitet? solitumst*, the emendation proposed to Mayor by Munro, and cited by Courtney (553).

19. For parricide in Rome and its punishment see Sat. VIII 214 and n. 27 ad loc.

20. The legend of pitched battles between the southward-flying cranes and the Pygmies (variously located in Ethiopia and Egypt) goes back at least as far as Homer's day: see *Il.* 3.3–6, Arist. *HA* 8.597a4 (cf. Hdt. 2.32.6), Strabo 15.1.57, C.711. Pliny and Pomponius Mela also refer to it. Aristotle believed it; Strabo was sceptical. Cranes do, in fact, migrate south in winter; and apparently the Akka dwarfs of

Central Africa do hunt them: the cranes are said to fight back with zest. This odd fact could have filtered back to Greece by way of Egypt or Cyrene, acquiring mythic accretions en route. The image also slily cuts Calvinus and his problems down to size: Morford 32.

21. At 178 I read *nimius* (some minor MSS, Martyn, Ferguson) rather than *minimus*: see Martyn, *Hermes* 102 (1974) 341−3. The obsession of Roman poets with the murder of Pompey in Alexandria by a Ptolemaic palace cabal after his defeat at Pharsalus (Green, *AA* 664−5) is remarkable, always circling back to the image of a headless corpse on the shore (Pompey's head was sent to Caesar, his body abandoned, see Sat. X n. 28). Virgil (*Aen.* 2.557−8) applied the image to Paris, but no one could mistake its resonance; and he returned to it in the closing line of Bk V (871), this time apropos the steersman who fell overboard and drowned while asleep: 'Nudus in ignota, Palinure, iacebis harena.' Lucan, on the other hand, applied it to Pompey directly (8.667). By J.'s day to evoke it at all would trigger instant literary associations.

22. Chrysippus (*c.* 280−*c.* 207 BC) succeeded Cleanthes, his teacher, as head of the Academy, and was regarded as the most distinguished Stoic after Zeno. There is a story that he saw a donkey eating a plate of figs set out for his own supper, and found the spectacle so amusing that he died of a fit of hysterics. Thales of Miletus (*c.* 640−*c.* 546 BC), the earliest of the Ionian 'pre-Socratic' philosophers, and one of the Seven Sages, believed that the original basic substance of all things was water. He could also predict eclipses, and made a fortune in the olive-oil business after being twitted with his impracticality. Apropos J.'s point, he argued that one lives best by not doing what one stigmatizes in others (Diog. Laert. 1.37). Both Ferguson (302) and Courtney (556) remind us that he also suggested that the most effective way of bearing misfortune was seeing your enemy having an even worse time of it (Diog. Laert. 1.36). As Courtney says, though this doesn't specifically contradict what J. is telling us, had the satirist known that particular apothegm (his philosophical reading seems to have been slight: cf. Sat. X 28 ff., and Introduction p. xlviii), he might well have chosen a different model.

The 'old man who dwelt by sweet Hymettus' was, of course, Socrates himself, seventy years of age at the time of his execution by drinking hemlock in 399 BC. Ferguson (302) points out that J.'s source for this Greek material is in fact Seneca (*Ep.* 24.4). If lines 187−9 represent a Hellenistic philosophical truism − how should one live, how best achieve one's goal (*telos*)? − we probably also owe the moral to Seneca. On J.'s general debt to Seneca's *Letters* see Morford 35 with n. 29.

23. This is not simply an example of J.'s personal anti-female chauvinism (though I am sure he found it highly congenial) but, alas, a well-worn literary topos: Sen. *De Clem.* 1.5.5, *Dial.* 3.20.3, Plut. *Moral.* 8.457b, cf. Courtney 557, Ferguson 302.

24. Rhadamanthus was the son of Zeus and Europa, and sometimes believed to have been a judge in Crete during his lifetime: after death he went, not to Hades but to Elysium (Hom. *Od.* 4.564), where he became a ruler and judge among the dead (Plato *Apol.* 41a). Renowned for his fair and impartial decisions, he was probably most familiar to J. from Virg. *Aen.* 6.566, where he is referred to as dispensing judgments in Tartarus.

25. This story seems to be taken from Herodotus, 6.86, where it is told of one Glaucus son of Epicydes. Glaucus considered withholding a sum deposited with him from the depositor's heirs, and made the mistake of asking Delphi whether this would be permissible. The oracle informed him, tartly, that such perjury would result in the eradication of the perjuror's family. He therefore returned the deposit. But to no avail: he had tempted the oracle, and his family became extinct anyhow.

What in fact is J. saying here? That the will to crime is as bad as the act itself (cf. Jesus on the contemplation of adultery)? That efforts to win acquiescence for one's peccadilloes from the gods constitute criminal blasphemy? Or simply (so Courtney 557) that conscience, itself the worst of punishments, is bad enough when a crime is merely considered, and thus *a fortiori* worse still when the act is committed? In any case, Calvinus can take comfort from the knowledge that the man who has bilked *him* can expect a singularly unpleasant future in consequence. Or can he? The moral fails of its effect in Herodotus: Leotychidas the Spartan king uses it to try and shame the Athenians into returning some hostages: they take no notice. Nor, clearly, did Calvinus' enemy. See Edmunds 71.

26. Cf. Sat. X 170 and n. 19 ad loc.

27. Courtney (560, cf. *BICS* 13, 1966, 42) queries *nec surdum nec Teresian* at line 249 and makes the attractive emendation *Drusum* for *surdum*, meaning 'that no god is either as blind as Tiresias or as deaf as the Emperor Claudius': cf. Sat. III 238. Edmunds (73) remarks, with shrewd irony, on J.'s conclusion, that yes, Calvinus' enemy, through his very corruption, will end up falling foul of the authorities (equally corrupt themselves), 'but Calvinus, for his part, will regard this vengeance as divine: his faith in the gods will be restored'. Even the myth of divine justice is a fraud suitable only for simpletons.

SATIRE XIV

Useful General Studies

Bellandi   Bellandi, F., 'Sulla struttura della satira 14 di Giovenale',
                Prometheus 10 (1984) 154–60.
O'Neil   O'Neil, E. N., 'The structure of Juvenal's Fourteenth Satire',
                CPh 55 (1960) 251–3.
Stein   Stein, J. P., 'The unity and scope of Juvenal's 14th satire', *CPh*
                65 (1970) 34–6.

1. Again, the dedicatee of this satire is a person otherwise unknown.

2. The literal translation of *ficedulas* is 'beccaficoes', but I have preferred, for English-speaking readers, more familiar delicacies: the only point of the reference here is that the dish should symbolize *gourmandise*.

3. It is often argued that in this poem J. has two themes, not very well combined, but rather treated, somewhat awkwardly, in succession: (i) irresponsible parental influence, and (ii) *avaritia*, combining miserliness and extravagance. Courtney (561–2) even cites Horace (*Serm.* 1.1) as a literary model for this uncomfortable structure. But the opening of the poem (1–14) demonstrates clearly that J. is launching a general satirical attack on every aspect of the acquisitive society, and that this acquisitiveness is engendered and perpetuated by parental example (cf. Bellandi, 154 ff.). Gluttony, sadism, infidelity, lavish entertainment – all are habits learnt early, and stamped on a child's character for life. Ferguson (315) has some sensible comments on this phenomenon.

4. It is likely (but by no means certain) that this Rutilus is the gluttonous spendthrift of Satire XI 1–11; see n. 1 ad loc.

5. The vocabulary ('material', 'elements') is Lucretian, and thus tinged with Epicureanism; but the sentiment – a fairly commonplace reflection – is, if anything, Stoic: Courtney 564 with reff., Ferguson 306. We may assume it was the kind of conventional *obiter dictum* to be expected from the 'bearded tutors' (12), i.e. those tame resident intellectuals who combined the roles, approximately, of schoolmaster and domestic chaplain.

6. Catullus (12) and Martial (12.29) both allude to light-fingered guests who make off with napkins. It is also possible that *lintea* could refer to towels in the public baths (also often stolen: Catull. 25, and cf. Courtney 565). The 'field-gang labour camps' were the notorious *ergastula*, semi-underground barracks in which fettered slaves who worked the large country estates were confined. Columella condemned this system, not for its inhumanity, but because it was uneconomical: Cato, in his *Res Rustica*, recommends in the same breath the dumping of worn-out harness and worn-out slaves.

7. The ancient cupping-glass was shaped like a gourd: hence its Latin name of *cucurbita*. One of its chief uses, surprisingly, was to draw blood from the head, a process thought to relieve madness (? cerebral congestion): Petr. *Sat.* 90, Celsus 3.18, cf. Courtney 568. The operation involved burning linen inside the cup to create a vacuum and thus draw out blood: the principle can still be seen in those 'burning cones' popularly used to extract earwax. Ferguson (307) deserves credit for unravelling J.'s joke here, the double play on a vacuum which is 'in the head where it should be in the glass – *cucurbita* too, since it is the Latin for a blockhead (Petr. 39): we are applying a *cucurbita* to a *cucurbita*!'

8. As both Ferguson (307) and Courtney (570) are quick to point out, vultures in fact nest among rocks, not in trees. Ovid (*Am.* 1.12.20) makes the same mistake.

9. A passion for extravagant building was one of the main forms of what Thorstein

Veblen calls 'conspicuous consumption' amongst wealthy Romans under the Empire. The tendency was satirized by Horace before J., and Martial also alludes to it. As Duff reminds us (419), even people of comparatively moderate fortune, such as Cicero or the Younger Pliny, were remarkable for the number and luxury of the country houses they owned.

10. This was 'Posides the eunuch, to whom [Claudius] actually awarded, at his British triumph, the honour of a headless spear, along with soldiers who had fought in the field' (Suet. *Claud.* 28). He also built baths at the seaside resort of Baiae (Plin. *NH* 31.5).

11. J., as Highet rightly points out (283), knew more about the Jews than any other Roman writer with the possible exception of Tacitus. Naturally he is most familiar with public rules or prohibitions: abstention from eating pork or worshipping images (Augustus once said he would rather be Herod's pig than his son: Macrob. 2.4.11), obedience to the commandments of the Torah. Circumcision, though less visible, was nevertheless a standing joke, not least since smart Hellenizing Jews, anxious to exercise in their local gymnasium, went to curious lengths to reverse the physical effects (Green, *AA* 510 with nn. 96–8). Line 97 (so reminiscent of the Aristophanic Socrates) enshrines a false deduction from the Jewish reluctance to name God, and consequent tendency to substitute the word 'heaven': that the Jews were sky-worshippers.

It has been suggested that in this passage he shows familiarity with a number of technical terms: e.g. 'the *numen* of the heavens' is the equivalent of *shamayim*, one of the periphrases for the Name of God (Tac. *Hist.* 5.5, had the same notion in mind when he said that 'the Jews worship with the mind alone'). There is a distinction between the two stages of Judaic conversion: the father is a Proselyte of the Gate, the son a Proselyte of Righteousness. Line 101 seems to parody biblical language; and J., like other Roman writers, emphasizes the negative and prohibitive aspects of Jewish law that would be most apparent to an outsider. Some authorities regard the request for water as an allusion to the practice of baptism (J. and his contemporaries made no clear distinction between Judaism and Christianity); but it seems more likely that J. is attacking 'prohibitions against showing the commonest offices of humanity . . . to any but co-religionists' (Duff 421: this charge of exclusive stand-offishness is also made by Tac. *Hist.* 5.5). Both J. and Tacitus, again, attribute the workless Jewish Sabbath to natural laziness and indolence.

12. The garden of the Hesperides, out in western Ocean beyond the Pillars of Hercules (perhaps the Azores or Canaries) contained a tree of golden apples (? oranges, lemons) guarded by the serpent Ladon: Hercules slew the serpent and carried off the apples. Colchis, at the E. end of the Black Sea, was where the Golden Fleece hung in a sacred grove, again guarded by a monstrous serpent. Medea drugged the serpent, after which she and Jason fled with the Fleece.

13. King Pyrrhus of Epirus (*c.* 318–272 BC) fought several successful campaigns against Rome from 280 BC onwards: he was, amongst other things, the first general

to introduce elephants into Italy. When he withdrew from Italy he remarked, with some prescience, 'What a battleground I am leaving to Rome and Carthage.' The subsequent Carthaginian or Punic Wars, in which Rome was opposed by Hannibal, were only concluded by the final defeat of Hannibal at Zama in 202 BC. (Half a century later came the fulfilment of Cato's dream: the total eradication of Carthage as a city.) J. is thus including all the veterans of a century's campaigning in his generalization.

14. The vinestaff was the centurion's badge of office: the rank itself is difficult for a modern reader to appreciate, since it combined the functions of a warrant officer and a company commander. For the plebeian recruit it was the summit of his ambition to attain centurion's rank: the boy described here would be lucky to begin his service with such status, even at the bottom of the list. The highest honour he could eventually hope for (197) was to become Centurion of the Standard (*primipilaris*). A person of equestrian rank, on the other hand, was obliged to serve in the army at four successive levels (of which centurion was the lowest) before becoming eligible for a post in the civil service. See Duff's useful note (427–8). Someone of senatorial rank began at the next level above centurion, as a military tribune.

15. The father's invocation of 'Moroccan encampments and British border forts' is a clever psychological touch on J.'s part. To begin with, he is a little out of date (as fathers so often are): this last, fifth, group of satires (XIII–XVI) can be dated to *c.* AD 130 or even later; but Hadrian had dealt with the rebellions in North Britain and Mauretania ten years before (120/1). Also the facts are a little shaky: the Brigantes (named by J.), up near the Scottish border, in fact had very few forts (Courtney 579). The boy is being encouraged by a not-too-accurate evocation of the past.

16. Certain commodities and activities (hides and tanning are an obvious example) were restricted by law to the further side of the Tiber, beyond the Janiculum.

17. We have a knowing allusion here to a famous anecdote. Vespasian slapped a tax on urine (which was collected and used by fullers). His son Titus found this method of augmenting revenue a trifle demeaning, and said so. Vespasian then asked him if he found that the money derived from this source smelt worse than any other (Suet. *Vesp.* 23, Dio Cass. 66.14.5).

18. Telamon and Peleus were brothers; exiled from Aegina for the murder of their half-brother Phocus, they both took part in the great Calydonian boar-hunt, and both accompanied Jason to Colchis as Argonauts. Achilles was the offspring of Peleus' unhappy marriage to the sea-nymph Thetis, who was fated to bear a son greater than his father. Telamon ended as King of Salamis, while his son Ajax (more properly Aias) earned surpassing fame as a warrior at Troy.

19. At line 229 I accept the emendation of D. A. Amyx (*CPh* 36, 1941, 278 f.) and read: *quippe et per fraudes patrimonia conduplicare.* This reading has also been adopted by Ferguson.

20. According to legend, when Cadmus reached Thebes, he killed the dragon of Ares guarding a spring where he had sent his followers to obtain water. Athena told him to sow the dragon's teeth, and when he did so armed men sprang up from the furrow. These were the Sparti, or 'Sown Men'. Cadmus threw stones in amongst them, and they thought they were being attacked by their fellow-Sparti: in the ensuing battle all but five of them were killed. These five helped Cadmus build his city. Courtney observes, tartly (582), that J. 'corroborates his doubts of the veracity of Greece by sarcastically suggesting that these are everyday occurrences at Thebes'. Cf. Ferguson 312.

Menoeceus, and his grandson of the same name, were descended from these Sparti. Menoeceus the elder was the father of Jocasta and Creon. After Jocasta's marriage to Oedipus plague struck Thebes, and Tiresias the prophet declared it could only be averted if one of the Sparti's descendants sacrificed himself for the city: Menoeceus thereupon jumped to his death from the walls. (For the magic nature of this *devotio* see Sat. VIII 254–8 and n. 35 ad loc.) The grandson, Creon's son, either committed suicide or was killed before the gates of the city during the War of the Seven Against Thebes, when Tiresias, again, declared that Thebes would only be saved if a descendant of the Sparti gave up his life to appease Ares, still rancorous, it seems, over the destruction of the Sparti by Cadmus. The two stories *may* be variant versions of the same myth – but not necessarily so: they are no odder a duplication than the parallel one of the Decii (on whom see Sat. VIII 254–8 and n. 35 ad loc.).

21. Another example of the ancient addiction to outrageous tall stories in the field of natural history: the scholiast solemnly declares that some stags lived to be nine hundred years old! But even this is eclipsed by Pliny's citation from Hesiod in the *Natural History* (7.153), that, while crows live nine times longer than humans, stags live four times as long as crows: thus 9 x 70 x 4 = 2,520 years! It comes as a relief to find that Aristotle, at least (*HA* 6.29.578b 23) was sceptical.

22. For the prophylactics of Mithridates see Sat. VI 660–61, and n. 72 ad loc. Cf. Aul. Gell. 17.66.6, Plin. *NH* 29.24. Mithridates, too (Courtney 583), had good reason to fear his sons.

23. For the praetor's function at the Games see above, Satire XI 193 ff. and n. 22 ad loc. The notion of life-as-theatre goes back to the Hellenistic era, when the visual arts in particular fostered the belief that 'all the world's a stage': see Green, *AA* 92–4, 342, 361, 579.

24. Money was regularly deposited in a temple for safe-keeping, just as we would deposit it in a bank. From this passage it appears that when J. wrote, the temple of Mars the Avenger had recently been burgled, and that the thieves had got away, not only with various citizens' cash-boxes, but also (supreme insult) with whatever they could prise loose from the god's own image. (For this practice see Sat. XIII 150–53.) The temple of Castor (and Pollux) was in the Forum: cf. Sat. X 24–5 and n. 3 ad loc. Apparently a military guard (*uigilem*) was posted there – as until 1973 at the Bank of England. It was located, conveniently, in the banking quarter, and had ample vaults (Courtney 583).

25. In 1967 I wrote: 'At line 269, for the meaningless †acullis† or scarcely more satisfactory *ac uilis* of the MSS [a view shared by Ferguson, 313] I conjecture *ac facilis*, and translate accordingly.' There have been other proposals. Griffith (1969, 386) suggested *fatuus*. Schreiber's *adquirens* (*Hermes* 99, 1971, 383–4) has been tentatively accepted by Ferguson (313), on the grounds of acquisitiveness being this satire's key leitmotiv. (Unfortunately, the emendation makes for bad Latin.) Courtney, however (584–5) argues convincingly that *perditus* here means 'reckless', not 'lost', and that there is no need for emendation at all. His 'reckless and contemptible' trader makes good sense in context, and has the great advantage of leaving the textual tradition intact: the 'recklessness' consists in the risks he is prepared to take (274–5: *temerarius*) in pursuit of cash and property. I therefore now retain *ac uilis*, and translate in accordance with Courtney's interpretation.

26. The idea of the sun hissing like red-hot metal as it dipped into Ocean was popular with Roman poets. Some thinkers, indeed, treated the idea as fact rather than poetic fiction: e.g. Epicurus (fr. 346b Usener), refuted by Posidonius (fr. 119 Edelstein-Kidd). Line 281 alludes to the fact that Hercules travelled to Spain (for the cattle of Geryon) and the Hesperides (for the golden apples: see above, line 113 and n. 12); it was on the former occasion that he traditionally established the famous Pillars of Hercules that served as a kind of formal gateway to the unknown. At 283 J. slily mocks tall travellers' tales, but also contrives to suggest a sexual substratum to the fantasy.

27. Orestes was pursued by the Furies after killing his mother Clytemnestra; Ajax went mad after being adjudged the loser in his contest with Odysseus for the arms of Achilles: see Sat. XI 31 and n. 6 ad loc. The scene described by J. approximates most closely in literature to Eur. *Orest.* 260–64. It is surprising that so visually dramatic a configuration does not seem to be represented in surviving art: see *LIMC* 7.1 (1994) 68–75 s.v. 'Orestes'.

28. The rivers in question were the Tagus in Spain (Catull. 29.19, Plin. *NH* 33.66) and the Pactolus in Lydia (Plin. ibid., Hor. *Epist.* 15.20). Both were believed – in all likelihood with justice – to wash down gold-dust.

29. For the very real dangers of fire in Rome see Sat. III 197–222 with n. 22 ad loc.

30. For the 'naked Cynic' Diogenes of Sinope see n. 16 to Sat. XIII 120 ff. The text here makes it clear that his 'tub' was not a wooden barrel but a huge pottery jar. It was, in fact, broken at least once: Diog. Laert. 6.43.

31. J. is referring to the famous – and perhaps not apocryphal – anecdote of the meeting between Alexander and Diogenes, which purportedly took place in Corinth (where Diogenes also spent much time: 'presumably he maintained a "tub" in each city', Courtney 588). Alexander asked what favour he could bestow on Diogenes, and was told to get out of the way, because he was blocking the sunlight. Note that for J. it is Diogenes, not Alexander, who is 'great' (311–12).

32. The words in square brackets are repeated from Sat. X 365–6; and though J. elsewhere repeats a line (e.g. the doublet of I 24 and X 226) the aphorism seems very much out of place here. Courtney (588), while conceding the awkwardness, supposes that J. is referring us back to the earlier poem ('remember what I said previously'), but this seems strained and unnatural. Ferguson (314) suspects that several lines have dropped out of the text here. Lacunae are a chronic problem in J.'s work (far more serious than those much-touted metrical interpolations), and this may well be the true explanation.

33. For Epicurus see n. 16 to Sat. XIII.

34. Basically a good Stoic truism; but Epicureans also shared this particular sentiment (Courtney 588 with reff.), and in any case J., as we have seen, was both amateur and eclectic (more often than not restricting himself to popular apothegms) in philosophical matters.

35. The 'legal minimum capital of a burgher', or member of the Equestrian Order, was 400,000 sesterces: see Sat. III 159 and n. 18 ad loc.

36. Narcissus was Claudius' immensely wealthy Imperial Secretary (*ab epistulis*), and a close confidant of his wife Messalina (Suet. *Claud.* 28, Plin. *NH* 33.134). But after Messalina contracted her lunatic 'marriage' with Gaius Silius (see Sat. X 329 ff. and n. 32 ad loc.), Narcissus and the other Palace freedmen determined to be rid of her. According to Tacitus (*Ann.* 11.30–38), Narcissus himself had her killed by an officer of the Praetorian Guard, and informed Claudius of the deed as a *fait accompli*. As a coda this story drives home J.'s bleak and pessimistic message: in Stein's words (36), 'before the many and varied forces marshalled by *avaritia* Rome goes down to defeat'. The acquisitive society ends by destroying itself.

SATIRE XV

Useful General Studies

Anderson	Anderson, W. S., 'Juvenal Sat. 15: Cannibals and culture', *Ramus* 16 (1987) 203–14.
Fredericks	Fredericks, S. C., 'Juvenal's fifteenth satire', *ICS* 1 (1976) 174–89.
Lindsay	Lindsay, J., *Daily Life in Roman Egypt* (London: 1963) 109–21.
McKim	McKim, R., 'Philosophers and cannibals: Juvenal's fifteenth satire', *Phoenix* 40 (1986) 58–71.
Powell	Powell, B. B., 'What Juvenal saw. Egyptian religion and anthropology in Sat. 15', *RhM* 122 (1979) 185–9.
Pryor	Pryor, A. D., 'The best satires . . . together with some observations on J.'s anthropophagous comedy', *AUMLA* 14 (1972) 44–55.

Singleton   Singleton, D., 'Juvenal's fifteenth satire. A reading', *G. & R.* 30
                   (1983) 198–207.

1. Once more we have an unknown dedicatee. The cognomen Bithynicus (attached
by J. to Volusius) was not uncommon, occurring in the Pompeian gens (Courtney
592). It was not exclusively noble. One Volusius Maecianus, a distinguished jurist,
served on the Privy Council of Antoninus Pius (reigned AD 138–61).

     The identity – or at least the nature, be he real or fictional – of the narrator
acquires some importance from the ambivalent nature of this satire. Is he joking
(Pryor) or serious (Singleton), anti-Egyptian (Courtney, Ferguson), or subtly anti-
Roman (McKim, Anderson)? If he 'proves to be a bigoted and irrational racist
Roman' (Anderson 204), is it then legitimate to conclude (as Anderson does) that
'he is not Juvenal'? Is he (Fredericks 174 ff.) modulating between the vice of *ira*
(anger) and the virtue of *humanitas*? Could he even (Powell 185 ff.) have witnessed
a ritual *sparagmos* ('dismemberment') and *omophagia* ('eating of raw flesh') the
significance of which he failed to grasp? Of recent studies, Anderson's strikes me as
by far the most persuasive: J. presents us with a narrator whose xenophobia is only
matched by his inaccuracy, tendentiousness, and prejudices, in order to slily suggest
that Rome's imperial militarists are in fact worse than the natives they dominate
(and thus lead into Sat. XVI). After all, the Spanish instances of starvation justifying
cannibalism he cites were brought about, in the first instance, by besieging Roman
armies. What is more, Petronius (*Sat.* 140) had already used these same Spanish
precedents to justify Eumolpus' decision to make his would-be heirs eat his dead
body first. My only worry about this persona is the feeling that, *pace* Anderson, it
could well be J. himself.

2. Egyptian gods were supposed to manifest themselves on earth in 'theophanies'
associated with specific animals. The crocodile-god Sebek (whom the Greeks called
Souchos) was worshipped in the Fayyum; Herodotus (2.69) confirms that 'some
Egyptians reverence the crocodile as a sacred beast; others do not, but treat it as an
enemy'. The ibis was associated with Thoth, the scribe-god of Khmunu (Hermo-
polis); Herodotus (2.75) claims that the ibis was worshipped because it killed flying
serpents (cf. Plin. *NH* 10.75: it does, in fact, eat snakes). Another of Thoth's
theophanies was the cynocephalous (*not* the long-tailed) ape, and the mummified
remains of these creatures have frequently been discovered. Ubastet or Bast was the
great cat-headed goddess of Bubastis (cf. Hdt. 2.66–7). Several river-fish were
regarded as sacred, in particular the *anet*, which announced the rise of the Nile, and
the eel (Hdt. 2.72). Herodotus (2.66–7) claims that the dog was sacred, but the
theophany here described is probably that of Anubis, the jackal-headed cemetery-god
whose cult was mainly observed at Abydos. The contrast with Diana, in this context,
is that – apart from being anthropo- rather than theriomorphic – she was, as huntress,
patron of (? hunting) dogs: whether these were frequently sacrificed to her (so Duff
440) is less certain. The half-destroyed statue of Memnon at Thebes (supposedly of

Memnon, actually of Amenophis III) used to produce noises at sunrise, like some sort of stringed instrument: rapid rise in temperature, it is believed, set up vibrations in the loosened mass of stone. When Septimus Severus restored the statue in AD 202 the musical effects stopped (Strabo 17.1.46, C.816; Paus. 1.42.2; Tac. *Ann.* 2.61). The ruins of hundred-gated Thebes were a great draw for Roman tourists.

3. 'In Egypt,' the Elder Pliny tells us (*NH* 19.101), 'people swear by garlic and onions as deities in taking an oath'. 'Leeks and onions' (*porrum et caepe*) is an echo of Horace (*Epist.* 1.12.21), where Pythagoreanism forms the target. There seems in fact to have been no abstention from leeks in Egypt, where they grew well and figured prominently in the normal diet (Plin. *NH* 19.110). Diodorus (1.89.4) mentions lentils and beans, as well as onions, as items of diet from which some Egyptians abstained: the common factor here may well be the flatulence which they cause (cf. below, n. 26).

Sheep were worshipped (Plin. *NH* 8.199), but goats apparently not: the 'goat of Mendes' associated with Pan (Hdt. 2.42, 46) was in fact a species of sheep closely resembling a goat (Courtney 595). Herodotus (2.45) explicitly denies that the Egyptians practised human sacrifice (or, by implication, cannibalism); J. (Courtney ibid.) 'infers the legitimacy of cannibalism from the fact that it had happened'. Quite apart from special cases of famine (e.g. that reported at Diod. Sic. 1.84.1) it may be worth recalling that cases of cannibalistic *omophagia* (eating of heart, liver and brains in particular), often in strikingly berserk circumstances, as with the case J. reports, have been noted throughout history, from Diomedes' father Tydeus sucking the brains out of a decapitated head on the battlefield to Cambodian mutineers in 1975, wolfing down their murdered officer's lungs, liver, heart, biceps and calves (E. Vermeule, *Aspects of Death in Early Greek Art and Poetry*, Berkeley: 1975, 94, 133).

Herodotus observed (2.42) that those in the province of Thebes never sacrificed sheep, but only goats; in the Mendesian province exactly the reverse was true.

4. Odysseus recounts his adventures, at length, to Alcinous and the other Phaeacians in Bks IX–XII of the *Odyssey*. In the first lines of Bk XIII we read that when he had finished, 'dead silence fell on all, and they were spell-bound throughout the shadowy halls'. J. suggests, wittily, that this silence was due, not so much to awed admiration as to sheer stunned disbelief. The next morning Odysseus was given gifts of departure and sent on his way – again, a reaction capable of more than one interpretation.

5. For the Cyclops see *Od.* 9.216 ff.; Laestrygonians, 10.80 ff.; Scylla (the tentacled sea-monster) and Charybdis, 12.80 ff. J. identifies the 'Clashing Rocks' of the Argonauts' voyage with Odysseus' 'Wandering Rocks' (*Od.* 12.59–72): in fact they are clearly distinguished, the Clashing Rocks (*Symplegades*) being at the entry to the Black Sea from the Bosphorus, and the Wandering Rocks (*Planktai*) in the Straits of Messina between Italy and Sicily. Aeolus and the bag of the winds: *Od.* 10.1 ff.; Circe, Elpenor, and the metamorphosis into swine, 10.210 ff. (thanks to Courtney, 597, for the nice oxymoron 'pig-oarsmen' (*remigibus . . . porcis*). Phaeacia from early times was identified with Corcyra (modern Corfu), lying off the coast of Albania.

6. Here we have one of the few datable references in J.'s work. The riot took place during the consulship of Aemilius Juncus: that is, between October and December, AD 127. This is described as *nuper*, 'recently' – though, as Duff (442) points out, 'recently' could stretch to a period of over thirty years. At all events, the date of the satire's composition is likely to have been about 130.

7. Pyrrha, Deucalion's consort, is chosen here for chronological reasons, as a characteristic example of a creation myth.

8. For many years it was thought that J. had got his geography wrong, and was writing on hearsay, since though the position of Tentyra (Dendereh), to the north of Coptos (mod. Negadeh) was not in question, Ombi had been identified with Kom-Ombo, 200 miles away on the other bank of the Nile. But in 1895 Flinders Petrie found the real Ombi not ten miles from Tentyra: see Highet, 28–9, with reff. Ombi worshipped Set, the pig-headed god of darkness, the evil killer of Osiris; Tentyra worshipped Hathor, the cow-headed goddess of love, and the Tentyrites also abominated the crocodile (Strabo 17.1.44 C.815; Sen. *NQ* 4.2.15), which was worshipped at Ombi: Courtney (598) identifies the crocodile as the source of the quarrel. 'Up-country' (*super*) places the battle near Ombi, so the Tentyrites (cf. 72–6) seem to have been the aggressors.

9. Lindsay (109–21) devotes a whole chapter to this incident, and the interested reader should consult it in detail. In particular he cites an apt parallel, shortly after the events here described, from Plutarch, *Isis and Osiris* 72 (380 BC): 'Within our memory, the Oxyrhynchites, on account of the people of Cynopolis presuming to eat their revered fish, in revenge seized on all the dogs, the sacred beasts of their foes, which came their way, offering them in sacrifice and eating their flesh just as they did the flesh of other victims. This brought about a civil war between the two cities . . .' Lindsay also cites a curious passage from Philo, *On the Contemplation of Life*, 5, in which it is asserted that the Egyptians, when drunk at a feast, 'bellow and roar like wild dogs, attack and bite each other and gnaw off noses, ears, | fingers, and other parts of the body'. J. Moreau, 'Une scène d'anthropophagie en Egypte en l'an 127 de notre ère', *Chronique d'Egypte* 15 (1940) 279–85, suggests that we have to do here with a magic rite designed to protect the living from the dead; but this (Ferguson 322) goes against the thrust of J.'s argument. Had there been a religious motive for the cannibalism, J. would not have wasted so welcome a chance to go Lucretius one better on the evils wrought by superstition.

10. Ever since late antiquity it has been generally assumed from this phrase – *quantum ipse notaui* in Latin – that J. is referring to his own residence in Egypt, and indeed this is possible. Courtney (599) points out that what the words mean is 'so far as my personal observation goes' rather than 'as I have noticed' (*quantum* in the sense of *ut* being a late development, after J.'s day), and argues that this simply implies 'to judge from the Egyptians I have met'. Perhaps; but to maintain that these Egyptians were *necessarily* observed in Rome rather than Egypt is a wholly unwarrantable assumption. J. may still have visited, or resided in, Egypt; the most we can say is that this evidence is one degree less clinching than was formerly supposed.

11. For these heavings of heroic boulders see Hom. *Il.* 5.307–8 (Diomedes at Aeneas), 7.268–70 (Ajax at Hector), 12.380; Virg. *Aen.* 12.896–902 (Turnus at Aeneas).

12. Reading *hinc* (P and O) rather than *hic*: see Courtney 602.

13. Reading *Prometheu, donasti*: Griffith (1969, 387), accepted by Courtney (602).

14. The Spanish tribe in question was that of the Vascones (Basques): after the death in 72 BC of the rebel Roman general Sertorius, whom they had supported, their capital, Calagurris (the birthplace of Quintilian) was besieged by the Romans under Afranius, and the sufferings they endured became proverbial: see e.g. Florus 2.10.9, Val. Max. 7.6.§3 (including cannibalism).

15. Readers should be warned that the sense of this couplet is at best approximate: the Latin is garbled and may well be spurious. Discussion in Courtney (603).

16. For Zeno see n. 16 to Sat. XIII. Here J. betrays his philosophical ignorance once again. In fact Zeno might well have vindicated the Vascones in their survival techniques: under such circumstances Stoics were permitted to practise cannibalism, though not to kill for food. See the discussions of Courtney (604) and Ferguson (319). As Ferguson says, 'J. obviously did not know this.'

17. This was the protracted war during which the Spaniards, led by the Roman general Sertorius, fought – with considerable·initial success – against the legions of Pompey and Q. Caecilius Metellus Pius (79–72 BC). At one point Sertorius held most of Roman Spain.

18. The reference to 'Iceland' (*Thyle* or *Thule*, an all-purpose term for the frozen islands of the far north, including material from the Orkneys, Shetlands and Faeroes) makes it clear that J. is mocking foreign/provincial pretensions. He probably felt much the same about Gallic intellectuals; but, as Ferguson stresses (320), by Hadrian's day the major cities of Gaul – Augustodunum (Autun), Lugdunum (Lyons: cf. Sat. I 44 and n. 5 ad loc.), and Massilia (Marseilles) – were indeed well-established cultural centres.

The reference at 113–15 is to Hannibal's siege and capture of Saguntum, in Hispania Tarraconensis, 219/8 BC: Livy 21.14–15. Though the city suffered much on this occasion (all adult males were executed), the story of cannibalism seems to be a late addition. Cf. Petr. *Sat.* 141, where it is referred to, together with the sieges of Petelia and Numantia.

19. The Tauri in the Crimea worshipped Artemis (or a goddess called Opis or Upis whom the Greeks identified as Artemis) with human sacrifices of any strangers who fell into their hands: see esp. Eur. *IT passim*, e.g. 28 ff. and 384, where the goddess is said to 'delight in human sacrifice'. J.'s point is that though they killed strangers, they at least refrained from eating them.

20. Most large Egyptian cargo vessels were made of acacia-wood, the *Mimosa nilotica* still used for this purpose; smaller rafts or punts were of papyrus reed, lashed together with rope. There is a good description of their construction in Herodotus (2.90). The painted earthenware wherries described by J. seem to have been tiny craft used on the network of streams and canals intersecting the Delta: Strabo, the geographer, who also visited Egypt, mentions them in this connection (17.1.4, C.788). It is possible that the clay was laid on a wicker base (or perhaps planks were set over pots lashed together: so Courtney 607), and that the boat is identical with the *pacton*, a kind of coracle, to which he later refers: cf. 17.1.50, C.818, and for their painted decorations, Virg. *Georg.* 4.287–9. J. imbues his entire description with contempt (note the jeering diminutives).

21. 'It is the universal custom of mankind,' Pliny tells us in the *Natural History*, 'not to cremate a person who dies before cutting his teeth' (7.72). The claim would appear to be true: see Courtney 609 for confirmatory reff. As Duff (450) reminds us, this custom still prevails among the Hindus; and cremation was not universal, even for adults.

22. i.e. worthy and pure enough to qualify as an initiate in the Mysteries of Demeter held at Eleusis, near Athens. The priest, or Hierophant, would pronounce what was known as the *prorrhesis*, a warning to the wicked and profane that they should withdraw before the ceremony began, and not participate in it: see Aristophanes, *Frogs* 354–71. Hadrian himself had been initiated a year or two before the composition of this satire. For a general account see G. E. Mylonas, *Eleusis and the Eleusinian Mysteries* (Princeton: 1962).

23. The ideals expressed in lines 143–7 are basically Stoic: indeed (Courtney 610) they can all be closely paralleled from Cicero (*De Legibus* 1.22–6), and one could legitimately speculate that it may have been this passage which J. had in mind when he wrote. The contrast between beasts on all fours (eyes on the ground) and men (upright, able to gaze skyward, hence divinely endowed) was a commonplace from early times: Xen. *Mem.* 1.4.11, Plato *Tim.* 90A (?), Arist. *PA* 4.686a 27, Cic. *ND* 2.140, Manil. 4.897–906 (Courtney 610), Ovid *Met.* 1.84–7.

24. Ferguson (321), always shrewd on J.'s popular philosophical borrowings, points out how eclectic this passage is: its general development comes from Lucretius Bk 5 (see esp. 1019–20), and hence has an Epicurean flavour; but J. also throws in a divine demiurge and teleological purpose, both anathema to Epicureans but a commonplace of Stoicism. Cf. Arist. *Pol.* 1.2.7 (1252b 15) ff., Cic. *De Inv.* 1.2 ff., *De Rep.* 1.39: other reff. in Courtney 610.

25. Duff (452) remarks on this passage, with demure accuracy: 'Moralists in all ages have pointed to the behaviour of animals to their own kind as an example to man; but the facts are not quite as the moralists have stated them.' As should by now be apparent, a collector of natural-history fallacies would do quite well out of J.

26. Pythagoreanism, with its mystical mathematics, belief in metempsychosis, and various exotic taboos, offered a natural target to irreverent ancient critics; but J.

here, in contrast to his usual attitude, prefers to elevate Pythagoras as a high example of civilized respect for human life: if he abstained even from beans, then *a fortiori* he must have regarded the eating of human flesh with peculiar horror.

There are various explanations given as to why the Pythagoreans abstained from beans. The pleasantest (known to my students as the '*Blazing Saddles* Syndrome') is because they caused flatulence (Diog. Laert. 8.24): the most ingenious that given by R. B. Onians, *The Origins of European Thought* (2nd edn, Cambridge: 1954) 112. Onians reminds us of the Orphic and Pythagorean saying that 'to eat beans is equal to eating the heads of one's parents' (Greek text in Courtney 611). They were symbolic of fertility, generation and intercourse, 'so that there is point and special emphasis in making them taboo as the heads of one's parents. The aim of these food prohibitions . . . seems to have been to prevent the eating of the *psyché* in its various abodes.'

However, like so many ritual prohibitions (e.g. the Jewish taboo on the eating of pork) this one may well have a solidly based original reason, medical rather than symbolic. The most convincing explanation is surely that offered by Richard and Eva Blum, *Health and Healing in Rural Greece* (Stanford: 1965) 78: 'The disease "favism" is associated with a genetic defect in which the enzyme glucose-6 phosphate dehydrogenase is lacking. Some people from the Mediterranean basin lack this enzyme, arnd when they eat the fava bean (horse bean) a hemolytic crisis occurs. We may presume that this reaction had been observed in ancient times and is reflected in the Pythagorean writings.' For other explanations see Ferguson 322. Amusingly enough, when we consider the setting of Sat. XV, Pythagoras was said in antiquity (Plut. *Moral.* 729a) to have derived this taboo from Egypt (cf., above, n. 3).

SATIRE XVI

Useful General Studies

Clark	Clark, M. E., 'Juvenal Sat. 16. Fragmentary justice', *ICS* 13 (1988) 113–25.
Durry	Durry, M., 'Juvénal et les prétoriens', *REL* 13 (1935) 95–106.
Highet	Highet, G., *Juvenal the Satirist* (Oxford: 1954) ch. xxvi ('The Luck of the Army') 154–60, 237–9.
Schnur	Schnur, H. C., 'Iuuenalis Saturae XVI fragmentum nuperrime repertum', *Silvae: Festschrift für Ernst Zinn zum 60. Geburtstag*, ed. M. von Albrecht, E. Heck (Tübingen: 1970) 211–15.*

*Non-classicist readers should perhaps be warned that this 'newly-discovered fragment' is in fact an imaginative, and witty, academic joke: a modern 'completion' of the satire which (like all such exercises in pastiche) draws heavily on the author's other work, but at the same time makes an intelligent guess at the line J. might have taken had he lived to finish it himself, and thus offers something more than mere curiosity value.

1. Gallius, J.'s last known dedicatee, is as anonymous as his predecessors. Inevitably, the suggestion has been made that these were fictitious pegs on which J. hung his homilies; and the practice of using such names is in fact well established by Martial (see esp. 1 *praef.* 2.23 and 10.33). The Younger Pliny mentions the blending of real and assumed names in satire (*Ep.* 6.21.5). But that J. did the same is no more than a possibility: we must not assume that Gallius, Volusius, Postumus and the rest did not exist simply because, in the deficient state of the record, we cannot identify them.

It is now generally agreed (see Durry, 95 ff.) that the troops J. had in mind were the Praetorians, which at once lends a political edge to this fragment. They certainly did well as far as pay went: two denarii *per diem* (Tac. *Ann.* 1.17), double the normal rate. Under Domitian this was increased to a thousand per annum, with a cash bonus of five thousand on discharge, and various other special allowances (Ferguson 324).

2. Jahn, followed by Knoche and Clausen, assumed – rightly, I believe – that something had dropped out of the text after line 2. I have accordingly supplied the line in square brackets as a possible approximation to the sense of what is missing.

3. There is sly irony (on top of the hyperbole) in the notion of a recruit being furnished with a letter of recommendation to Mars the War God, since the Emperor himself was ex officio C.-in-C. of Rome's armed forces. In the same spirit Ovid had equated Augustus with Jupiter.

Virgil (*Aen.* 1.16) tells us that Samos stood at least second in the affections of Juno (Hera); this was almost entirely due to her great temple there, which stood at the mouth of the R. Imbrasos, some four miles south-west of the modern port of Tigani. It was the fourth Heraeum built on the site (its predecessor was burnt *c.* 530 BC) and the largest Greek temple known to us, measuring 179 by 365 feet; it was never completed. By J.'s day it had degenerated into a kind of art-gallery and museum (Strabo, 14.1.14, C.637). Lucretius (1.30–40) emphasizes Venus' ability to soothe angry Mars, in language which suggests he may have had some conventional statue-group in mind.

4. This alone would suffice to prove the satire incomplete, since no other categories are listed. Presumably J. also intended to deal with individuals or special groups (Ferguson 324, Courtney 617–18).

5. Highet (287) points out that 'the poem seems to reflect Hadrian's own new measures to keep the army contented': the cases J. mentions are directly occasioned by his legislation. It was Hadrian who laid down (Just. *Dig.* 22.5.3.6) that soldiers could not leave their units to engage in legal activity in the civilian courts; he was also responsible for the law enabling a soldier to dispose of his property during his father's lifetime. J. is at pains to emphasize the threat to civilians posed by military privileges (Clark 116): Persius too (3.77–85, 5.189–91) stresses the brutal nature of centurions. Still, the civilian lawyers J. portrays (41–7) are scarcely an improvement.

6. At line 18 I accept Kilpatrick's emendation (*CPh* 66, 1971, 115), reading *agitur* for *igitur* of the MSS, involving repunctuation with a semi-colon after *cognito*. Sullivan's additional tinkering (*CPh* 79, 1984, 229) is no improvement, while Shackleton Bailey (*CPh* 81, 1986, 60–61) reverts to the (for once) even less satisfactory suggestions of Housman. It is, of course, impossible to determine whether the remark should be taken ironically, as naïve optimism, or as an ironic J. commenting on naïve optimism.

7. This would have struck J.'s audience as comic: the Praetorians' camp was just outside the city wall, no more than 4–500 yards distant. The 'friends' are thus shown to be making excuses (Courtney 617–18).

8. Boundary-stones were worshipped as images of the god Terminus: for the ritual associated with this somewhat indeterminate deity see Ovid, *Fasti* 2.641–4. The occasion here described will have been the feast of the Terminalia, which took place on 23 February. Cf. Plutarch, *Roman Questions* 15. In a farming culture that lacked defining hedgerows, these stones played an important role. Despite their religious significance, we find necessary legislation against their being surreptitiously shifted by neighbours as impious as they were dishonest (Courtney 618 with reff.).

9. For this privilege, and the exceptions to it, see Just. *Dig.* 49.17 and *Institutes* 2.12 pr., cited at length by Friedländer 599–600.

10. The satire breaks off abruptly at this point. No known MS contains any more of it, and the ancient commentators possessed a similarly deficient version. Three explanations have been advanced: (i) the poem was censored, perhaps by Hadrian; (ii) J. died before he could complete it, and the surviving fragment was published as it stood; or (iii) at some early point in the tradition the end of what turned out to be the one surviving MS was mutilated or lost. Highet (156–9) rejects (ii), the most popular theory, and is very cautious (correctly, in my opinion) about (i). He plumps for (iii), arguing that where fragments survived an author's death in antiquity his editors always tried to polish them up into some sort of completion before publishing, and that the loss of either one or two parchment quires would (at an average of 30 lines a page) produce a poem of just the right length, either 300 or 540 lines.

His second point has more cogency than his first (Bk VIII of Thucydides, for instance, also breaks off *in mediis rebus*). (i) is generally rejected nowadays, and with good reason: censorship would have destroyed the whole poem, not part of it (and that part beginning in mid-sentence): besides, what we have is hardly complimentary. (iii), at first sight the most plausible theory, has two drawbacks. First, it is odd 'that no trace of even a single line has been preserved in either quotation or allusion' (Ferguson 323), and second, the loss of one (or *a fortiori* two) quires from a codex would bulk out Book V suspiciously large. The most common MS page for J. averaged 29 or 30 lines to the page: an 8–page quire would thus contain up to 240 lines. XIII–XV contain 813 lines. If XVI contained either 300 (60 + 240) or 540 (60 + 480) lines, the total would run to 1113 lines minimum, perhaps 1353. Lucretius apart, books that long are virtually unknown in Latin, and in fact no book of J.'s runs over 1000 lines. (ii) thus offers by far the most natural explanation, and is not to be rejected merely because ancient editors tried, more often than not, to give an author's posthumous *oeuvre* some appearance of completeness.

It is interesting that Schnur, when composing his witty (if not always wholly Juvenalian) supplement to the fragment, both conceived a satire of 174 lines only, thus bringing Book V in at the average length overall of 987 lines, and by and large followed Highet's speculation, which critics had figured – wrongly, it now appears – was bound to produce an over-long text. He even concluded (lines 136 ff.) with a section (pp. 214–15) on military service as a road to the purple: 'Maxima sed lucri spes atque occasio fiet / si uacet imperium' – 'But there'll be the highest hope and occasion of profit / if the emperor's throne is vacant.' A plausible, but, as Highet (159) stresses, also a distinctly dangerous peroration.

ABBREVIATIONS

Act. Class.	*Acta Classica* (South Africa)
Ael.	Aelian (Claudius Aelianus), AD 165/70–230/5, essayist
NA	*De Natura Animalium*
AJAH	*American Journal of Ancient History*
AJPh	*American Journal of Philology*
Anc. Soc.	*Ancient Society*
ANRW	*Aufstieg und Niedergang der römischen Welt* (Berlin: 1972–)
App.	Appian[os], *fl.* 2nd c. AD, historian
Bell. Civ.	*Civil Wars*
Mithr.	*Mithridatic Wars*
Ap. Rhod.	Apollonios Rhodios, ?305–?230 BC, epic poet
Arg.	*Argonautika*
Apul.	Apuleius of Madaurus, AD 123–?170, orator and novelist
Met.	*Metamorphoses* (also known as 'The Golden Ass')
Arat.	Aratos of Soloi, *c.* 315–*c.* 240 BC, didactic poet
Phaen.	*Phaenomena*
Arist.	Aristotle of Stagira, 384–322 BC, philosopher
HA	*Historia Animalium*
PA	*De Partibus Animalium*
Pol.	*Politica* ('Politics')
Aristoph.	Aristophanes, *c.* 450–*c.* 385 BC, comic playwright
ASNP	*Annali della Scuola Normale Superiore di Pisa (Classe di Lettere e Filosofia)*
Athen.	Athenaeus of Naukratis, *fl. c.* AD 200, polymath
Aug.	St Augustine (Aurelius Augustinus) of Hippo, AD 354–430, theologian
Civ. Dei	*De Civitate Dei*
Aul. Gell.	Aulus Gellius, *c.* AD 130–*c.* 180, essayist

AUMLA	*Journal of the Australasian Universities' Language and Literature Association*
Aur. Vict.	Aurelius Victor, Sextus, *fl. c.* AD 370, historian
Caes.	*Caesares*
BICS	*Bulletin of the Institute of Classical Studies* (London)
Boll. di Stud. Lat.	*Bollettino di Studi Latini*
Braund, *JS I*	S. Braund, *Juvenal: Satires, Book I* (Cambridge: 1996)
Caes.	G. Julius Caesar, 100–44 BC, statesman and historian
Bell. Gall.	*De Bello Gallico*
Catull.	G. Valerius Catullus of Verona, 84–54 BC, poet
CB	*Classical Bulletin*
Cic.	Marcus Tullius Cicero, 106–43 BC, statesman, orator
Att.	*Ad Atticum*
De Amic.	*De Amicitia*
De Div.	*De Divinatione*
De Fin.	*De Finibus*
De Inv.	*De Inventione Rhetorica*
De Offic.	*De Officiis*
De Rep.	*De Republica*
ND	*De Natura Deorum*
CIL	*Corpus Inscriptionum Latinarum* (Berlin: 1863–)
CJ	*Classical Journal*
Class. & Med.	*Classica et Medievalia* (Copenhagen)
Colum.	Lucius Iunius Moderatus Columella of Gades, *fl.* 1st c. AD, agricultural writer
Courtney	E. Courtney, *A Commentary on the Satires of Juvenal* (London: 1980)
CPh	*Classical Philology*
CQ	*Classical Quarterly*
CR	*Classical Review*
CSCA	*California Studies in Classical Antiquity*
CW	*Classical Weekly*
Dem.	Demosthenes, 384–322 BC, Athenian orator
Dial. di Arch.	*Dialoghi di Archeologia*
Dio Cass.	Cassius Dio Cocceianus of Nicaea, *c.* AD 160–*c.* 235, historian
Epit.	*Epitome Historiarum*
Diod. Sic.	Diodorus Siculus of Agyrium, *fl. c.* 50 BC, historian
Diog. Laert.	Diogenes Laertius, early 3rd c. AD philosophical biographer
Dion. Hal.	Dionysius of Halicarnassos, *c.* 50 BC–?*c.* AD 25, rhetor and historian
RA	*Antiquitates Romanae*
Diss. Abs.	*Dissertation Abstracts*

Eur.	Euripides, *c.* 485–*c.* 406 BC, Athenian tragedian
IT	*Iphigenia Taurica* ('Iphigeneia in Tauris')
Orest.	*Orestes*
Ferguson	J. Ferguson, *Juvenal: The Satires* (New York: 1979)
G. & R.	*Greece & Rome*
GIF	*Giornale Italiano di Filologia*
Green, *AA*	Peter Green, *Alexander to Actium: The Historical Evolution of the Hellenistic Age* (revd, impr., Berkeley: 1993)
JR	'Juvenal Revisited' in *Classical Bearings: Interpreting Ancient History and Culture* (London: 1989) 240–55
Hdt.	Herodotos of Halicarnassos, *c.* 485–*c.* 425 BC, historian
Hes.	Hesiod of Ascra, *fl. c.* 700 BC, epic poet
WD	*Works and Days*
Highet	G. Highet, *Juvenal the Satirist: A Study* (Oxford: 1954)
Hom.	Homer, *fl.* ?*c.* 750 BC, epic poet
Il.	*Iliad*
Od.	*Odyssey*
Hor.	Horace: Q. Horatius Flaccus, 65–8 BC, poet
Epist.	*Epistulae*
Sat., *Serm.*	*Satirae* or *Sermones*
HSCPh	*Harvard Studies in Classical Philology*
ICS	*Illinois Classical Studies*
Id.	*Idyll*
JHS	*Journal of Hellenic Studies*
JRS	*Journal of Roman Studies*
Just. *Dig.*	*Iustiniani Digesta* ('The Digest of Justinian')
LCM	*Liverpool Classical Monthly*
LIMC	*Lexicon Iconographicum Mythologiae Classicae* (Zurich/Munich: 1981–)
Livy	Titus Livius of Patavium, 64/59 BC–AD 12/17, historian
Epit.	*Epitomae*
Lucan	Marcus Annaeus Lucanus of Cordoba, AD 39–65, epic poet
Lucian	Lucian (Λουκιανός) of Samosata, ?AD 120–?190, satirist
Apol.	*Apologia*
Dial. Mer.	*Dialogi Meretricii*
Rhet. Praec.	*Rhetorum Praeceptor*
Macrob.	Ambrosius Theodosius Macrobius, *fl.* early 5th c. AD, scholar
Manil.	Marcus Manilius, *fl. c.* AD 10, didactic poet
Mart.	Marcus Valerius Martialis, *c.* AD 40–*c.* 104, epigrammatist
Epigr. [*Lib.*]	*Epigrammata*
MD	*Materiali e Discussioni per l'Analisi dei Testi Classici*
OLD	*Oxford Latin Dictionary*

Ovid	Publius Ovidius Naso, 43 BC–AD 17/8, elegiac poet
AA	*Ars Amatoria*
Am.	*Amores*
EP	*Epistulae ex Ponto*
Met.	*Metamorphoses*
Trist.	*Tristia*
PACA	*Proceedings of the African Classical Associations*
Paus.	Pausanias, *fl. c.* AD 150, travel writer, geographer
PCPhS	*Proceedings of the Cambridge Philological Society*
Petr.	T. Petronius Arbiter, *fl. c.* AD 60, courtier and novelist
Sat.	*Satyricon* [*Liber*]
Pindar	Pindar (Πίνδαρος), 518–438 BC, lyric poet
Pyth.	*Pythian Odes*
Plato	Plato (Πλάτων), *c.* 429–347 BC, philosopher
Apol.	*Apologia*
Rep.	*Republic*
Tim.	*Timaeus*
Plin.	G. Plinius Caecilius Secundus [the 'Younger'], *c.* AD 61–*c.* 112, lawyer and imperial administrator
Ep.	*Epistulae*
Pan.	*Panegyricus*
Plin.	G. Plinius Secundus [the 'Elder'], AD 24–79, polymath and imperial administrator
NH	*Natural History*
Plut.	Plutarch (Μέστριος Πλούταρχος) of Chaeronea, *c.* AD 45–*c.* 120, biographer and essayist
Cic.	*Vita Ciceronis*
Dem.	*Vita Demosthenis*
Mar.	*Vita Marii*
Moral.	*Moralia*
Quint.	Marcus Fabius Quintilianus, *c.* AD 30–?110, advocate, teacher, rhetorician
Inst. Orat.	*Institutio Oratoria*
RASB	*Rendiconto. Accademia delle Scienze dell'Istituto di Bologna (Classe di Scienze Morali)*
REL	*Revue des Études Latines*
RhM	*Rheinisches Museum für Philologie*
Riv. Stor. dell'Ant.	*Rivista storica dell'Antichità*
Sal.	Gaius Sallustius, 86–35 BC, historian
Cat.	*Bellum Catilinae*
Sat.	*Satura*, satire

schol.	scholion, scholiast
SCO	*Studi Classici e Orientali*
Sen.	Lucius Annaeus Seneca, *c.* 4 BC–AD 65, orator, man of letters, imperial minister [the 'Younger']
Apoc.	*Apocolocyntosis*
Cons. Helv.	*Ad Helviam de Consolatione*
De Clem.	*De Clementia*
Dial.	*Dialogi*
Ep.	*Epistulae*
NQ	*Naturales Questiones*
Suas.	*Suasoria*
Sen.	Lucius Annaeus Seneca, *c.* 50 BC – AD 40, writer on declamation [the 'Elder']
Serv.	Servius (Marius Servius Honoratus), *fl.* late 4th c. AD, grammarian and commentator
SIFC	*Studi Italiani di Filologia Classica*
Sil. Ital.	Tib. Catius Asconius Silius Italicus, AD 26–101, epic poet
SO	*Symbolae Osloenses*
Stat.	Publius Papinius Statius, *c.* AD 45–96, epic and occasional poet
Silv.	*Silvae*
Theb.	*Thebaïs*
Strabo	Strabo (Στράβων) of Amaseia, 64/3 BC–*c.* AD 25, geographer
Suet.	G. Suetonius Tranquillus, AD 69–*c.* 130, imperial civil servant and biographer
Claud.	*Divus Claudius*
Dom.	*Domitianus*
Tib.	*Tiberius*
Verg.	*Vita Vergilii*
Vesp.	*Vespasianus*
Tac.	Cornelius Tacitus, *c.* AD 56–?120, consular and historian
Agric.	*Agricola*
Ann.	*Annales*
Cal.	*Caligula*
Dial.	*Dialogus de Oratoribus*
Germ.	*De Origine et Situ Germanorum* [*Germania*]
Hist.	*Historiae*
TAPhA	*Transactions and Proceedings of the American Philological Association*
Theophr.	Theophrastos of Eresos, *c.* 370–288/5 BC, philosopher
De Lapid.	*De Lapidibus*
UCPCP	*University of California Publications in Classical Philology*
Val. Max.	Valerius Maximus, *fl. c.* AD 30, rhetorician

Varro · Marcus Terentius Varro, 116–27 BC, statesman and polymath
   RR · *Rerum Rusticarum Libri III*
Vell. Pat. · Velleius Paterculus, *c.* 19 BC–*c.* AD 35, historian
Virg. · Publius Vergilius Maro, 70–19 BC, epic and bucolic poet
   Aen. · *Aeneid*
   Ecl. · *Eclogues*
   Georg. · *Georgics*
Vitruv. · Vitruvius Pollio, ?50 BC–?AD 20, architect and military engineer
WS · *Wiener Studien: Zeitschrift für klassische Philologie*
Xen. · Xenophon, *c.* 428/7–*c.* 354 BC, Athenian soldier and historian
   Mem. · *Memorabilia*
YClS · *Yale Classical Studies*

SELECT BIBLIOGRAPHY

This bibliography, heavily revised from its 1974 predecessor, is restricted to basic general titles. Those items dealing with specific satires are listed as Useful General Studies immediately before the notes to the poem concerned. Very occasionally a work of general *and* local interest will be listed in both categories. The titles of texts, commentaries, translations and scholia, etc. are set out chronologically. General studies appear in alphabetical order.

BIBLIOGRAPHICAL SURVEYS

Anderson, W. S., 'Recent work in Roman Satire', for (i) 1937–1955, (ii) 1955–1962, (iii) 1962–1968 and (iv) 1968–1978, all in *Classical Weekly*: 50 (1956) 33–40; 57 (1964) 293–301, 343–8; 63 (1970) 181–94, 199, 217–22; 75 (1981/2) 273–99.

Coffey, M., 'Juvenal 1941–1961', *Lustrum* 8 (1963/8) 161–215.

Rodriguez, M. T. M., 'Juvenal (1979–1992)', *Tempus* 5 (1993) 5–38.

TEXTS AND COMMENTARIES

Ruperti, G. A., *D. Iunii Iuvenalis Aquinatis satirae XVI ad optimorum exemplarium fidem recensitae, varietate lectionum perpetuóque commentario illustratae et indice uberrimo instructae* (2nd edn, Leipzig: 1818).

Jahn, O., *A Persii Flacci D. Iunii Iuvenalis Sulpiciaer Saturae* (Berlin: 1868).

Mayor, J. E. B., *Thirteen Satires of Juvenal* (2nd edn, London: 1872–3).

Duff, J. D., *D. Iunii Iuuenalis saturae XIV: Fourteen Satires of Juvenal* (Cambridge: 1898; revd edn with new introduction by M. Coffey, London: 1970).

Friedländer, L., *Junii Juvenalis Sat. Lib. V mit erklärenden Anmerkungen*, 2 vols (Leipzig: 1905; repr. 1 vol., Amsterdam: 1962).

Housman, A. E., *D. Iunii Iuuenalis saturae, editorum in usum edidit* (Cambridge: 1905; corr. repr. 1931).

Knoche, U., *D. Iunius Iuvenalis Saturae mit kritischem Apparat* (Munich: 1950).

Rudd, N., Courtney, E., *Juvenal: Satires I, III, X* (Bristol: 1977).

Ferguson, J., *Juvenal: The Satires*, edited with Introduction and Commentary (New York: 1979).

Courtney, E., *A Commentary on the Satires of Juvenal* (London: 1980).

Courtney, E., *Juvenal: The Satires* (Rome: 1984).

Martyn, J. R. C., *D. Iuni Iuuenalis saturae* (Amsterdam: 1987).

Clausen, W. V., *A. Persi Flacci et D. Iuni Iuuenalis Saturae edidit breuique adnotatione critica instruxit* (2nd edn, Oxford: 1992).

Braund, S., *Juvenal: Satires, Book I* (Cambridge: 1996).

Willis, J. A., *D. Iunii Iuuenalis saturae sedecim* (Stuttgart & Leipzig: 1997).

TRANSLATIONS, SCHOLIA, ETC.

Wessner, P., *Scholia in Iuvenalem Vetustiora* (Leipzig: 1931).

Knoche, U., *Juvenal: Satiren* (Munich: 1951).

Humphries, R., *The Satires of Juvenal* (Indiana: 1958).

Dubrocard, M., *Juvénal, Satires: Index Verborum, relevés statistiques* (Hildesheim: 1976).

Ferguson, J., *A Prosopography to the poems of Juvenal* (Brussels: 1987).

Viansino, G., *Decimo Giunio Giovenale: Satire* (Milan: 1990).

Rudd, N., *Juvenal: The Satires*, Introduction and Notes by W. Barr (Oxford: 1992).

GENERAL STUDIES

Adamietz, J., *Untersuchungen zu Juvenal* (*Hermes Einzelschriften* 26) (Wiesbaden: 1972).
'Juvenal' in *Die römische Satire*, ed. J. Adamietz (Darmstadt 1986) 231–307.

Adams, J. N., *The Latin Sexual Vocabulary* (London: 1990).

Anderson, W. S., 'Imagery in the Satires of Horace and Juvenal', *AJPh* 81 (1960) 225–60.
'Juvenal and Quintilian', *YClS* 17 (1961) 1–93.
'Venusina Lucerna. The Horatian Model for Juvenal', *TAPhA* 92 (1961) 1–12.
'*Lascivia vs. ira*: Martial and Juvenal', *CSCA* 3 (1970) 1–34.
Essays on Roman Satire (Princeton: 1982).

Bardon, H., 'Reflexions sur réalité et imaginaire chez Juvénal', *Latomus* 36 (1977) 996–1002.

Beaujeu, J., 'La réligion de Juvénal' in *Mélanges d'archéologie, d'épigraphie et d'histoire offerts à J. Carcopino* (Paris: 1966) 71–81.

Bellandi, F., 'Poetica dell' "*Indignatio*" e del "*Sublime*" satirico in Giovenale', *ASNP* series III, 3 (1973) 53–94.
Etica diatribica e protesta sociale nelle satire di Giovenale (Bologna: 1980).

'Mito e ideologia: età dell'oro e mos maiorum in Giovenale', *MD* 27 (1991) 89–128.

Bodoh, J. J., An analysis of the Ideas of Juvenal, diss. University of Wisconsin: 1966 (available on microfilm).

'Artistic control in the Satires of Juvenal', *Aevum* 44 (1970) 475–82.

Bracciali Magnini, M. L., 'Grecismi dotti nelle Satire di Giovenale', *Atene e Roma* 27 (1982) 11–25.

Bradshaw, A. T. von S., '*Glacie Aspersus Meculis*: Juvenal 5.104', *CQ* NS 15 (1965) 121–5.

Braun, L., 'Juvenal und die Überredungskunst', *ANRW* II 33.1 (1989) 770–810.

Braund, S., *Beyond Anger: A Study of Juvenal's Third Book of Satires* (Cambridge: 1988).

Carcopino, J., *Daily Life in Ancient Rome*, ed. H. T. Rowell, tr. E. O. Lorimer (revd Pelican edn, Harmondsworth: 1956).

Clausen, W. V., 'Juvenal and Virgil', *HSCPh* 80 (1976) 181–6.

Cloud, J. D., 'The client–patron relationship: emblem and reality in Juvenal's first book' in Wallace-Hadrill (1989) 205–18.

Coffey, M., 'Turnus and Juvenal', *BICS* 26 (1979) 88–94.

Roman Satire (2nd edn, Bristol: 1989).

Colin, J., 'Juvénal, les baladins et les rétiaires d'après le MS d'Oxford', *Atti dell'Accademia Scientifica di Torino (class. sci. mor., stor. e filol.)* 87 (1952/3) 315–86.

'Galerus: pièce d'armament du gladiateur ou coiffure de prêtre salien?', *Les Études Classiques* 23 (1955) 409–15.

'Juvénal et le mariage mystique de Gracchus', *Atti dell'Accademia Scientifica di Torino* 90 (1955/6) 114–216.

Colton, R. E., *Juvenal's Use of Martial's Epigrams* (Amsterdam: 1991).

Courtney, E., 'The interpolations in Juvenal', *BICS* 26 (1979) 146–62.

'The progress of emendation in the text of Juvenal since the Renaissance', *ANRW* II 33.1 (1989) 824–47.

Dill, S., *Roman Society from Nero to Marcus Aurelius* (London: 1905).

Dubrocard, M., 'Quelques remarques sur la distribution et la signification des hapax dans les Satires de Juvénal', *Annales de la Faculté des Lettres et Sciences humaines de Nice* 11 (1970) 131–40.

Duret, L., 'Juvénal réplique à Trébatius . . .', *REL* 61 (1983) 201–26.

Fabrini, P., Lami, A., 'La paupertas di Orazio e l'indignatio di Giovenale', *SCO* 31 (1981) 163–76.

Fletcher, G. B., 'Alliteration in Juvenal', *Durham University Journal* 5 (1944) 59–64.

Fredericks, S. C., 'Irony of overstatement in the Satires of Juvenal', *ICS* 4 (1979) 178–91.

Friedländer, L., *Roman Life and Manners under the Early Empire*, tr. J. H. Freese, L. A. Magnus, S. B. Gough, 4 vols (London: 1908–13).

Fruelund Jensen, B., 'Crime, vice and retribution in Juvenal's satires', *Class. & Med.* 33 (1981/2) 155–68.

Gérard, J., *Juvénal et la réalité contemporaine* (Paris: 1976).

'La richesse et le rang dans les satires de Juvénal', *Index* 13 (1985) 273–88.

'Des droits et des devoirs du poète satirique à l'âge d'argent de la latinité', *ICS* 14 (1989) 265–84.

Giangrande, G., 'Textkritische Beiträge zu Lateinischen Dichtern', *Hermes* 95 (1967) 110–21.

Gowers, E. J., *The Loaded Table: Representations of Food in Roman Literature* (Oxford: 1993).

Grant, M. (tr.), Tacitus: *On Imperial Rome* (Penguin Classics, Harmondsworth: 1956).

Graves, R. (tr.), Lucan: *Pharsalia* (Penguin Classics, Harmondsworth: 1956).

Suetonius: *The Twelve Caesars* (Penguin Classics, Harmondsworth: 1957).

Green, P. M., 'Juvenal Revisited' in *Classical Bearings: Interpreting Ancient History and Culture* (London: 1989) 240–55.

Griffith, J. G., 'Juvenal and the stage-struck patricians', *Mnemosyne* 4/15 (1962) 256–61.

'Frustula Iuvenalia' *CQ* NS 19 (1969) 379–87.

Grimal, P., 'Juvénal rhéteur', *Vita Latina* 101 (1986) 2–9.

Hellegouarc'h, J., 'Les idées politiques et l'appartenance sociale de Juvénal' in *Studi in onore di Edoardo Volterra* (Rome: 1971) 233–45.

'Juvénal, poète épique' in *Au miroir de la culture antique: mélanges offertes au Prés. René Marache* (Rennes: 1992) 269–85.

Helmbold, W. C., 'The Structure of Juvenal I', *UCPCP* 14/2 (1951) 47–60.

Highet, G., 'The philosophy of Juvenal', *TAPhA* 80 (1949) 254–70.

'Juvenal's bookcase', *AJPh* 72 (1951) 369–94.

Juvenal the Satirist (Oxford: 1954).

'Masks and Faces in Satire', *Hermes* 102 (1974) 321–37.

Iverson, S. A., The military theme in Juvenal's satires, diss. Vanderbilt University: 1975; *Diss. Abs.* 37 (1976) 279A–80A.

Jachmann, G., 'Studien zu Juvenal', *Nachrichten von der Akademie der Wissenschaften in Göttingen (phil.-hist. Kl.)* 6 (1943) 187–266.

Jenkyns, R., 'Juvenal the Poet' in *Three Classical Poets* (London: 1982) 151–221.

Jones, F. M. A., The protagonists in the satires of Juvenal, diss. University of St Andrews: 1986; *Diss. Abs.* 49 (1988) 248A.

Kenney, E. J., 'The First Satire of Juvenal', *PCPhS* (1962) 29–40.

'Juvenal, Satirist or Rhetorician?', *Latomus* 22 (1963) 704–20.

Kernan, A., *The cankered Muse: Satire of the English Renaissance* (Yale Studies in English 142) (New Haven: 1959).

Knoche, U., *Roman Satire*, tr. E. S. Ramage (Bloomington: 1975).

Labriolle, P. de, *Les Satires de Juvenal: étude et analyse* (Paris: 1932).

Lelièvre, F. J., 'Parody in Juvenal and T. S. Eliot', *CPh* 53 (1958) 22–5.

Lindo, J., 'The evolution of Juvenal's later satires', *CPh* 69 (1974) 17–27.

Lorenzo, E. di, *Il valore del diminutivo in Giovenale* (Naples: 1972).

Malnati, T. P., 'Juvenal and Martial on social mobility', *CJ* 83 (1988) 133–41.

Marache, R., 'La revendication sociale chez Martial et Juvénal', *Rivista di cultura classica e medievale* 3 (1961) 30–67.

  'Juvénal et le client pauvre', *REL* 58 (1980) 363–9.

  'Juvénal, peintre de la société de son temps', *ANRW* II 33.1 (1989) 592–639.

Marongiu, A., 'Giovenale e il diritto', *Studia et Documenta Historiae et Iuris* 43 (1977) 167–87.

Martyn, J. R. C., 'Juvenal's wit', *Grazer Beiträge* 8 (1979) 219–38.

Mason, H. A., 'Is Juvenal a Classic?' in *Critical Essays on Roman Literature (Satire)*, ed. J. P. Sullivan (London: 1963) 93–167.

Mattingly, H., *Roman Imperial Civilisation* (London: 1957).

Nisbet, R. G. M., 'On Housman's Juvenal', *ICS* 14 (1989) 285–302.

Paoli, U. E., *Rome: Its People, Life and Customs*, tr. R. D. Macnaughten (London: 1963).

Pepe, L., 'Questioni adrianee. Giovenale e Adriano', *GIF* 14 (1961) 163–73.

Pyne, J. J., A study of Juvenal's use of personal names, diss. Tufts University: 1979; *Diss. Abs.* 40 (1979) 1449A.

Ramage, E. S., 'Juvenal and the Establishment. Denigration of predecessors in the *Satires*', *ANRW* II 33.1 (1989) 640–707.

Ramage, E. S., Sigsbee, D. L., Fredericks, S. C., *Roman Satirists and their Satire* (New Jersey: 1974).

Rebert, H. F., 'The literary influence of Cicero on Juvenal', *TAPhA* 57 (1926) 181–94.

Reekmans, T., 'Juvenal's views on social change', *Anc. Soc.* 2 (1971) 117–61.

Ribbeck, O., *Der echte und der unechte Juvenal. Eine kritische Untersuchung* (Berlin: 1865).

Robertson, D. S., 'Juvenal V 103–6', *CR* 60 (1946) 19–20.

Rochefort, G. R., Laughter as a satirical device in Juvenal, diss. Tufts University: 1972; *Diss. Abs.* 33 (1972) 2913A.

Romano, A. C., *Irony in Juvenal* (Hildesheim: 1979).

Rooy, C. A. van, *Studies in classical satire and related literary theory* (Leiden: 1965).

Rudd, N., *Lines of Enquiry: Studies in Latin Poetry* (Cambridge: 1976).

  Themes in Roman Satire (London: 1986).

Saller, R. P., *Personal Patronage under the Early Empire* (Cambridge: 1982).

Scivoletti, N., 'Plinio il Giovane e Giovenale', *GIF* 10 (1957) 133–46.

  'Presenze di Persio in Giovenale', *GIF* 16 (1963) 60–72.

Scott, J. G., *The Grand Style in the Satires of Juvenal* (Northampton, Mass.: 1927).

Seager, R., 'Amicitia in Tacitus and Juvenal', *AJAH* 2 (1977) 40–50.

Serafini, A., *Studio sulla satira di Giovenale* (Florence: 1957).

Settis, S., 'Qui multas facies pingit cito (Iuven. 9.146)', *Atene e Roma* 15 (1970) 117–21.

Shero, L., 'The *cena* in Roman satire', *CPh* 18 (1923) 126–43.

Smemo, E., 'Zur Technik der Personenzeichung bei Juvenal', *SO* 16 (1937) 77–102.

Smith, W. S., 'Heroic models for the sordid present: Juvenal's view of tragedy', *ANRW* II 33.1 (1989) 811–23.

Syme, R., 'Pliny's less successful friends', *Historia* 9 (1960) 362–79.

'Juvenal, Pliny, Tacitus', *AJPh* 100 (1979) 250–73.

'The patria of Juvenal', *CPh* 74 (1979) 1–15.

Tarrant, R. J., 'Towards a Typology of Interpolation in Latin Poetry', *TAPhA* 117 (1987) 281–98.

Thomas, E., 'Ovidian Echoes in Juvenal' in *Ovidiana*, ed. N. Herescu (Paris: 1958) 505–25.

'Some aspects of Ovidian influence on Juvenal', *Orpheus* 7 (1960) 35–44.

Townend, G. B., 'The earliest scholiast on Juvenal', *CQ* NS 22 (1972) 376–87.

'The literary substrata to Juvenal's Satires', *JRS* 63 (1973) 148–60.

Vahlen, J., 'Quaestiones Iuvenalianae' in *Opuscula Academica*, vol. i (Leipzig: 1907) 223–53.

'Juvenal und Paris' in *Gesammelte philologische Schriften*, vol. ii (Leipzig: 1923) 181–201.

Wallace-Hadrill, A. (ed.), *Patronage in Ancient Society* (London: 1989).

Watts, W. J., 'Race prejudice in the satires of Juvenal', *Act. Class.* 19 (1976) 83–104.

White, P., '*Amicitia* and the profession of poetry in early Imperial Rome', *JRS* 68 (1978) 74–92.

Wiesen, D. S., 'Juvenal's moral character, an introduction', *Latomus* 22 (1963) 440–71.

'Juvenal and the blacks', *Class. & Med.* 31 (1970 [1976]) 132–50.

'The verbal basis of Juvenal's satiric vision', *ANRW* II 33.1 (1989) 708–33.

Winkler, M. M., *The persona in three satires of Juvenal* (Hildesheim: 1983).

'The function of epic in Juvenal's Satires' in *Studies in Latin Literature and Roman History* V, ed. C. Deroux (*Coll. Latomus* no. 206) (Brussels: 1989) 414–43.

Witke, C., *Latin Satire: The Structure of Persuasion* (Leiden: 1970).

Woodman, A. J., 'Juvenal and Horace', *G. & R.* 30 (1983) 81–4.

INDEX

Piso, C. Calpurnius, and conspiracy, 150, 166, 173, 175, 182

pitch, shirt of (*tunica molesta*), 7, 68, 176

pity, 118

Plato, 128, 179, 181, 205, 207, 218

Pliny the Elder (C. Plinius Secundus), 130, 131, 132, 134, 135, 139, 142, 145, 148, 149, 150, 159, 162, 163, 167, 176, 177, 179, 181, 195, 198, 205, 209, 211, 212, 213, 214, 215, 217

Pliny the Younger (C. Plinius Caecilius Secundus), xxv, xxvi, xlvii-xlviii, 125, 209; writings, 124, 129, 141, 143, 146, 148, 165, 167, 169, 173, 183, 203, 220

Plutarch, 159, 176, 177, 184, 185, 186, 199, 206, 216, 217, 221

Pluto, 98

poisoning, 101, 110, 135; of relatives, 7, 15, 125, 175; suicide by, 80; Mithridates' prophylaxis, 54, 112, 163, 211; women, 5, 53-4, 125, 163, 175

Poland, 118

Polyclitus, 20, 138

Polyphemus, 72-3, 179; *see also* Cyclopes

Polyxena, 83

Pompeius (member of Domitian's Cabinet), 27, 145

Pompey the Great (Cn. Pompeius Magnus), 79, 84, 184-5, 188, 206

Pomptine marshes, 22, 139

Pontia, 53, 163

Ponticus, 64, 62, 171

Pontifex Maximus, 25, 142

portents, 99, 203-4

Poseidon, *see* Neptune

Posides (Claudius' freedman), 107, 209

Postumus, 35, 152

Praeneste, 19, 107, 138

Praetorian Guard, xxxi, 78, 126, 184, 220

praetors, xxxiv, 6, 17, 157; ceremonial role, 77, 92, 112, 183, 196

Prefects: City, 26, 101, 143-4; of Egypt, xxxi, 6, 126, 140; Praetorian, xxxiv, 126

Priam, 44, 83, 187

priests: of Cybele, 179; eunuch, 9, 136; of Isis, 50, 161; of Mars, 12, 131; Salii, 131, 175

Priscus, Helvidius, xx, 148

Priscus, Marius, xv, 4, 65, 125, 173

prisons, 23, 45, 139

Probus, Valerius, xiv

Procne, 53, 163

prodigies, 99, 203-4

Prometheus, 28, 66, 117, 146, 173

Propertius, Sex., 130, 132, 153, 162, 187

prostitutes, 10, 15, 17, 38, 39, 52, 82, 91-2, 155

Prudentius Aurelius Clemens, xiv

Prusias, king of Bithynia, 80, 186

Prussians, 28

publication of *Satires*, xv-xviii, xxv, xxvi, xli

purple, 3, 16, 91, 136, 195

Pygmies, 101-2, 205-6

Pyrenees, 80

Pyrrha, 5, 116, 125, 216

Pyrrhus, king of Epirus, 96, 109, 157, 200, 209-10

Pythagoreanism, 120, 218-19

Pythian oracle, 51, 87-8, 102-3, 161, 192, 207

quaestiones, 169

Quartilla, 166

questions, J's rhetorical, 170

Quinquatrus, 185